WEB OF DREAMS

On their return to Farthinggale Manor, the mystery-shrouded luxury home of the Tatterton family, Annie and Luke believe that they will be putting the past finally to rest, and bringing peace to the spirit of Annie's mother, Heaven.

But Annie discovers a diary at Farthinggale — 'Leigh's Book'. There she finds the story of her grandmother, Leigh, and of her grandparents. Born into the privileged life of Boston's wealthy classes, Leigh hopes for happiness in her life. Her dreams are shattered, however, when, at the age of twelve, her adored parents divorce and her mother, Jillian, marries Tony Tatterton. The awful shadow cast by the Tatterton family over the lives of the next three generations begins to spread . . .

In *Web of Dreams*, Virginia Andrews brings her best-selling Casteel-Tatterton saga to a passionate, romantic, tragic conclusion.

By the same author

FLOWERS IN THE ATTIC
PETALS ON THE WIND
IF THERE BE THORNS
MY SWEET AUDRINA
SEEDS OF YESTERDAY
HEAVEN
DARK ANGEL
GARDEN OF SHADOWS
FALLEN HEARTS
GATES OF PARADISE

WEB OF DREAMS

Virginia Andrews

HarperCollins*Publishers*

This edition published in 1999 by HarperCollins Publishers

HarperCollins*Publishers*
77-85 Fulham Palace Road
Hammersmith, London W6 8JB

First published in Great Britain by
Collins 1990

This reprint published 1995

ISBN 0-261-67271-1

Set in Times

Printed and bound in Great Britain by
Caledonian International Book Manufacturing Ltd, Glasgow

WEB OF DREAMS

Prologue

Luke and I pass through the tall wrought-iron gates that spell out FARTHINGGALE MANOR. Patches of rust have broken out along the letters like a skin rash and the pounding of sea storms and winter winds have bent the gates back. Now they lean against the somber gray skies and the great house itself looks oppressed, weighed down by time and the heavy and bleak history that lives in its hallways and grand rooms. There are a few employees kept on to look after the house and grounds, but no one really checks on their work and they do relatively little to keep things up.

Luke squeezes my hand. It has been years, centuries, it seems, since we have been here. The dismal skies are appropriate for our arrival, for this is not a nostalgic journey. We would rather not remember my stay here, my imprisonment I should say, after the dreadful accident that took my parents' lives.

But our journey is sadder yet. The funeral air is correct. We have come to bury my real father, to put Troy Tatterton finally to rest alongside his true love, my mother Heaven. He had remained in his little cottage all these years, continuing his intricate artistic work on the wonderful Tatterton Toys, leaving only for special occasions like the births of my children. But whenever he visited us, no matter what the occasion, he could never stay away from Farthinggale long. Something always called him back.

Now he will never leave.

Even though the great house looms forever in my nightmares, and the memories of those tortured days remain remarkably vivid still, once I look upon this grand estate, I understand why Troy had the need to return. Even I, who have every reason not to, feel a need to re-enter the house and walk through its long corridors, up its great stairway to view the room that had been my cell.

Luke doesn't want me to go inside.

'Annie,' he says, 'it's not necessary. We'll wait for the burial ceremony to start and greet whoever there is to greet outside.'

But I can't help myself. Something draws me on.

I don't enter what was my bedroom. There are cobwebs everywhere and everywhere there is dust and grime. Curtains are faded and hang loose. Linens look stained, dirty.

I shake my head and walk on, pausing at Jillian's suite, the famous suite Tony had kept up with a fanatical urgency, refusing to face up to Jillian's passing and all that had gone with it. The suite has always intrigued me. It intrigues me now. I walk in, look up at the mirrors without their glass, gaze at the clothing still draped over chairs, the toiletries still on the vanity table. I pass it all, slowly, moving like one through a dream, the air like gauze.

And then I stop at Jillian's desk. I do not know why I do, but perhaps it's because the drawer is slightly open. Everything about this suite intrigues me and I wonder if there is something in that drawer that Jillian might have written during her days of madness.

Curiosity takes hold of me and I open the drawer. I blow away the dust and peer inside to see blank paper, pens and ink. Nothing unusual I think and then I spot the cloth bag toward the rear of the drawer and reach in.

There's a book in it. I take it out slowly.

'LEIGH'S BOOK', it says on the front. I hold my breath. It is my grandmother's diary. I open to the first page and find myself falling back through time.

ONE

Leigh's Book of Memories

I think it first started with a dream. No, not a dream, but more of a nightmare. In it I was standing with my parents – I don't know where. They were talking with each other and sometimes they would turn and say something to me. The only thing was, whenever I tried to talk to them, they seemed unable to hear me. As I kept trying to get into their conversation I reached up to push my hair back. Yet instead of my hair falling into place, I was horrified to discover a large clump of hair falling into my hand. Again and again I pushed back at my hair and each time I did another clump of my hair came free. I stared at the large strands of hair in my hand with horrified eyes. What was going on? Suddenly, a mirror appeared before me and in it I could see my image. I choked back a scream. My beautiful cashmere sweater was filled with holes and my skirt was torn and dirty. Then, before my already disbelieving eyes, I watched my features bloat. As I became fatter and fatter I started to cry. A trail of tears streamed down my smudged cheeks. I tore my eyes from my ugly image and turned to my parents, screaming for their help. My screams reverberated and bounced off the walls. Yet my parents did nothing. Why wouldn't they help me?

I couldn't stop screaming. Finally, when I thought my voice was gone and I was unable to utter a sound, they turned to me. Looks of astonishment broke across their faces. I wanted to call to Daddy . . . to have him cover me with hugs and kisses . . . to protect me as he always had . . . but before I could open my mouth, a look of disgust came over his face! I cringed in horror and then he disappeared. Only Momma remained. At least, I thought it was Momma. This stranger looked exactly like her . . . except for her eyes. Her eyes were so cold! Cold and calculating . . . empty of the love and warmth I saw daily. Where had it gone? Why was she looking at me this way? My beautiful Momma would never look at me with such hatred. Yes, hatred . . . and jealousy! My Momma wouldn't fail to help me in my most desperate moment. Yet she did nothing. First, a look of disgust, identical to the look Daddy had given me, appeared. Soon it was replaced by a smirk . . . a smirk of satisfaction. And then she turned her back on me . . . starting to walk away . . . leaving . . . leaving me alone in the darkness.

Somehow I found my voice and cried for her help. But she only kept walking, becoming smaller and smaller. I tried to follow, but was unable to move. Then I turned back to my image and before I could blink an eye, the mirror shattered and shards of glass came directly at my face.

With my last bit of strength I screamed, raising my hands to shield my face as I kept screaming and screaming.

When I awoke I was still screaming and my heart was beating furiously. For a moment I couldn't figure out where I was. Then, as the familiar surroundings of my bedroom came into view, I remembered. I was home in my bedroom in Boston. Today was my birthday. My twelfth birthday. Glad to be out of my awful dream, I put my fears behind me and pushed away the images that had terrified me only seconds ago. I headed downstairs with only thoughts of the day ahead.

On my twelfth birthday, I opened what would be my most precious gift: this book for memories. At the last moment, Daddy slipped it into the small mountain of wonderful and expensive gifts he and Momma had bought me. I knew he had put it there himself after Momma had arranged everything because she was just as curious about it as I was. Daddy usually left the buying of gifts completely in Momma's hands, just as he left her in charge of buying things for the house and buying all my clothes because he admittedly knew absolutely nothing when it came to fashions. He said Momma was an artist, so she would know better about color coordinations and designs, but

I think he was just happy not to have to go to department stores and clothing stores.

On a few occasions when I was younger, Daddy brought me models of his steamships, but Momma thought those were silly gifts for a little girl, especially the one that you took apart to learn about the workings of the engine. But I couldn't help being intrigued and very interested and played with it all the time, except when Momma was around.

Everything was stacked on one side of the dining room table at breakfast, just as it always had been on every birthday I could remember. I had woken early, of course, because of the dream. Birthday mornings were usually like Christmas mornings to me, although this morning I was still a little upset by the nightmare, and now I tried hard to forget its scariness.

Daddy had the surprise gift wrapped in light pink paper with birthday candles painted in dark blue that spelled out HAPPY BIRTHDAY all over it. Just knowing he had bought it for me all by himself made it the most important gift there. I tried not to rip the paper as I unwrapped it. I loved saving things like that, mementoes of all my special occasions: the candles from my tenth birthday cake, the one that was so big it took both Clarence the butler and Svenson the cook to carry it into the dining room; the candy angel on the top of the four-foot Christmas tree Momma bought to have placed in my playroom when I was only five; tickets from the circus Daddy took me to when it came to Boston last year; a play program from the Punch and Judy puppet show at the museum Momma and I went to when I was seven; and dozens of odds and ends like buttons and pins and even old shoe laces. So Daddy already knew that memories were precious to me.

I took the book out slowly and ran the tips of my fingers over the cover, over my name. I just loved the feel of the butter soft, rose colored leather cover with the gilded edging, and I especially loved seeing my name in print written like the title of a book: LEIGH'S BOOK.

I looked up with excitement. Daddy, already dressed in his dark gray three-piece suit and tie, stood back smiling, standing there the way he usually stood with his hands clasped behind his back, rocking on his heels like an old sea captain. Usually, Momma made him stop, claiming it made her nervous. Because Daddy was the owner of a big luxury ocean liner company and was on one ship or another so often, he said he spent more time on the water than on the land and he was used to rocking.

'What is that?' Momma asked when I opened the cover to blank page after blank page.

'I call it a log book,' Daddy said and winked at me. 'Captain's log. Keep track of the major events. Memories are more precious than jewels,' Daddy said.

'It's just a diary,' Momma said shaking her head. 'Log book. She's a little girl, not a sailor.'

Daddy winked at me again. Momma had bought me so many very expensive things, I knew I should pay more attention to them, but I clutched the book called LEIGH's BOOK to my heart and got up quickly to kiss Daddy thank you. He knelt down and I kissed him on his rosy cheek just above his gray beard, and his shimmering rust brown eyes brightened. Momma claimed Daddy was on one or another of his ships or at the ocean so much, his skin tasted salty, but I never tasted it whenever I kissed him.

'Thank you, Daddy,' I whispered. 'I'll write about you all the time.'

There were so many things to write down, so many private and precious thoughts, I couldn't wait to do it.

But Momma was anxious for me to unwrap the other gifts. There were a dozen cashmere sweaters in a variety of pinks and blues and greens, each with a matching pencil-slim skirt, the skirts Momma said everyone was wearing even though they were so narrow you couldn't walk very quickly in them. There were silk blouses and gold hoop earrings and a matching bracelet splattered with diamond flecks from Tiffany's. There was Chanel perfume and scented soaps, as well as a pearl comb and brush set.

And lipstick! I was finally going to be able to wear it, lightly of course, and only on special occasions. But I had my very own. Momma always promised she would show me how to wear make-up correctly when the time came.

There was one package she said I couldn't open now. It had to wait until we were alone, later.

'Girl business,' she said eyeing my father. She thought it was horrible of him to rush off to his office on my birthday morning, but he said he could spend the rest of the day with me and then take Momma and me to dinner, so I forgave him. There was always one sort of crisis or another for him these days. He blamed it on commercial jet airline travel that was increasingly cutting into the luxury ocean liner business. Momma always criticized him for how much time he spent working, and this all made it worse.

Although we had gone on many trips, she claimed we were like shoemakers without shoes because we didn't go on the trips she wanted.

'My husband's in the vacation travel business and we rarely vacation. We have to check out new routes or new ships, rather than enjoy them the way we should,' she complained, sometimes bitterly.

I knew my last big package had something to do with all this because she said she bought what was in it, hoping I would have an opportunity to use it, and then she scowled at Daddy and said, 'I still haven't had an opportunity to use mine.'

I tore open the package quickly and opened the box. It was a skiing outfit: a heavy cashmere sweater and tailored ski trousers with a matching Italian silk blouse. Many times during the summer, Momma had voiced her desire to go for a winter holiday to St Moritz and stay at the Palace Hotel, 'where all the best of society stopped'. It was a beautiful outfit.

I looked over all my wonderful presents, squealed with delight and hugged her. She vowed she was always going to make sure I would have better birthdays than she had when she was growing up in Texas. Even though her family wasn't poor, she said her mother, my grandma Jana, was as austere as a Puritan minister. She had told me over and over the sad story of how she wasn't even allowed to have a doll when she was a little girl, and she said her sisters, both older, were just like her mother because they were both so plain looking, they didn't care about being feminine and having dainty and beautiful things.

Aunt Peggy and Aunt Beatrice really were as ugly as the wicked witch in the *Wizard of Oz*. We didn't see them very often, but whenever we did, I hated the way they gaped at me through their thick-rimmed spectacles. Both wore the same ugly black frame glasses that magnified their dull brown eyes making them look like frogs. The way Momma always clumped them together when she spoke about them made me think of them as twins. They did have identical shapes. 'Ironing boards', Momma called them. She said Grandma Jana found them husbands – spineless, homely men themselves: one the owner of a department store in Ludville, Texas, and the other an undertaker in nearby Fairfax.

According to Momma, both Texas towns as well as her own 'were so dusty and dirty, you had to take a bath after a walk through Main Street'. It didn't take Daddy long to win Momma away from all that. I made her tell me the story again and again, never minding that each time she told it, she added something new or changed or forgot something she had told me before. The main part of the story was always the same and it was one of the first things I wanted to put into my book.

So in the early evening, when she came into my room to talk while we both got ready to go out to a fancy Boston restaurant for my birthday dinner, I asked her to tell me the story again.

'Don't you ever get tired of hearing about that?' she asked, throwing me a quick look.

'Oh no, Momma. I think it's a wonderful story, a dream story. No one could ever write one as beautiful as that,' I said, which made her very happy.

'All right,' she said, sitting down at my vanity table. She began to brush her beautiful hair, till it shone like spun gold. 'I lived like poor Cinderella did before her prince arrived,' she began as always. 'But it wasn't always like that. I was the apple of my father's eye. He was a foreman in charge of everything at a nearby oil field, a very important man. Although he wasn't afraid to get his hands dirty when he had to, he was a very elegant man. I hope some day you'll find a man like my father.'

'Isn't Daddy like him then? He doesn't mind working on his ships, getting down in the engine room with his men?'

'Yes,' she said dryly, 'he doesn't care. But I want someone different for you, someone who is a real executive, who orders men about and lives in a mansion and . . .'

'But don't we live in a mansion, Momma?' I protested. Ours was the biggest, most luxurious town house on the street, a classic Georgian Colonial with oversized entryways and fourteen-foot ceilings. All my friends loved my house and were especially impressed with the dining room because it had a domed ceiling and was encircled by Ionic columns. Momma had had it redone two years ago when she saw one just like it in one of her art magazines.

'Yes, yes, but I want you to live on an estate with acres and acres of land, and horses, and pools and dozens and dozens of servants and its own private beach. And . . .' Her eyes grew soft and dreamy and faraway as she conjured up this wonderful mansion and grounds, 'it will even have an English maze.'

She shook her head as though to clear it of its daydreams and began to brush her cascading hair again with long, graceful strokes. She said you had to brush your hair at least one hundred times a night to keep it soft and healthy, and a woman's hair was her crown. She usually wore it up or pulled back from her face to show her sculptured profile.

'Anyway, my sisters, the iron board twins, were terribly jealous of the love my father had for me. Often, he would bring something beautiful home for me and nothing but practical things like sewing kits or crochet hooks for them. They didn't want pretty ribbons or new earrings or combs anyway. They hated me for being pretty, don't you see? They still do.'

'But then your father died, and your older brother went into the army,' I said, impatient to get to the romantic part of the story.

'Yes, and how things changed. Then I really became poor Cinderella, you see. They made me do all the chores around the house and hid my beautiful things whenever they could. If

I didn't do what they wanted, they broke my combs or buried my jewelry. They threw out all my cosmetics,' she declared hatefully.

'But what about your mother? What did Grandma Jana do?' I knew the answer, but I had to hear it.

'Nothing. She approved. She thought my father had been spoiling me anyway. She's just like them, no matter how she acts now. And don't think that because she gave you that cameo pin for your birthday,' she added eyeing the cameo on my vanity table, 'she has changed in any way.'

'It is beautiful and Daddy says it's very, very valuable.'

'Yes. I asked her for it years ago, but she refused me,' she said bitterly.

'Oh, do you want it, Momma?'

'No. It's yours,' she said after a moment. 'She gave it to you. Be careful with it, that's all. Anyway, where was I?'

'They were burying your jewelry.'

'Burying my . . . oh, yes, yes. And they tore my best dresses, my most expensive dresses, too. Once, Beatrice, in a fit of temper, sneaked into my room and hacked one of my dresses with a kitchen knife.'

'How cruel!' I exclaimed.

'Of course, to this day they deny doing all that. But they did, believe me. They even tried to cut off my beautiful hair once, sneak in on me while I was sleeping and chop it with their long sewing scissors, but I woke up just in time and . . .' She shuddered as if what followed was too terrible to mention. Then she began stroking her hair again and continued. 'Your father had come to Texas on some business venture, and my mother, who was still mingling with the blue bloods, met him at a dinner and invited him to our house, intending for him to fall in love with your aunt Peggy.

'But when he set eyes on me . . .' She stopped and sat back, looking at herself in the mirror. Momma always had the smoothest skin, not a wrinkle daring to show itself. She had an elegant face, a face that you could find on a cameo or on the cover of *Vogue*. She had shining blue eyes that revealed her moods: brightening like Christmas lights when she was happy, cold like icicles when she was angry, and soft and sad like a lost puppy when she was unhappy.

'When he looked at me,' she said to her own image in the mirror, 'his heart became an instant slave to my beauty.

'Of course,' she added turning to me quickly, 'your aunts were insanely jealous. They made me wear this faded, dull brown dress that came down to my ankles and hid my figure, and they wouldn't let me wear any jewelry. I had to have my hair up in a granny's bun and could wear no make-up, not even a dab of lipstick.

'But Cleave saw right through all that. His eyes were fixed on me all night, and every time I spoke, even if it was to say, "Please pass the salt", he would stop whatever he was saying to listen as if my words were pearls of wisdom.' She sighed and then so did I. How wonderful, I thought, to have such romantic memories. More than anything, I wanted one day to have memories just as romantic for my own.

'Did you fall in love with him right away too?' I knew that answer too, but I had to hear it again because I wanted to get it right for my book.

'Not right away, although I did feel myself turning to him more and more. I thought he had a funny accent, you know, that Boston accent, so I was intrigued with everything he said. He was distinguished and had the look of a successful businessman: confident of himself, but not stiff; he wore expensive clothing, and had a thick gold pocket watch with the longest gold chain I had ever seen. When he opened it, it played the tune of "Greensleeves".'

'Did he look like an old sea salt?' I asked, laughing. Daddy always told me he did.

'I didn't know anything about the sea or his business, having lived in central Texas all my life, but he had the same beard he has now, only it wasn't all gray and it was much more neatly trimmed, I might add. Anyway he did talk on and on about his growing steamship line. Grandma found that interesting,' she added with a smirk. 'Planning on the rich suitor she was going to have for Peggy.'

'Then what happened?'

'He asked to see our gardens and before Grandma could get Peggy to guide him, he turned to me and asked if I would do so. You should have seen their faces then. Peggy's dropped even lower, her chin stretched down to her ugly Adam's apple, and Beatrice actually groaned.

'Of course, I agreed to do it, first just to torment them, but after we walked out into the warm Texas night . . .'

'Yes?'

'And he began to speak softly. I realized Cleave VanVoreen was more than a stuffy, New England businessman. He was rich and clever and handsome in his own way, yes, but he was also very lonely and very taken with me, so taken that he actually proposed that first night. We were standing by the baby roses.'

'I thought you were on the swing and it wasn't until the second night.'

'No, no, it was by the roses, and it was the first night. The stars . . . the night was bursting with stars. It was an explosion of light above us. It took my breath away,' she said putting her fingers on her throat softly and closing her eyes as if the memory was too much for anyone to bear.

I held my breath. Tonight she had told the story better than ever before. She's making it special for me because it's my twelfth birthday. How wonderful of her. Maybe she changed the story from time to time because as I got older, she thought I could hear more and more.

'And suddenly, Cleave took my hand into his and said, "Jillian, I have traveled all through this country and seen many other lands, many people and many beautiful women, from the Orient to South America, Hawaiian princesses and Russian princesses and English princesses, but never have I feasted my eyes on someone as beautiful as you. You're a jewel as magnificent as any of the stars above us."

'"I am a man of action, he went on, who, once he realizes what is valuable in this world and what is not, makes immediate decisions, but fervent decisions, decisions he will stand by through any controversy or turmoil."

'Then he took my other hand into his and said, "I won't leave this town until I have you for my wife." ' I mouthed the words in a silent chorus along with her. I had heard that sentence so many times and found it thrilling every time. To think, my daddy would have remained in that dusty Texas town and neglected his business forever and forever until he had the woman he loved . . . their romance did belong in a story book, and now it was in mine.

'Well, of course, Leigh, I was overwhelmed by such an expression of love. He asked permission to court me and I granted it. Then he went in and spoke to Grandma Jana privately, asking her permission as well. She was shocked, but I suppose she thought she would at least get this rich suitor for one of her daughters.

'He came to the house every day for a week after that and my sisters died with envy, but there was nothing they could do. Grandma Jana was ashamed to let Cleave see me in rags doing menial chores about the house, so I got a reprieve from all that and your aunts had to do them.

'About the fifth day, Cleave formally proposed. He got down on his knees while I sat on the couch in our living room, and I accepted,' she said ending the story abruptly. 'I left Texas with him and said good riddance to all that.

'Once your grandmother and aunts found out how rich I was, they became as sweet as honey.' She looked at my memory book. 'Are you going to put all this in there?'

'Oh yes. All my most important memories. Did you ever have a diary, Momma?'

'Never. But that's all right,' she added quickly, 'I have my memories stored right here,' she said pointing to her heart. 'Some of them, I have told only you,' she said, her voice so low it made my heart skip a beat. She trusted me more than anyone.

'I won't ever keep secrets from you, Momma.'

'I know you won't, Leigh. We're too alike, you and I, to hide anything important from each other,' she said stroking my hair with her fingers. 'You're going to be a very beautiful young woman someday soon, do you know that?'

'I want to be as beautiful as you are, but I don't think I will be. My nose is too long and I don't have your soft mouth. My lips are too thin, aren't they?'

'Of course not. Anyway, your features aren't fully shaped yet. Just follow my directions, do the things I tell you to do and you will be very attractive. Will you promise to do that?'

'I promise.'

'Good,' she said and finally turned to the birthday package that she had declared was 'girl business'. 'It's time to open this now and talk about it,' she said. She unwrapped it herself and opened the box.

I couldn't believe my eyes. It was a bra. My breasts had started to grow lately, and some of my friends were already wearing bras. She held it up between us.

'Your figure is developing and you've just had your first period,' she declared. 'It's time you learned a woman's ways and learned some things about men.'

I nodded, practically holding my breath. Such a grown-up conversation between us made my heart pitter-patter.

'You don't wear this all the time, just on occasions when you will meet elegant people and handsome, wealthy suitors, and when you put this on under your new cashmere sweaters . . .'

I took the new bra gingerly. My heart was still racing.

'Men, especially men of position and wealth, like to be seen with women who are stunning. It strokes their egos, understand?' She laughed and tossed her hair back over her shoulders.

'I think so.'

'Even your father, who is oblivious to almost everything but his ships, enjoys walking into a fine restaurant with me on his arm. Men see women as ornaments.'

'But is that good?' I wondered aloud.

'Of course it's good. Let them think what they want, as long as they work themselves to the bone making you happy. Never let a man know exactly what you're thinking.' Suddenly she turned to me and her soft face became something cold and hard. 'Always remember, Leigh, women can *never* be as promiscuous as men. Never.'

My heart began to beat madly again. She was about to discuss the most intimate things.

'It's all right for men to be that way. It's expected. They want to prove their manhood, but if a woman is that way, she will lose everything important. Nice girls don't go all the way. Not until they're married,' she added. 'Promise you won't forget that.'

'I promise,' I said, my voice barely above a whisper.

'Good.' She looked at herself in the mirror again and her ice-hard expression melted into my sweet, pretty mother once again. 'You have opportunities I never had, if I could just get your father to take advantage of them.

'Did your father take us to Jamaica like I asked him to? Did we go to Deauville to the races? We have luxury liners, but do we have our own yacht on which to sail to the Riviera? No, he takes us to London three times because that trip can combine business with pleasure and expects me to cater to the passengers like the wife of a hotel owner or something. I want to go away at least once and be on a real vacation, no business. Nothing but enjoyment. How does he expect me to introduce you to the right kind of people if we don't go to these other places?'

She turned back to me again, her face flushed with anger. 'Don't marry a man who is more in love with his business than he is with you.'

I didn't know what to say. She had told me so much and overwhelmed me with so many new ideas and things to think about. And I had new questions to ask. When do men start trying to get you to go 'all the way' and how do you know which men to trust and which not?

I wasn't ready, I thought and felt a panic coming over me.

Momma stood up and swept toward the door. 'I'm so glad we've had this talk, darling, but we have to get dressed now, I'm afraid. You know how impatient your father gets when he has to wait. Everything's a schedule with him. He treats us like his ships. I'm sure he's downstairs in his office pacing about and mumbling to himself.'

'I'll hurry.'

'No, take your time,' she said as if she were unaware she was contradicting herself. 'It's good practice to keep a man waiting for you. Spend time on your hair, put the lipstick on lightly, as I've shown you before, not pressing down, but gently running it over your lips as if you were caressing it with a kiss,' she said demonstrating. 'Understand?' I nodded. 'Good.'

'And don't forget, put on your stockings and wear your new high-heeled shoes that are just like mine. Always wear high heels, they are much more flattering to one's legs,' she said.

She started out and stopped again in the doorway.

'Oh, I almost forgot. I have another surprise for you,' she announced.

'Something more? But you and Daddy have given me so much today.'

'It's not another gift, Leigh. It's a trip, a place I want you to see,' she explained. 'I'm taking you with me this weekend.'

'Where?'

'To that mansion I told you about, the one called Farthinggale Manor.'

'Where you're painting the murals in the music room?' I asked. She had told me about it very quickly one day. Momma was doing illustrations for children's books, working for Patrick and Clarissa Darrow, the husband and wife owners of a publishing company here in Boston, who were neighbors of ours. Their decorator, Elizabeth Deveroe, was hired to do some work in a fabulous mansion outside of Boston. Momma and Elizabeth were good friends and Momma had accompanied her out there one day and made suggestions, which the owner apparently loved. She said Elizabeth then asked her to carry out the order, which was to paint murals depicting scenes from fairy tales, something Momma had been doing on the covers of books.

'Yes. I'm more than half done and I want you to see that as well as meet Tony.'

'Tony?'

'Mr Tatterton, the owner, and I want you to see his estate. If you would like to go, of course.'

'Oh, I do! I can't wait to see what you've painted.'

'Good.' She smiled. 'Now we both better get dressed before your father walks a hole in the floor.'

I laughed, thinking about poor Daddy and how it would be for him to have to live with two mature women now, instead of only one. But I could never be cruel to Daddy, I thought. I could never deceive him or not tell him what I was really thinking. Wasn't there ever a time, I wondered, a time after you were in love and married, when you could trust your husband and be honest with him?

I put on the new bra and one of my new cashmere sweaters and the matching skirt. I brushed my hair back and put on the lipstick just the way Momma had instructed and then I found the shoes with the high heels and stood before my mirror to gaze at myself.

I looked so different. It was as if I had grown up overnight. People who didn't know me might not be able to guess my true age. How exciting, I thought, and yet, in a way it was a little scary. I looked older, but could I act older? I always watched Momma in public, how she seemed to slip in and out of parts, become this and become that, sometimes giggle and act silly and sometimes look so elegant and aristocratic anyone would think she was a member of royalty. Always, she was beautiful; she was the center of attention. Whenever she walked into a room, men stopped their conversations and spun their heads around so quickly, they nearly snapped them off their necks.

It made me nervous to think that the moment we entered the restaurant for my birthday dinner, all eyes would be turned our way and men and women would gaze closely upon me, too. Would they laugh? Would they think there's a young girl trying to be like her mother?

When I finally walked downstairs to Daddy's office, I was filled with apprehension. He would be the first man to see me so dressed up and he was the most important man in my life right now. Momma was still getting ready.

He was behind his desk, reading one of his reports. Two years ago, Momma had redesigned and redecorated the entire house, except for his office. That was the one room he wouldn't let her touch, even though its floor was covered with a rather worn looking rectangular rug Momma considered an embarrassment. His desk had been his father's and was scratched and chipped, yet he would permit nothing to be done with it. His office did look cluttered because he had shelves of models of ships and nautical books on all the walls. There was one small dark brown leather settee and a worn hickory rocker with an oval maple table beside it. He worked by the light of a brass oil lamp.

The only art in the room consisted of pictures of ships: Yankee clippers and some of the first luxury liners, and some dried and treated driftwood pieces he had on his cluttered desk and on the oval table. On the wall behind him was a portrait of his father. Grandpa VanVoreen, who died two years before I was born, had a hard stern face with deep wrinkles and windblown cheeks. Daddy always said that he took after his mother, who had also died before I was born. In her photographs she looked like a diminutive, soft woman, from whom Daddy had probably inherited his quiet, conservative manner.

I often studied the photographs of Daddy's parents, searching for some resemblances to myself. I thought his mother's eyes were like mine in some pictures, but in others, they looked quite different.

He looked up slowly from his desk when he realized I had entered his office. For the first few moments, it was as if he didn't recognize me. Then he stood up quickly, his face filled with amazement.

'How do I look, Daddy?' I asked tentatively.

'You look so . . . grown up. What has your mother done to you?'

'Is it all right?' I asked anxiously.

'Oh yes. I didn't realize how beautiful you were becoming, Leigh. I guess I'd better stop thinking of you as being a little girl.' He simply stared a little longer. It made me very self-conscious. I felt myself blush. 'Well now,' he said finally coming around his desk to me. 'I'll have two beautiful women on my arms tonight. How wonderful.' He hugged me to him, and warmed my cheeks with kisses.

'Are you sure I look all right, Daddy?'

'Of course, I'm sure. Come on now, let's see how many more hours it will be before your mother comes down those stairs.' He put his arm around me and we walked out to the staircase hall and looked up at the suspended staircase because Momma was descending.

She looked as pretty as ever. Her eyes were sparkling so brightly, they were luminous. Her color was radiant and her hair had an angelic sheen to it. She winked at me as she made the turn.

'Good grief, Cleave, you could have at least changed into a different suit from the one you wore all day,' she said stepping down.

'I did!' Daddy protested.

Momma shook her head.

'One is so much like the other, no one could tell.' She brushed back a strand of my hair. 'Doesn't Leigh look beautiful?'

'Absolutely. Overwhelming. I can't think of when you looked more like mother and daughter,' he said, but she seemed hurt by that. He saw it too and corrected himself quickly. 'Actually, you look too young to have a daughter who looks this old. You look more like sisters,' he concluded. Momma beamed.

'See,' she whispered as we started out, 'you can always get them to do and say the right things if you want to.'

My heart fluttered and my breath caught in my throat and seemed to stay. Momma was really doing it: she was really sharing her womanly secrets with me. Dressed the way I was, going off to a fancy restaurant, I felt more thrilled and excited than I could remember.

And then, at the restaurant, Daddy gave us another surprise. He announced that he had initiated a new Caribbean vacation cruise in hopes of stimulating more business. Primarily it was a cruise to Jamaica and he had made plans for us to go on the commencing voyage. We would leave next week with a *bon voyage* party and all.

Momma was so speechless, she didn't look happy at first, even though just today she had complained about never going to Jamaica, which had become a vacation spot for the rich and famous.

'But what about Leigh's schooling?' she asked.

'We'll take her tutor along, just like the other times,' Daddy replied and looked perplexed about her sudden concern.

I thought it was peculiar for her to be concerned about that, too. She had never been worried about it before.

'I thought you'd be pleased,' Daddy said. He looked heartbroken that Momma hadn't gotten more excited over his announcement.

'I am pleased. It's just . . . just so unusual for you, Cleave, to do anything spontaneous.' Her voice sounded strange to me, brittle. 'It takes a moment to get used to.' She looked at me and after a moment, she laughed and we went on with our birthday celebration.

What a wonderful birthday this has been, I thought. And how perfect it was that Daddy had given me this diary in which to record these precious memories. It was as if he knew I would have so many special ones from now on and would want more than ever to put them down to save forever and forever.

Today I have felt some of what it would be to feel like a woman instead of a little girl. Deep in my heart, I wondered if Daddy would still bring me home little presents and call me his little princess. Oh, part of me feared that if I grew up, his love for me would change, would lessen.

Momma came by after I had put out my lights and crawled into bed. She wanted to remind me about going to see Farthinggale Manor. I sensed how important it was to her that I like it. How could I not like the place she described. It sounded like a fairy tale kingdom.

And this Tony Tatterton . . . he sounded like a king!

TWO

An Enchanted Kingdom

I was hoping Daddy would come along with us to see Momma's murals, but even though it was a weekend, he had to go down to his office. He usually spent Saturdays there and often a part of Sunday afternoon. This particular weekend he was more depressed than ever about his business because it looked certain that he would have to sell off one of his ocean liners and cut staff. Airline companies were expanding even faster than he had first thought they would and continued to eat away his clientele. He said the airlines were going to offer people gourmet meals on board, food even made by famous chefs, and people were more and more in a rush to get places. I didn't want to tell him that some of my girlfriends at school were dreaming of becoming airline stewardesses.

Momma told him to invest in something else besides steamships and luxury liners, but he shook his head and replied that that was all he knew.

'The Captain goes down with his ship,' he told me. 'Right, Princess?' I felt terrible for him, but Momma didn't seem upset or concerned at all. She thought the new Caribbean cruises would help. She said she had been encouraging him to start them for some time.

'But like all men,' she told me, 'he hates to let a woman tell him what to do. Really,' she said, 'men never stop being little boys. They like to be babied, pampered, and they are always so stubborn.'

I listened to what she said, but I didn't think Daddy was so stubborn, except about his office at home. But everyone is stubborn about something, I thought. Momma was stubborn about a lot of things too, and when I asked her about that, she said it was a woman's prerogative to be difficult at times. She said that it made men appreciate women more.

'Never let a man take you for granted,' she advised. We were having this discussion on the way to Farthinggale Manor. Usually we had a driver take us places, but this time Momma wanted to drive herself.

It was a very bright and unusually warm day. Daddy said we were having an extended Indian summer and if it continued like this, we wouldn't see snow until January. I hoped we would see it for Christmas. It made such a difference to hear the sound of sleigh bells or hear the singing of carols while snowflakes fell. When I mentioned that to Momma, she laughed and said, 'Tony Tatterton is planning to have a Christmas party and if Tony Tatterton wants to see snow on Christmas and it hasn't snowed, he'll have it flown in.'

'He must be very, very rich!' I exclaimed.

'When you feast your eyes on Farthy, and see the sports cars and Rolls Royces, the Arabian horses and the grounds with the Olympic size pool, you'll understand why even that is an understatement,' she said. We left the city and headed toward the ocean.

'Farthy? What's Farthy?'

'Oh,' she laughed again, a thin, short laugh, the kind of sound people make when they are thinking of something quite private, something only they or someone close to them would appreciate. 'It's Tony's nickname for his home. I told you, it's called Farthinggale Manor.'

'It sounds like a storybook place. Only in stories do people name their homes.'

'Oh no,' Momma explained. 'People with histories, with houses that have histories really do name their homes. You'll see other grand estates, and I hope you'll meet these sort of people more often now.'

'Did you always want to live in a grand style, Momma, even when you were my age back in Texas?' I asked. I had never dreamed about living on an estate or going to parties with aristocratic people whose homes were so old and famous they had their own names like Tara in *Gone With the Wind*. Was I supposed to want these things? Or was this something that happens when you get older, more mature? I wondered.

'Hardly,' Momma said. She laughed at a private thought again. 'I wanted to live in a garret, be the lover of a poor poet in Paris and be a starving artist displaying her works along the River Seine. At night I would sit at outdoor cafés and listen to my lover read his poetry to friends, but when I told my mother these things, she laughed and ridiculed them. She thought it was silly for me to want to be an artist. A woman had only one purpose in life to her, to be a wife and a mother.'

'But couldn't she see how talented you were? Wasn't she proud of your paintings and drawings?' I asked, even though it was very hard for me to imagine Momma living in a garret and not having fine clothes and jewels and all her make-up.

'She didn't even want to look at them and yelled at me for spending too much time drawing or painting. My sisters were not above sabotaging something I had drawn or painted. You have no idea how I suffered when I was your age, Leigh.'

How horrible, I thought, for your own mother to ignore you and not support you. Poor Momma, living with those terrible sisters and a mother who didn't care about the things that were her passion and most important to her. She was really all alone until Daddy arrived to sweep her away, to rescue her so she could become an artist and still have the things she loved and wanted.

'But now you're happy, aren't you, Momma? You have all the things you want, don't you? And you're able to be an artist, aren't you?' I asked, pressing for her to agree. She took a while to respond, but I kept silent because I sensed that she would.

'I have many expensive things, Leigh, but I did think my life would be different.' She smiled softly. I loved this smile, the way her eyes twinkled because of some precious memory. Daddy was so right when he said memories are more precious than jewels.

'I used to imagine going to all sorts of gala events, parties, christening ships while the newsreel cameras and reporters surrounded me,' she said.

'But you've done some of that. I saw the pictures, the newspaper clippings.'

'Yes, yes, here and there, we had an event, but I always had to talk your father into doing such things. He comes from such a practical, puritanical background. Look at how he keeps his office at home. Everything in it is all right, according to him. Everything's good enough because it was good enough for his father, who probably died with the first nickel he ever made still clutched in his fist. Honestly, I have to keep his office door closed whenever I have anyone at the house, but he doesn't care. Do you know anyone who loves to work more than he does?' she asked.

'He's just trying to make his business successful so we'll be happy,' I said in his defense.

'Yes, yes. So we'll be happy,' she said and let her voice trail off. 'We're getting closer, Leigh. Now turn your head to the right and look for a break in the tree line. The first glimpse of Farthinggale Manor is a sight to remember,' she added, her voice full of excitement.

The sun was just over the tops of the trees now and as we made a turn to the right on a private road, the rays lit up an enormous wrought-iron gate that arched overhead and spelled out with ornate embellishments the words FARTHINGGALE MANOR. I gasped at the imps and fairies and gnomes that peeked between the iron leaves. I did feel as if I were entering a special place, a magical kingdom. Even before I saw the great house looming ahead, I understood Momma's excitement. Our town house in the city was large and luxurious, but there was something different about having acres and acres of land with fields and hills and great fences around you. Back in Boston, we lived in a rich part of the city, but here . . . here we would have our own private city, our own private world.

'Farthinggale Manor,' I whispered. Those words had an enchanted ring to them. It was as if uttering them changed the world around me. The grass did look richer, greener and thicker here. Most of the lawns in the city had already begun to turn yellow and brown. Along the way, I had seen many trees that had already lost their autumn gold and brown leaves, but the trees on the grounds of Farthy still clung to their precious leaves, made more precious by the way the sunlight caressed them and lit them like jewels in the bright light. A part of Farthy was nestled protectively in the embrace of surrounding hills, protecting the trees from the harsh winds off the ocean. Some of the leaves were so still, they looked as if they were painted on the branches.

I saw at least a half dozen groundsmen raking, trimming and nurturing plants and saplings. Some were on their hands and knees around sparkling fountains with small statues of Cupid and Neptune and Venus at their centers. Elsewhere, workers were trucking wheelbarrows of landscaping stone and dust to new locations. There was such a sense of activity and life on the grounds, it was hard to believe that we were at the end of October and approaching winter. Riding down the long drive-way, I felt as if Momma and I were re-entering spring, as if we had turned back time or entered a kingdom that never experienced a bleak, dreary day.

And then I looked up at the great house and thought I was right to think of this place as a storybook realm. The huge building made of gray stone did resemble a castle. The roof was red and soared, forming turrets and small red bridges connecting portions of the high roof that would have been inaccessible otherwise. I could just imagine the views from the windows on the upper floors. Surely, you could see the ocean from there.

As we drew closer and closer, the house seemed to grow taller and wider. I thought it was at least as big as half a city block. Our town house could easily fit inside it with room for a few more. As we got closer, Momma cut her eyes toward me, watching for my reaction. She stayed silent but drove right up to the wide stone steps that led to an enormous arching front door, a door that looked so heavy and thick, I imagined it must have taken ten men to bring it there.

'We're here,' Momma declared and shut off the engine. Almost instantly, an attendant came around to open her door for her. He was a tall, dark man, perhaps only in his early twenties. He wore a chauffeur's uniform and took his hat off as we stepped out of the car.

'Good afternoon, Miles,' Momma said. 'This is my daughter Leigh.'

Miles looked at me quickly. I thought he was rather shy, but cute and quickly tried to imagine what it would be like to have him as a boyfriend. I wondered nervously whether he thought I was pretty and I couldn't keep my face from turning crimson. I wondered if Momma noticed.

'Pleased to meet you, Miss Leigh,' he said and nodded. It sounded so funny and so stuffy to be greeted so formally, but before I could even think of smiling, Momma shot a look of expectation at me.

'Thank you, Miles,' I said. 'I'm pleased to meet you, too.' He moved quickly behind the steering wheel to park our car.

'Miles is Mr Tatterton's chauffeur,' Momma explained as we started up the steps. 'He's only been here two weeks.'

Before we reached the door, it was opened by the butler, a very tall, thin man with a sad, deeply creased face that made me think of Abraham Lincoln. He had his thin, dark brown hair brushed back and lying flat with a parting nearly at center. He moved so slowly and so softly, he made me think of an undertaker.

'Good afternoon, Curtis,' Momma said. 'This is my daughter Leigh.'

'Good afternoon.' Curtis nodded, his eyes down as if he were greeting royalty, and then stepped back to let us enter. 'Mr Tatterton is awaiting you in the music room.'

'Thank you,' Momma said and we moved down the enormous entryway. 'He's only in his late twenties, but he looks like someone's grandfather,' she whispered and then giggled. Momma was acting more excited than I'd ever seen her, almost like a little girl, or someone my very own age. It made me nervous, almost scared but I didn't know why. I only knew I wanted her to stop, to act like a mother again.

Trying to take my mind off my silly uneasiness I looked at the dozens of enormous ancestral portraits we were passing as well as pictures of beautiful horses, pictures of the ocean, pictures, pictures, pictures, and great drapes spread over the marble walls, too. Against the walls were white and black marble tables and ornamental stone benches, obviously far too uncomfortable and cold to sit upon. Ahead of us was a long, circular staircase twice, no, three times as long and as wide as ours. Above us was a tremendous chandelier with so many bulbs in it, I imagined it was as bright as the sun whenever it was turned on. The floors of the entryway were covered with enormous Persian rugs that looked so clean and new, it seemed sinful to walk over them.

'Come along,' Momma urged, and I followed beside her as we walked past an enormous living room. I caught a glimpse of a grand piano. We stopped at the doorway of the music room and I gazed up at the domed ceiling arching overhead. There was a tall ladder with scaffolding hanging just at the point where the paintings still had to be completed.

So far, Momma had painted a bright blue sky with terns and doves flying. At the center was a man riding a magic carpet and just ahead of him was the drawing of a mystical, air castle, half-hidden by clouds. That had yet to be painted.

I looked at the murals on the walls and recognized some of the scenes because they were pictures she had done to illustrate various children's books. The far wall consisted entirely of a shadowed wood with sunlight drizzling through and winding paths leading into misty mountain ranges topped with castles.

'What do you think?' she asked softly.

'Oh Momma, it's beautiful, just beautiful. I love it!'

I had been so entranced by the murals and paintings on the ceiling, I hadn't noticed the man sitting on the small sofa with an elaborately decorated frame. The sofa was facing the doorway, so that he had been looking at the two of us while I had been turning in slow circles, my breath caught, my eyes wide, gaping in awe.

'Oh,' I said retreating a step closer to Momma. I couldn't help blushing with embarrassment.

The handsome young man with the brightest blue eyes I had ever seen laughed. He was dressed in a burgundy velvet smoking jacket and dark slacks and had thick, richly dark brown hair.

His lips were full and even I could see they were more than a little sensual and his face was as tanned as a movie star's. I thought he had an air of elegance and celebrity about him.

When he stood up, I saw that he was strong-looking with wide shoulders. He was tall, maybe an inch or so taller than Daddy, and had long, graceful-looking hands. There was power emanating from him and a confidence and certainty he seemed too young to possess.

'Forgive me,' he said, 'but I had to look at the two of you freely for a moment. There is no question this is your daughter, Jillian. She has inherited your *joie de vivre* and her eyes sparkle with your exuberance.' I looked at Momma to see how she reacted to such lavish compliments. Oh, she seemed to blossom under them, like a flower in a warm summer rain. 'Welcome to Farthy.'

'This is Mr Tatterton, Leigh,' Momma said not taking her eyes from him.

Mr Tatterton? I was astonished. From the way Momma had spoken about him, I just assumed he was a much older, gray-haired man. I thought all millionaires somehow looked like the men in our history text: the Rockefellers and Carnegies, and oil barons, stuffy old men who cared only about Wall Street or cartels and monopolies.

I looked at Momma and saw from the brightness in her face that she was amused with my reaction and she liked Tony Tatterton very much.

'Hello, Mr Tatterton,' I said.

'Oh, please, please, call me Tony. So, how do you like your mother's work?' he asked, gesturing toward the ceiling and then toward the walls.

'It's wonderful. I love it!'

'Yes.' He turned back to me and gazed at me with a sharp, penetrating look that made my heart pound and brought a warmth to my neck. I hoped I hadn't broken out in blotches. Ever since I was a little girl, the slightest bit of excitement could make me do that.

'I love it too,' Tony said, 'and I am forever indebted to Mrs Deveroe for bringing your mother around. Well,' he said clasping his hands together. 'First things, first. I'm sure you want a tour of Farthy.'

'Me, too,' I heard a small voice cry and turned to my left to see a small boy with dark, inquisitive eyes as big as half dollars staring up at me from the corner of the couch. He had obviously been hiding behind it. He had the very same dark brown hair that Tony Tatterton had and he wore it long, but cut neatly around, making him look like a little prince. He was dressed in a dark blue sailor suit.

'Come over here, Troy,' Tony Tatterton urged, 'and let me introduce you properly. Come on.'

The little boy hesitated and continued to stare up at me.

'Hi,' I said. 'My name's Leigh. Want to shake hands?' He nodded quickly and stood up to rush over.

'Well, we can see that Troy has already developed good taste at the age of four. Troy is my little brother,' Tony explained as I took Troy's little hand into mine. Troy looked up at me anxiously. 'I suppose you might say I'm more like a father than a brother to him since both our parents are gone,' Tony added.

'Oh.' I looked down at this cute little boy and felt sorry for him. He looked as fragile and as tiny as a small bird that had fallen from its nest and lost the warmth and care of its mother. There was a longing in his eyes, a cry for someone warm and loving.

'Troy, meet Jillian's daughter Leigh. Leigh, this is Troy Langdon Tatterton,' Tony said and smiled widely, for Troy had not let go of my hand. I knelt down to look into his face.

'You want to go on the tour, too?' I asked and he nodded quickly and reached out for me to take him into my arms. I hugged him to me and lifted him. I looked up and caught Tony Tatterton staring at me with his intense blue eyes. His eyes held mine for a moment, making me very uncomfortable, then he laughed.

'A lady killer. I knew it,' Tony said. 'You must be someone very special though, Leigh. He's usually rather shy around people he first meets.'

I blushed and looked away quickly. If anything, I was the

shy one, I thought. But little Troy looked so delicate, I didn't want to do anything to hurt his feelings.

'Oh he won't be shy around me. Will you, Troy?' He shook his head.

'Great,' Tony said. 'Let's tour the house and then go outside to see the pool and the horses. After lunch, we'll all take a walk to the beach. But Leigh can't carry you everywhere, Troy. You're too big and heavy now.'

'It's all right,' I said. 'I'm sure Troy will want to walk by himself soon anyway, right Troy?' He nodded and studied me closely. I saw a fear in his eyes, a fear that I would drop him and ignore him. 'Maybe Troy can tell me about things and show me things too. Can you, Troy?' He nodded. 'Okay, we're ready.'

Tony laughed again and he and Momma led us out. Perhaps no room in the big house was as impressive as the dining room. It was as big as a banquet hall with the longest table I had ever seen. While we were there, the cook came out of the kitchen and Tony introduced him to us. I could see Tony was very proud of him. He had discovered him on a trip to New Orleans and brought him back to be his personal chef. His name was Ryse Williams and he was a very warm and happy black man who had a way of speaking that made his words sound like music. He promised to fix us 'a lunch so special, our stomiks wouldn't stop thankin' us fer days'.

My arms got so tired I thought they might have stretched several inches. I put Troy down for our walk up the marble staircase. He was anxious for me to see his room. All the bedrooms upstairs were really suites, each with its own sitting room. Troy's sitting room was so filled with toys, it looked like a toy store.

'Hasn't your mother told you about my business?' Tony asked, seeing my astonishment. I shook my head. 'You mean, she didn't tell you you were going to see the king of the toy makers?' He and Momma looked at each other as if that were a private joke. I shook my head again, confused by both the conversation and the amused looks between Momma and this intense, handsome young man.

‘Why would she call you king of the toy makers?’ I asked while Troy went to his pile of toys to pick something special out to show me.

‘It’s how we’ve built our fortune,’ he said. He saw the way my eyes widened with interest and he smiled, a small tight smile . . . amused. ‘I can see you have been a deprived child, not to have ever been given a Tatterton toy. Jillian, you should be ashamed of yourself,’ he kidded.

‘Please, I have enough trouble getting her father to buy her the proper things for a young girl,’ Momma replied archly. Tony and she stared at each other for a moment as if they had discussed this before and then he turned back to me.

‘Our toys are special, Leigh. They are not ordinary toys made of plastic. What we make is really meant for collectors, for wealthy people who cannot grow up and forget they are no longer children. Perhaps some still regret their memories of being poor when there was barely anything under their Christmas trees or anything for their birthdays.

‘Do you see the castle with the moat there?’ he said pointing to the far left corner of Troy’s bedroom. ‘That was handmade by one of my craftsmen. If you look closely at it, you’ll see the detailed work. Each toy is only one of a kind, so each is special and valuable. Those who can afford it set up their own kingdom, you might say.’

I walked over to look at the castle.

‘There are even tiny people, servants, peasants, lords and ladies!’ I exclaimed. ‘Are all your toys so perfect?’

‘Yes, they are, or I won’t let them be sold.’ His velvet sleeve brushed mine as he stepped beside me and I caught the rich scent of his expensive cologne and aftershave. ‘And we make games too, but games that are so difficult they keep the best minds intrigued for hours and hours.’ He looked at Momma again and they smiled at each other as before, as if they shared a private joke.

‘Rich people tend to get bored faster. Some of them are always bored, and that’s when they turn to collectibles, be they antiques or my toys. There are people in this country who have so much money, they don't have the time to spend it. I provide them another outlet, a place to find fantasy.

'If you came with me to one of my toy shops, you'd think you were stepping into a fairyland. In my stores people can enter any time period they desire, be it the past or the future. We find they are more interested in the past. Maybe they're afraid of the future,' he concluded philosophically.

I stared at him. He spoke about his customers as if they were to be pitied. I didn't think he really respected them, and yet, they provided the income for him to keep up this magnificent estate.

'See,' Troy urged and pulled on my skirt. I looked down to see him clutching a metal fire truck almost as big as he was. All the parts on it were moveable and some were detachable. The small firemen had faces molded and painted in such detail, each had a distinctly different look. Troy pressed a button and a siren went off.

'That's wonderful, Troy,' I said. 'I bet you have so much fun with it.'

'Wanna play?' he asked.

'Leigh can't play with your toys right now, Troy,' Tony explained. 'We're taking her on a tour, remember?'

He looked heart-broken.

'We'll play later,' I said. 'I promise, okay?'

He nodded, his hope revived.

From his room we went to the other suites, each more luxurious and larger than the last. All the sitting rooms were fully furnished with restored nineteenth-century pieces, some looking as if they had never been used. There was art work everywhere, too. The bathrooms were big and ornate with brass fittings and tubs as big as small pools. There were mirrors everywhere, which made the bathrooms and the bedrooms look even larger.

Momma and Tony Tatterton walked ahead of us when we went outside to tour the grounds. They spoke so low when they talked to each other, I couldn't hear what they were saying, but I probably wouldn't have heard anything anyway because of Troy. I held his hand as we walked along the pathways through the landscaped gardens and lawn toward the pool and cabana, and he began a remarkable monologue for a little boy his age. Once he had warmed up to me, he revealed just how precocious he was.

'Boris the garden man is going to make little trees grow there,' he said pointing off to the right where two groundsmen were working. 'The flowers are dead, but after the winter, they'll be more and more 'cause Boris says he's going to plant more different ones this time.

'He's the boss of the maze, too,' Troy said, obviously very impressed with that.

'The maze?'

He pointed off to my right and I saw it. The walls of hedges looked twelve or thirteen feet high at least.

'How far does it go?' I asked.

'All the way down there,' Troy pointed, 'and to the little cottage.'

'Little cottage?'

'Uh huh.' He nodded and then let go of my hand and ran up to Tony, pulling on the bottom of his smoking jacket.

'Leigh wants to go in the maze! Leigh wants to go in the maze!' he chanted.

'Oh?' Tony and Momma turned back to me.

'I didn't say that. He's a little imp. But it might be fun,' I added looking toward it.

'You've got to be careful going in there,' Tony warned. 'People actually get lost in there.'

'It's that big and deep?' I asked, intrigued.

'Oh yes. I never actually measured it, but Boris, my head groundskeeper, thinks it's at least a half an acre, if not more.'

'Let's go in the maze, Tony!' Troy cried. 'Let's go in the maze!'

'Maybe afterward, Troy. We've got to show Leigh the pool and the stables and take her down to the beach, don't we? There's just too much to do in one day,' he added shaking his head. 'I'm afraid you'll have to come back here again and again, otherwise Troy will get very upset.'

I looked at Momma. She was smiling like a Cheshire cat, grinning from ear to ear.

'Maybe you'll return next weekend,' Tony said.

'Yes, please, please,' Troy pleaded.

'I . . . we're going away next weekend, but when we come back . . .'

'Going away?' Tony turned abruptly to Momma. 'I don't remember you mentioning any trip.'

'I learned about it myself only last night,' she said. I was surprised at how displeased about it she sounded. But why? I wondered. She had wanted this trip so much. 'We'll talk about it later,' she added softly to Tony and turned so they would continue the tour. Their conversation, although just as low, became more animated with both of them gesturing. Tony was probably just worried about his unfinished murals, I told myself.

Little Troy began to whine about the maze again.

'All right,' I told him. 'You and I will just run in and out of it after we look at the pool, okay?'

'Okay.' He took my hand again and looked up at me, very pleased.

'You're a little charmer, aren't you, Troy Langdon Tatterton?'

He shrugged as if he understood exactly what I meant and I laughed and laughed.

What a strange and yet wonderful place this was, I thought as we went on. It was vast and beautiful and had so many things to offer its inhabitants, but Farthinggale was so immense a place for just a bachelor and his tiny little brother. Even with an army of servants around them, they must be very lonely, I thought. Poor little Troy, I thought, by the age of four to have lost both his parents. I shivered to think of losing my own dear parents, whom I loved so much. Momma often made it sound as if money could buy happiness, but I was sure if little Troy could choose, he would choose to give up all this to get his parents back. I knew I would.

Tony let Troy run down into the Olympic size pool which had recently been emptied. He thought it was funny to go where the deep water had once been.

'The little tyke swims, you know,' Tony whispered in my ear. 'Ever since he was a year and a half old.'

'Really?'

'Leigh, come in. Come in, Leigh. The water's fine.' Troy laughed at his own joke. He stopped about midway and beckoned.

'It's too cold to go swimming,' I cried. He looked up at me with the most grown-up expression of amazement on his face.

'I was teasing. There's no water in it,' he said holding his arms out as if he were talking to a complete idiot. I had to laugh, and so did Momma and Tony.

'All right,' I said. 'I'll take a dip.' I walked down the steps and into the pool. He took my hand and led me to the deep end.

'I can swim from here to here,' he said, pointing. After he touched the far wall, we turned to go back and out. Momma and Tony were off somewhere else. When we went up the steps, I saw them over by the cabana, again conversing in a very animated fashion and standing very close to each other. I thought Tony looked upset. Momma saw that Troy and I had reappeared and put her hand on his forearm to interrupt.

'Oh Leigh,' she called, 'look, there's even a small stage out here for a band to play while people swim.'

'That's right,' Tony said. 'We have wonderful pool parties all summer: sumptuous foods and dancing into the night. Did you ever go swimming under the stars?' he asked me and pointed to the sky as if it were the middle of the night and the stars were out. I shook my head, but just talking about it sounded wonderful.

Troy tugged my arm and I looked down at his pleading eyes.

'Tony, would it be all right for Troy to take me just a little ways into the maze on the way to the stables?' I asked and nodded toward him.

'All right,' he told Troy. 'You can take Leigh into the maze. Enter just over there,' he said pointing, 'but don't go beyond the first turn,' he instructed me.

'You make it sound as if it can swallow you up,' I exclaimed.

His face grew serious, his cerulean blue eyes narrowing.

'It can,' he warned. I nodded, impressed with his concern.

'All right, Troy. We can go, but you heard what your brother said. Hold my hand and don't run off in there, understand?'

'Uh huh.' He shook his head emphatically.

'Momma?' I thought she might want to come along.

'Go on,' she said. 'We'll wait for you.'

I took Troy's hand and we walked across the grounds to the maze.

I saw from the precise, careful way little Troy entered it that he was quite taken with the maze. There was suddenly an expression of reverence and awe on his face. He held my hand tightly, and for a moment, I felt as if I had entered a church. It was so quiet. Even the chirps of the small garden birds sounded distant and faded, and the melancholy cries of the sea gulls flying overhead were muffled, faraway. The hedges were so tall that at one point, they shut off the warmth of the sun and cast long, dark shadows in our path. Yet, I found the maze serene, quietly beautiful and mysterious. When we arrived at the first turn and I looked down the next pathway that had branches leading off right and left, presenting choices that could lead a wanderer around in circles or eventually to a destination, I realized the challenge and couldn't help being just a bit excited and curious. This was probably what Tony meant when he warned the maze could swallow you up. It had a way of tempting, drawing, daring any intruder to solve its secrets. I thought I would love to come back some day by myself and try it.

'Have you ever gone farther in, Troy?' I asked.

'Oh sure. Tony takes me to the cottage sometimes. He can go right through,' he said, illustrating by zigzagging his palm in front of me. Then he leaned toward me, his eyes bursting with excitement and whispered, 'Wanna try it?'

'You little devil. You heard what your brother said. Now come on, let's go back. I want to see the horses next.'

He pulled back and smirked like a young man at least four times his age. Then, his mind switched excited thoughts instantly, and he started me back toward the entrance.

'Come on, I'll show you my pony, Sniffles, and you can ride him, okay?'

'Sniffles?' I followed him out, my laughter trailing behind, left to fade in the shadows of the maze.

Tony and Momma had walked on a ways and were having one of their animated talks again. Butterflies started in my stomach at the sight of Momma throwing back her lovely head and laughing her beautiful throaty laugh at something Tony had said. I tried to tell myself that I was just hungry for lunch. But oh, part of me was enthralled by everything in this fairy-tale kingdom and part wanted to run from its mysterious spell.

'Tony! Tony!' Troy cried, releasing his hold on my hand and running toward them. 'Leigh wants to ride Sniffles. Can she? Huh? Can she?'

I shook my head.

'Leigh wants to ride? Or you want her to ride?' Tony asked him. Troy shrugged, not seeing the difference. 'Now Troy, you know it takes time to get the pony ready. We've got to tell Curly first and Leigh really isn't dressed to ride a horse anyway, is she?' he asked. Troy looked back at me. I was wearing one of my new cashmere sweaters with one of my flared skirts instead of one of the new slim ones.

Momma snapped her fingers.

'I knew there was something I forgot. I was going to buy her a riding outfit for her birthday.'

'Her birthday?' Tony said. 'Oh, that's right, yesterday was Leigh's birthday.' He winked at Momma and stepped forward. 'I knew there was some reason I was carrying this,' he told me and took a small box out from his jacket pocket. It was wrapped in gold foil with a black ribbon tied in a bow around it.

'What's that?'

'It's obviously a birthday present, Leigh,' Momma said, a little snappishly. 'Take it and say thank you.'

'But . . .' I took it slowly.

'What is it? What is it?' Troy demanded.

I untied the bow and unwrapped the small box. Then I opened it to look upon a gold pendant in the shape of an ocean liner with a gold necklace. There were two tiny diamonds on the pendant, one atop each smokestack.

'Oh, look,' I said holding it out. Momma shook her head and smiled.

'Beautiful.'

'Me too. Show me, too,' Troy cried. I knelt down and he gazed at it with short-lived interest.

'It won't float,' he said.

'It's not supposed to float, Troy. You wear it around your neck, see,' I said taking it out and holding it up.

'Look at the back of the charm,' Tony said.

I turned it over and read, 'The Princess Leigh'.

'That is beautiful, Tony,' Momma said, no longer sounding at all snappish. 'I wish her father would give her things like that instead of actual working ship models to take apart and study,' she added.

'Daddies are always the last to see how grown up their daughters have become.' I looked up quickly. He gazed at me with those intense blue eyes, and it made me feel older. The feeling made me blush and, my heart racing, I looked down just as quickly as I had looked up.

'Anyway, I hope you like it, Leigh,' Tony said, almost in a whisper.

'Oh, I love it. Thank you. Thank you so much.' I looked at Momma who nodded and I knew she wanted me to kiss him. Because I hardly knew him, I felt funny doing it even though he had just given me a very expensive gift. But Momma looked as if she expected it and I wanted to do everything right, if not for myself, then for her.

Tony anticipated the thank you kiss. He leaned toward me and turned his cheek toward my lips. I kissed him quickly, but closed my eyes and inhaled the scent of his aftershave. He was really the first man I had ever kissed, other than Daddy. I couldn't stop my heart from pounding. It made me feel a little dizzy. I hoped he hadn't noticed.

'Thank you,' I murmured.

'Here, let me help you put it on,' Tony said and took it from my hands. My fingers were actually trembling. He opened the chain and put it around my neck. I felt his warm breath at the back of my neck as he studied the clasp. 'These things are so tiny. There, I have it.' He stepped back beside Momma and they looked at the charm on me. It fell just between my breasts.

Momma looked faraway and almost sad as if she had suddenly become a little jealous.

'Good.' Tony clapped his hands. 'Well then,' he said, 'let's go on and look at the stables so that when you do have that riding outfit, you can see what you can do.'

When we arrived at the stables, Troy called out for Curly, who turned out to be a short, stout Scotsman who indeed had very curly red hair. I thought he was about fifty years old. Each of his chubby cheeks had two bright red spots, so bright they looked like he had put on clown make-up.

'You wanna take a gander at Sniffles, I imagine,' he said leading the way.

Curly opened the stall door and I looked in at the black and white Shetland pony. She was so precious, I fell in love with her instantly. Troy offered her some hay and she took it gingerly and began to chew, her eyes on me.

'You can pet her if you'd like, Miss.'

'I will. Thank you.' I stroked the little horse, again thinking what a magical place Farthinggale Manor was with its beautiful grounds, its enormous pool and cabana with a stage, its maze and now its riding stables. I began to understand why Momma was so taken with it. Perhaps she would try to get Daddy to move out of the city and buy an estate too, I thought.

'Will you come back tomorrow and ride her?' Troy asked. 'Will you?'

'Maybe not tomorrow, Troy, but soon.'

He looked disappointed again. Oh, how desperately he needed a mother, someone who could be soft and loving. Tony was probably a good brother to him, but he couldn't give him the comfort a mother could give him. I wished we could bring him home with us. I had always wanted a little brother.

It took Momma and Tony quite a while to join us at the stables. I had begun to wonder if we should start back to find them. When they did arrive, Tony announced it was time to see about lunch. Momma had decided she wanted to put in two hours of work on the murals after we ate, so Tony offered to take me and Troy to the beach without her. Tony saw I was disappointed. I had wanted to watch Momma work.

'I'll show you all my special places on the beach,' Tony promised. 'I love the ocean.' His expression changed, darkened. 'It's full of magic and mystery and changes every day.'

'My father loves it too,' I said.

'I'm sure he does. But I'm glad I don't depend on it for my living,' he added. 'The ocean can be so finicky . . . just like a woman.' I was surprised when Momma laughed at that. If Daddy had said it I was sure she would have scowled or said nothing. But it seemed no matter what Tony Tatterton did or said, she thought it was wonderful. 'Beautiful, all-powerful and untrustworthy,' he continued, smiling a broad smile that didn't seem to reach his eyes. 'But there's nothing lovelier. Except, of course, your mother,' he added looking at Momma. I turned quickly to see her reaction, but instead of embarrassment, she wore a look of pride.

Shouldn't it be embarrassing when you're married and another man compliments you so lavishly, I wondered.

It was so much easier just being a little girl, I almost wished I could return to being just that; but I knew Time and Fate weren't about to let me go back.

THREE

A Very Private Place

Lunch was as wonderful as Ryse Williams had predicted and Tony made it into such a formal affair. Suddenly we were surrounded by servants, new faces that seemed to come out of the woodwork – two waiters and a maid. I felt as if I were in a fancy restaurant.

The table was set with very expensive-looking china that Tony explained had been passed down from his grandparents. We all sat at one end of the tremendous table, Troy and I on Tony's left, Momma on his right. Each setting had a wine goblet, even Troy's. Tony winked at me when he poured a few drops into his brother's glass. Troy acted very grown up about it, showing no surprise at all. I saw from the way he studied Tony's every move, that he was trying to act just like him. He took his napkin off the table, unfolded it and placed it neatly in his little lap. Then he sat back with the same perfect posture.

Beside the fruit cup, with each piece of fruit cut into a fancy shape, we had a delicious salad that included ingredients I had never tasted nor seen. Some of it looked like flower petals, but it all tasted wonderful. The main dish was a Cajun shrimp platter on a bed of wild rice. It was spicy but scrumptious. For dessert, Ryse Williams brought out a peach melba himself. I was so full, I looked forward to the walk on the beach.

'Leigh,' Tony said, 'why don't you take Troy out and I will join the two of you in a moment. Your mother and I just have one more thing or two to discuss concerning the murals.'

'Come on, Leigh,' Troy cried jumping off his seat. I looked at Momma. She had her elbows on the table, her hands clasped, the fingers pressed up against her lips, but there was a smile of contentment around her eyes. Here amidst this enchantment she looked more than ever like a princess in a fairy tale, I thought.

'I'm going to go change into my smock,' she said softly.

I followed Troy out of the front door.

'Where are you going, Troy?' I asked. He had started off to the right and then had gone in behind a shrub. He answered by showing me the little pail and shovel he had fetched.

'I left it here yesterday when I was working with Boris. We need it on the beach.'

'Oh. Yes, we do.'

'Come on,' he said, 'Tony will catch up.'

'I think we had better wait.'

'I'm always waiting, waiting, waiting,' he said and stamped his foot. Then he plopped himself down on the grass and folded his arms across his chest in a sulk.

'He won't be long, I'm sure,' I said and smiled reassuringly.

'If your Momma's going to paint, he won't come out.' What an odd thing for him to say, I thought. Surely Tony didn't look over Momma's shoulder the whole time she worked. He had his own business to tend, and Momma had never liked an audience when she drew and painted.

Troy turned his eyes to me suspiciously.

'Where's your Daddy?' he asked. 'Did he die and go to heaven to be with angels, too?'

'No, he's working. I wanted him to come with us today, but he couldn't,' I added. He continued to stare at me with curiosity. Then he looked toward the front door of the mansion, his eyes growing smaller.

'*Hello!*' Tony called from the top of the steps. Troy jumped to his feet. 'Okay, let's go,' Tony said coming down quickly, and Troy shot forward. 'Do you get to the ocean much, Leigh?' he asked as we started after Troy.

'I go down to the harbor to my father's office frequently and we've gone on a number of ocean voyages,' I said.

I couldn't believe how nervous I was without Momma to accompany us. I was so afraid I would say or do the wrong thing and embarrass her, as well as myself. Tony seemed so self-assured. With the kind of wealth he possessed, and the big business he ran, he had to be a very cosmopolitan and sophisticated young man, I thought. Because of Daddy's business, I had traveled a great deal more than most of my friends and met many more people from different countries, but still, I didn't feel confident.

'Oh, of course,' Tony said. 'Silly of me to ask. What I really meant is, do you get to the beach in the summer?'

'Not that much, no. Momma's not fond of the beach. She hates getting sand all over her. But a friend of mine, Michele Almstead, has a swimming pool.'

'Ah.' We walked on. Troy ambled ahead, wobbling on his little legs, his pail swinging back and forth with his determined arm movements.

'He's so cute,' I said.

'Yes,' Tony replied in a sad voice. 'It's been hard for the little tyke. He was very sickly at birth. There was a time there when we didn't think he would make it.'

'Oh. What happened to . . .'

'To our parents?'

I nodded.

'Our mother died only a year and a half after Troy's birth. She had a rare blood disease. My father passed away a year ago next month, heart attack.' His eyes went from a warm sky blue to frosty ice, as he must have remembered tragedy. 'It happened in the maze.'

'The maze!'

'Yes, and unfortunately, little Troy was with him at the time.'

'Oh no,' I cried.

'They were going to the other side. We have a little cottage there. No one uses it now, but it's so quaint and special, we keep it up and Troy thinks it's a magical place from one of his children's stories. Do you know he was reading when he was only about two and a half. A nanny we had working for us then, Mrs Habersham, a delightful elderly lady from London, spent hours patiently teaching him. He's very, very bright, far ahead of his age.'

'I know, but how horrible it must have been for him to be

there in the maze when such a thing happened!' I exclaimed. 'What did he do?'

'Amazingly, he didn't panic. Another child his age would have most probably sat there beside his father's body, crying and crying until someone eventually found him. But Troy realized something was seriously wrong with our father and found his way out of the maze quickly. I can still hear him screaming for me as he came running toward the front door. We rushed to my father, but it was too late.'

'I'm sorry. How sad,' I said, thinking again of what it would be like to lose my own daddy, even now when I was old enough to understand what death was.

'It's been harder for Troy, of course. No nanny I hire can replace a mother and no matter what I do, I can't substitute for a father. I can't spend enough time with him, not the kind of time he needs.'

'Is Mrs Habersham still here?'

'No, she got sick and had to return to England. Right now I have Mrs Hastings doubling as nanny and maid. Here,' he said, 'we just go over this hill. Troy's already on the beach.'

As soon as we walked over a little knoll, we confronted the ocean. It was breathtaking the way we just stepped up and there it was, the vast Atlantic spread out before us. Troy was down on the beach already digging. The beach went on and on in both directions.

'All this is your private beach?' I asked in amazement.

'Yes. There is a little inlet there,' he said pointing to the right, 'a very private, quiet place I used to go to when I wanted to be alone.'

'How wonderful.'

'Do you like it here, Leigh?' he asked, gazing at me with those sharp, penetrating eyes again.

'Very much.'

'I'm glad,' he said. He smiled at me with so much warmth in his eyes, his stare almost drinking me in. How old was he? I wondered. At times he seemed worldly, so very wise, and at times he seemed no older than a high school boy. He looked out at the ocean again.

'It *is* wonderful here,' he said. 'When I was seven, I was sent to Eton because my father thought the English knew more about discipline than our private schools do. He was right, but I was always dreaming of coming home to Farthy.' He closed his eyes and in a soft voice added, 'Whenever I felt homesick, which was most of the time, I'd close my eyes and pretend I could smell the balsam, fir, and pine trees, and more than anything, the briny scent of the sea and I'd wake up aching, wanting to feel the damp, cool morning air on my face, wanting my home so badly, it physically hurt.'

I held my breath as he spoke. I had never heard anyone speak of his home so romantically. Tony Tatterton was capable of such deep passion, I thought. It brought tingles to my spine to listen to him. He snapped open his eyes as if someone had slapped his cheek.

'But it's a lot of responsibility running an estate this size and a business that's growing in leaps and bounds all by yourself. And with a small child to look after, as well,' he added.

'For someone so young,' I said. It just blurted out. He laughed.

'How old do you think I am?'

'I don't know . . . twenty.'

'Twenty-three.'

Twenty-three, I thought. Momma was nearly twice his age yet she seemed only a few years older, if that.

'Come, let's stroll along the beach here and listen to the ocean's roar. We can't go back to the house too early and interrupt the artist. You know how artists are – sensitive, moody,' he said and laughed.

We had a nice walk. He told me about the plans he had to expand his business and asked me many questions about my school and life in Boston. Afterward, Troy and I went searching for sea shells while Tony lay back on the beach, his hands behind his head, his eyes closed. By the time we returned to the house, Momma had cleaned up and changed again. Most of the castle on the dome was painted.

'I have a day or so of work left,' she declared. 'We have to start back to Boston now. I'd like to get home before dark.'

Troy lowered his head in disappointment.

'Leigh will come back another day, Troy. It's not nice to act this way in front of guests,' Tony instructed. Troy looked up at me, tears building up in the corners of his eyes. 'Now thank them for visiting us and wish them a good trip home.'

'Thank you,' Troy said. 'Have a good trip home,' he recited.

'Thank you, Troy,' I said.

'I'll have Miles bring your car around,' Tony said and started out.

'Want to walk us to the car?' I asked Troy. He nodded and took my hand.

I knelt down before getting in the car and gave Troy a kiss on his cheek. He touched his cheek, thought a moment and then gave me a kiss on mine before turning around abruptly and charging up the steps to go back into the house. Curtis opened the door for him, but he hesitated at the front door and looked back longingly.

Tony and Momma spoke quietly behind the car and then she got in behind the wheel.

'So long, Leigh,' he said, his eyes seeming to look into me and read my thoughts. 'I hope you enjoyed your day at Farthy and will return soon.'

I looked away, hoping Momma didn't think I was rude. 'Bye, and thank you again for the wonderful birthday present,' I said lifting the gold pendant.

'It's all been my pleasure.' He stepped back and we started away. I looked back and saw little Troy still standing by the front door, waving his little hand. It brought tears to my eyes. We drove down the long drive and back under the great arch and I indeed felt as if I had just left a magical kingdom, full of wonderful things, and yet full of mystery and sadness, too. I hadn't been wrong. It was just like a storybook place after all.

'Isn't Tony wonderful?' Momma said as soon as we pulled away. 'And wasn't it sweet of him to remember your birthday and buy you such an expensive gift? I just happened to mention your birthday was coming up, not expecting he would remember, and certainly not expecting him to buy you something.'

'It was nice.' I didn't say that I thought it was unusual for a man I had never known before to buy me such an expensive present, even if he was very wealthy.

'Did you have a good time at Farthy? Wasn't it everything I promised it would be?' Momma's face was still bright with excitement.

'Oh yes. Troy is so cute, isn't he?'

'He's cute, but Tony spoils him. It's only going to make things more difficult for him later on.' I was surprised at how stern she sounded.

'Tony feels so bad for him, losing both of his parents so young. Don't you think that's it?' I waited, but she didn't answer. Suddenly she laughed.

'Tony swears we look more like sisters than a mother and daughter. It's because I take such good care of my complexion. I drink a lot of water and I stay away from greasy, heavy foods and always leave the dinner table a little hungry. Never stuff yourself, Leigh. It's unladylike, besides being ruinous to your figure.'

'I know. You always tell me that.'

'Well, it's true. Look at me. Aren't I proof that it's true?' She twisted herself around in the driver's seat as if she were showing me her figure for the first time.

'Yes.'

'Do any of your friends' mothers look like me?' she demanded.

'No, Momma.' It wasn't the first time we'd had this conversation. I didn't understand why I had to keep telling her she looked so beautiful.

'I don't intend to ever look old,' she declared with determination.

'But you can't stop yourself from growing old, can you?'

'I can't stop myself from getting older in years, but I can stop myself from looking older,' she boasted. 'How old do you think I look? Go on, tell me what you think.'

'I know how old you are, Momma. I was talking to Tony and . . .'

'You didn't tell him how old I was, did you?' she demanded, her face suddenly screwed into an expression of panic, her eyes glittering at me. 'Did you!' Her delicate eyebrows rose.

'No. He just told me how old he was.'

'Good. Good,' she repeated with relief. 'He thinks I'm only twenty-eight.'

'Twenty-eight! But Momma, he knows I'm twelve. That would mean you had me when you were only sixteen!'

'So?' She shrugged. 'It was very common in the South, Texas especially, for girls to get married at young ages. I knew girls who were only a few years older than you and already married with their first child.'

'Really?' I tried to imagine myself already married. It seemed like such a big responsibility to have a husband, much less have a husband and children too. What would my husband be like? I wondered. I had never really thought about it. Oh, I dreamt and fantasized about movie stars and singers but I never mused about actually setting up house and living every day with the same man. Of course, I would want him to be as loving and considerate as Daddy. I wouldn't want him to work as hard or as much, so if we weren't as rich, I wouldn't demand things all the time the way Momma did; but if we were rich, I would want the same things, I imagined.

He should be as debonair and sophisticated as Tony Tatterton was, too, I thought, and certainly as handsome. And I would want him to love and care for our children just as much as I did. He didn't have to be a movie star or a big businessman, as long as he loved me more than anything else in the world.

But what about me? I wondered. Could I care for someone else as much as I cared for myself? Was I capable of loving someone the way a wife should love a husband? I hadn't even graduated from high school, and I wanted to go to college too. Lately, I had been thinking about becoming a teacher and my day with little Troy had reaffirmed those ambitions. I enjoyed little children, loved their innocence and their inquisitiveness. Most children asked anything they wanted, even the most embarrassing questions. They were unpredictable and I found that delightful, even exciting at times.

'I don't want to get married for a long time,' I declared.

'What? Why not?' Momma asked, a smirk on her face as if I had declared I wanted to be an atheist.

'I was thinking of going to college to become a teacher, a grade school teacher,' I announced boldly. Momma's unhappy expression didn't change at all, as I had hoped it would; if anything it deepened.

'That's ridiculous, Leigh. You know who becomes grade school teachers – spinsters, women who look like my sisters or dumpy women with poor complexions. Just think for a moment. Can you imagine someone like me being a grade school teacher? Can you? It would be a terrible waste, wouldn't it? Well, it will be the same for you, for I expect you to develop into a beautiful young woman. I told you – you're going to be a debutante. You're going to go to the finest finishing schools and meet wealthy, aristocratic young men so someday you will live on an estate just like Farthy. I know I should be living on one,' she added, an ominous tone in her voice.

'But Momma, I like little children. I just loved spending the day with little Troy.'

'Liking little children is one thing. I like little children at times. There is a time and a place for them, but to condemn yourself to a life with them, stuffed away in some public school where you have no opportunity to meet people of the finer classes . . . ugh,' she said shaking her head as if I had suggested working in a coal mine. 'Little children are always sick. They sneeze and cough all over you. That's why those grade school teachers look so yellow and anemic.'

I thought about some of mine. They hadn't appeared sickly and pale to me. Mrs Wilson was a beautiful woman with long, dark brown hair and warm, green eyes. I loved her smile of sunshine. She was so nice, it was hard for her to get real mad, even when the boys pulled pranks like putting tacks on someone's seat.

'Put such thoughts out of your mind. You want to study the arts, music. You want to travel more. Next thing I know,' she said, 'is you'll tell me you want to be one of your father's ship engineers.'

'I did once dream of becoming the first woman to captain an ocean liner,' I confessed. 'And I told Daddy.'

'Yes, and what brilliant thing did your father say?'

'He said someday that might just happen. There are women doctors and women lawyers, why not women as ship captains?'

'Just like him to encourage such thoughts. Next thing you'll know, there'll be women electricians and plumbers and telephone linemen. Oh, they'll have to be known as telephone women, though, won't they?' she asked and laughed. 'Really, Leigh, I'm afraid we're going to have to get you away from the shipyards sooner than I thought, and off to some decent girls' school. It's just not healthy for you to be hanging around your father's office or going down into engine rooms surrounded by all those sweaty, greasy men. Do you see me doing that? When was the last time I went to your father's office? I can't recall it myself.

'Now let me think about this *bon voyage* party your father wants to have for the Caribbean cruise. I've already invited Tony Tatterton.'

'You have?'

'Of course. And I'm going to invite a number of his wealthy friends, too. But let me think now. If I don't plan out this party, your father will make it look like a funeral.'

She became silent for most of the remainder of our trip home, planning the party in her mind as she said she would. I thought about all the things she said and wondered if there was something wrong with me for not feeling as passionately as she did about certain things. I decided only time would tell and with the speed at which I was changing and developing, that wouldn't be so long a wait.

Since the *bon voyage* party was to be held in the ship's ballroom, Momma demanded that Daddy assign a different, larger vessel to the Caribbean cruise. He didn't want to do that because it would cut down on the profit since the ship was far too big for the anticipated number of passengers and required a much bigger crew. But she was insistent.

'You must learn to do things in a splashy way, Cleave,' she

told him. 'The impression you make on the public is what matters now, not worrying about the profit and loss column. We have the press coming and you showed me the passenger list – some of the finest families will be on this inaugural trip. It's worth the added expense.'

In the end Daddy gave in to her demands and assigned *The Jillian*, his second biggest luxury liner. Momma went down to the ship every day before the *bon voyage* party to oversee the decorations for the ballroom and to check on the entertainment, the menu, and the guest list. Many dignitaries from Boston were being invited even though they weren't taking the cruise. Then Momma came up with a very exciting idea.

There was a new musical being tried out in Boston for its eventual opening in New York, and it had already gotten rave reviews, *The Pajama Game*. We had gone to opening night. Momma talked Daddy into spending even more money to hire members of the cast to come to the *bon voyage* party and sing some of the highlights like 'Steam Heat'. That brought us a lot more newspaper and magazine attention.

I went along with her to the printers to put in the order for the invitations she had designed herself. The front of them had a picture of a couple dressed in evening clothes standing on the deck and looking out over an inky blue ocean with a sky full of stars. You could just feel the warmth and the romance. The inside of the cover had copy from a recent magazine advertisement.

TOMORROW . . . 1500 MILES AT SEA . . .

> Each day of a VanVoreen cruise is an open invitation. The luxury of breakfast in bed . . . games, or just loafing on the broad decks . . . shopping, dancing and fun . . . time to refresh . . . and plan for a busy schedule after arrival.
>
> Whether this is your second honeymoon or your first, what better tonic than the enveloping peace of sea, sky, and ship – the infinite resources of VanVoreen food and service.

BON VOYAGE!

And then on the inside page read the invitation:

THE PLEASURE OF YOUR COMPANY IS REQUESTED
FOR THE BON VOYAGE BALL
INAUGURATING THE NEW CARIBBEAN CRUISE
ON THE VANVOREEN LINES.
THE JILLIAN
8 P.M.

BLACK TIE

It was going to be very exciting. Momma bought a strapless black Christian Dior original that had a charcoal gray-colored velvet fur strip diagonally across the bodice and a billowing skirt. She wore her Tiffany necklace with the oval diamonds and matching oval diamond earrings and oval diamond bracelet. She spent all afternoon preparing herself, twice rejecting and changing the hairstyle her personal hairdresser created. She finally brought out magazines that had run features on members of the royal family in England and chose a style worn by one of the beautiful women, a real English duchess. Her hair was swept back off her forehead and down with the strands brushed behind her ear so her beautiful earrings would show.

When she finally stepped out of her suite to attend the ball, I thought she looked stunning. It was as if she were about to be crowned queen herself and I was to be one of her ladies-in-waiting.

I couldn't help but feel self-conscious in the dress she had picked out for me. It, too, was strapless, but I didn't feel as secure, even with the formfitting bra. I thought my shoulders were too bony, my collar bone was too prominent and my breasts looked obviously artificial, even silly, to my critical eyes. The dress was a deep, dark blue with a billowing skirt, under which I wore layers of crinoline. Momma had asked me to wear the necklace Tony had given me and then loaned me small gold button earrings that went with the necklace very well. I put on the gold bracelet she and Daddy had given me last year. I had my hair combed and brushed into a long page boy.

Daddy, dressed in his tuxedo, was pacing back and forth below as usual. When we started down the stairs together, he stopped and gazed up with a smile of awe. 'Magnificent, magnificent,' he cried. 'You look more beautiful than ever, Jillian.

'And you Leigh, tonight you are the princess for sure.' He kissed me quickly on the cheek and went to kiss Momma too, but she said he would spoil her make-up.

'Right, right. Anyway, we're quite late.'

Tonight, at Momma's insistence, we had a limousine waiting to take us to the ship. All our suitcases had been taken during the day and placed in our suites on board. It couldn't have been a more perfect night for a shipboard party. The sky was covered with stars and there were only wisps of clouds passing over them. Even the breeze down at the dock was unusually warm.

As soon as we arrived, we took our places at the ballroom's great entryway to greet everyone. As well as being one of Daddy's bigger ships, *The Jillian* was one of the most luxurious. The corridor leading to the ballroom was paneled in the finest wood, highly polished and inlaid with marble. Enormous mirrors in gilded frames lined the wall and there were pieces of antique French furniture – cushioned chairs, settees and dark pine tables along the way. Anyone entering surely felt that he or she were entering a palace.

The ballroom itself was an enormous room with burgundy velvet wall hangings draped from the high ceiling, and there was silver and gold-colored molding everywhere.

The room was lit by a dozen or so great chandeliers with fake candlesticks topped by flame-shaped bulbs. On the far right was a bar that extended nearly halfway across the room. A dozen or so bartenders dressed in starch white shirts and black bow ties with shiny black pants were getting the guests in the Caribbean mood with Margaritas and Piña Coladas.

Food was provided in buffet style on tables organized by courses: salad tables, soup tables, tables with duck, prime ribs, chicken and fish. An entire section was devoted to desserts like flaming baked Alaska, all sorts of cream and fruit pies, cakes and *petits fours*, and ice cream. Waiters and waitresses in Caribbean garb, the women wearing colorful headpieces, served hot *hors d'oeuvres* and glasses of champagne.

On the stage was a sixteen-piece Swing dance band with a female singer. They began playing as soon as we took our places and the guests began to arrive. Some guests moved right to the tiled floor in front of the stage and began to dance. There was an immediate air of festivity around us. Never had I seen so many fancy-dressed people, even on our other voyages and *bon voyage* parties. The women dressed in an array of styles, each trying to look more lovely and more fashionable than the others. Many wore embroidered ball gowns and were bedecked in diamonds and gold, some wearing diamond tiaras, but I didn't think anyone was as pretty as Momma.

Tony Tatterton was one of the last to arrive. He looked so tall and handsome in his elegant tuxedo. He came towards us quickly, a small and amused smile on his sensual lips and his cerulean blue eyes sparkling.

'Miss Leigh VanVoreen,' he said taking my hand and kissing it. I blushed and turned quickly to Momma. She had the beginnings of that excited little girl look on her face again, a look that immediately woke up the butterflies in my stomach.

'Cleave, I would like to introduce you to Townsend Anthony Tatterton, who you've heard me speak so much of,' she said. Daddy scrutinized Tony quickly and then smiled as warmly as he had smiled at everyone else.

'Pleased to meet you, Mr Tatterton. Thank you for giving my wife employment she enjoys.'

'Oh, it is I who should thank you, sir, for permitting her to demonstrate her talent on the walls of my home.'

Daddy nodded, his lips tight, his eyes small. I wasn't sure whether he was going to laugh or cry. Momma broke the scary silence by suggesting Tony get himself a drink. He turned as if noticing the party for the first time.

'Looks like quite an affair,' he said. 'Thank you for inviting me. Leigh,' he added turning my way, 'perhaps you will do me the honor of dancing with me later.'

I was speechless. Why me with all these incredibly beautiful, sophisticated women about? I couldn't go out there and dance with him in front of all these people. I wasn't that good. Oh, the very thought of doing it terrified me. He must have seen my fear in my face, for he smiled even more widely and then nodded at Momma and Daddy before heading toward the bar.

'Well,' Daddy said immediately, 'I think most of our guests have arrived. I have to meet the ship's captain for a while to discuss the itinerary and other matters.

'Now, Cleave?' Momma asked with irritation in her voice.

'I'm afraid so. You can hold things down here for a while, Jillian. Leigh, would you like to come along? You should learn about the business. Someday, all this will be yours. If it lasts,' he added.

'Now don't go taking her down to the engine room,' Momma ordered, 'as you did last time. She doesn't have to know how things work.'

'Of course she does. She should know things inside out, and besides,' Daddy said, 'she seems to have a proclivity toward mechanical things. I bet she could take apart an engine and put it back together in no time now, couldn't you, Leigh?'

'Hardly an accomplishment for a young lady to brag about,' Momma snapped. 'I wish you would treat her more like what she is and not like some tomboy. Really, Cleave.' There was an extra edge of annoyance in Momma's voice, as though she had forgotten even about the fancy party going on all around us. I held my breath for fear they were going to get into an argument about it right then and there.

'We're not going down to the engine room, Momma. I'm not dressed for that.'

'I'm glad you have that much sense at least, which is far more than your father has,' she said glaring at Daddy.

'Well, let's get started then, so we can come right back,' he said to me, and we went off to the bridge of the ship, leaving Momma fuming, I knew.

I had met the captain of *The Jillian* before, Captain Thomas Willshaw, an ex-British Navy officer, and I liked him very much because he always looked and spoke to me when Daddy and I were with him, and he seemed to enjoy explaining things to me. While Daddy and he discussed the journey, the navigator took out the nautical maps and traced our route for me.

'I'm happy that you're not bored with all this, Leigh,' Daddy said. 'There is no reason why you won't be able to run a big business when you are out of school.'

I nodded, but I thought how different Daddy and Momma really are and how differently they see things, especially things for me.

When we stepped out on the deck again on our way back to the ballroom, Daddy took my hand and we looked out over the great ship.

'You see, Leigh, a man has to have a deeper reason for working, for striving and building all this. His ego is not enough. He has to believe he is building it all for a more substantial reason. I'm building it all for you. I should say battling it all for you, since the entire luxury liner industry is in turmoil right now.

'I know I work too hard and don't get to spend enough time with you, but do you understand what I mean, Leigh?' he asked, his face as tight and as serious as I had ever seen it.

'Yes, Daddy.'

'I mean, I don't mean to pull you away from all the things girls love. Your mother thinks I'm always trying to make you into a son instead of a daughter, but I just want you to be capable of owning all this and overseeing it. I wouldn't want it placed in the hands of some trusteeship just because I hadn't given you adequate preparation.'

'Daddy, I'm so proud that you think I'm smart enough and that you think one day I will be capable of helping you here. It means more to me than all the parties, dances and dresses in the world.'

His face relaxed and broke into smiles. 'Good,' he said. He kissed me twice and pulled me to him and for the first time in days I realized suddenly that I felt warm and safe.

'Well, my little Princess, we'd better get back to the party or your mother will have me strung up on the yardarm.'

When we returned, the party was in full swing. The dance floor was crowded, and everyone was indulging in the fine foods.

Daddy got right into conversations with people and I wandered about looking for Momma, but I couldn't find her. I looked for Tony, too, but couldn't find him either. I decided to have something to eat. A little while later, I spotted Momma and Tony entering the ballroom. Tony went off to speak to some people and Momma joined me at my table.

'I was showing Tony the ship,' she explained with a giggle. 'Well, I'm glad there's no grease on your elbows this time.'

'Daddy just wants me to understand things.'

'You pay people to understand things for you. That's the point in being the owner,' she replied. She kept gazing Tony's way, clearly waiting for him to turn toward her. It wasn't like her not to circulate among all the guests, I thought. Usually, for all her complaining she enjoyed being the owner's wife and helping to decide who would be invited to the Captain's table later on in the voyage. Momma saw the way I was staring at her.

'Why are you gorging on all this food?' she asked me. 'It's never too early to start worrying about your figure.'

'I'm not gorging, Momma. I haven't eaten very much all day and I just took . . .' Suddenly, her face got funny and cold and her eyes got small.

'How do I really look tonight, Leigh? Do I look prettier than any woman here? Have you seen anyone who looks younger or more beautiful?' She seemed almost in a frenzy. Then her voice changed. 'You can tell me the truth,' she purred. But her eyes were still hard, like ice chips. She gripped my arm hurtingly.

'Momma,' I began, but she didn't hear me.

'Just look at some of these women,' she said, nodding toward the party crowd. 'Some have become so fat, they've lost all their femininity. No wonder their husbands hover above me like panting dogs.' Her face softened back to the mother I was used to. She looked back at Tony and he turned her way. Even across the vast room, they seemed to be able to communicate, for she turned back to me to say she would see me later and hurried off to join him.

I watched them for a while. Daddy brought over some people to introduce to me and then I stayed with him until he went back to talk to the head chef. I was standing by myself feeling a little lost when suddenly someone tapped me on the shoulder and I turned to look into Tony's blue eyes.

'Time for our dance,' he said and held out his arms.

'Oh, but I'm not good at ballroom dancing,' I pleaded, even as he took me in his powerful arms and swept me onto the floor.

'Nonsense. Just follow my lead.'

I caught a glimpse of Momma off to the side, standing with some people and smiling, but I felt so nervous and stiff, I was sure I looked silly out on the dance floor.

'I'm happy you decided to wear my gift tonight,' Tony said. 'It looks so pretty on you.'

'Thank you.' My heart was pounding. I was sure everyone was looking at me and laughing because I looked so awkward in his arms. He was so tall and graceful and sure and I moved like a girl who had been crippled all her life. It was hard to relax on a dance floor with all these elegantly dressed adults around me. This was nothing like a school dance.

'This is a wonderful party,' he said. 'I can't imagine what it must have been like for you growing up in all this.'

'It's a very hard business,' I replied, thinking of my daddy. 'Especially these days.'

'Oh, I see.' He smiled as if he had to humor me. 'You're thinking of becoming a businesswoman then?'

'There's no reason why a woman can't.' I knew I was being rude, but for some reason I couldn't stop myself.

'No, none at all.' His eyes brightened and he laughed. I was glad when the music ended and he bowed and thanked me. He disappeared in the crowd and left me standing there, feeling even more self-conscious. I retreated to a corner of the ball room. A little while later the cast of *Pajama Game* performed. They were as wonderful as they had been on the stage. After the show, many people began to leave. By the time the horn was sounded for visitors to depart, many already had. The ship's staff began to clean away some tables. I joined Daddy who was speaking with the Captain and the First Officer, just as the band announced its final number, which was to be a waltz.

Suddenly, I saw Daddy's eyes grow small and his lips tighten so that a whiteness formed under them. When I turned about, I saw what had caught his attention. Momma and Tony were practically the only couple left dancing and they were dancing so gracefully and so closely, all the remaining guests and visitors had their eyes on them.

I couldn't help but feel sorry for Daddy because Momma and Tony did look so beautiful together, moving as if they had been dancing together for years and years. Momma seemed to bloom in Tony's arms. Never had she looked more radiant, and tonight she looked so young. I hadn't realized until this moment how young she looked in contrast to Daddy. The years between them had never seemed so vast as they suddenly did.

Daddy appeared to sense that too, for he looked tired, resigned, defeated as if he had just aged an additional ten years. Oh, there was such sadness in Daddy's handsome face. He saw the way I was gazing at him and he forced a smile. Then he leaned over to me and shook his head.

'Somehow or another, your mother is always the life of the party, isn't she, Leigh?'

I nodded. He didn't sound angry; he sounded melancholy. I was relieved when the music finally ended and Momma and Tony stopped dancing. Tony followed Momma back to our table to say good night.

'It was a wonderful party,' he said. 'Best of luck on your maiden voyage.'

'Thank you,' Daddy replied, his voice sounding neither bitter nor pleasant. 'I'm glad you enjoyed yourself.'

'Leigh,' Tony said turning to me, 'don't get too sunburnt. Good night.' He turned to Momma. 'Jillian,' he said nodding.

'I'll walk you to the gate,' she offered and followed him out.

Daddy watched them with cold eyes. Instinctively, I reached

across the table and squeezed his hand. He smiled at me as if to say 'I'm all right.' But I couldn't keep my heart from pounding out its ominous warnings. Like some old seafaring soul, I sensed an impending storm over the horizon and felt the need to batten down the hatches.

FOUR

Rough Seas

A little over a year ago, Momma decided that if Daddy wanted us to go along on his cruises, he would have to permit her to redecorate the suites we would have on the liners. She designed the suites in only two ships before losing interest, but one of the two was, of course, *The Jillian*. In one of her fashion magazines, Momma had seen a spread done on a celebrity's New York apartment and she decided to model her shipboard suite after it. Our suite was decorated in serene, neutral colours – taupes and honeyed beiges – with bleached, light-colored woods that all provided the perfect backdrop for Momma's cool blonde good looks.

The liner was a floating resort. On one level there were all sorts of shops, including beauty shops and barber shops, drugstores and boutiques featuring the latest fashions from home and abroad. There was a continuous schedule of activities for guests, including dance instruction, exercise classes, art exhibits and lectures, teas, endless meals, games of competition, shuffleboard, and of course, once we sailed into the warm weather, swimming in one of the three pools on *The Jillian*. At night there were dances with entertainment provided by singers and comedians, and even the latest movies.

Momma slept late every morning, so that Daddy and I usually went to breakfast without her. We always ate with the Captain, or when he wasn't available, the First Officer, plus guests. Some days, Momma didn't come out of her suite until early afternoon and had her breakfast brought in. Usually she had only a small glass of juice, one poached egg and one piece of toast.

She was very disciplined about how much she would expose herself to sunlight, actually timing it so she would just have some slight color on her face. She had read somewhere that sunlight hastened wrinkling and nothing terrified Momma more than the possibility of a wrinkle appearing. Her vanity table was covered with every skin cream and body lotion available, especially the ones that promised eternal youthfulness. Most of her morning was taken up with working creams into her skin and preparing her make-up. She was often in the steam room and scheduled herself a massage every day and a facial once a week.

From the day we left Boston Harbor, Momma complained continually about the devastating effect the salty sea air was having on her hair. She had to go to the beauty parlor almost every day to keep her hair from 'kinking'. She said the sea air robbed her hair of its softness and chapped her skin because her face was too sensitive. She was rarely on deck in the evening, even when we had sailed into the warmer climate and the evenings were tepid. I thought there were few sights as beautiful as the calm ocean on a warm night with the moonlight painted over the water. The waves bobbed under an unobstructed night sky so dazzling it took my breath away. I was always trying to get Momma out on deck with me to look at it, but she told me she could see it through the windows whenever she wanted.

Although Daddy was busier than usual on this voyage because it was a maiden voyage establishing a new cruise, he made every effort to spend more time with both Momma and me, always promising to meet us here or there. Momma didn't seem to care if he was with her or not. Whenever he had time to do something with us, she always found something else to do. Daddy and I spent many evenings without her, watching a movie or attending one of the shows. She would promise to join us, but never appear. When I inquired, she told me she was too tired or had a headache. I would find her in bed reading one of her many magazines or scribbling letters. Whenever I asked her to whom she was writing, she would simply reply, 'Just friends,' and put everything away as if she had become instantaneously bored with what she had been doing.

Even when I sat on her bed and described the singers and

the comedians and the activities, she seemed very distracted and not very interested, so I knew she wasn't very happy. And then, one night nearly a week after our cruise had begun, I was woken by the sound of Momma and Daddy shouting at each other.

'I do everything you ask of me,' Daddy complained, 'but still you act as if you're suffering. You wanted to remake the suite, I let you and spent the money; foolishly, I thought, but spent it anyway. You're the owner's wife, but do you attend to some of our more important guests? No. And when you do come to the dining room to sit with me and the Captain and one of the guests you yourself chose, what do you do? Complain about the sea and living on board a liner as if you were some negro slave being brought over from Africa and kept chained below.

'How do you think that makes luxury liner travel seem . . . my own wife despises it!'

'I'm not built to be confined,' she retorted.

'That's your own choosing. I don't tell you you can't come out of this room. Why don't you enjoy the activities more, enjoy what the ship has to offer?'

'I told you how the sea air affects me, but you don't care about me; you care only about your precious ship and your business. You would sacrifice me to it, endanger my beauty, my looks and health, just to use me as some sort of public relations person.'

'That's not fair! You were the one who suggested this cruise.'

'I didn't suggest we take it.'

'But . . . I thought . . . you always wanted me to take you to Jamaica,' Daddy blurted in confusion. 'Honestly, Jillian, you're driving me mad. I don't know what you want and don't want anymore.'

'I don't want to stay up all night arguing. I need my rest to combat the elements,' she said and there was a deep silence. When Daddy spoke, he sounded so frustrated and angry. What was happening to them? I wondered. Was it because of the pressures of the business?

There was an uneasy peace between them for a day or so afterward and then one morning I went with Daddy down to his engine room when the chief engineer reported a problem. I was wearing one of the new outfits Momma had bought me for the cruise. It was a pair of knee length white shorts with a matching blue and white sailor blouse. The shorts had blue embroidery over the pockets.

I always enjoyed going down to the engine room to see the great machines that made so large a ship move through the ocean. Some of the passageways were quite narrow, as was the scaffolding, but I found it adventurous and fun. I knew the men who worked down there were amused by my interest in their work, but they were all quite friendly and eager to describe their responsibilities and explain the purposes of different gauges and levers and wheels.

One of our engines had to be shut down for repair, but the others could pick up the slack for the time it would take. I listened to the questions Daddy asked the chief engineer and followed him about to see what the problems were. I lost myself in the discussions and didn't realize I was leaning up against a very greasy railing until we came up from the engine room and met Momma in the corridor by our suite. She was just coming out to have some breakfast and she looked fresh and exuberant for the first time since we had left Boston.

But the moment she set eyes on me, she froze in the corridor and screamed so hard and so viciously, she frightened me.

'Where have you been? Look at the grease on your arms and on your outfit!' She pointed and I looked down to see a thick line of engine grease along the side and front of my shorts. She looked up at Daddy accusingly. 'Where have you taken her, you fool?' she demanded.

A shiver raced down my spine. I told myself over and over it's all right. It's all right.

Daddy's face turned crimson. I had never heard her call him a name to his face before, and I knew he was especially embarrassed because she had done it in front of me. He snapped his head back as if she had actually slapped him across the face, but his reaction didn't slow her down.

'I picked out this outfit for her at one of the more expensive Boston department stores because I wanted her to look like a young lady in fashion, not a grease monkey. You continually sabotage my efforts to teach her the finer things, to help her realize her potential as a woman. You insist on trying to make her into a tomboy,' she accused.

'Now, just hold on there, Jillian . . .'

'Don't tell me to hold on there. Leigh, get to your room and clean yourself up. I'll have the maid take that outfit to the laundry immediately to see if it can be salvaged.'

'Momma, it wasn't Daddy's fault. I just wasn't careful, I . . .'

'Of course it was his fault,' she insisted, glaring at him. 'If he hadn't taken you to where he did take you, it wouldn't have happened.'

'But I wanted to go, Momma. I wanted to see the engines and . . .'

'You wanted to see the engines?' She rolled her eyes. 'Look at what you are turning her into,' she said, her palms out toward me as if I had changed into some sort of creature on the spot. Daddy closed and opened his eyes patiently.

'It won't hurt her to know a little about the workings of the ship and the things that can go wrong. The day will come . . .'

'The day will come when all this will end,' Momma snapped and pulled me toward my suite, leaving Daddy standing behind us with his mouth open. I felt so sorry for him, but Momma was in a rage and babbled on and on about how he was ruining me, ruining my chances of becoming a debutante, a young and desirable young lady. She said he was 'suffocating my femininity'.

I tried to defend him, but she wouldn't listen. I got out of my outfit quickly and changed into something else while she went off to give the grease streaked shorts and blouse to a maid. By the time I emerged from my suite, Daddy was already gone. I spent the remainder of the day feeling terrible because I thought it had all been my fault. Oh, why hadn't I been more careful? Why wasn't I as concerned about my clothing and my looks as Momma was? There were cracks appearing all over my fragile world, but I was trying desperately to hold it together.

I couldn't remember seeing Momma shout at Daddy that way or Daddy so embarrassed and angry. This cruise, which was supposed to make Momma happy and cheer Daddy up by helping his business, was turning out to be a disaster for all of us.

That evening things became even worse when Momma developed a bad case of seasickness. Not only didn't she come out to dinner, but she didn't come out to enjoy any of the entertainment, which included ballroom dancing, one of the few things she enjoyed doing on the ship. Every time I went down to her suite to see how she was, I found her moaning and groaning.

'Why did I agree to this? Why did I come on this ship? I wish I could just fade away,' she wailed. I couldn't do anything to help her. The ship's doctor was called twice. He gave her double doses of everything, but she wasn't much better the next day, and once again, she wouldn't get out of her bed. I went down to read to her and keep her company. She was very depressed because she looked so pale and sickly that no amount of make-up could help.

'I don't even want the servants to see me,' she cried. 'It will take me weeks to get over this,' she claimed. 'Weeks!' She pulled on strands of her hair. 'Just look at what's happening to me. Look!'

'But Momma, this never happened before. Why is it happening on this trip?' I asked. Her eyes cut toward me sharply and for a moment grew small. Then she fell back against her large, fluffy pillow and crossed her arms under her bosom, pouting.

'How would I know? I was just lucky before.' She turned on me quickly. 'You don't remember your first trip across the Atlantic, I suppose,' she added in a biting tone. It was as if I had accused her of faking it and she wanted to punish me. 'You were so sick the first two days, I thought we would have to turn the liner around and go back to Boston. Then, as your father would say, you got your sea legs. He was so happy about it, as if walking around looking like a bow-legged sailor is an accomplishment.'

She turned to the wall to catch her breath. Her face was brightened with emotion as she encouraged her own anger.

When she looked at me again, she had a very ugly, but determined look on her face.

'Well, I never wanted sea legs,' she said smirking. 'Oh, I don't know why I didn't insist Cleave get out of this stupid business years ago. We could have had a respectable business in the city . . . maybe a chain of department stores, something like Tony Tatterton has. Then you're not at the mercy of the weather and the finicky ocean,' she concluded.

'But Daddy's always been a shipman. It's all he really knows,' I protested in a low, scared voice.

'Nonsense. A man learns what he has to learn if he's a man. It's just been easier for your father to remain what he is. He's lazy, that's what?'

'Lazy? Daddy?'

'Yes,' she insisted. 'Just because he works hard at what he likes, doesn't mean he's not lazy. And he's not brilliant when it comes to investments. We should be twice, no, three times as wealthy as we are.'

I was shocked at the way she spoke about Daddy. She often complained about this or that, but her complaints were never so vehement, so vicious. She was so angry and looked so hateful, it made my heart pound for Daddy. I was happy he wasn't nearby to hear all this, but I wondered if she hadn't said things like it to him before. Maybe that was another reason why he was walking around with a sad face so much of the time.

'But don't you just love having all this, Momma? The big ships, the glamorous cruises, all these wealthy passengers and . . .'

'*Love it? No! I don't love it!*' she screamed. 'Thank God, I'm not on the ships that often. When you're on one of these extended cruises, you miss all the social activity back in Boston. *I* think the people who have discovered airplane travel are *right*. You get to your vacation resort quickly, enjoy it, and return so you don't miss the important things at home.

'Anyway,' she said, calming down a little, 'I can't tell you often enough – never marry anyone who is a slave to his business, no matter how rich or handsome he might be. *You* have to come first, even if it means he might sacrifice a little money here and there.'

'But . . .' She had just complained about not being rich enough, I thought, and now she was willing to sacrifice money. But she didn't care about her contradictions.

'The smart executive has people he can trust doing all the real work,' she rambled on. 'But not your father.

'Your father,' she said pulling the blanket up to her chin, 'is a peasant in rich man's clothing, I'm afraid.' She turned her back to me and pulled the blanket nearly over her head. 'I have to close my eyes and imagine I'm not here now, Leigh. Go on upstairs, but don't go fiddling around with mechanical things or go down into the engine room again.'

'Yes, Momma. If you feel better, will you try to come to dinner tonight? It's a special dinner because we'll be in Jamaica tomorrow,' I said.

'Thank God for that. I'll see. If I feel better,' she muttered with little enthusiasm.

She really didn't come out of the suite until we sailed into Montego Bay and Daddy went down to announce we had arrived. It was a magnificent day, the kind the Caribbean islands were famous for – rich blue sky with only a passing cloud, a luscious warm breeze, and music everywhere. I was on the upper deck playing ping pong with two girls I had met during the voyage, the Spenser sisters, Clara and Melanie, who were both about my age, so I didn't know what went on between Momma and Daddy below, but the next thing I knew, the porters were carrying Momma's luggage off the ship to a waiting taxi.

I watched in disbelief. Oh, Momma, what are you doing? We weren't supposed to be checking into a hotel here. The ship was going to dock at the harbor for three days and nights. Passengers would disembark to shop and go to the restaurants, and then we would sail back to Boston.

Daddy signaled to me to come to him.

'Your mother wants to see you below,' he said. He looked so tired and depressed with his sad, unhappy eyes cast downward at the deck. My butterflies started waking up, but this time they felt less like flutterings, more like birds flying and crashing around in my stomach. I was scared that I might be sick.

When I entered their suite, I found Momma dressed in one of her olive green, silk cardigan suits with a Lily-of-the-Valley beaded pin on the bodice, a silk scarf and matching silk gloves. She had her hair brushed back and up away from her face and put on her eggshell white bell bonnet just as she turned to face me. The suite reeked with her jasmine perfume.

All the paleness and gloom was gone from her face. Her cheeks were rosy, her lips bright. She had put on all her make-up and even darkened her eyelashes. I thought she looked as healthy as ever. It was a miraculous recovery, and one that filled me with anxiety and dread.

'Oh Leigh,' she said when she set eyes on me. 'I've made a decision. I'm going back to Boston,' she announced. Her words fell like thunder and my heart became a heavy lead drum in my chest.

'Back? But how, Momma?'

'I had the ship's captain inquire as to airplane schedules and found a flight going into Miami, Florida. From there, I will take another flight into Boston.'

'But Momma, what about our vacation in Jamaica?' I couldn't believe what I was hearing, and what made it even more difficult to swallow was that she had already made all these travel plans, plotting here in the suite while I thought she was groggy and sick. 'Why are you doing this?' I cried, unable to hide my disappointment.

'This has turned out to be anything but a vacation for me, Leigh. I'm not enjoying a moment of it, as you know.' She straightened the fingers of her gloves. She was obviously determined to walk off the ship in style, knowing many people would be looking at her and wondering what was happening, since she was the owner's wife.

'But Momma, we're in the harbor now. We're not sailing. You won't be seasick.'

'What about the trip back, Leigh? Do you want to put me through all that?'

'No, but I wanted us all to be together, to go shopping

together and go to the fine restaurants and see the shows and swim in the ocean and . . .'

'Your father wouldn't have the time for much of that anyway. He wouldn't leave the ship. Don't you remember how we had to twist his arm to get him off the ship in London, and if we hadn't taken that tour, we wouldn't have seen half the city?'

'He arranged for the tour, Momma, and we had such a good time. I have all those pictures of us at London Bridge and Big Ben and the Tower of London. We did have a lot of fun there. We'll have a good time now, too. Please, stay with us, Momma. Please,' I begged, silently praying that she'd reconsider.

'I can't.' She turned away. 'I'm sorry. I just can't. You'll understand later.'

'Why? What do you mean?' My heart was in a frantic pitter-patter. Why later? What horrible news awaited.

'For now, just let it be, Leigh. Enjoy the rest of this vacation. I'll meet you at the dock when you return.' She took my face between her hands and kissed my cheek. 'Now, be a good girl and promise you won't do any repair work while I'm not around.'

'Oh, Momma.' I was crying now, crying so hard I thought I might not ever stop, and I couldn't keep myself from calling her by the name from my childhood. Oh, why couldn't I be back in that happy, safer, childhood!

'I've left you some of my costume jewelry to wear on your nights out. Be careful with it.' She absent-mindedly stroked my head a bit but I could tell she was intent on her plans.

'Thank you, Momma.' I lowered my head in defeat. Nothing I could do or say would make her change her mind. I felt so helpless and alone, but more than feel sorry for myself, I felt sorry for Daddy. It would be so embarrassing for him to face his passengers once they all learned that his wife had left the ship and taken an airplane back to Boston. And he couldn't very well say she was so sick she had to leave. Looking like a fashion plate she was walking off the liner. There could easily have been photographers from one of the glamour magazines snapping her picture as she descended to the dock. I decided right then to try hard not to embarrass him myself, to try to pull myself together.

'You're only going to be here three days, Leigh, and you have made some friends aboard, haven't you? You told me about the Spenser sisters and I had the Captain report to me about their family. They're quite well-to-do.

'I'm only in everyone's way here,' she added. 'It's not fair to you and it's not fair to me. Understand?'

I nodded, reluctantly. I couldn't believe she was making these feeble excuses to me. I didn't understand. Why was she doing this? Why was she doing something that would hurt Daddy and me so much? It seemed the older a person became, the more difficult it was to be happy. Would that be the way for me as well?

'Good. Now help me leave. Take that small bag that contains my make-up, please.'

We walked out together. I felt so empty inside. Oh, Momma, it hurts so that you're leaving. Doesn't she care about us, I thought. There was something in the way Momma turned at the door to look back at the suite that told me she was saying, 'Good riddance.'

I was surprised that Daddy wasn't waiting on the deck. How could she leave without kissing him goodbye? She didn't even look for him. She just started down the gangway to the dock and the awaiting taxi cab.

'Momma, where's Daddy?' My eyes looked frantically over the deck, but he wasn't in sight.

'We said our goodbyes earlier,' she replied quickly. She took the make-up bag from me. 'Be a good girl. See you soon. I promise, I will make this up to you in ways you could never begin to imagine, Leigh.'

It sounded like a good thing, but it frightened me even more to hear her say it.

She kissed me again and then hurried to get into the taxi, looking ever so happy when she peeked out of the window to wave. I stood watching her go off. Then I turned back to the ship. High up in the bridge, Daddy peered down, his face like the face of a stone statue – cold, lifeless, dejected, aged and worn by sorrowful times. He looked so gray and so old to me. The tears that streaked down my cheeks felt like drops of ice. What was happening to our happy, wonderful life? I used to believe the words 'Once upon a time' had been created just for me. Now, I was afraid to include them in my own diary, afraid of what they had come to mean.

Even though I was angry at Momma for walking off the ship and leaving Daddy and me this way, I couldn't help but miss her. Whenever we had gone on one of Daddy's cruises, we always did so much together. It was so much fun shopping with her, and she would always find some fashionable place for us to lunch, no matter where we were. While we sat there, Momma would look about and comment about this person or that, describing who she thought they were, what they did for a living, how much money they made, how sophisticated they were. Whenever I was with Momma, people became interesting.

She had a way of carrying herself in restaurants and stores when we were on vacation that made waiters and *maître d*'s and sales clerks think they were waiting on someone either very famous or royal. She spoke a little French and a little Italian, learning from the 'Teach Yourself a Language' records she played over and over back home. Even if she mispronounced something or said something totally incorrect, she did it in such a way that the French person or the Italian person didn't correct her. And whenever she made a purchase or gave an order at a restaurant, she always made a point of leaning toward me and whispering something about what she had done, so I would learn from it.

It was no wonder then that I felt this great emptiness in my heart when she walked off the ship. Suddenly all the things I was looking forward to held no interest for me. And now there was Daddy to cheer up.

The first day he kept himself busy with all the arrangements for the excursions the passengers would make and the docking of the ship. The Spenser sisters and their parents invited me to go to dinner with them in Montego Bay, but I didn't want to leave Daddy this first night without Momma, even though he insisted I go. Mrs Spenser had asked him for permission to take me, so he knew about it. We didn't get a chance to really talk until late in the afternoon. I joined him in the Captain's office, and after he and the Captain had completed their discussions and the Captain left, we remained.

'You should go to dinner with your girlfriends, Leigh. I want you to enjoy yourself here.'

'But Daddy, I thought we would go to dinner together.'

'I have to stay on board and do some other things,' he replied. 'I intend to just grab a quick bite.'

'I'll grab one with you and help you do whatever you have to do,' I insisted.

'No, that's not right,' Daddy said. He shook his head. He looked so tired, so worn down by the day's events. Shadows deep and dark settled in his eyes. The walls of my heart quivered. I held the tears within and swallowed, and then I tried to find a voice that wouldn't tremble and sound like a little girl's voice.

'Why did Momma have to leave us like that, Daddy? Couldn't you have gotten the ship's doctor to talk to her?'

He shook his head.

'It wasn't just her bout with seasickness, Leigh. She wasn't very happy about this cruise from the start.'

'But why, Daddy? She always talked about it, didn't she? She wanted to come to Jamaica. So many of her friends had been here,' I insisted. 'Didn't she once pin up that magazine ad in your office, the one that said "Come to Jamaica – it's no place like home"?'

Daddy nodded, remembering. Then he sighed.

'If she could have been a passenger instead of the owner's wife, she would have been happier about it,' he said sadly.

'But why, Daddy? She didn't really have to work and we have the best ship's quarters anyone can have. You did everything she wanted you to do.'

'I'm afraid not, Leigh. Your mother continues to be disappointed in me.'

'But why?' I cried. 'You give us everything. We have a beautiful home and we can buy almost anything we want. All my friends are envious.'

'Sometimes, those things are just not enough,' he said. He looked at me for a long moment and then he warmed me with a smile. 'Sometimes, especially when you are frustrated, you look so much like her, and yet, you are so different.'

'We are?' I was surprised to hear him say that. He was always saying we were like sisters now, especially in front of Momma. Was it because I hadn't yet grown to like all the things she liked as much as she liked them?

'How are we different, Daddy? I know she's so pretty and . . .'

'Oh no,' he said quickly, 'it has nothing to do with that. You're going to be far more beautiful than your mother.' It shocked me to hear him say that so sincerely. Me? More beautiful than Momma? 'And you won't have to work at it as hard or as long. Not that your mother isn't blessed with natural beauty. Far from it. She's just more involved in herself than you will be.'

'How can you be so sure, Daddy?' I really wanted to know because although I believed he was right, I wasn't sure myself.

'You've got other interests, Leigh. You have an inquisitive mind. You'll be too impatient to learn about other things. Not that you're anything near the tomboy your mother thinks I'm turning you into. No sir. You're every bit a young lady.'

Even though our subject was an unhappy one, these words from him went straight to my heart and filled it with warmth and love.

He sat back in the Captain's oxblood leather chair.

'Your mother is still a very young woman, Leigh. Years ago, when I first set eyes on her in Texas, I didn't seriously consider the difference in our age or think it would be a problem. Perhaps that was the blindness of love.

'Love can be like that, you know, like a blast of sunlight reflecting off the water. You can't look directly into it; you've got to shade your eyes or close them altogether, and when you do that, you see only what you want to see. Do you understand? Are you old enough to understand what I'm saying, Leigh?' he asked.

I nodded. Daddy and I rarely had this sort of serious, adult conversation. If ever he would begin to tell me something very serious, he would stop and say, 'Oh well, I suppose your mother will tell you about that soon.'

'Maybe you do understand,' he said smiling. 'I think you're a lot brighter than your mother or I think.'

'But Daddy, what does all this have to do with what's happening now?'

'Well, as I said, your mother was still quite young. She matured quickly, of course, but I was already quite settled in my ways. When a man is settled in his ways, it's difficult, if not impossible for him to change. As your mother grew older, she wanted me to make some changes, be a different person in many ways. I tried, but it's not in my nature, I'm afraid, and that has made your mother very unhappy.'

'What ways, Daddy?'

'What ways? Well for example, she would love me to take her on one of these cruises and act like just another passenger . . . sleep late every day, eat and then recline on the deck or play shuffleboard. In the evening, she would like me to take her dancing and dance all night into the wee hours, drinking champagne, and then sleep late again, and not ask one question about the business or the conduct of the voyage.'

He smiled.

'At times she can be so childlike, so hungry for excitement and fun. I've never seen a woman who has your mother's appetite when it comes to enjoyment and pleasure. I couldn't give her enough diamonds or take her to too many fine restaurants. She's insatiable.

'Oh, I understand her. Your mother is young, beautiful, vivacious. On the other hand, here I am working long hours, deeply involved in a major family-owned enterprise, with little time for frivolities. If your mother had her way,' he added shaking his head, 'I'd play five hours for every hour worked.

But, I'm afraid I can't do that, and even if I could, I probably wouldn't, not only because I'm too old for it, but because it's not part of who I am.

'And so, to answer your question, that's why your mother is disappointed,' he concluded and smiled softly at me.

I couldn't keep the tears hidden any longer. As soon as the first one appeared, Daddy got up and came to me.

'Now, now, let's not have any of that. Don't make me regret having this grown-up talk with you, Leigh.'

'I won't, Daddy.' I wiped my eyes quickly and held back the rest of my tears. My heart ached, but I smiled. 'What's going to happen now, Daddy?' I asked.

'We'll see. Your mother wanted to have some time by herself to think things out. In the meantime, young Captain Van Voreen, you and I have a cruise to run, understand?'

'Yes, Daddy.'

'Now, here's my first command. You go with your girlfriends and their parents to dinner and enjoy yourself.'

'But what if they start asking me questions about Momma?' I asked. He thought for a moment.

'You say, there were some serious family matters back home that had to have immediate attention. No one would ask you any more than that, and if they did, just tell them your parents didn't tell you more.

'So,' he said clapping his hands together, 'that should take care of that. Tomorrow you can go shopping in the bazaar and buy all your friends back home something, if you'd like. In the afternoon you can go swimming on the beach, and then in the evening, you and I will go to an authentic Jamaican restaurant and eat something called Jerk-chicken. One of the porters who happens to come from Jamaica was telling me about it. How does all that sound?'

'Wonderful, Daddy.'

'Good. Now get on with you. I want a full report afterward. How's that log book of yours? Filling up?'

'Oh yes, I write in it every day.'

'Good.' He kissed me on the cheek and I hugged him tightly and inhaled his familiar scents – the fragrance of his aftershave and cologne, the aroma of his pipe tobacco, and that fresh, clean smell of the sea.

I wished he and I had had talks like this before. In one way Momma was very right to be jealous of the time he spent on his business. I wished he had spent more time with me and told me about himself when he was my age and younger. I realized he had never really given me his version of the Cinderella story between him and Momma. Perhaps I could get him to do that someday. Daddy was so modest though. Would he really describe what it was like when he first set eyes on Momma? And would he be willing to describe himself proposing on his knees? He never really expressed any dislike for Grandma Jana or Momma's two sisters. Whenever she ranted and raved about them in front of him and me, he would simply nod or look away. I wanted to know so much more. Hopefully, now that he saw me as older and more mature, he would talk about these things.

My little talk with Daddy in the Captain's office did cheer me up enough so that I could go to dinner with the Spensers. They took me to a delightful Italian restaurant called The Casablanca. The tables were set out under the stars and there was a small three-piece band and a singer who crooned romantic songs. Mr and Mrs Spenser danced so closely and were so loving and tender with each other, my girlfriends were embarrassed. They giggled like grade school children. I could understand why they were self-conscious about their parents, but I thought it was wonderful to see a husband and wife so loving and affectionate with each other. I couldn't help but close my eyes and imagine they were my parents, imagine Momma and Daddy on this small dance floor with the stars twinkling above and the singer serenading them with songs of love.

Daddy had said love blinds you. When you fall in love, do you have a chance to think about all these things? Do you have a chance to envision what it will be like years and years from now? The way Momma now spoke about Daddy made me feel that if she could have seen what it would be like when he first proposed, she might not have accepted, even if it meant her remaining in Texas with her dreadful sisters.

'When I fall in love,' I told the Spenser sisters, 'I want it to be just like it is for your parents.' They both looked at me, undecided as to whether or not to laugh. They were laughing at everything at this point. My serious expression kept them from doing much more than smiling, although I imagined they would talk about me later in their stateroom. It was true we were all about the same age, but I felt so much older than they were.

It was all so confusing for me. Maybe age wasn't important if you had grown up. Maybe what Daddy was telling me back on the ship was that he thought Momma hadn't yet grown up, or grown up the way he had hoped she would.

The music and the stars began to make me sad now. I was happy when it was time to return to the ship. Daddy saw us come aboard and spoke with Mr and Mrs Spenser for a while, thanking them for taking me to dinner. Then he asked me how I enjoyed it.

'It was fun,' I told him, half-telling the truth, half-lying. 'But I can't wait until tomorrow night when it will just be you and me, Daddy.'

'Oh dear,' he said, 'it will have to be the following night. I'm sorry. But we have a very important guest coming to dinner aboard ship tomorrow night – the governor of the island. You understand, don't you, Princess?'

I swallowed my disappointment quickly and put on a mask of smiles just the way Momma could.

'Yes, Daddy. I'm tired,' I told him. 'I'll just go to sleep.'

He kissed me goodnight and then went off to check on something in the kitchen. I hurried down to my suite and shut the door behind me. Then I fell on my bed and cried. I wasn't crying over any one thing, but all of it – crying over Momma's leaving us, crying over seeing someone else's parents so happily in love, crying over Daddy's frustration and unhappiness with Momma and her unhappiness with him, crying over his not being able to be with only me.

After I had cried ten oceans of tears, my warm, sad tears finally tired me out and I curled up in my bed, hugging my stuffed sailor teddy bear. I could hear the ballroom dance-band playing something soft and lovely above and I could hear the water lapping against the sides of the ship below, and if I listened even harder, I could hear the beating of my heart.

Nothing could have made me feel more lonely. I was happy to fall asleep.

FIVE

Almost an Orphan

I tried very hard to keep myself occupied during our remaining time in Montego Bay so that I wouldn't keep thinking about Momma's going home, because whenever I did, my heart felt like a brick in my chest. The Spenser sisters and I finally made friends with two boys who at first seemed very uninterested in us, probably because they were high school age and thought it was beneath them to associate with younger girls. They both attended a prep school outside of Boston and had their noses in the air. A number of times before, I had seen them side by side in lounge chairs on the deck or playing chess, but they never paid me or the Spenser sisters the slightest attention.

The taller of the two, a boy with thin, light brown hair and hazel eyes, introduced himself as Fulton Wittington, Jr. His friend, Raymond Hunt, was much stouter and far less good-looking, but a lot more informal and relaxed. I think he liked me because it was he who brought us together when he saw Clara, Melanie and me playing shuffleboard. He began to tease me.

'You push that like you're pushing a broom,' he said. Although he wasn't very good-looking because his mouth was too long and his nose was too thin, he did have a friendly, warm smile, once he let himself smile.

'I wouldn't know. I never pushed a broom,' I retorted and turned my back to them. That made them both laugh.

'You better not make fun of her,' Clara said with her hands on her hips. 'Her father owns the ship.'

'Oh?' Fulton suddenly became more interested and very soon after, they joined our game, first to give us instructions, and then just to have fun. We all had lunch together and decided to go to the beach together that afternoon. The Spenser sisters giggled and whispered most of the time, which I thought was very impolite and immature. Before the afternoon ended, they were off by themselves, splashing and frolicking in the water and I was left with both boys, lying between them on a great beach towel.

It was a cloudless day with the sea breeze making the sun seem less intense than it really was, but I had all Momma's suntan oils and skin creams. Fulton, Raymond and I talked about many things, including school, the new movies and fashions. For the most part, I found they liked and disliked many of the same things I did.

Fulton's family had a seaside home on Cape Cod, and when I mentioned having been to the sea recently at Farthinggale Manor, I was surprised to learn that not only did he know of it, but his father had purchased two Tatteron toys, a replica of the Tower of London, and a replica of the Bastille.

'They're wonderful!' Fulton exclaimed. 'There's even a working guillotine. If you put your pinky finger under it, it would cut the tip off.'

'I think I can do without that,' I said grimacing.

'A number of my parents' friends have Tatterton collector's toys. My father instructed the manager of the Tatterton Toy Store to inform him the moment any other famous prison has been made.'

'My mother wants my father to get a Tatterton toy,' Raymond said. 'He's supposed to buy one this Christmas.'

'My parents are very proud of them,' Fulton added. He wanted to know what Farthinggale Manor was like, so I described it and told them both about Tony and Troy and the maze. They seemed fascinated and I was very proud of myself for being so interesting and attractive to two older boys, both of whom were obviously very rich and very well traveled. I thought Momma would be very proud of me as well.

I kept calling to the Spenser sisters and telling them to put on some skin creams, but they didn't listen so both of them got bad shoulder and neck burns before we quit the beach and returned to the ship.

'You know,' Fulton said while he looked out at the Spenser

sisters, 'it's very difficult, if not impossible to believe you are their age.'

'You could pass for a high school senior,' Raymond said and Fulton agreed. In the bright sunlight my blushing was undetected, but I felt a tingle of excitement in the way they both gazed at me now.

That night I waved to them from the Captain's table where I sat with Daddy and the governor of the island. Everyone talked about the tourist industry and how Jamaica was growing to be one of the most popular spots in the Caribbean. When the governor described his hope that it would be the sort of vacation paradise not only the very rich and glamorous would enjoy, but the middle class as well, I thought it was good Momma wasn't here. She would be very disappointed in learning that, for she was always looking for special places that only the very rich or famous visited.

I saw that Clara and Melanie hadn't come to dinner. When I inquired about them, Mr and Mrs Spenser told me they were back in their suite suffering with their very bad sunburns. After dinner Raymond and Fulton escorted me to the Caribbean show, which turned out to be one of the most exciting shows I had ever seen on any of Daddy's luxury cruises. There were folk dancers in colorful costumes and straw hats, calypso musicians with a twenty-piece steel drum band and folk-singers who sang songs about love on the islands.

After the entertainment portion, guests were invited to try the limbo. They had to dance and lean back and slip under this bamboo pole without touching it. It was lowered and lowered until there was barely anyone left in the game. At that point an island dancer dropped his body until he was barely inches from the floor and moved under the pole with the agility of a snake. The audience loved it.

I spent the entire next day with Fulton and Raymond. They taught me how to play chess and we went swimming on the beach again. In the cooler, later afternoon, we went shopping in the street markets and I found a beautiful hand-painted silk scarf I knew Momma would love. I bought Daddy an ornamental cane covered with carved fish.

Fulton and Raymond wanted to take me on a glass-bottomed boat and tour the harbor, but I was anxious to get back to the ship and dress for dinner because this was the night Daddy was taking me to a Jamaican restaurant instead of our eating aboard. I was looking forward to the two of us having a wonderful evening together, talking. I put on some of the costume jewelry Momma had left me and sat before my mirror brushing my hair just the way she always did, counting out one hundred strokes. I put on the lipstick just the way she showed me and sprayed myself with jasmine perfume. I wore a bright blue silk blouse with a lace embroidered collar and a full pleated matching skirt. So that I would look older and more sophisticated, I unbuttoned the first two buttons of my blouse.

My face was evenly tanned and the silver earrings and bright blouse highlighted it well. I felt that I looked sensational and I hoped against hope that Daddy would think so too. Older boys liked me and found me fun and interesting and mature. I was wearing Momma's jewelry and perfume and I admitted to myself for the first time that there were strong resemblances between us. Perhaps I really was going to be beautiful after all. Was it vain to think it? I couldn't help admiring my own image in the mirror, even though I knew it wasn't very nice to be conceited. But there was no one here, no one would know, I thought.

I stood there assuming different poses, trying to imitate some of Momma's expressions and looks. I sucked in my cheeks, turned my shoulders, drew my shoulders back and thrust out my breasts until they looked more prominent. I pretended a handsome, young man was looking at me across the dance floor. Should I smile back and encourage him? Momma probably would, I thought, even though Daddy wouldn't like it. I turned slowly and smiled. Then I laughed at myself. But it was fun to be silly.

I took a deep breath, gazed at myself in the mirror one more time to check my hair, and then went out to meet my date, Daddy.

He was waiting for me on deck. Suddenly I felt all quivery over how I would look to him, but he took one glance at me and smiled widely, his eyes brightening just the way they often did when Momma appeared all dressed up to go to a gala or to a fancy restaurant.

'Do I look all right?' I could almost hear Momma whispering behind me: *'It's all right to fish for compliments, Leigh. A woman should sound a little insecure, no matter how sure of herself she might be.'*

'You look gorgeous, Princess.' He turned to his right. 'We have the prettiest date in Jamaica tonight,' he declared to Captain Willshaw.

'No question about that,' Captain Willshaw said stepping forward. I had been so anxious about how I looked to Daddy when he first saw me, that I hadn't even noticed the Captain standing on the sidelines.

I couldn't help my look of confusion, nor my look of disappointment when Daddy added, 'The Captain has recommended what he has found to be the best restaurant in Jamaica, and he has agreed to join us for dinner, Leigh. Isn't that nice?'

'Join us for dinner? Oh. Yes.'

But Daddy, I thought, what happened to our private date? Don't you understand what is in my heart of hearts? Couldn't you see that I needed you and you alone with me tonight? What happened to what was supposed to be our wonderful night in Jamaica when we would comfort each other and grow closer to each other? Oh, I had so many private and personal things to tell him. I wanted to tell him about Fulton and Raymond and about Tatterton Toys and what I had bought for Momma. I wanted to tell him how I was planning to try harder not to displease her and do things that would cause them to fight.

Mostly, I wanted him to look at me and be reminded of her and then I wanted to hear him tell me how much he missed her and needed her. I hoped to have him tell me about their first days together when their romance was intense and true, the way I hoped love would be for me someday.

We would walk hand in hand through the Jamaican night after dinner and feel happy again under the stars.

But instead, Daddy and Captain Willshaw talked about the

cruise. They went through it all endlessly, evaluating each and every day, each and every event, reviewing what they would change, what they would improve or increase. I listened politely. Normally I might have been interested but tonight I had wanted my father to treat me like a woman. I was bored and terribly unhappy. Even though the food was delicious, I lost my appetite and had to force myself to eat, but Daddy didn't seem to notice.

We had to return to the ship immediately after dinner because it was the last night in Jamaica and a show and a ball had been planned. I told Daddy I had to go to my suite for a while and I would meet him later.

'Just like your mother, you've got to go powder your nose, eh Princess?' he asked. He winked at the Captain.

'Yes Daddy,' I said, my eyes down. I felt two small tears in the corners of my eyes. They lingered without falling.

'You all right? That food wasn't too spicy, was it? You're not overtired, are you?' he asked, his voice filled with fatherly concern.

'No Daddy.' I had to bite the inside of my mouth to keep from crying or screaming. Why was he talking to me as if I were a little girl again? Why couldn't he see what was really wrong? Were men simply insensitive to the things women felt? I had so many questions running through my mind, questions that I guess only another woman could answer.

When I entered my suite, I felt so let down and alone that all I could do was sit on the bed and cry. I caught a glimpse of myself in the mirror – my hair brushed and shining, my beautiful clothing, Momma's jewelry and my evenly-tanned face now changed by sadness and tears. I thought I looked pathetic and ridiculous, like some little girl trying to imitate her mother. I had hoped that when Daddy set eyes on me and had inhaled Momma's jasmine perfume, he would have lost himself in the memories of her and be soft and precious with me. But none of that had happened.

Never had I felt I needed Momma more. I wanted her to tell me what she felt like when she had dressed herself up and not dazzled a man the way she had planned to. What could I do?

I couldn't talk intimately with anyone on this ship, certainly not the Spenser sisters, or someone else's mother.

How horrible it must be for a real orphan, I thought, never to have anyone you trust and who loves you and will not laugh at you when you told her your deepest, most heartfelt feelings. Tonight, I felt like an orphan, cast out on the sea, floating aimlessly about, lost in the waves to be tossed here and there with no one to hear my cries.

I wiped my tear-streaked face and looked at myself in the mirror. Maybe Daddy and I would have our private chat in a day or so on the way home. Maybe it was very hard for him to talk about these things and he was deliberately finding ways to avoid talking about them. He had so much on his mind, so much responsibility and worry and didn't need me to add to the list. I would have to be more understanding and more patient, I thought. I straightened up.

'No one cares about someone who is pathetic and weak,' Momma once told me. 'Pity is the most degrading emotion. Even if you are upset, don't give anyone the satisfaction of knowing it. It makes them feel superior.'

'All right, Momma,' I whispered as if she were here in my suite beside me. 'I'll do what I must do. No one will know my secret, sad thoughts. I'll do it for Daddy and I'll do it for you, and I'll do it for myself.'

I stood up with determination, but in my secret, putaway heart I knew that when I returned to my suite at the end of the evening and crawled under the covers and put out the lights, I would sob like a baby in the darkness until I cried myself asleep.

The journey home seemed so much longer because I was so anxious to get there to see Momma and to see Momma greet Daddy. I got down on my knees every night and prayed that she would be less angry with him. I did a lot of reading and worked on my lessons with my tutor, Mr Abrams. I played chess with Raymond and Fulton and went to the movies and shows with them and spent time with the Spenser sisters. Daddy seemed busier than ever. I barely caught a glimpse of him all during the last day at sea. He didn't eat lunch with me, and when we finally sat down together at dinner, he was distracted by so many people: guests who came by to tell him how much they had enjoyed the cruise and members of the crew and staff who came by with questions.

The night before we were to sail into Boston Harbor, Raymond and Fulton came to see me separately to give me their addresses and get mine. They each promised to write and even visit, first chance each had. I was very flattered by their attention. Raymond kissed me on the cheek, pecking it quickly and pulling away, his face red. It was the first time a high school age boy had kissed me and I couldn't stop the flutter of butterfly wings under my heart. Fulton just shook my hand, but he kept his shoulders back and his eyes fixed on me as if he wanted to drink in my face and never forget it.

After they left me, I saw to my packing. Daddy told me to leave my bags just inside the suite door and the porters would come by to pick them up while I was having breakfast. Our schedule called for us to dock shortly after breakfast. I was so excited, I had a terrible time falling asleep. I wrote and wrote in this diary until my eyelids drooped, but even after I put out the lights and closed my eyes, I kept thinking about all the things I wanted to tell Momma. I didn't want to forget a thing.

As soon as the first rays of morning light came through my window, I hopped out of bed and took my shower. I wanted to have my breakfast quickly and go out on deck to watch us approach Boston. But after I had gotten dressed and had just finished brushing my hair, I heard a knock on my door. It was Daddy.

He was dressed in his dark suit, but he didn't look as handsome as he usually did. He looked like he had been up all night and had gotten dressed in the dark. His tie knot was not tied tightly and his suit jacket looked wrinkled. His hair looked a little bit mussed.

'Good morning, Princess,' he said softly. My heart began to pitter-patter. He looked so sad; his face was as gray as his hair.

'Morning, Daddy. Isn't everything on schedule?' I felt so

very afraid suddenly, but I tried to tell myself that something had gone wrong and our docking had been postponed.

'Yes, yes.' He smiled weakly and closed the door behind him. 'I wanted to see you before you went to breakfast and we docked.'

I turned completely round in my vanity table chair. Daddy fidgeted nervously for a moment and looked around my suite as if he were unsure of where he should sit. Finally, he sat on the end of my bed. He clasped his hands and leaned toward me. He was quite upset about something – I could tell because the small muscles in his jaw were jumping and the veins in his temples were pressing so hard against his skin, they looked as if they would pop out. For a long time he said nothing until I got so nervous I thought I would scream.

'What's wrong, Daddy?' I held my breath.

'Leigh,' he began, 'I waited until the last possible moment to come here to tell you this. I wanted to hold off as long as I could to hold sadness away for as long as I could.'

'Sadness?' I brought my hands to the base of my throat and sat so still, waiting, unable to breathe, for him to say more. I heard the pounding of my heart and felt the slight rocking of the ocean liner in the water. Above and around us were the sounds of the guests and the crew preparing for the final morning aboard ship – people talking loudly and excitedly on their way to have their breakfasts, porters getting instructions, doors closing, children laughing and running. Excitement and tumult rained down around us making the silence between us that much deeper and more disturbing. Inside my blood felt that it was freezing, leaving me a stiff ice princess instead of flesh and blood.

'You'll remember when you and I had that little discussion right after your mother left us in Jamaica that I told you she was going off to do some thinking,' he began again.

'Yes?' My voice sounded so tiny, so frightened.

'I told you she was disappointed in me, disappointed in the way things were between us.' He swallowed hard. I nodded, just so he would continue because he seemed to be swallowing back his words. 'Well, a few days ago, Leigh, I received a telegram on board ship. It was from your mother and she informed me she had gone ahead with one of her possible choices.'

'What choices? What has she done?' I shot out in dismay.

'She flew from Miami to Mexico, instead of from Miami to Boston, and processed a divorce,' he said quickly, as quickly as a doctor would give a patient bad news, so as not to draw out something so painful.

But his words hung in the air as if they had been frozen there. My heart fluttered beneath my breast and then became a thumping drum. Numbness tingled in my fingers because I had them locked so tightly together.

'Divorce?' It was such a forbidden word, such a foreign word. I had read about the divorces of movie stars and other entertainers. It seemed to be a natural course of events for them, almost something expected; but I had no friends whose parents had divorced, and the students in school whose parents were divorced were somehow thought of as different, sometimes avoided as if they had leprosy.

'Actually,' Daddy said sighing, 'I almost feel relieved. For months now I've been waiting for that second shoe to drop over my head. Barely a day has gone by without your mother expressing her unhappiness with me or without us having angry, bitter words between us. I did my best to hide it all from you, as I think your mother did as well.

'I submerged myself even deeper in my work just so I wouldn't dwell on matters at home all the time. In a way it has been something of a blessing to have all these financial and business crises occurring. It's kept my mind off my marital problems.' He pressed a smile back on his face, but it was such a sad, soft, and weak smile, the kind that can't last more than a moment or two. For his sake I closed off my own emotions, clamped down hard on them just so I could speak.

'Is Momma still in Mexico?'

'No, she's back in Boston, at home. She sent me the telegram from Boston. But,' he said after a deep breath, 'I did promise her that I would go along with whatever she had decided. There's no point in trying to force someone to stay with you, if she doesn't want to anymore.'

'But why doesn't she?' I demanded. 'How can she want to leave you after all these years?'

What I really wanted to know was how could a love that had begun so magnificently, so romantically, die? How could two people be so sure of each other at one point and then so unsure of one another? Was this what Daddy really meant when he told me love blinds you?

But then, how can anyone know he or she is really, truly in love? If feelings betrayed you and words were like thin bubbles that burst in the memory and disappeared, what could anyone do to be sure? You promise someone you will be with him and he promises he will be with you until death do you part, and then . . . something else parts you. What is the value of a promise, even a promise that comes with a kiss?

'Your mother is still a very young woman. She thinks she still has a chance for a happier life, and I won't stand in her way of achieving that. Ironically, I love her too much to do that,' he said. 'I know that doesn't make sense to you right now, none of this does; but later in your life, you might think about what I said and you might understand why I say, I love her too much to stop her from leaving me.'

'But Daddy, what will become of us?' I was frantic now, and I was surprised that my voice hadn't come out in a shriek. What I really meant was 'What will become of me?' He understood.

'You will stay with your mother. The two of you will live in our house for as long as your mother wants to.' He paused, sighed, then went on, 'I have much to occupy myself with these days. In fact, after a very short shore leave, I'm taking another cruise, an exploratory one to a place called the Canary Islands. I've got to search for new and exotic places to attract my clientele and keep myself competitive.

'I guess your mother is right about one thing, Leigh – I am devoted to my business. I can't sit by and just let it die,' he confessed.

'I want to go with you, Daddy,' I choked out through my sobs.

'Now, now, sweetheart. That would be impossible and wrong. You have your school and your friends and you should be with your mother in your own home where you will be comfortable. There's nothing to worry about financially, although the way your mother spends money, there's never enough,' he added dryly.

There were no tears in Daddy's eyes. If he had cried over this, he had done it privately and he had put it aside. Even now he was so in control over his emotions, when I never was. I could see that his love affair with Momma was already dead and gone, buried in a cemetery filled with once happy moments, happy things. He was already thinking of other things. The funeral was over.

His tired face was so filled with resignation that one look at him snuffed out the small candle of hope I tried to keep bright and alive in my heart. It shocked me to learn that the love between Momma and Daddy had been dying in small, slow ways for a long time. But now that he told me this, I thought back and remembered things Momma had said about him and the way she had said them. When I recalled her words now, I recalled them in their true color, and I heard the unhappiness and the warnings I had refused to listen to before.

But I could ignore them no longer.

'Daddy, won't I ever see you again?' I pleaded. I had to wet my lips which had gone dry. My hands betrayed me and began to shake so I had to clasp them together and press them down in my lap.

'Oh sure you will. Sure, sure. This trip will only be about a month and then I'll come by.'

'Come by?' The words sounded so silly coming from my father. He would 'come by' – to his own home? Like a visitor, a stranger, he would ring the doorbell and be greeted by a butler and then be announced?

'And I'll call you and write you whenever I can,' he added. He reached out to take my hand. 'You're growing very quickly now, Leigh. You are a young woman and have a young woman's concerns. You need your mother more than ever, need her advice and companionship. You'll be growing more interested in boys and they'll be growing more interested in you.

'Perhaps your mother's right about one thing – I shouldn't

be filling your head with business things and mechanical things at this point.'

'Oh no, Daddy, I never minded that. I enjoyed it,' I protested fervently.

'I know.' He patted my hand. I yearned to have him hold me so tight I couldn't breathe, to warm my lips with his kisses and to make me feel that everything would be okay.

'Oh Daddy, I don't want you to go. I don't want you to just *come by*,' I choked. The tears were streaming freely down my face now. No matter how I tried, I couldn't hold back the sobs. My shoulders shook. Finally Daddy embraced me and held me tighter than he had ever held me and he kissed my hair and stroked me.

'There, there, my darling Princess. It will be all right. You'll see. Once we're over the hump, it will be all right.' He held me and wiped away my tears. 'You're the owner's daughter. You want to put on a good face and go upstairs to say goodbye to people alongside me. Will you do that for me?'

'Of course I will, Daddy.' I swallowed my cries, but I started to hiccup. Daddy laughed. 'I'll hold my breath,' I said. 'That usually works.'

'That's the spirit.' He stood up. 'Take your time and then come up and join me for breakfast. After that, we'll go to the bridge and watch Captain Willshaw bring the ship to the harbor. Okay? And no matter what, Princess, always remember I love you. Promise?'

'I promise, Daddy, and I'll always love you.'

'That's the spirit, the spirit of the sea. I'll wait for you upstairs.' After he closed the door, I sat there staring at it.

My heart was an aching ruin, but I was too emotionally exhausted to cry anymore, even though a part of me wanted to bawl and bawl until my body was dried out. Then I felt angry, furious at Momma for doing this. How selfish she was. Now I saw how selfish she'd always been. How could she care only about herself like this? How could she do this to Daddy and to me? Who cares how young she was or how young she looked? She wouldn't be young forever and she would never find anyone who loved her as much as Daddy had, and still did!

Oh, it was so ungrateful of her to turn her back on him now that the years had passed. He had rescued her from a horrible life. She'd told me all that herself, and now she was casting him aside, just because she wanted to have more fun. Maybe it wasn't too late. Maybe I could talk Momma into changing her mind, I thought. No one even has to know she went to Mexico to get that horrible divorce. She could go back and change it again. Once she saw she had ruined my life . . .

My heart sunk like a rock in a pond because I knew Momma obviously had to have considered all this before and it hadn't made her stop. She had left me in Jamaica, hadn't she? This was too important to her. She wouldn't listen to anything I had to say, I thought, and no amount of crying, not even gallons and gallons of tears, would convince her she was wrong.

Daddy had accepted it; there was no hope left in him, I concluded. I got up slowly and looked at myself in the mirror. I looked horrible, my face streaked, my eyes bloodshot. I still had the hiccups, too. It kept happening so fast and so hard, it actually began to hurt. I drank a glass of water and then held my breath, but it didn't go away until I had washed my face again and was ready to go up to the dining room to join Daddy. I had no appetite but I would do what he asked of me.

After breakfast Daddy and I went to the bridge just as he had promised and we stood beside Captain Willshaw watching him and the officers oversee the docking of the cruise liner. How sad it must be for Daddy, I thought, to think of the ship's name now. I remembered the day he had taken Momma and me for a ride without telling us the reason. He had turned down to the dock pretending he had a short errand to run, and suddenly there it was before us . . . the new ocean liner being readied for christening. Both Momma and I were excited, but it wasn't until Daddy pulled right alongside the ship that we understood why he was so insistent we take this ride. There were the words brightly painted over the sides of the new liner: *The Jillian*.

How Momma had squealed with delight and covered Daddy's face with kisses. But that seemed so long ago, ages ago.

Now as we drew closer and closer to the dock, I could see the crowd of people that had gathered to greet the returning voyagers. There were taxi cabs lined up alongside limousines and private vehicles. Down below on the decks, passengers were waving and shouting at people who were waving hats and handkerchiefs, taking pictures and calling to them. I looked for Momma, but I didn't see her anywhere. Finally, I saw one of our cars, but there was just Paul Roberts, a driver we used frequently, standing beside the car, waiting.

'Isn't Momma coming for me, Daddy?'

'I had an idea she might just send Paul with the car. She's not anxious to set eyes on me.'

'But what about me! She should be here like everyone else's relatives.'

'She's just avoiding a scene,' Daddy said. He was defending her even now, I thought. If she only knew how much he really loved her. I was determined to tell her.

'You're not coming home at all now, Daddy?' I asked quietly. I knew he was depending on me not to cry and not to give away our personal problems in front of the passengers and crew members.

'No. I have some work to do yet. You just go on ahead. I'll come by later.'

There was that expression again: 'come by'.

I nodded quickly. When the ship was finally docked and people were permitted to disembark, I turned to Daddy. He just closed his eyes and opened them and then nodded.

'Go on,' he said softly. 'I'll be all right.'

'Daddy.' My throat closed up. He nodded again toward the door. I saw that he was doing all he could to keep himself together, too. He kissed me quickly on the cheek. I started to reach for him, but he pulled back and then I charged out the door and down to the deck.

It was a partly cloudy morning, but to me it was dismal and gray. The sea breeze felt like a snowman's breath against my cheeks, making the warm tears cold instantly. I closed my coat around myself and started for the gangplank when I felt someone pull my arm.

It was Clara Spenser and her sister Melanie. Their parents were right behind them and they were all so close to each other, their mother resting her hand on Clara's shoulder and their father resting his hand on Melanie's. It was like a family portrait with a caption underneath that read, *'The Happy Family'*.

'Goodbye, Leigh,' Clara said. 'We'll write to you.'

'Bye. I'll write back,' I called and started away. I wanted to run away from them.

'Leigh!' Clara yelled. 'It was fun, but isn't it wonderful to be home again?'

I just waved and hurried on to the car as fast as I could. My bags had already been loaded.

'Is my mother all right?' I asked. Perhaps she was so upset over what she had done, she was sick in bed at home, I thought, hopefully.

'Oh, yes. She called me this morning and sounded fine. You were lucky to be away; it's been so cold here this past week. Did you have a nice time?' he asked when I didn't reply.

'Yes,' I said and turned to look back as we drove off. I could see Daddy on the bridge talking with Captain Willshaw, but he stopped in the middle of his conversation and looked my way. I waved from the window. He lifted his hand slowly and held it up like a flag of surrender and defeat.

Clarence came out to greet me and fetch my luggage as soon as we drove up, but Momma was nowhere to be seen. I rushed into the house and called for her, demanded her.

'Momma! Momma! Where are you?'

Clarence came up behind me with my bags.

'Mrs VanVoreen went for a ride to the seashore this morning,' he said. 'She has not yet returned.'

'What? The seashore? But . . . didn't she know I would be back this morning?' I shot out. Clarence looked overwhelmed by the ferocity with which I demanded answers to my questions.

'I'll just bring your luggage to your room, Miss Leigh.' He started up the staircase. Confused, I just stood there for a few moments. My gaze fell on the doorway to Daddy's office. He won't be using it anymore, I thought, my throat aching. What would Momma do now – just close it up? I knew how much she hated that room the way it was.

But to me it suddenly became as precious as a church. I stepped into it and gazed at Daddy's things. I inhaled the scents – the aroma of his tobacco still lingered, as did the smell of the driftwood and the old furniture and carpet. Even though much of it was worn and faded, it was beautiful to me because it was Daddy.

In my mind I could see him crouched over his desk, the thin column of smoke rising from the bowl of his carved pipe, the first pipe his father had given him. On the front right corner of his desk was a model of *The Jillian*. He had been so proud of it, so proud of naming it after Momma. The rest of his desk looked as cluttered and as disorganized as ever, but now the sight of it heartened me, because it meant he would have to come back soon to get his important papers.

I walked out slowly and slowly went up the stairs. Clarence was coming down. He seemed very anxious to get away from me.

'Everything's in your room, Miss Leigh.'

'Thank you, Clarence. Oh Clarence,' I called after he had gone past me.

'Yes?'

'Didn't my mother leave any word as to when she would return?'

'No.'

'Thank you, Clarence.' I continued upstairs and went into my room.

How different my world looked to me now. I had been so anxious to hurry home, to get back to my own, precious room and sleep in my own bed, cuddling the stuffed animals given to me over the years. I had looked forward to calling my friends and finding out all the news I had missed while I was on the cruise. I had wanted to tell them about Fulton and Raymond, and the shows and the dances and being kissed by one boy and exchanging addresses with both. But none of that mattered now; none of that was important anymore.

I felt like someone who had been hypnotized. Mechanically,

I unpacked, sifting through my clothing and separating those things that had to be cleaned and washed from those that didn't. Then I sat on my bed like one in a daze. Finally, out of curiosity and boredom, I got up and went into Momma's suite.

She had still not returned. There was nothing different about her bedroom. Her long vanity table was still cluttered with her creams and make-up, her brushes and combs.

And she hadn't put away her and Daddy's wedding picture! The two of them were still there, encased in that solid gold frame, both looking young and happy, Momma so beautiful, Daddy so handsome and distinguished.

The word 'Divorce' had such a mystical ring to it for me. I had half-imagined that now that Momma had gotten a divorce from Daddy, the house itself had undergone some enchantment as if divorce put us all in the grip of some sorceress. The house would be different; the servants would be different; Momma and Daddy would certainly be different, and I . . . I was still afraid of how I would change.

I started out of Momma's suite, but stopped in the sitting room when something on Momma's desk caught my eye. It looked like a pile of books containing samples from a printing company. We had nothing to celebrate soon, no birthdays, and certainly, no anniversaries now. What was Momma doing: planning to announce her divorce? I approached the desk and opened the first book of samples.

At first it made no sense at all, but my heart understood faster than my mind, for it began to thump so hard, it took my breath away. The pounding sounded like thunder in my mind. I choked back my tears, tears that had been threatening to burst forth from the moment I entered my house, and I continued to thumb through the books. They were all the same.

They were all samples of wedding invitations!

SIX

A New Best Friend

Momma didn't come home for hours. I went up to my room and waited and waited until I heard her entering the house. Her laughter preceded her footsteps on the stairway. I couldn't imagine how or why she would be in such a jolly mood. The world was crumpling around us and her voice rang out with a musical cadence as if it were Christmas morning or the morning of her birthday. I stepped out of my room just as she reached the top of the stairway.

She looked just as beautiful as ever, if anything her beauty had flourished since she had left Daddy and me. She seemed invigorated, full of life and energy, her eyes sparkling, her soft, golden hair glistening under the white, fur cap. She was wearing her white mink fur coat, the one Daddy had imported from Russia. Her cheeks were rosy, having been caressed by the crisp November air. I didn't realize until I saw her how much I had wanted to see her sickly and pale, ravaged by the decision she had made.

Her burst of exuberance and her brightness overwhelmed me. I could just stand and stare. But Momma's face wasn't drawn, her eyes weren't bloodshot. Instead, she looked like someone who had been liberated from a dark and dismal castle dungeon, unchained and free to be young and lovely and alive once more. She misunderstood my look of surprise and sadness.

'Oh Leigh, I'm so sorry I wasn't here when you arrived, but you'd never believe the traffic.' She smiled as if she expected me to forget everything horrible instantly.

'Why didn't you come down to the dock? Where were you?'

'Where was I? I was at Farthy,' she sang and started for her suite. 'You know how undependable those dockings can be . . .

half an hour late, an hour late. Something's always going wrong. I could just envision myself stuck in that stuffy automobile, waiting, waiting, waiting.' She turned back to flash a quick smile. 'I didn't think you would mind and it's so much nicer out at the seashore today,' she said as she took off her coat. 'There, the sky is all blue,' she added and threw her fur coat over one of the rococo chairs. 'But it's always blue there to me, even when it's gray,' she whispered, making her sentence sound like the words from a love song.

Then, still wearing her fur cap, she fell back over her bed and flung her arms to her sides as she bounced on the mattress. I had never seen her so cheerful. She seemed years younger, more like one of my girlfriends, silly and full of giggles. Her eyes were twinkling as she smiled up at the ceiling. I stood there speechless, staring down at her. Could it be that she was unaware Daddy had told me everything?

'Daddy told me about your telegram,' I blurted.

She looked up at me, her smile slowly fading, the glimmer in her eyes dying. The vigor and brightness lifted from her face. It was as if she were coming back to earth, back to reality. Her eyes grew cold, her mouth tight. She took a deep breath and sat up slowly and with great effort. Then she took off her cap, unpinned her hair and shook her head to let the strands fall free.

'He was supposed to leave it to me to tell you,' she said with remarkable calmness. 'But I'm not surprised. I'm sure he put it all horribly, making it sound like the failure of some business venture. What did he tell you, our marriage was bankrupt?'

'Oh no, Momma, Daddy is heartbroken,' I cried. She smirked and got up to go to her vanity table. 'Did you really go to Mexico and get a divorce?' Some stupid childish part of me was still hoping beyond hope that perhaps it wasn't all true.

'Yes, Leigh, I did. And I'm not sorry.' Her words felt like needles being poked in all over my body.

'But why did you do it? How can you do it?' I screamed, enraged at my mother. I hated how little she seemed to care about how I was affected by her selfish decision. She sat down and turned to me.

'Leigh, I was hoping you would be adult about all this now,' she said calmly, but firmly. 'I have been wanting to do this for some time, but I held off until I thought you were old enough to deal with it on a mature level. I've gone through months, years of added suffering just so you would be old enough to understand when I took this action,' she added and shook her head as if she had just slipped out from under some terribly heavy load.

'Well I don't understand,' I snapped. 'I'll never understand. Never.' I hoped that my words fell like daggers. She pulled her shoulders back and her eyes widened with fire.

'Exactly what did you father tell you?'

'That you left us to think things over and he received a telegram from you that you had flown to Mexico to get a divorce.'

'And did he tell you why?'

'He said you were very disappointed in him and you were still young and wanted a chance to be happy. But why can't you be happy with Daddy?' I moaned.

'Now, Leigh, you've got to try to understand my point of view. It should be easier for you to understand now that you are becoming a woman yourself.

'You don't know, you can't imagine what it's been like for me these last few years. Whenever your father takes me on one of his cruises it's because he wants to make an impression, to use me for his own advantage. I've felt like a caged bird, encased in a gilded cage, yes, but nevertheless, imprisoned.'

Imprisoned? What did she mean? She could come and go as she wanted, buy whatever she wanted, do whatever she wanted. We had such a beautiful home, I couldn't imagine anyone thinking of it as a prison.

'The other passengers pity me, Leigh. I see it in their faces.' She threaded her fingers through her hair madly. 'They know I rarely do what they can do anytime they want. I hate their pity! I hate it!' She clenched her hands into small fists and pounded the top of her thighs.

It's been this way for years and years and I've tried to keep my sanity just so you would grow up in a happy home, but I can't sacrifice anymore. I won't! I won't give up what is so precious and fleeting – my youth and my beauty. I won't wilt away like some flower closed off from the sun.

'I belong out there on the dance floors, at the operas and the theatre, at the seashore resorts, at the parties with my picture being taken for the society pages.

'Do you have any idea how many affairs I had to miss because your father was too busy to attend? Do you?' She then took a breath. Her face was scarlet and her eyes were screwed so tight that I was frightened. I was stunned by her outburst. Never had I imagined she harbored such resentment and despair.

I wanted to hate her for what she was doing to Daddy and to me, but seeing her in such a state, her eyes bulging, her hair pulled out, her face red with frustration, all I could think was that this terrifying creature wasn't my mother.

'Daddy is sorry about all that. He really is.'

'I'm sure he is . . . for the moment, but tomorrow some crisis at his business will take up his attention and he will forget what has happened between us.'

'No, Momma, he won't. Can't you let him try again? Can't you?' I pleaded.

'I have let him try again, Leigh. Many, many times. This didn't just start recently. It started almost as soon as we got married.

'Oh,' she said sighing and sitting back, 'it wasn't so bad in the early years because you were born right away and I had you to care for and your father was very attentive and quite devoted to me. Of course, he was twelve years younger then, but you must remember, he was already well along in his years. I bet you never realized that he is old enough to be my father.'

The idea was so preposterous and strange that I almost laughed, but she didn't crack a smile. Daddy, her father? My grandfather?

'His age has caught up with him. I admit this is all partly my fault because I agreed to marry him, but I was so young and so unhappy then that I didn't think of what the future would be like.

'And your father made all sorts of wonderful promises . . . promises he has never kept . . . promises he can't even remember having made!'

'But you were so in love. You told me so yourself.' My little lifeboat of hope was sinking rapidly. Everything she told me punched holes in it.

'I was young; I didn't know what love was then.' She smiled. 'But now, now I understand. Completely,' she added, the brightness and sparkle returning to her face. 'Oh Leigh . . . Leigh,' she cried, 'don't hate me, but I'm in love, really and truly in love.'

'What?' I looked back toward the sitting room and thought about those invitations. 'You've fallen in love with someone else? Those sample invitations . . .' I muttered, the realization falling over me like ice cold rain.

'You saw them?'

I nodded.

'Well you might as well know it all,' she said, pulling herself up firmly. 'I'm in love with Tony Tatterton and he is madly in love with me, and we're going to have a Christmas wedding and live at Farthy!' All at once the face that had seemed a monster version of my beautiful Momma relaxed. Then she smiled, her eyes filled with happiness.

Even though I had anticipated something like this, actually hearing her say these words was devastating. I felt my face whiten and drain. A combination of shock and sorrow numbed my legs and nailed my feet to the floor. I couldn't speak, couldn't swallow, I think my breathing stopped and my heart froze. It was as if two giant hands of ice had clasped over my chest.

'You must not hate me and you must try to understand, Leigh. Please. I'm speaking to you as one woman to another.'

'But Momma, how could you fall in love with someone else?' My mind was racing about, trying to understand. When I recalled the way Momma and Tony had been dancing together, every moment he held her there, every look he gave her had more meaning, had its true meaning. I had felt something when I went to Farthy with her and saw the way they walked together and whispered, but I had not understood what it was I had felt. Why is it the heart knows things so much quicker than the mind? I wondered. Perhaps I didn't want to know, didn't want to understand. Now, I had no choice.

'It's not hard to understand why or how this happened, Leigh. Tony adores me, worships me. He says I'm like some mythical goddess who has descended from the heavens above to make his life worthwhile, for even men with all his money and power feel incomplete if they don't have a woman to love and a woman who can love them.

'Love, true love, is what makes life fulfilling, Leigh. This is something you will understand, and when you do, you will appreciate all the things I am telling you.

'Can I tell you more? Will you listen like a best friend, a close girlfriend? I've never had a truly good friend. I grew up with two terrible sisters who were always so jealous of me, I would never tell them one good thing or share one good feeling with them. Leigh?'

'I'm your best friend, Momma. I . . . just . . .'

'Oh good,' she said, her eyes taking on a faraway look. 'The first time I set eyes on Tony and he set eyes on me, it was as if the clouds were swept off the blue sky. Everything became more vivid, more alive around me. Colors brightened, birds sang, and the breeze, no matter how cool, was refreshing and soft. I couldn't wait to awaken every morning and get myself to Farthy, just so I would be around him, hear his voice, and feel his eyes on me.

'That's what love is, Leigh, true love.' She reached out for me. Her words were so magical, her thoughts so wonderful, I couldn't help but step closer until she could take my hand and look into my eyes.

'I know he had opened his heart to me and that I had found a place there. Whenever he spoke to me, his voice grew so soft, so loving. There was a longing in his eyes that made me tingle all over,' she said, confessing to me like a school girl who had just found her first love. Only this was Momma talking . . . Momma . . . and to me!

'Oh, I tried to resist at first, Leigh. I wasn't unfaithful to your father. I told myself over and over that I was a married woman, that I had a husband and a child to think about, but as Tony and I drew closer and closer, all restraint weakened until I could deny what was happening no longer.

'It happened one night after I had finished working and had cleaned up to go home. It was a warm day, a warm late afternoon. He asked me to take a walk with him to look at the ocean. I hesitated, but he pleaded, promising to bring me right back. I relented and we walked to a small hill and looked out over the sea. The sun was red and low, the bottom of it just touching the ocean. The sight was breathtaking. Suddenly, I felt his hand in mine, and when we touched, my heart cried . . . no . . . demanded to be heard.

'I confessed my unhappiness to him, but I told him I couldn't rush into anything. He was very understanding, but determined.

'I tried on three or four occasions to explain things to your father, but he either ignored it or didn't really listen. His mind's always on his business. Finally, at the *bon voyage* ball, I made Tony a promise. Even so, I tried to break it. I suffered so on that trip to Jamaica, but love will not be denied, when it is as real and sincere as it is between Tony and myself, and I knew at the end that I had to do something dramatic or I would pine away in the darkness like a flower.

'Will you try to understand? Will you, Leigh? It could happen to you someday and you might need someone, someone you love and who loves you to understand.' She squeezed my hand and pleaded with her eyes.

'Oh Momma. This is all happening so fast. It might not have happened overnight to you, but it is to me.'

'I know, Leigh. I appreciate what you're going through, but I'm going to need you to help me, too. I need your support and love. Will you be more than my daughter? Will you be my best friend, too?'

Her eyes were glassy, tear-filled, but warm. I couldn't help reaching out to her. She kissed my cheek.

'I'll try. But Momma, what will happen to Daddy?'

'Nothing will happen to him, Leigh. Believe me. He has his business and that keeps him busy day and night. You'll see him and he'll see you just as much as you do now, which isn't all that much,' she added dryly.

I didn't say anything. She might be right about that, I thought, but still, it felt like a sword through the heart to hear her say it.

'And Leigh, most important of all, will you try to like Tony? Will you give him a chance? If you do, you will see how sweet he is and you will understand why I love him so.' I couldn't help my feelings. Every time she said she loved Tony, I thought about Daddy and how cruel it all was. To think of Tony made my stomach butterflies flutter a bit, stir from their restless sleep. As I sat there it slowly dawned on me, sank like water into concrete, that this was all Tony's fault. *I hated Tony!*

Oh, why did this rich, handsome man have to come into Momma's life and sweep her off her feet so quickly and so completely? I wanted more than any other want to make him regret tearing my happy loving world asunder.

'Leigh, will you?' Momma repeated, her voice a little desperate now. Once again today her wants would battle with mine and win. I nodded. 'Thank you. Oh, thank you so much, honey.' She embraced me and I was so starved for this affection, so needed to be warmed by her touch that I knew that if she asked me now I might agree to anything. But, I couldn't help feeling cold, lifeless in her arms. It was horrible for me to agree to this. I was betraying Daddy.

'And there is one other thing I have to ask of you, Leigh, one thing, a secret to be kept between two best friends like us now because I trust you with keeping it. Will you promise to keep it secret? A bosom buddy promise,' she added, placing her hand on her breast.

What could it be? I wondered.

'I promise, Momma.'

'Good.' She leaned toward me and whispered as if there were other people in the room. 'Tony doesn't know my true age, even now, even though he has proposed and I have accepted. I don't want him to know. As I told you after we left Farthy, he believes I'm twenty-eight.'

'Won't you ever tell him the truth?'

'Someday, but not right now. Okay?'

I nodded, but wondered if they were so much in love, why was it necessary to lie? Didn't being in love, true love, mean you would have no lies between you, that you trusted each other so completely nothing could break you apart?

'Thank you, Leigh. I knew you would understand. I knew you were grown up. I told Tony. He likes you very much, by the way. He talked about you continually, about how sweet you were and how much Troy likes you and what a wonderful time he had with you when the three of you walked to the beach.

'Oh, I just can't wait until we're all together at Farthy. It's a dream life come true, Leigh. You'll see. You'll be a princess, a true debutante yet.' She got up.

'I'm going to take a warm bubble bath now because I can relax now that I know my little girl is understanding and loves me. Afterward, we'll sit and talk and you'll tell me all about Jamaica and the things you did. Okay?' I nodded and remembered her gift.

'I bought you something in the street market, Momma.'

'Really? How sweet for you to think of me even after I had deserted you like that. You're such a warm, wonderful child, Leigh. I'm very lucky to have you.'

'Let me get it,' I cried and rushed back to my room. 'It's not very much,' I told her when I returned, 'but I thought it was beautiful.'

She unwrapped it quickly.

'I just love gifts, love surprises, no matter how much they cost. Tony's like that, too. He wants to give me something new and beautiful every day of our lives together,' she squealed. Because of my promises I tried as hard as I could not to harden myself against her new-found happiness. She looked down at the hand-painted scarf. 'Oh, this is great, Leigh. How clever of you to pick it out. It will go with so many of my outfits. I'm sorry I wasn't there with you, but I will make it up to you in a thousand ways. You'll see.'

'I bought Daddy a hand-carved cane,' I said softly.

'That's nice.' She went into her bathroom to run her water.

I stood there for a moment listening to her hum to herself and then left.

Daddy arrived shortly before dinner. Momma was still in her suite talking to her friends on the telephone and doing her nails and hair. I still hadn't had an opportunity to tell her about the Spenser sisters and Fulton and Raymond, but I expected to tell her everything at dinner. Suddenly, I heard the front door open and heard Clarence say, 'Hello, Mr VanVoreen.'

Daddy! I thought and jumped up. He was already in his office, gathering some papers.

'Daddy!'

'Hello Leigh. All settled back, are you?'

'Yes. Momma's here. She's upstairs.'

'I see.' He went back to his papers quickly.

'Are you staying here for a while?' I felt so sorry for him. He looked tired and worn, older than ever, and I kept thinking how much worse it would be for him once he learned about Momma's love for Tony Tatterton. Maybe he still held on to some hope, like I had, even though she had gotten the divorce.

'No, Leigh. I've got to get back to the office and prepare for my next journey.'

'But where will you sleep tonight?'

'I have rooms at the Hilton. You must not worry about me. I want you to take good care of yourself and . . .' His eyes rose as if he could see through the ceiling into Momma's suite. 'And your mother.' He went back to his papers, sorted through folders, opened file cabinet drawers, and began to fill a briefcase.

I sat on the leather settee watching him, and I felt terrible. I felt as though I were betraying him by not telling him what I knew about Momma and Tony. I felt split in half. If I smiled at Momma or felt good with her, I couldn't help feeling guilty, feeling that I was hurting Daddy; and the same was true if I smiled at him and felt good with him. Momma would hate me. She would certainly hate me if I told him any of her secrets. What was I to do?

Daddy saw the troubled look on my face.

'Now, now,' he said. 'You must not do this to yourself. I told you, once we're through the storm, it will be clear sailing again. Button up against the wind. Be hearty. You've been around sailors and seamen too long to be anything else.'

'I'll try, Daddy.'

'That's my girl. Well,' he said looking about, 'I guess I have what I need for now.' He closed his briefcase. My heart began to pound. I didn't think I had the strength in my legs to stand up. He started around his desk and then stopped abruptly, the expression on his face changing quickly from a soft, loving one, to a look of firmness, even anger. I spun around. Momma was standing in the doorway.

'Hello, Cleave,' she said.

'I've just come by to get some of my papers.'

'I'm glad you did,' she said. 'There are some matters to discuss. I was going to leave them for later, but perhaps this is as good a time as ever.'

'Yes,' he said.

'Leigh, would you excuse us for a while, please,' Momma said and then smiled coldly. I looked at Daddy. He nodded and suddenly my legs that had felt like two overcooked pieces of spaghetti found their firmness again and I got up and rushed out of the office. I turned back to see Momma close the door.

I wanted to go back and put my ear to it, but I was afraid they would find me there.

It seemed like hours, but finally Momma came in to get me. I looked behind her, anticipating Daddy too. Maybe, somehow they had worked out their differences and they were going to give our family another chance. Maybe Daddy had said some magical things and they had both thought about their early days together when they were so much in love. I waited for the words; I prayed for them.

'I bet you're famished,' Momma said. 'I know I am.'

'Is Daddy going to eat with us?' I asked hopefully.

'No, it's just like old times,' she said dryly. 'He's off to his shipyards.'

'Off? Did he leave?' I cried. Oh, surely, he didn't leave without saying goodbye, without giving me a last kiss.

'Yes, he's gone. Let's go to dinner.' She turned away.

But he can't be gone, my brain screamed. Not without saying goodbye. I hurried out behind her, but instead of going straight to the dining room, I went to his office.

The door was closed and when I opened it, I looked into a dark room. Momma waited in the hallway. I spun around, the tears streaming down my face.

'Where is he?'

'I told you, Leigh. He left.'

'But he didn't . . . he didn't kiss me goodbye,' I bawled.

'He wasn't in the mood to kiss anyone. Now please, honey. Pull yourself together. Go wash your face. Freshen up. We don't want to show the servants we're unhappy, do we? After you have something in your stomach, you will feel a lot better anyway, I'm sure.'

'I'm not hungry,' I cried. I ran to the staircase.

'Leigh!'

I didn't turn back. I couldn't. I ran up the stairs and into my room. I rushed to my window to look out in hopes of catching sight of Daddy leaving the house, but the street below was empty, the streetlights casting long dark and lonely shadows over the sidewalks. I clenched my hands into fists to grind away my tears and then I looked about my room. I looked at all the things I had that reminded me of Daddy, looked at his picture, looked at the models of ships. It was over. This life I had known had passed on into that empty night below.

Daddy had a saying when he met someone new, especially someone he liked.

'Let's not be like two ships passing in the night. Call again. Stop by.'

Oh Daddy, I thought, will we now become like two ships passing in the night?

One day slipped into another. I returned to school and described my Jamaican trip to all my girlfriends. Everyone was interested in my stories about Fulton and Raymond, and a week after I had returned home, I received a nice letter from Raymond. I brought it with me to school to show my friends, especially the ones who had looked skeptical when I had told them about the two older boys who said I could pass for a high school girl.

Most of Raymond's letter was about his work at school, but he did say how much he had enjoyed spending time with me, and at the end, he signed it, 'Fondly, Raymond'.

Toward the end of the first week, Daddy called me to tell me about his plans for his next voyage. There was a lot of noise around him in his office, and even though it was a short talk, we were interrupted several times. He said he would try to write or call as soon as he reached the Canary Islands. Oh, how I missed him and how I tried not to hate Momma for driving him out of my life.

A few nights later, Momma came into my room to announce that we were going to go to Farthinggale Manor for Thanksgiving dinner.

'It's going to be the most magnificent Thanksgiving dinner we ever had. Many of Tony's wealthy friends will be there and he's even invited Patrick and Clarissa Darrow, the publishers of my illustrations, and of course, Elizabeth Deveroe, the decorator, and her husband, so there will be people we already know. Isn't that nice?'

'But we've always had Thanksgiving here, Momma.' It hadn't occurred to me until just this moment that Daddy wouldn't be home and with us for Thanksgiving. It would be the first time, for no matter where his business took him or what he had to do, he always managed to be home for Thanksgiving.

'I know, but I want to be with Tony and he has a large affair every year. We'll have pheasant, instead of turkey, and champagne, and desserts beyond imagination. You remember how well his chef cooks.'

'But it won't be Thanksgiving without a turkey.'

'Oh, there will be so many other delectable things, you'll never miss it. I know what we'll do,' she continued, 'we'll buy new dresses, just for the occasion.'

'But I haven't worn many of the things you bought me for my birthday yet.'

'This is different,' she said, turning slowly and thinking. 'We need to stand out . . . Get your coat,' she said suddenly, her face lit with excitement. 'We're going to André's Boutique and pick out something original for both of us.'

'But Mommy . . .' I knew that dresses and gowns at André's began somewhere around eight hundred dollars and went as high as ten thousand. 'Can we afford it now that Daddy's . . . Daddy's not here?'

'Of course, we can. Your father is still responsible for all our expenses,' she replied firmly. 'Until I remarry. Then, he's just responsible for yours, not that you will need to worry. Tony is very generous. Come on,' she said beckoning. 'Let's get started.'

Momma bought a black velvet dress with spaghetti straps and a wide charcoal silk belt. She wore black satin elbow length gloves. She put on her biggest diamond necklace and matching pear shaped diamond earrings.

For me she bought a beautiful aqua-colored dress in an airy fabric. I never felt so dressed up for a Thanksgiving dinner.

Tony sent Miles in his limousine to pick us up early in the afternoon, but he had to sit in the hallway and wait for at least an additional forty-five minutes for Momma to finish with her hair and make-up. Finally, wearing her sable fur piece, she came down the stairs. Never had her hair looked as soft or gleamed as brightly. I saw by the way Miles rose from his seat that he was stunned by her beauty. I thought she looked just like a movie star.

How I wished Daddy could be here to see her, I thought, but then I thought that would only bring him more pain because she was so beautiful and she was gone from his life.

'How do I look?' she asked me and spun around.

'Prettier than anyone.'

'Oh honey, thank you. And you look beautiful too. We're going to dazzle everyone,' she added and we went out to the limousine.

During the trip to Farthy, she told me about some of Tony's

friends she had met. Everyone seemed to be known by what business or profession he was in.

'And wait until you see their wives,' she said. 'With all their wealth and position, they don't know very much about fashion and make-up. You and I will stand out like . . . like roses in a bed of weeds.' She giggled and hugged me. As sad as I felt going to a Thanksgiving dinner without Daddy, I couldn't help but be fascinated by the way Momma spoke to me. She was acting more like my older sister than my mother. I felt, perhaps for the first time in my life, that she was treating me like her closest friend.

'Now don't be nervous just because these people have so much money. You will see they aren't so clever when it comes to socializing. When they ask you a question, answer politely, but don't offer more information than they request. Men appreciate women who are not talkative and gossipy around the dinner table. Men like to dominate the conversations with their talk of politics and business.'

'But Daddy was never like that.' Poor Daddy, I thought, with no family around him, out on the ocean on one of his ships, having a Thanksgiving dinner with strangers.

'Don't look so sad,' Momma advised. 'You are so pretty when you smile.'

Mrs Deveroe and her husband and the Darrows were already there when we arrived. Everyone said Momma and I looked like sisters. The men made me feel very grown up with their compliments and approving eyes, and Momma entered the great house as if she were the queen arriving. There were servants everywhere, just waiting to do her bidding – take her and my coats, show us into the music room where the others were already gathered, and get us some champagne punch.

'Jillian! You're finally here,' Tony cried coming quickly to greet us at the entryway to the music room. He took her hand into his and gazed into her eyes, his blue eyes burning with love and appreciation. 'You are undoubtedly the most beautiful woman I have ever seen. I don't think I'll ever tire of saying it.' I had thought all morning about how much I hated Tony but now a warm, electric feeling shot through my body. I had never been so close to anything so romantic. It was as if I had stepped into a movie, and I couldn't take my eyes off the two of them. No one in the room could. There was a great pause, as though we were all sighing and then everyone burst out into conversation. Tony turned his heavenly blue eyes to me.

'And Leigh, you look very beautiful too. I'm so lucky to have both of you here. Farthinggale Manor will sparkle like it never has.' He scooped our arms into his, placing himself between us, but I stood as stiffly as I could, touched him as little as possible, hoping to hurt him as he introduced us to everyone.

Little Troy sat in a huge cushioned easy chair in the corner, his feet dangling over the edge. He looked lost and alone, but so cute in his tiny tuxedo and black tie. As soon as he saw me, his eyes lit up.

'Hi Troy. Happy Thanksgiving.' I shook his little hand.

'Hi. Tony says you're going to come here to live and be my big sister now. Are you? Are you really?' I had to smile at his enthusiasm, even though the words he spoke were still so alien and so frightening to me.

'Yes, it looks that way, Troy.'

'Good. I have so many things to show you, secret things,' he added in a whisper, his eyes turning to be sure no one overheard.

When the time came for all of us to go into the great dining room and gather around the long table, Troy and I indeed sat beside each other. Momma sat on Tony's right and I sat on his left with Troy on my left. There were thirty-three people for dinner. I had never seen so many people at a dining-room table.

At the center was a great chopped-liver swan. There were large goblets for wine and settings of Wedgwood china with little figures and country scenes on them. The silver was heavy, but sparkling bright with floral designs. The heavy blue, napkins had an embroidered *F.M.* done in white thread.

After a while Momma began to announce her plans for her and Tony's wedding.

'It will be like a royal coronation,' she said and followed it with a trail of laughter. But then she elaborated. 'The invitation will become a collector's item, for I am designing it myself, based upon one of the illustrations I've done for Darrow Publishing,' she added and nodded toward the Darrows.

'We're going to have a twenty-six-piece orchestra and flowers flown in from South America and Tony has come up with a wonderful added touch. Tell them, Tony.'

'Well, you're ruining the surprise,' he said gently and smiled. 'But I suppose it's all right since these are special friends tonight. I'm having a commemorative Tatterton toy created for each and every guest. It has the date of our wedding carved into it.'

'It's a wonderful idea.' Momma beamed. 'Two figures modeled after us . . .' She reached for the hand of her handsome young husband-to-be. 'Dancing on the top of the world.'

Everyone 'oohed' their appreciation. Even I had been taken by surprise hearing it for the first time. Tony tried to catch my eye with his own intense ones, but I looked away. How easily Momma had captured the whole table's attention, I thought. They all looked envious – men envious of Tony's having her as his wife; women envious of Momma's beauty and exuberance.

These plans for the wedding did sound exciting and glamorous, but even now, even at this Thanksgiving dinner table at Farthy that seemed so far away from our intimate family Thanksgivings of the past, I couldn't help but feel alone and lost.

The wedding dominated the conversation for the rest of the dinner. Little Troy got a face full of whipped cream when he dipped into the chocolate cream pie. I laughed and wiped his mouth.

After dinner everyone returned to the music room. Troy asked me to go to his playroom to help him color his drawings. When we got there and I saw that he had created the pictures himself, I stared in amazement. He was remarkably talented for a small child. There were pictures of the great house and the grounds and some pictures of groundsmen.

'This is Henderson and this is Margaret Stone and this is Edgar.' He pointed at his different drawings.

'They're wonderful, Troy. Very, very good.' I said. His eyes brightened.

‘Here,’ he said handing me a brown crayon. ‘Edgar always wears a brown shirt. You do Edgar.’

I laughed and began. I lost my sense of time sitting there and coloring and listening to Troy chatter away about the servants and the pool and maze and Tony, but perhaps an hour or so later, I heard Momma’s voice just down the hall from Troy’s playroom. Then I heard Tony. He sounded annoyed. Troy didn’t notice because he was too engrossed in his work. I saw how intent he would get when he did something creative, and I thought it was remarkable for a little boy to be able to shut the world out so completely. He didn’t even see me rise from my seat and go to the doorway.

Tony and Momma were standing a half-dozen yards away. Tony stood tall and masculine and had his hands on her hips, trying to keep her close to him. They didn’t know I was there, silent, watching.

‘Come on Jillian.’ His full lips looked sulky. ‘We’re practically married.’

‘But we’re not married, not yet. That’s why not. And there’s Leigh to think about.’

‘I’ll put her on the other side of the house. She won’t even know you’ve come into my room. He bent his dark head to nuzzle her neck.

‘No,’ Momma pushed him away. ‘I told you, not until after we’re married. And besides, I have things to do in Boston tomorrow. We can’t stay over and that’s that. Now don’t be difficult.’

‘All right,’ he said shaking his head, ‘but you’re tormenting me . . . and on Thanksgiving,’ he half-joked I thought. I had a funny feeling in the pit of my stomach and I felt bad watching them but I couldn’t stop. Just before they turned to go back to the others, Tony caught sight of me peering out of Troy’s playroom door. For a long moment his eyes burned into mine and I felt like he had stroked my hair or the delicate, airy fabric of my dress. I returned to Troy for another half hour or so and then Momma came to fetch me.

‘It’s time to head back to Boston.’

Little Troy grimaced. 'When are you going to stay here forever and ever?'

'Very soon now, Troy,' Momma told him. 'It's late and you should be thinking about going to bed anyway.'

'I'm not tired,' he wailed.

'That's not for you to decide,' she said. 'You've been sickly and need your rest. Come along, Leigh.' She turned and left quickly.

'I'll be back soon and we'll finish it all,' I told him. He wasn't placated, but his sour expression left him when I kissed him on the cheek goodbye.

I joined Momma and Tony in the entrance hall. Most of the guests had already left.

'Thanks for entertaining Troy tonight, Leigh,' Tony said. 'He adores you.'

'He's very talented.'

'Yes,' Tony's lips were curled into an amused smile. 'He'll be designing Tatterton toys in no time.' He stepped close enough to kiss my forehead. 'Good night, Leigh,' he said, his hand lingering on my shoulder. I felt myself tremble. How could I ever consider such a handsome young man my step-father?

'Good night,' I muttered and quickly stepped out the door. Momma lingered behind whispering with Tony for a few moments. Then he kissed her softly on the lips and she turned to join me. We went down the steps and it occurred to me that very soon now, this would be my home, yet it all still seemed so strange to me. There were so many empty rooms, so many dark shadows. I wondered if I could ever call such a place my home.

Apparently Momma had none of these feelings. She was bubbling over with excitement.

'Wasn't it the most wonderful Thanksgiving you've ever had? All those people . . . all that food. Did you see the jewelry on Lillian Rumford?'

'I don't remember who she was, Momma.'

'You don't remember? Oh, Leigh, how could you not notice that diamond tiara and those bracelets and that cameo?'

'I don't know. I guess I just missed it,' I snapped. She heard the sadness in my voice and her smile wilted. I was glad in a mean way. All of a sudden my heart hardened against her – against my beautiful mother and her desire for fun and a rich, handsome husband.

I wouldn't speak to her anymore. I turned to look out of the window at the night. She was quiet also for a while then she started rattling on about the clothing the other women wore, what fantastic things were said to her and things she said, how much Tony adored her and how their wedding would be the talk of the town . . .

As I gazed out the window into the darkness, I was hardly listening. There was a break in the landscape and we could see the ocean. It was a clear, cool night. Far off, I saw the small lights of a ship and I thought about Daddy someplace out there in the darkness – a lonely light against the velvet black night, like a single star in the evening sky.

SEVEN

Lost

Two weeks after Thanksgiving, I was on my way back to Farthy for a wedding ceremony rehearsal. It had snowed very heavily up and down the New England coast two days before. The landscape we passed through on our way to Farthy was covered with a white blanket that sparkled, crisp and clean, in the morning sunlight. When we entered the wooded area just before the estate, I saw that many trees had changed shape, leaning over like old men because of the weight of the snow, or standing frozen against the blue sky, their branches looking more like bones because of the snow that clung to them. Some had icicles hanging from the tips of their branches, like large teardrops frozen in the air.

Momma wasn't very interested in Nature. She had taken command of her wedding, planning every moment, every little detail as if it really was going to be the most important social event of the decade. Tony provided her with one of his secretaries, Mrs Walker, a very tall, very slim, dark-haired woman who was all business and no smiles. I guessed she just wasn't very happy about her assignment. She sat across from us in the limousine taking notes as Momma thought of things she still wanted added or changed. The reading of the guest list was the opening activity each morning. Mrs Walker had been asked to do it again as soon as we had gotten into the back of the limo and begun our journey to Farthy.

Momma had decided that once she and Tony were married, she would never drive herself anywhere again. It would be chauffeurs and limousines from now on, and whenever Miles wasn't available because he was driving Tony somewhere, Momma would simply hire a temporary limo and driver.

During the days that followed our Thanksgiving dinner at Farthinggale Manor, I noticed other changes in her as well. She spent even more time on her hair and make-up, as impossible as that seemed, because she believed she had an even greater responsibility to look good now.

'People know I'm to be Mrs Tony Tatterton. They are looking at me more closely, expecting more. I am really in society now, Leigh.'

I didn't think her spending all this extra time on herself made any real difference. Her hair couldn't be any softer, her complexion any more peaches and cream. But I didn't say anything to her because I saw how important it all was to her. What made me feel bad was the way she talked about some of her old friends, even someone like Elizabeth Deveroe. I could tell she thought they had been all right to know when she had been married to Daddy, but now that she was to be Mrs Tony Tatterton, they were just not good enough. After all, Elizabeth Deveroe was someone for whom she had once worked but would now be working for her.

She always hesitated by her name and some of the other names of old friends when Mrs Walker read down the list.

'I'm a little sorry I invited them,' she would say. 'They are going to feel so out of place.'

On our way to Farthy for the rehearsal, she did cross off one particular couple who had not been mailed their invitation yet and added a new couple, the Kingsleys, because Louise Avery told her, 'Martin Kingsley, publisher of the *Globe*, had just returned from Moscow and he and his wife were among the most sought-after dinner guests in town.' She would add these little explanations whenever she told Mrs Walker to write a new name, but Mrs Walker didn't seem to be impressed. Momma didn't notice or care. She was in her own world, happier than I had ever seen her.

As we drove through the gates of Farthy, she was reviewing the menu again, wondering aloud if we needed an additional selection of hot *hors d'oeuvres*. Even though I wasn't really listening while she rattled on and on during our ride to Farthy, I said I thought it sounded as if there was enough of everything.

I made the mistake of adding, 'There will be more food than on one of Daddy's cruise ships.' She squinted and pulled her mouth in as if she had been slapped.

'Leigh, there will be no comparison. We're not preparing just to stuff people to give them the impression they're getting more for their money; I have hired some of the best gourmet chefs in Boston, each with a specialty. Why, the Frenchman who's preparing the Lobster Bisque is known everywhere, and . . .'

'But Ryse Williams is such a wonderful chef, Momma. Couldn't he have done it all?'

'Done it all?' She laughed and smiled at Mrs Walker as if I were five years old. 'Hardly. There is enough to keep ten chefs of Ryse William's calibre busy. Don't you worry about any of this,' she said patting me on the knee. 'You just worry about looking good in your dress.'

I had to admit I was nervous about it. As one of the bridesmaids, I was to wear a light pink strapless chiffon dress with white lace trim over the bodice and a full skirt. All of Momma's other bridesmaids were grown women. None would have my small shoulders, shoulders I still thought looked too bony, and none would be as dependent on a foam bra to give them a womanly shape. I was sure I would look silly in this dress when I stood among the others, but Momma had chosen it herself to compliment her wedding gown. None of the bridesmaids were permitted to wear necklaces and earrings either. Momma wanted her own jewelry to stand out and she wanted to be sure no one would upstage her, for some of these women were very wealthy and possessed famous diamonds.

When the limo pulled up to the front steps of Farthinggale Manor, little Troy was outside with Mrs Hastings, his nanny. She was nice enough, but the few times I had met her, I had had the feeling she was somewhat overwhelmed by the responsibilities. Troy was very clever for his age and had already figured out ways to outsmart her and get his own way. I saw from the way she was standing beside him as he worked on making a snowman that she was trying to coax him back into the house.

But I also saw from the expression of intensity on his face that he was too involved in his creation even to hear her. He wore the same look he had worn while he and I colored in the pictures he had drawn: his eyes fixed, his face as still as the face of a granite statue. He was working on the details of the snowman's face, carving out the features with the back of a silver spoon.

'Leigh!' he cried the moment I stepped out. 'Come see my snowman. Come see.'

'You have to get right upstairs and get dressed,' Momma warned. Mrs Walker had gone to the car trunk with Miles to gather the garments. Curtis was already coming down the steps to help, little puffs of air popping from his mouth as he stepped down as quickly as I had ever seen him move. He hadn't put on a coat and in his vest, shirt and pants, he looked like an underdressed scarecrow.

'That's the best snowman I've ever seen,' I told Troy. He straightened up proudly and glanced at Mrs Hastings, who had her gloved hands stuffed so deeply into her coat pockets, she looked as though she might tear the pockets out. 'But we've all got to go inside and prepare for the wedding rehearsal. You too,' I added, noticing Mrs Hastings' eyes grow warmer and more appreciative with my every word. 'You're the best man, remember.'

'I know. Tony already told me I have to carry the ring.'

'Come on then. Let's get dressed. We'll come out and play in the snow later.'

'Promise?'

'I promise,' I said holding out my hand. He took it quickly and we followed Momma and Mrs Walker into the house, Mrs Hastings right behind us, her face in a wide smile.

The wedding itself was to be held in the great entry hall. Momma would come down the stairway when the pianist played 'Here Comes the Bride', and everyone would be forced to look up and watch her descend like some angel. Just under the stairway the minister would take his place and Tony and little Troy would wait. Cushioned folding chairs for the guests were already placed in the hallway. Tony had told Momma that this would be the fourth wedding ceremony held here. His great-grandfather, grandfather, and father were all married in Farthy. The hallway would reek of tradition, the great portraits of Tony's ancestors looking down as he and Momma recited the oaths of love and loyalty to each other.

Tony emerged from his office as soon as our arrival had been announced. He wore his tuxedo pants and white shirt without a tie, his sleeves still open and without cufflinks. It was the first time I had seen him so informally dressed. For some reason, this way he reminded me even more of a movie star; he looked so tall and dashing.

It bothered me that Tony was so handsome. Daddy wasn't an ugly man, but he was so much older, his face weathered by hours, days, months at sea. He wasn't as glamorous looking; he never looked like a movie star, not that I loved him any less for it. But when Tony and Momma stood beside each other, they commanded everyone's attention. It was as if they had stepped off the cover of a fan magazine. It was very painful to admit that they looked so right for each other. It made me think of Daddy as farther and farther away, dwindling like some distant star that had died a million years ago. I desperately hoped that one day I would marry a man just like him, except maybe a man who was less obsessed by his business.

'Darling.' Tony took Momma's hands and kissed her quickly on the lips. He smiled, his eyes looking mischievous. 'Are you ready for the rehearsal?'

'Of course.'

'Your dressing suite is all prepared.' He turned to me. 'Hi, Leigh. I bet you're not as nervous as I am.'

'Of course I am,' I said sharply. I couldn't help it. How could he think I wouldn't be nervous . . . more than nervous . . . upset? I didn't want to have anything to do with this wedding, and in order to keep from screaming this fact at him I swung my eyes away from his.

'I'm not nervous,' Troy chirped. That made everyone laugh, except me.

'That's because you're not the one getting married,' Tony told him. Troy just shrugged, but held onto my hand tightly.

'Well, now is as good a time as any for me to show Leigh her suite of rooms,' Tony said, slapping his hands together.

'Yes, that would be wonderful. Won't it, Leigh?'

'I've had them all redone as a surprise for you,' Tony said, cutting his eyes sharply towards me. He held out his arm for me to take.

I looked at Momma. She nodded and gestured with her eyes that I should take Tony's arm. I did so quickly.

'Can I come too?' Troy begged.

'You've got to get dressed yourself, young man. This is a full dress rehearsal,' Tony said. 'Except for the bride, of course,' he added. 'It's bad luck for the groom to see her in her wedding gown before the wedding.'

'I wanna . . .'

'Now Troy,' Tony said and looked to Mrs Hastings.

'Come on, Troy. I'll help you get dressed.'

'I don't need help,' he said petulantly. Momma scowled down at him and shook her head.

'Right this way,' Tony commanded and we ascended the stairway. Something about holding his arm made me nervous. My stomach butterflies were careering all over the place and I was sure I was blushing.

Tony led me down left on the second floor and stopped before a set of double doors.

'Here we are,' he announced and threw open the double doors dramatically. 'Leigh,' he started. He reached his hand up and I thought he would touch my hair, but he quickly took his hand away. 'I tried to make these rooms feminine, but not girlish. I hope you enjoy them,' he added, his voice dropping into almost a whisper. His head was turned in a way that kept me from reading his eyes.

The sunlight through the pale ivory sheers was misted and frail and gave the sitting room an unreal quality. The walls were covered in some delicate ivory silk fabric, woven through subtly with faint oriental designs of green, violet, and blue, and the two small sofas were covered with the same fabric, the cushions soft blue to match the Chinese rug on the floor.

Despite my desire to dislike anything from this man I had to admit to myself that this was the most lovely room I had ever seen. I could easily picture myself in this room, cuddled down before that little fireplace.

'What do you think?' He leaned back against the wall and formed a temple with his hands under his chin. He looked as though he were studying me.

'It's a very pretty room. I never had my own sitting room,' I added and then regretted saying that. It sounded as if I had been deprived.

'Well, now you do,' Tony said standing up quickly. A smile touched his full, sensuous lips. 'Come, see your bedroom.' He moved ahead of me and opened the bedroom doors.

What could I do? I didn't want to like it, to be impressed, to be thrilled and excited by my new home, but there before me was the loveliest, most darling double bed, a four-poster with an arching canopy of heavy lace. The two rooms were done in my favourite colors: blue and ivory.

There was a blue chaise and three chairs that matched those in the sitting room. I wandered on into the dressing and bathroom area. There were mirrors and lights everywhere, it seemed. And there were crystal chandeliers and hidden lights in all the walk-in closets, one of them almost as big as my entire Boston bedroom.

I sensed Tony right behind me and turned. He was standing so close, I felt his breath on my forehead and inhaled his aftershave lotion.

'I hope you can be happy here, Leigh. It's almost as important to me as making your mother happy,' he said softly. He was silent as I stared up at him.

I wanted to scream back at him. I wanted to demand to know how he expected me to be happy. He had won my mother's heart away from my father and destroyed the only life, the only family I had known. Daddy was off somewhere wandering the world, dazed and saddened by events that were taking place with lightning speed. Tony's good looks and sophisticated ways, his enormous wealth and family name, had stolen my mother away from my father, and now he was raining down all sorts of luxuries on me, as though that were all it took to make him as important to me as my father, as though I could forgive all because of a beautiful room. I clenched and unclenched my hands at my sides to keep from striking him, but just then I may have hated him more than ever before!

Tony continued to gaze into my eyes. I think he read the rage that lingered just below the surface, for his face softened and he backed away.

'I know it's not easy for you right now, but I'm going to try to make things work between us. It will take a while, I know, but in time, I hope you will consider me more than just a stepfather. I want to be your friend too.'

Before I could reply we heard a knock on the outside door. It was Mrs Walker bringing in my dress, my shoes and undergarments to be worn for the rehearsal. I heard Momma's voice out in the hallway too, as she gave people orders on her way to her suite.

'Yes, yes,' Tony said annoyed by the interruption. 'Bring it all in.' He turned back to me. 'We'll talk more later. We'll have lots of time to talk and grow to know each other well. If you will let it happen.' He turned and walked out.

'What a nice room!' Mrs Walker exclaimed. She put my garments on the bed and spun around. 'You're a very lucky girl to have such a place to live.'

'Thank you, Mrs Walker, but there is nothing wrong with the way we live in Boston,' I said sharply. She saw the look on my face and left to assist Momma.

I stood there alone, staring at everything. This would be my new world, the place where I would think and have dreams and build my hopes, the place where I would cry and laugh, feel lonely and sad, and maybe, someday, feel happy again. I loved and hated it at the same time.

Daddy would never come through these doors to say good night or greet me after he came home from a long day's work at the shipping office. In a way I was glad he wouldn't ever see this suite. It would sadden him because he would think I had been won away from him by all this wealth.

I wouldn't let any of this make me forget Daddy, my heart cried. I would line the long dressing table with all my framed photographs: the one with me sitting on Daddy's knee, the one with Momma and me sitting and Daddy standing right behind us. When I was only five, I wrote 'Daddy, Momma and me', at the bottom of it. I would surround myself with all my happy memories – pictures of our trips, pictures at the zoo, pictures aboard Daddy's ships, the one with Daddy trying to teach me to dance. Never, never would I let soft, expensive materials, rich and plush furniture, enormous rooms and luxuries cause me to forget Daddy. And most of all, Tony Tatterton would see immediately that he had no chance, no chance in the world, of replacing him.

With little enthusiasm, I started to undress. Standing before the large dressing mirror, I gazed quickly at my growing breasts.

I put on a special strapless bra and then slipped into the dress. It fit snugly around my waist, but every time I reached back to pull up the zipper, the bodice fell forward. It was a very awkward thing to do alone. Frustrated, I slipped into the matching shoes and started out, intending to go into Momma's suite and have her help me, but when I walked out of my bedroom, I walked right into Tony. He had put on his tie and cufflinks, but not his tuxedo jacket. I stepped back with surprise and clung to the front of my bodice.

'Sorry to startle you, but your mother asked me to check on how you were getting along.'

For a moment I couldn't reply; my breath had caught in my throat. How long had he been right by my bedroom doorway? Could he have come back and seen me gazing at myself? And why had Momma sent him? She hadn't ever sent Daddy to do such a thing.

'I . . . I'm just on my way to her suite to have her help me zip up my dress,' I said and started out.

'Let me do that. That's why you beautiful women keep us men around . . . just for such chores.' He put his hands on my shoulders to stop me from walking around him and out. I nearly gasped and felt a surge of heat climb into my neck. If he could see my embarrassment, he ignored it and turned me around. 'Now let me see . . . oh, this is easy.'

He pulled the zipper up slowly, taking great care not to pinch my skin, and when he had it up all the way, he planted a quick kiss on the top of my head.

'Done,' he announced. 'Anything else you need help with?'

'No,' I said quickly, so quickly, it brought a wide smile to his face and laughter to his eyes. I allowed my eyes to meet his briefly before they fled again to gaze down at the floor. 'I've got to fix my hair,' I said and retreated to my bedroom. I sat down at the dressing table to catch my breath. When I looked at myself in the mirror, I saw I was still clinging to the top of my bodice, even though I had no need to. I let go and looked back at the doorway, half expecting him to be there.

But he was gone.

My mind went chasing my feelings. There were so many different ones to try to understand. I hated the way he spoke, trying to sound like a father, and I cringed at his kissing me on my head like Daddy would, but I had to admit to myself that when his fingers touched my shoulders and when his lips grazed my hair, I felt a pleasing tingle through my body.

And his eyes! When he shifted them to mine, the blue in his had brightened as if he could see the tingle I had felt. I had to be careful with a man as sophisticated as Tony, I thought. I should think more about what my eyes might reveal. After all, he was the man who had won Momma's heart, the heart of a woman so beautiful most any man would give his right arm for it. I was no match for a man with such power.

And yet his soft blue eyes and handsome face lingered before me, pleading for understanding and love, begging me to consider him my new daddy. How could I ever think of someone that young as a daddy, and when he finds out how old Momma really is, he will feel foolish himself, I thought.

Life that had once been as simple and pleasing as a child's storybook tale was now so complicated and hard. I hated it here, *hated it*! I hated being in this dress preparing for this rehearsal, hated the idea that I would be a bridesmaid at my own mother's wedding, hated this house, and the servants, and the grounds, and . . .

'Hi. Are you ready?'

My building rage was interrupted. I turned to see little Troy in his tuxedo and tiny black tie, his hair brushed neatly, standing in my bedroom doorway. He wore a gold signet ring on his left hand and he looked like a miniature version of his handsome and elegant big brother. All my fury wilted.

'Almost,' I said.

'We can get back into our "good" clothes as soon as the rehearsal's over, Tony says,' Troy told me eagerly. I laughed at the way he widened his eyes and nodded his head.

'Good clothes?'

'I have to be very careful when I'm dressed like this, careful about what I touch and where I go,' he recited. He scrunched up his nose to indicate how much he hated it. He was so cute, I wanted to hug him to me like one of my Teddy bears.

'Right. I can't wait to get back to my "good" clothes, too.' I stood up, took one last look at myself in the mirror, and then started out. He gave me his hand and we went downstairs to begin the rehearsal.

Throughout the entire rehearsal, I felt as if I were moving through a dream. Surrounded by all these strangers, watching Momma and Tony play act their upcoming ceremony, I couldn't help looking around every once in a while, searching for Daddy, half-expecting him to come charging through the great front doors. I permitted my imagination to take over. In my dream, the music stopped and everyone turned Daddy's way.

'Jillian,' he screamed. 'You can't do this. And you,' he said, turning to Tony, 'you must end this spell you have thrown over my wife.' In my daydream, Daddy looked bigger and more powerful than ever. He held his arm out and pointed accusingly at Tony, who backed away in awe of such strength. Suddenly, Momma's eyes blinked. She looked from Daddy to Tony and back to Daddy.

'Cleave? Oh Cleave, Cleave, thank God you've come. I don't know what came over me. I don't know what I'm doing here.'

She ran to his arms and I ran after her. Then Daddy put his arm around me, too, and the three of us walked out of this castle and were on our way home, safe and sound forever and ever.

My reverie ended, burst like a bubble, when little Troy tugged demandingly on my hand. I was standing behind the other bridesmaids. We had come down the stairway in front of Momma and taken our positions while the minister reviewed the ceremony. Now all that had apparently come to an end and Troy was reminding me of my earlier promise to go out with him.

'Come back in about an hour for lunch,' Tony said.

The two of them went off to Tony's office. I went to change and was barely dressed when Troy came charging in again, all bundled up and ready to go out in the snow.

'Will you need me to come along, too?' Mrs Hastings asked, the answer she hoped for written all over her face.

'No, Mrs Hastings. We'll be fine,' I replied. She looked as if I had given her a reprieve from ten years at hard labor. Little boys had to be a handful, I thought, laughing to myself. I put on my coat and gloves and took Troy's hand. We went down the stairs and out to his snowman.

Although it was still quite bright, the sky had become overcast and snow was falling. I watched Troy work diligently on the snowman's fingers, and I listened to him chatter away about the toys Tony had promised him for Christmas. He skipped from one topic to another, at one point telling me a story Ryse Williams told him about a little boy in New Orleans who had a magical flute. He kept calling Ryse 'Rye', and when I asked him about that, he said he had heard the other servants call him that.

'They said his name was Rye Whiskey, not Ryse Williams.'

'Rye Whiskey? You don't call him that, do you?'

'Uh huh,' he said, and then he looked toward the front door and added, 'when Tony's not there. He doesn't like me to.'

'Oh, I see. Well, maybe you shouldn't do it then.'

He shrugged. Then his eyes brightened with a new idea. He dropped his silver spoon and stepped back.

'We gotta go get some pieces of hedge to make the snowman's clothes. We gotta, Leigh.'

'Pieces of hedge?'

'Uh huh. Boris trims the maze all the time and there's pieces of hedge there. We gotta get some, okay? Please. Okay?'

I sighed. It was cold just standing around and the snowflakes were falling faster and getting bigger every moment. A walk would do us both good, I thought.

'Okay.'

He grabbed my mittened hand and started us away from the house.

'I'll show you. Don't be afraid. I'll show you.'

'All right, all right. Slow down, Troy. Your snowman won't melt. That's for sure.'

I looked back at the house because I overheard two women from Tony's offices in Boston who were serving as bridesmaids talking about Momma as they walked to their car.

'She was married to a man old enough to be her grandfather,' one said. 'I heard he's practically senile and doesn't even realize she's left him.'

'The only reason a woman like that would marry a man that old is for his money.'

'She won't need to worry about money anymore,' the first woman said. 'And now she has a devastatingly handsome young man as well. That's one shrewd woman.' They both laughed and got into their car.

Despite the cold air and the falling snow, my face felt hot with rage. I wanted to run over to their car and pound on the windows. They were making fun of my father. How dare they? Who told them such a story? They didn't deserve to be in the wedding party. Jealous, envious, vicious gossips . . .

'Come on, Leigh,' Troy said pulling me forward.

'What? Oh, yes.' I followed him, looking back once to see their car drive off.

We stopped at the entrance to the maze.

'I don't see any hedge trimmings, Troy. Let's go back.'

'No, there's always some. We'll go in a little and look, okay?' he pleaded.

'Your brother doesn't want us to, Troy.'

'It's okay. I know how to go in and out.'

'Is that right?' Sometimes, he looked so mature for a little boy, so self-assured.

'Tony won't be mad. Tony's going to be your daddy now.'

'No, he's not,' I snapped. Little Troy looked up confused. 'He's marrying my mother, but that doesn't make him my daddy. I have a daddy.'

'Where is he?' Troy asked, lifting his little shoulders.

'He works with big ships and he's out on the oceans.'

'Is he coming here, too?'

'No. My mother doesn't want to live with him anymore. She wants to live with your brother, so we're living here and my father lives someplace else. That's called a divorce. People who are married stop being married. Understand?'

He shook his head.

'To tell you the truth,' I said bitterly, 'neither do I.' I looked back at the house again. A group of Tony's male friends came out laughing and patting each other on the arms and shoulders. 'All right,' I said, 'we'll go into the maze and look for pieces of trimmed hedges. We can't get lost anyway,' I added, 'because we can just follow our footsteps in the snow back.'

'That's right.' He charged ahead of me into the maze. I hesitated a moment and then followed.

Actually, I welcomed the serenity of the maze. I wanted to be cut off from all the noise and activity. I felt very irritated; my stomach churned, my heart pounded. I recalled the piano playing 'Here Comes the Bride', and that made me more and more furious.

But as we made the turn in the maze and went deeper and deeper into the belly of it, the world beyond fell farther and farther away. The tall hedges served as great walls, cutting us off from the sounds at the front of the house. The thickened snowflakes that fell floated into the corridors clinging to the hedges. Troy surged ahead, looking back every few moments to be sure I was still following him. I lost track of how many sharp right angles we took. One corridor looked the same as another, especially dressed in the newly forming coats of snow. I was glad we were doing this through snow though, for now I understood how easily it would be for someone to get lost. The maze was indeed deep and seemingly endless.

'Troy,' I finally called. 'We'd better turn back. There are no hedge trimmings and we're just wandering about in circles, I think.'

'No we're not. We're going toward the cottage.'

'What is this cottage? Who lives in it?'

'Nobody now. It's one of my secret places,' he whispered.

'Well, we'd better not try to find it,' I said looking back.

'Just a little more, please. Please, Leigh,' he pleaded.

'All right,' I said. 'We'll go just a little more, but if we don't find it soon, we have to turn back, okay?'

He nodded quickly and ran ahead, disappearing around a turn. He was moving so rapidly through the corridors, I had to depend on seeing his little footsteps in the snow.

'Troy, don't go so quickly,' I shouted. 'Troy.' I quickened my pace, but he was being mischievous and remained a turn ahead of me. 'Troy!'

Finally, I made a turn and found myself out of the maze, on the other side. And there it was – just as Troy had said, a little house that looked like something Momma might have drawn in one of her children's book illustrations. Some magician had touched the pages and made it real. Surrounded by tall pines was a small stone cottage with a red slate roof. There was a path of pale flagstones leading to the front door.

'Come on, Leigh,' Troy called and hurried down the path.

'Wait,' I cried, but he had already turned the door knob and entered. I followed and found him sitting in a hard maple rocking chair next to the fireplace. He wore this big smile of self-satisfaction. I looked around the small room and imagined it could be very cozy when the fireplace was burning. There were just some simple pieces of furniture, an old couch, an easy chair, a rectangular brown rug, some small tables and empty dark pine wooden shelves. The thin, white cotton curtains hung sadly over the frosted windows. It was so cold in the cottage that I could see both Troy's breath and mine. I hugged myself to keep warm.

'No one lives here now?' I asked as I wandered through to look at the one small bedroom and the small kitchen. There was a single bed in the bedroom and a small dresser, but no rug on the floor and no mirrors. The kitchen had an old coal stove, a small sink, and instead of a refrigerator, an ice box, its doors wide open. Nothing was in it, however. Troy jumped off the rocker to follow me.

'Boris lives here in the summer sometimes, but it's really my secret place,' Troy said.

'You don't come here by yourself? How did you find your way through the maze?' I asked him. He shrugged. I understood, it had just been luck.

'Lucky for us we only have to trace our footsteps back.' I continued to look around. 'This must be nice in the spring and summer though.'

'Will we come here again? Will we, Leigh?'

'I suppose,' I said. Maybe it would become my secret place, too, I thought, especially when things became too difficult for me back at the mansion.

'I can bring in some logs from the pile outside,' Troy said. 'And we can make a fire in the fireplace.'

'No, no, I think we had better just head back. We've been gone a long time. Everyone will wonder where we've gone and it's starting to snow harder.'

'Don't you want to make a fire and warm up first? There are matches here,' he said, shooting around me and into the kitchen. He pulled a chair over to the stove and stood up on it to reach onto the shelves above and came down with a box of wooden matches. 'See.'

'Yes.'

'Let's make a fire and warm up, Leigh. I'll get the kindling wood, too,' he said and dropped the matches on the table and ran out.

'Troy.' He was already out the front door. I shook my head and laughed at his enthusiasm. I didn't think we had been gone all that long. Maybe warming up with a small fire would be all right. It seemed like fun, too. Troy came rushing back in with an armload of kindling wood. He brushed the snow off it.

'Want me to do it or do you know how?' he asked.

'You know how?'

'Sure I do. Boris showed me lots of times.' He placed the kindling wood in the fireplace and carefully arranged the sticks. Then he pushed open the vent and taking great pains to get it right the first time, lit some small twigs under some large ones. Soon he had quite a little fire going. He ran out and brought in two logs and placed them carefully on the fire.

'Very good, Troy.' I was amazed. 'You're very grown up.'

'I'm like the daddy here,' he said proudly. 'You can be like the mommy and make us supper and clean.'

I laughed and thought how I wish I could create a happy family in this small cottage. I would give up all the big rooms and glamorous things.

'And what will you do besides make the fire?'

He shrugged. 'Eat the supper.'

'Is that all?'

'I don't know. What else should I do? What else does a daddy do?'

Poor Troy, I thought, he never really had a chance to know his father and know how important a daddy was. I pulled the rocker up close to our small fire. Troy came to me and I sat him in my lap.

'A daddy makes you feel safe and secure; he gives you just as much love as a mommy, and if you're a little boy like you, he plays ball with you or teaches you things and takes you places,' I told him.

'What if you're a little girl?'

'He makes you into his little princess and buys you things and makes you feel special because he loves you so much.'

'And does daddy love mommy and mommy love daddy?'

'Oh yes, very much. For them, there are no people who are more important in the whole world. Because love brings them together, you see, and love is . . . love is . . .' I couldn't go on. I found myself sobbing, shoulders shaking.

'What?' He looked up at me. 'Leigh, why are you crying?'

'I cry sometimes when I think about my daddy.'

'Why? 'Cause he's not here?'

'Yes.' I sniffled several times, trying to stop crying.

'I'll be your daddy when he's not here, okay?'

'Oh Troy.' I hugged him to me. 'You're very precious and sweet, but I'm afraid you can't because . . . oh no.'

'What?'

'Look at how hard it's snowing,' I said pointing to the window. It was almost impossible to see the pine trees through the shower of heavy flakes. 'We better get going.' I lifted him to the floor. 'Come, quickly.'

I took his hand and we left the cottage. It seemed like nearly an inch of snow had fallen over the flagstones already. I hurried him down the path and to the maze, rushing into it, the snow blinding me with its fury. We stepped quickly to the first right angle and turned and then started down the next corridor of hedges and turned and then . . . I stopped.

'Oh no,' I said looking at the fork in the path ahead of us, one corridor going to the left, the other to the right.

'What's the matter?' Troy asked,

'Our footsteps! They're gone! The new snow has covered them already, and I can't remember if we came from the right side or left side here.'

'It's all right,' Troy said bravely. 'We'll find our way.' He started down the corridor and turned back. 'Come on,' he beckoned.

'I don't know. I'm afraid,' I said, hesitant. Troy looked at the path ahead. The snow was falling so fast it was hard to see where the turn was anyway. 'What will we do?' I asked myself. I thought about going back to the cottage, but the snow might continue for a long time and no one knew we had come through the maze. Reluctantly, I plodded forward, took Troy's hand, and made my first guess. Then I made another and another and another. The snow never slowed for a moment and soon, all the turns and all the corridors looked alike. When I made another turn and came upon our freshly made footsteps, I realized we had just gone around in a circle.

'We're lost,' I cried. Troy began to sob. 'Don't cry, Troy. Someone will help us. We'll get out soon.' I lifted him up and started down another corridor, the flakes of snow sticking to my cheeks and forehead. My feet were very cold; I wasn't prepared for a trek through deep snow. Little Troy clung to me and I clung to him.

And like two orphans cast out in an unforgiving storm, we searched for a sign of home.

EIGHT

Lies, Lies, Lies

I heard the shouts and shouted back at the top of my voice, until my throat ached. There was another shout and another. I recognized Tony's voice and then I heard him scream some commands. Suddenly, a stout, elderly man appeared through the snow showers in front of us and little Troy exclaimed, 'Boris!'

The kindly gardener hurried to us.

'Are ye all right, Miss?'

'Yes, just . . . cold, very . . . cold,' I said, shivering.

'Naturally. Here, let me take Master Tatterton,' he offered, and Troy went eagerly into his arms. 'Just follow me, Miss. Stay close behind,' Boris advised. He didn't have to tell me twice. I practically clung to the back of his coat as he led us on and out of the maze. Tony and Miles were waiting at the entrance.

'What happened? Why did you go into the maze?' Tony demanded quickly. Instead of responding, I started to cry. His face softened instantly. 'Are you all right?'

'I'm freezing,' I said. My legs felt numb and my toes ached. I felt a strange combination of heat and cold in my cheeks, and that frightened me.

'Let's get them inside,' Tony snapped. He put his arm around my shoulders and he and I, Miles and Boris, still carrying Troy, hurried back through the snow storm to the big house. Momma came out of the music room the moment Curtis opened the front doors. She looked distraught and confused.

'They got lost in the maze,' Tony explained quickly.

'The maze!' Her face contorted and looked pained.

'Mrs Hastings, please take Troy up to his suite and get him

into a warm bath,' Tony commanded. 'He's very susceptible to colds.' Momma was staring at me, her face still twisted in disbelief, her eyes wild, her mouth slightly opened. She shook her head as if to deny what was happening. 'Jillian,' Tony said seizing her hand, 'you should get Leigh into a warm bath too. She wasn't properly dressed to be out in a snow storm for hours.'

'I can't believe this. Why did you go into the maze, Leigh?' she grilled.

My teeth were still chattering. My gloves were soaking wet as were my shoes and stockings and melted snow was trickling off my hair and down the sides of my face and over my forehead and down the back of my neck. It felt as if Troy's snowman had come to life and was running the tips of his fingers over my body to torment me.

'I . . . we . . . went to look for pieces of trimmed hedges and . . .'

'Jillian, you should get her into a warm bath,' Tony repeated.

'But Tony warned you about going into the maze and this wasn't the time for such things. All these people here,' she said turning about as if we were surrounded by the wedding party. 'We were getting frantic, looking for you. How embarrassing,' she said, bringing her hands to her face just like someone who wanted to hide behind them.

'The girl's freezing in her shoes,' Tony prodded.

'What?'

'Jillian, get her into a warm bath and into a change of clothing.'

Momma shook her head. 'I can't believe you did this to me, Leigh. I can't believe it,' she repeated, her voice growing shrill.

Tony seized my left arm at the elbow and started me for the stairway. I looked back at Momma who was still gaping at me in astonishment. One of the bridesmaids, Cecilia Benson, was standing just behind her. Momma turned to her.

'Do you believe this?' she asked her. Cecilia looked my way, but said nothing as Tony hurried me up the stairs. He rushed me to my suite and helped me take off my cold, wet coat in the sitting room. Then he tossed it over the settee and moved immediately into the bedroom and toward the bathroom.

'You'll find a terry cloth robe with the Farthinggale Manor emblem on it in your closet,' he gestured. 'Get out of those wet clothes as fast as you can.'

A moment later, he was running my bath water. My fingers trembled as I peeled off my soaked mittens. The effect of the warmth in the house was to make me aware of just how cold I had been and still was. I shivered even more and heard my teeth click.

I started to pull my sweater up and over my head, but my arms were shaking so, I couldn't manipulate well. Just as I had it over my face, I felt Tony seize it and help pull it off.

'Are you all right? Your lips are so blue.'

I nodded, dazed by all that was happening and happening fast. Momma hated me now. She was sure to think I had done it all deliberately, and I was still so cold I couldn't think straight and speak quickly enough to explain.

'Sit on the bed,' Tony commanded. After I did, he squatted before me and pulled off my shoes and took off my stockings. 'Your feet are soaked and your toes are so red,' he said and held my right foot between his hands, rubbing it vigorously and then rubbing my left. 'You have to get into that water or you'll catch pneumonia.' He got up and went back to check the bath.

I slipped my damp skirt down and stepped gingerly out of it. My slip felt cold and damp too. My arms ached and it was still hard to control my fingers, but I got my slip off and sat back on the bed. Where was Momma? Why didn't she come up to help me? Why was she leaving this to Tony? Was this her way of punishing me?

'It's ready,' Tony announced in the bathroom doorway. I brought my fingers to my blouse, but the buttons felt so big and so secure and the tips of my fingers itched madly, I fumbled helplessly.

'Let me help you,' Tony offered.

'No, I . . .'

'I know. It's embarrassing. But I'll just get you started, and you can do the rest.'

I gazed into his warm blue eyes and handsome face. He was so close to me, my cold breath was instantly warmed by his. He undid the top button of my blouse and then the next and the next, working gracefully, but quickly. When the blouse was completely undone, he paused and looked into my eyes. My whole body was still trembling, but not only from the cold. He smiled softly and took my right hand into his and then rubbed it quickly.

'You'll be all right,' he said. 'Once you're soaking in the bath water.'

'My mother . . .'

'She's just upset. I'll calm her down and send her right up. Don't worry,' he said. He seemed so considerate, so gentle. I felt the wall of hatred I had built between us begin to crumble, but I fought that back. I wanted my daddy. More than ever, I needed my daddy, but he wasn't here. He was far, far away, too far to even hear my voice on a telephone.

'Come on,' he urged. He stood up, still holding my hand. I lowered my feet to the floor and stood up. As I did so, he brought his fingers to the collar of my blouse and gently pulled it back over my shoulders and down my arms. In a moment I was only in my bra and panties. 'Go on,' he whispered, his breath hot on the base of my neck. Without looking back, I walked to the bathroom.

The huge whirlpool tub was filled and bubbling. Nothing could have been more inviting. I turned around and started to close the door. He was standing there, still holding my blouse in his hands, a wry smile on his face.

After I closed the door, I got out of my bra and panties and stepped into the warm, blue-tinted water. At first my ankles ached, but moments after I lowered myself completely in, I felt a wonderful flush of heat drive away the chill. I moaned with delight and closed my eyes. Then came the relief, flooding over me, inundating me so I could breathe, relax, and even manage a tremulous smile. I heard a knock on the door and opened my eyes.

Momma has finally come up, I thought.

'Yes?'

The door opened, but it wasn't Momma. It was Tony. He poked his head in.

'You forgot the robe,' he said and opened the door wider. I lowered my body as far as I could into the water. The foam hid some of my nakedness, but I still felt so exposed and terribly flustered when he entered to place the robe on a hook. 'How is it?'

'It's good.'

'I knew it would be,' he said gazing down at me. I didn't see how he could be so blind to my embarrassment, but he acted as if he really were my father. 'Don't feel bad. Troy will be all right,' he said as though he thought that were the reason for my look of discomfort.

'I didn't think we would get lost because we would be able to trace our footsteps back in the snow, but the new snow came so fast, it covered everything and . . .'

'It's all right. Really,' he said kneeling beside the tub. 'Water still warm enough?' He put his fingers into it, only inches from my thigh. 'Yes, that's okay. Well, will you be all right, now?'

'Yes,' I said quickly. I folded my arms over my breasts.

'I could wash your back for you. I'm an expert when it comes to washing backs,' he added, widening his smile.

'No. I'm going to get out soon.'

'Take your time. You're not embarrassed, are you? We're family now,' he added. 'We'll be as intimate and close to each other as possible, just as if we have been living together our whole lives. You'll see.' He leaned forward to kiss my forehead tenderly, cupping my face between his palms. He kept his face close to mine and stared into my eyes, his luminous and deep. Then he stood up and wiped his hands on a towel.

'Well, it's a good thing you have most of your things here already. Do you want me to get anything out for you? I can play the valet, too, you know,' he added with an amused smile.

'No. I'll be all right now.'

He nodded, but continued to look down at me.

'Okay,' he finally said. 'I'll see about your mother and Troy.'

I released a deeply held breath when he stepped out. My heart was pounding so, I thought it would make the water over my chest splash. No man, even Daddy, since I was ten, had ever seen me naked, and here I was covered only with this foamy warm water and Tony just inches away. It had been mortifying, but it had also excited me in a way I had not expected. How confusing this was all going to be with him thinking he could be my daddy. I closed my eyes again, and the moment I did so, I envisioned his blue eyes searching my face, almost touching me with his intense gaze.

When I brought the soapy washcloth to my breasts, I was surprised at how hard my nipples had become. Was that because of the cold and the heat or did it have something to do with the tingling that moved up my thighs and down the small of my stomach when I thought about Tony's fingers in the water, just an inch or two from my naked body?

Before I could think any more about it, Momma came bursting into the bathroom. She had regained her composure, but she was still very angry.

'How could you do such a stupid thing, Leigh? And you, a bright girl who gets such high marks in school?' she asked pacing back and forth.

'I thought we would be all right. We would have our footsteps to follow and . . .'

'Mrs Hastings went out to look for Troy and then came in and asked if anyone had seen you two come back inside. So Tony sent the help out to search, and they returned claiming no sign of either of you.

'You know how Tony is about his little brother, unreasonable and obviously overprotective as it is, but when he heard you and Troy were missing, he went wild with worry. A search party was formed and sent out into the storm. And I had all these people here.' Was that what she was worried about – being shown up in front of others? Didn't she care any longer?

'But when they brought you two in and Tony said you had gotten lost in the maze . . .'

'Momma, just listen . . .'

'To go in there during a storm, no less. What were you thinking? Was this a deliberate act, an attempt to embarrass me because you feel sorry for your father? Or maybe you just aren't getting enough attention today, is that it? Maybe having these beautiful rooms from Tony just isn't enough, and little miss princess had to cause some trouble so everyone would notice her!'

'*No!*' I cried. 'It just happened. The snow came so quickly, we didn't realize our footsteps would be covered.'

'Why did you go into the maze?' she asked, her eyes tight with suspicion.

'Troy wanted to show me the cottage and I thought . . .'

'Oh, that child. He's so spoiled.'

'No, Momma, he's lonely and . . .'

'All that boy needs is some discipline. You've got to be firmer with him, Leigh. I insist. You're to think of yourself as his big sister, who knows better, understand? If you have any doubts at all about anything he wants, ask me or Tony, but don't cater to his whims. Oh dear,' she said, catching sight of herself in the mirror. 'Look at me. And all this happening right before my wedding.'

'I'm sorry, Momma.' I lowered myself into the water again.

'Well . . . you should be. This wedding is the most important thing that has ever happened to me . . . or to you, young lady. It will be perfect. You don't want to get sick right before my wedding, do you? Can you imagine what it will look like if you are sniffling behind me, sneezing and coughing during the wedding procession?' She grimaced as if it were happening this very moment.

'All right, Momma. I'll get into bed after I get out of the bath.'

'Good. Oh, Leigh,' she said pressing her palm against her chest, 'what a fright.' She sighed and then smiled as if someone had closed the book on this episode. 'Afterward, I'll come up and sit with you and we will have a good talk about my honeymoon. I'll tell you all the details and we'll discuss my wardrobe, what I should bring along, what jewelry, make-up, okay?

'Poor thing. I'm sure you were terrified out there. But, it's over,' she added quickly and with a swipe of her hand as if she were shooing away flies. 'Let's put it behind us. We have too many wonderful things to think about, don't we?'

'Yes, Momma.'

'Good. I don't want to have a sad day here after this, not one sad day. Why should I? I've got everything anyone could want – youth, money, and a handsome, doting husband.' She gazed down at me. 'I'm sure you will have the same things someday, too. Well, get out and dry off or you will turn into a prune,' she added and laughed. 'I'll see about some hot tea for you.'

She left and I got out of the tub. I dried myself off and put on the terry cloth robe. Then I went into my bedroom and picked out the warmest nightgown. I slipped it on and crawled under the covers.

Momma had been right about one thing – I was very tired. The moment I closed my eyes, I fell asleep and didn't even hear the maid bring in the tea.

Momma was true to her word – she refused to hear any more about the incident in the maze, as she called it. As soon as Tony and she returned to my suite to see how I was and he brought it up, she snapped at him with surprising fury.

'Please, Tony, let's not talk about it anymore. It happened and it's over. Thank goodness, everyone's all right.'

One result of the incident was that Momma and I would sleep over at Farthy. She explained it to me when Tony left us.

'I've decided Tony's right,' she said. 'It's best we remain here tonight. It's still snowing quite heavily and I shouldn't take you back into the storm. In the morning after breakfast, we'll return to Boston and complete our packing for the move to Farthy. Tony promises to honor my wishes and remain in his own suite this evening,' she added with a coquettish turn of her shoulders and smile. The situation was fascinating.

'Will you have your own rooms after you're married, too?'

'Of course.'

'But you didn't have your own room back in Boston. You always shared one with Daddy,' I said. If she was so in love with Tony, I thought, why did she want to be separated? When I fell in love, I knew that I would never want that; because I would want to be with my husband every single moment of every day.

'I always wanted my own suite, but your father could never understand. A woman needs her privacy. I don't want my husband standing over me while I go through my beauty rituals. There are things I'd rather he didn't know,' she added, gazing at herself in one of my dresser mirrors. 'I have my secret ways of keeping my skin wrinkle-free, ways I'll share with you when the time comes, of course, but a husband need not know.

'A woman has to keep herself somewhat mysterious. If a man knows every little thing about you, he will lose interest in you. But if you can surprise him every once in a while, he will think you're exciting forever. That's why there are things I will tell you that we will never tell men, even men we love. Understand?' she asked smiling.

'Yes.' I knew that one of the secrets she wanted to guard closely was the secret of her age. Perhaps, if Tony saw her at her dressing table every night, he would figure out that she was much older than she claimed, I thought.

'And besides,' she continued, pacing slowly at the side of my bed as she lectured like a college professor, 'there are times you just don't feel like having intimate contact with your husband. Men can be so insistent, so annoying with their male drives and needs. They'll pester you to death until you give in to their lust.

'If you have your own rooms, you can simply close the door and shut off all that vexatious, irritating, and aggravating behavior. If you want to remain youthful and beautiful, you've got to be a little selfish, Leigh. You would think a man could be considerate and understand, especially a man who claims to love you, but men can't control themselves sometimes. The sexual urge is much more demanding for them.

'But,' she said, waving her hand in the air, 'I'm sure you know most of this by now.'

'Oh no, Momma. I don't.'

'Really? How innocent and sweet you are,' she said looking at me as if she saw me for the first time. 'When I was your age . . .' She paused and bit down on her lower lip. 'Well, those were different times. I didn't have a quarter of what you had and I was exposed to a different crowd of people. We grew up faster.

'In fact,' she added after a deep sigh, 'I lost half my childhood, lost that wonderful innocent time when the world looks so rosy and nothing seems more tragic than not being invited to a party or having a pimple on your face.'

I started to laugh, but then thought, if Momma found a pimple on her face now, she would think it was the end of the world. In that way she wasn't so different from my girlfriends.

'So,' she said returning to the moment, 'just remain in bed. Stay cozy and warm. Tony's having your dinner sent up.'

'I could get dressed and join you in the dining room. I feel fine,' I protested.

'No, no. You've had a shock. I'll stop by after dinner, we'll have that talk about my honeymoon.' She left.

A little while later, Tony had my dinner sent up. He made it into a major production, just to amuse me, I was sure. A different maid brought each course. Curtis brought up my *entrée*. Then Tony appeared with the dessert himself, a short towel over his arm like a waiter. I found myself unable to resist laughing.

'Now that's the face I need to see,' he responded. He stepped back after placing the custard pie on my bed table. I felt myself blush. 'I'm glad you're feeling better. Had enough to eat?'

'Oh yes, thank you. But I could have easily come down.'

'That's all right. You have to get used to being pampered. You're going to live like a princess now,' he said, his voice soft, enticing. 'Farthy is a palace; the Tattertons are like royalty.' He looked so serious, I didn't crack a smile. 'I wanted to buy you an entirely new wardrobe and told Jillian not to even bother moving any of your things from Boston, but she insisted on bringing some things.'

'I have a lot of new things, things I haven't even worn yet,' I said. 'I don't need an entire new wardrobe.'

'We'll see. Anyway, can I get you anything else?'

'No thank you. Is Troy all right?'

'Fast asleep, but I expect he'll be one of the first up in the morning, so expect him to come crashing through your door once he learns you've slept over. I didn't tell him, but he's a Tatterton, and like me, he senses everything new and different in Farthy. It's a part of us and we are a part of it. There's an uncanny, almost eerie connection between the Tattertons and our home,' he said, looking about my room as if the house indeed could feel and listen and know the things that happened in it and were said in it. 'It absorbs us, our history, our passions, our hopes and dreams,' he added in a voice barely above a whisper. His eyes were dreamy and faraway-looking and I thought he'd forgotten I was in the room with him. His love of his home was so intense, it was frightening.

'That's why I hope you will forget the bad experience you had today in the maze,' he said looking down at me, his eyes narrow, ice-blue. 'Don't blame Farthy. I want you to grow to love this place as much as I do.'

'I don't blame anyone or anything. It was just a stupid mistake,' I said.

He was silent, and I grew nervous and felt I should say more.

'From the moment I saw it, I thought Farthy was beautiful . . . like a storybook kingdom.'

'Yes,' he said. 'A storybook kingdom,' he whispered, his eyes glassy, far-off. There was another long moment of silence between us and then he slapped his hands together. 'Okay, I'll leave you to eat your delectable dessert. Someone will be up shortly to collect your dishes. Have a good night's sleep, Leigh,' he said coming over to me. 'Can I kiss you good night?'

I hesitated. Was this another betrayal of Daddy? Whenever he was home, he came to kiss me goodnight. But Tony looked so sincere and sorry, I couldn't refuse him. He had been so concerned about me. It wasn't fair to him either, I thought. I nodded and he leaned over and kissed me softly on the forehead, his lips lingering a little longer than I expected.

And then he was gone.

The servants arrived and took away my dishes. I stared at the empty door, listening to the vague sounds from below. I drifted in and out of sleep, dozing off a few minutes at a time and then waking with a sudden start and realizing where I was and what had happened.

Momma came into my bedroom just before going to her own suite, as she had promised. But instead of talking about her honeymoon plans, she told me all about the dinner, some of the guests they had, rambling on about the service, the dishes, the various topics of conversation. Her monologue made me even sleepier, and when my eyes closed in the middle of one of her sentences, she declared it was time for her to go to sleep, too.

'We want to have an early breakfast and go off to Boston,' she said and kissed me good night. At the doorway, she turned and laughed, a thin, high-pitched laugh.

'What a strange and yet wonderful day this has been,' she said. 'I have a feeling all our days will be just as exciting from now on. You'll help me see to that, won't you Leigh?'

I opened my eyes and looked at Momma in puzzlement. What could she possibly mean? Wouldn't marrying Tony make her every dream come true? What did I have to do with her happiness?

'Won't you Leigh?' It wasn't a question but a sharp demand.

After an exhausting day all I wanted to do was sleep. 'Of course Momma,' I weakly agreed, unable to find the strength to refuse before slipping into a trouble-filled sleep.

We left for Boston right after breakfast, just as Momma had planned. The snow storm had ended shortly after midnight, but it had been so severe, and fast, that there was nearly a foot of new snow. Farthy resembled a winter wonderland in the bright morning sunlight. Some of the pine trees looked as if they had had giant sheets tossed over them, because so little green was visible.

During the ride back to Boston, Momma finally elaborated on her honeymoon plans. She and Tony were flying to St Moritz to stay at the Palace Hotel, something I knew she had always wanted to do. Since Tony was such a good skier, and had been there before, he was very agreeable.

'It's a wonderful place for a honeymoon,' she told me. 'Members of Europe's aristocracy will be there, and you know how much I've wanted to go to the Palace Hotel.

'I never really had a honeymoon,' she continued. 'After your father and I were married, we came directly to Boston. He had promised to take me to Havana, but wouldn't you know it, as soon as we returned, he claimed he had a major business crisis, partially brought about because of his prolonged stay in Texas. Can you imagine? He was indirectly blaming me because he had remained in Texas longer than he had planned, just so he could win my hand in marriage.

'But finally,' she said, 'I'm going to have the honeymoon I deserve. Unfortunately, we'll be away for Christmas and New Year, but you will have everything at your disposal at Farthy and mountains of gifts. If you want Miles to take you someplace, he will. You understand, don't you?' she asked without pausing to take a breath. She was almost pleading for my approval.

'Yes, Momma,' I said, but couldn't help feeling horrible about beginning my life at Farthy, which for the most part still remained a strange place, during the holidays, without Daddy or her.

'We'll make it up to you when we return. You know, of course, that Tony's working behind the scenes to get you right into the best private girls' school around,' she added quickly. I hadn't known, not until this very moment. I had just assumed I would go to a public school close to Farthy.

'No, I didn't know. What school, Momma?'

'It's called Winterhaven. Isn't that a wonderful name for a private school? It just rings of class and wealth, doesn't it? You know it's special because it has a waiting list yards long, but Tony is sure he can pull a few strings and get you in, especially since you're such a good student. It's a boarding school,' she added quickly.

'A boarding school? You mean, I'll live there . . . like at a college?'

'Miles will drive you there every Sunday night and you can return every Friday, if you like. Doesn't that sound wonderful? Think of all the new friends you will make, and all girls from well-known, rich families. And you will meet fine young men, too. They have dances and get-togethers with a nearby boys' finishing school. You will finally be around people of your class, Leigh. Finally,' she added with a breath. And then, as if that was all there was to it, she turned away and began reviewing her wedding plans again.

I sat back, stunned. All these changes being rushed over me – I would spend Christmas and New Year alone at Farthy, I would go to an all-girls boarding school, and have to make all new friends. My life was truly topsy-turvy. I should have anticipated it, I thought. I should have realized all this was going to happen, but I kept avoiding reality, dreaming that it would all go back to the way it was. Now that I heard the hard details, my dreams burst like balloons. And there was nothing I could do.

I felt even sadder and more depressed when we arrived at our house in Boston. Because Daddy was going to be away so much, and because we were now leaving it for good, our servants would have to go. I was especially fond of Clarence and Svenson, and they were fond of me. They had been with us for as long as I could remember. This trip home might very well be the last time we would see each other.

I was happy to learn, however, that Daddy was employing them to work on one of his ships. There was always a need for a good chef on an ocean liner and since Clarence was such a perfect house servant, he would be assigned to the captain of the ship.

A second thing that made me happy was the discovery of a letter from Daddy. It had just arrived from the Canary Islands. Clarence brought it to my bedroom moments after we arrived. I could see by the look on his face that he hadn't told Momma. Perhaps this had been Daddy's instructions. I didn't like keeping secrets from Momma, but I thought perhaps this was better. She wouldn't have anything to feel bad about.

I opened it quickly and read.

Dearest Leigh,

I hope this letter finds you safe and well. I know you can't be happy with your life having been upset so, but

I hope things have settled down somewhat for you, and that, in time, you will find happiness again. I, of course, will do anything in my power to make that happen.

My trip to the Canary Islands was uneventful. This is a beautiful place, however, and I am happy I was talked into considering it. I will definitely be adding it to our route structure.

We will be leaving here shortly and heading for Miami, Florida, where I will be working on my Caribbean itineraries with travel experts and the like. It looks like I will be there during the holidays, but I will call you on New Year's Eve. I know where you will be.

Yes, Leigh, I know about your mother's plans to remarry. That was part of what we discussed when she came into my office and asked you to leave us. I knew this would only add to your sorrow, so I didn't want to bring it all up. Perhaps now, your mother will find that world of happiness she dreams of. She also told me of her plans for you to attend one of the finest finishing schools in the East. I rest easier knowing you will at least have all the material comforts life has to offer.

I promise to visit you every chance I get. For a while I would like to bury myself in my work. It has helped me get over the emotional crisis and tragedy. However, it is a consolation for me to know that you will be there when I return.

Now you are the only remaining soft and beautiful part of my life. I don't want to say anything that will make you cry, so batten down the hatches and wait for my ship to come back.

I promise it will.

Love,
Daddy

The walls of my heart quivered. I held the tears within and swallowed the cries that tried to emerge from my throbbing throat. Daddy didn't want me to cry; he didn't want his letters to leave me sad and distraught, but it was so hard to read his words and not hear his voice and see his gray beard, his rosy cheeks, and his eyes filled with pride and love. It was hard to hear these words in my mind and not think of him downstairs in his office, scribbling away on his old desk. I wanted to shout *'No, no, none of this has happened!'* I wanted my shouts to wipe away all the unhappy moments and return us to the happy ones. I won't put up with it; I won't, I won't.

My heart pounded with my anger and frustration, but my fragile, weak fists landed insignificantly on the top of my desk. Who would hear them? Who would care? What could I change? I dropped my head to my arms over Daddy's letter and gasped back my cries in deep breaths. Then I raised my head, folded Daddy's first letter neatly, and placed it in my diary. I knew it would grow thin and tattered at its edges from my frequent unfolding and folding after I read it again and again.

By the time Momma came by, I had regained my composure and I was busy packing the last few things I wanted taken to Farthy. Of course, we were going to leave many things here in Boston. Momma had decided some weren't good enough for Farthy; others, she would rather replace with new ones.

'You won't believe this,' she said, laughter trailing her words like a tail of smoke. She waved a letter. 'But my mother has decided she will attend my wedding after all, even though my horrible sisters won't.

'In fact,' she continued, gazing at the letter, 'if she keeps to this schedule, she will be arriving here in Boston today.'

'When? What time?' A visit from Grandma Jana was always a special occasion. Her visits were infrequent because she hated to travel and she wasn't fond of the North, especially the Northeast, but when she arrived, she always made quite a stir. Momma was less than happy to have her, and always breathed a sigh of relief when she left.

Momma checked her watch.

'It could be any time now. I'd better warn the servants, especially Svenson. You know how finicky she can be when it comes to eating. Oh damn. I was hoping she and my witch-face sisters would arrive together on the day of my wedding, attend and leave. I just don't have the time to cater to her right now.

You'll have to help me, Leigh. She likes you more than she likes me.'

'Oh Momma, she doesn't,' I protested.

'She does, but it doesn't matter. I don't mind. It's a wonder she likes anyone. Now please,' Momma begged, 'don't put on any long faces. I know she's going to be horrible about my divorce and quick remarriage as it is. If she sees you moping about . . .'

'I won't be moping about,' I said, turning away quickly so she wouldn't see my eyes.

'Good. That's my girl, my darling little girl,' she said. 'Now, what was I going to do? Oh yes, warn the servants,' she said and hurried out of my room.

Grandma Jana did arrive a little less than two hours later, complaining bitterly about planes and trains and taxicabs as she entered the house behind her baggage. I heard her shouting at the cab driver who struggled with her luggage, scraping a bag against the door as they came in. Clarence came rushing to the poor man's aid.

It was hard to believe that an elderly woman hardly five feet tall, a thin wisp of a woman, could make grown men jump and stutter so, but her voice snapped like a bullwhip when she was angry and her small, sharp eyes flashed. She had her silvery gold hair pinned back so tightly in a bun that the skin at the corners of her eyes and the top of her forehead looked strained, something which only added to her fierce and fiery demeanor. Even Momma looked terrified and stood back, her hands clasped against her breasts as Grandma Jana swung her cane threateningly at the driver, who was eager to turn over his responsibilities to Clarence. I stood on the stairway, watching.

'Those bags survived baboons handling them at the airport. I don't intend to have them damaged coming into my daughter's home,' she screeched as the driver scurried out.

'Hello Mother,' Momma said. She hugged her awkwardly, Grandma Jana keeping her attention on Clarence who now struggled to carry the bags as gingerly as he could up the stairway. Her eyes found me.

'Well don't just stand there, child. Greet your grandma,' she instructed. I hurried down the remaining steps. Grandma Jana gave me a real hug and kiss that warmed me to the bottom of my heart, and held me back. 'Goodness, look at you. You've grown nearly a foot and in other ways too, I see.'

'I haven't grown that much, Grandma,' I said smiling. She grunted and spun around to Momma.

'Before I settle in, I want to hear what's going on . . . every detail,' she commanded. Momma's lips trembled as she forced a smile. Grandma looked about. 'I don't imagine Cleave is still in his own house,' she added.

'No, he's on one of his voyages.'

'Humph,' Grandma said. She went directly to Daddy's office and threw open the door, pointing inside with her cane. Momma gazed at me quickly, hoping I might think of something to say to help her, but I was just as shocked by Grandma Jana's abruptness.

'Don't you want a cup of tea or to wash up first, Mother?'

'Absolutely not. We'll use Cleave's office,' she insisted and walked in. '*Jillian!*' she shouted.

'All right, Mother.' Momma shook her head helplessly and followed Grandma Jana into Daddy's office. What had Momma told her about the divorce and remarriage to get her so excited? I wondered.

'Close the door behind you,' Grandma Jana commanded as Momma entered Daddy's office. Momma closed it but not properly, and it snapped open enough for me to hear their voices. I glanced up the stairway as Clarence came down, wiping his face. He smiled at me and then went off. There was no one left in the entry hall. I couldn't help my curiosity. I sat on the Colonial bench that was just to the left of Daddy's office doorway, pretending I was waiting for them to come out.

'Now, what is all this about Cleave not loving you?' Grandma Jana began. 'You weren't worried about that when I got him to marry you quickly in Texas. You were damned lucky to find someone so well off who wanted you.'

'You know I was never happy about this marriage, Mother. You know I never loved Cleave and never could.' I couldn't believe my ears. Never loved Daddy? Never could? But the story . . . the dazzling stars . . . Cinderella . . .

'Never could?' Grandma spit. 'I suppose you would have been happier now if I'd let you marry that worthless Chester Godwin after he had gotten you pregnant, huh? You could love him, I suppose. The two of you could be in a nice shack in shanty town and Leigh could be running around in rags.

'But instead of being grateful that I found you a rich, decent man who would provide you a more than comfortable life, what do you do . . . hate me and finally throw it all away for a man nearly twenty years younger!'

The words stung my ears. ' . . . after he had gotten you pregnant?' What was Grandma Jana saying? Had Momma been pregnant once before she had me? Did she have an abortion? Was there another child?

'I didn't expect you would understand anything,' Momma said haltingly, 'and least of all, care about what I felt, what I needed and wanted. Cleave's an old man now; he doesn't care about anything but his business. I'm too young to bury myself and I'm lucky to find a man like Tony Tatterton. Wait until you see Farthinggale Manor, wait until you see . . .'

'How much does this young man know about your past? Does he know the truth? Have you ever told Cleave the truth or does he still think Leigh's his child?' Grandma Jana demanded.

It was as if some giant, invisible pair of hands had grasped me at the waist and squeezed. I bent over in agony, embracing myself. What was Grandma saying . . . Daddy wasn't my real daddy? Another man had made Momma pregnant and Daddy married her not knowing? Who was I? What a horrible, horrible secret to keep from Daddy and from me!

'Why should they know these things?' Momma said, her voice weakening.

'Thought so.' I could imagine Grandma Jana's eyes burning into Momma's face. 'Does this Tony Tatterton know how old you really are?'

'No,' Momma said, her voice small. 'And please, don't tell him. Don't spoil this for me.'

'Disgusting. Another life built on lies. I have a good mind to turn right around and head straight home, but I came and I'll stay for Leigh's sake. That poor child having to be dragged through one thing after another by her selfish, vain, foolish mother.'

'That's not fair,' Momma cried. 'I've done everything I can to make her life happy, happier than my own miserable life was. Now she will live like a princess and go to the finest schools and meet the best of society, and all because of me, because of my beauty and what that beauty can do to a man!'

'This will come to no good,' Grandma Jana predicted in a biblical voice. 'Mark my words. You are a sinner, Jillian!' she said. 'And a wicked, dishonest person, too – the worst I've ever met.'

'Well it's all done, signed and sealed, and there's nothing you can do or say about it. You're not running my life like you did in Texas, and I won't have you sneering at everything. This is going to be the most wonderful wedding, maybe the most important social event of the year in New England.'

'Humph,' Grandma Jana said.

Momma began to describe her wedding plans. I got up slowly from the bench, resembling a sleepwalker as I started up the stairway, still hugging myself.

I would never tell Daddy, I thought. I would never break his heart, and I didn't care what was true and what was not – in my mind and my heart, he would always be my daddy. But Momma, all those lies, those stories. It was as if bubbles were bursting all around me, lights shattering, streamers floating down, my world crumbling like a house of cards, or as Grandma Jana said, a life of lies.

And Momma living the biggest lie of all. Her advice came up in my throat like sour milk. I could still see her face when she said it, wearing the mask of sincerity, false sincerity.

'Remember this, Leigh: nice girls don't go all the way. Not until they're married. Promise you won't forget that.'

I won't forget it, Momma.

I turned at the top of the stairway. I wanted to shout it out, let her know what I had overheard.

I won't forget it, Momma!

NINE

Here Comes the Bride

I did nothing to let Momma know what I had overheard while sitting outside Daddy's office; but whenever I looked at her now, I saw someone different from the woman I had wanted so much to resemble. It was almost as if my real mother had gone away and left this look-alike, this woman who had Momma's hair and Momma's eyes and Momma's beautiful skin but who was empty inside.

Most of our time was spent discussing the final wedding details anyway. Actually, it was all we talked about. Even Grandma Jana was drawn into the discussions when Momma cleverly asked for her opinion about this or that. And then Farthy, with its magical powers, its mystical presence, overwhelmed her. Despite the way she felt about Momma's leaving Daddy and marrying a man so much younger, Grandma Jana was impressed. The size and the opulence of Farthinggale Manor took her breath away. When we drove through the gates, she wore a look of amazement, wondering aloud as I had wondered how one man could own so much.

Tony charmed her as well, treating her as if she were royalty. If he had had a red carpet to roll out over the steps and snow, he would have done it. He placed her left hand on his right arm and escorted her through the large rooms, explaining who was in this ancestral portrait and that, spending a great deal of time reviewing his history and talking about his parents and grandparents.

At lunch he had the waiters and waitresses hovering around her like hummingbirds. She couldn't lift a spoon or reach for a dish without a servant anticipating her wants and getting it for her. And all the while, Momma stood back quietly with her

Mona Lisa smile. Whatever resistance and reservation had been in Grandma Jana when she had arrived slipped away. After I saw the way Tony Tatterton doted on her, flattered her, charmed her with his manners, his good looks, and his wealth, I understood why such a man could win the heart of any woman, especially a woman like Momma.

'I knew Tony would tame her,' Momma whispered in my ear when we left Farthy for what would be the final time, for tomorrow was the wedding and when I returned, it would be for good. In the evening, just before I went to sleep, I packed all my photographs and precious mementoes. I had left them for the very last moment, clinging to some hope that this really wasn't going to happen. But now my fate was sealed.

In the morning the house was a hive of activity. Momma buzzed about from room to room like a bee in a field of wild flowers. She was so flustered and excited that if I asked the simplest question, she would go into a panic and beg me to solve the problem myself. She refused to eat anything for breakfast. I had little appetite, too, but I ate what I could. This was the last meal Svenson would prepare for me; the last meal Clarence would serve. It wasn't until we all headed for the limousine that I realized Momma hadn't invited Clarence and Svenson to her wedding. The two of them stood side by side in the doorway as Miles loaded our things into the trunk.

'Good luck to you, Miss,' Clarence told me. There were tears stuck in the corners of his eyes.

'And don't forget to come by to say hello when you come aboard your father's ship,' Svenson said.

I mouthed a goodbye and hurried in behind Momma. I felt my own tears sting behind my eyes. Momma took one look at my face and moaned.

'Oh Leigh, please, don't look so downhearted on my wedding day. What will people think?'

'Leave her be,' Grandma Jana said. 'It's not her wedding day. She can look the way she wants.'

'Well I can't spend my time cheering her up. Not today. I have too much to do,' Momma declared petulantly. Then she pursed her lips in a pout and looked the other way. I never realized how much like a spoiled child she could be if she didn't get everything exactly how she wanted.

I gazed back at our Boston house. Clarence and Svenson were still standing on the front steps watching us drive off. I thought about the times when I was little and I knew that Daddy was coming home any moment from one of his voyages. I would play in the living room and keep one ear tuned toward the front door. The moment I heard Clarence open it, I would rush out to greet Daddy and no matter how tired he looked, he always broke into a wide smile and held his arms out for me to rush into them. I would give him a big, loud kiss on the cheek.

'That's the way to greet a sailor!' he would exclaim. 'Eh, Clarence?'

I could hear him saying it even now. Then, the house disappeared from sight as we rounded a corner, and it seemed my childhood was over in an instant.

This time when we passed under the great arch at the front gates of Farthy, I felt the significance of it. The great estate was now my home, I thought, whether I wanted it to be or not. The groundsmen were busy clearing every last flake of snow from the driveway and stairs. Two maids were absorbed in polishing every bit of brass and iron in sight, and a half dozen men were touching up shutters and cleaning windows.

The wedding preparations combined with the Christmas decorations created an overwhelmingly festive atmosphere. There were lights strewn over the hedges, lanterns dangling from evergreen trees, and tinsel and gold everywhere. Little Troy's snowman, although diminished considerably by the sunlight, still stood in front of the big house. He had placed a top hat on its head and draped a black tie around its neck. The sight of it brought a welcome smile to my face, even though Momma thought someone should have taken it down by now.

'Oh, it would break Troy's heart. He worked on it so hard.'

'There's a time and a place for these things, Leigh. Tony's got to stop catering to his little brother's whims.' She smiled quickly at Grandma Jana. 'Now that I'm here, that will all change.'

Inside the orchestra was practising in the ballroom; the kitchen staff was setting up the giant tables of food. Ushers were gathered around the minister like football players around their coach getting final instructions. Momma went directly upstairs to her suite to make her final preparations with the assistance of her hairdressers. There was a constant traffic of people in the corridors – bridesmaids, escorts, flower girls and photographers. A society editor from the *Globe* stood outside the door to Momma's suite trying to get an interview with Momma.

Troy was very excited. Every chance he had, he marched people in to see his toy collection. Relatives stopped by, cousins and aunts and uncles. I never would have believed that a house this big could be so crowded. I didn't think the wedding would have any sense of order, but when the time came, everyone and everything fell into place.

I joined the other bridesmaids in the upstairs corridor. We were each given a bouquet of sweetheart roses to carry. Troy, as cute as ever in his tuxedo and black tie, was hurried downstairs to take his place next to Tony by the altar. Finally, there was a deep hush. We heard the first piano notes. Excitement rippled through the faces of everyone in the wedding party.

Looking angelic in her Victorian wedding gown with a lace neck smothered in pearls, Momma emerged from her suite. She smiled through her veil and paused to squeeze my hand when she stepped beside me. My heart began to pound so hard and my face felt so hot, I thought I would faint. I felt terrible knowing I should be saying something sweet, something loving to her, but my throat ached from swallowed tears.

'Wish me luck,' she begged.

Luck? What does luck have to do with love and marriage? I thought. Was it bad luck that Momma had gotten pregnant with me or was it just stupidity? Was it just bad luck for Daddy that had brought him to her that fateful night in Texas, or was it Grandma Jana's manipulations? Was it good luck or bad luck that Elizabeth Deveroe had thought of her one day at Farthy and then brought her out here to meet Tony? Was it good luck or bad luck that he took one look at her and fell in love? Did

Daddy think it had all been bad luck? Was he thinking that now?

Where was Daddy this very moment? I wondered. Was he halfway to Florida, perhaps standing on the bridge of his ship, looking out at the sea and wondering about us back here at Farthy? Was he thinking of me?

'Good luck, Momma,' I muttered quickly and she continued on to the back of the line.

We heard 'Here Comes the Bride', and the procession began. As we descended the great staircase, I looked down at the sea of faces, at all these elegantly dressed men and women who were all gazing up at us, and I felt as if I were part of a great show.

Momma, of course, was the star. Eventually, all eyes were on her. I was already in my place so when she made the turn at the foot of the stairway, I could see her face. She looked beautiful and ecstatic. She was just where she had always wanted to be, I thought, at the center of attention.

And all at once, I wanted to shout *'Stop!'* I wanted to end everything, scream my discomfort and agony. 'How can you all be so gleeful and excited! How can you all want to be part of this?' I dreamed of shouting. I wanted to tell all these rich and refined people the truth. 'My mother never told my father the truth about me. We've been living a lie all this time, and now she has taken me from him and brought me here to live with a man twenty years younger than she is. More lies. Everything is lies, lies, lies!'

But like the coward I am I swallowed my dream words. The power of the music, the lights, the excitement and the sight of Tony standing so tall and handsome at the altar with little Troy looking so grown up and serious beside him stopped me. I felt utterly caught up in this madness, tossed about by its waves. I glanced at Grandma Jana sitting in the front row and saw her nod and smile at me. Even she was lost in the ceremony now. Events were flowing over us. We couldn't hold them back.

Little Troy peeped out from behind Tony, searching for me. When he saw me, he smiled and waved. Tony looked down at him and he drew back smartly. Then Momma took her place at the altar; the music stopped, and the words began. My heart pounded at the sound of them, especially the sound of 'To have and to hold from this day forward, for richer or poorer, in sickness and in health, till death do you part.'

Momma had taken the same oaths with Daddy and it hadn't mattered a bit. What did it mean to say those words, even before an altar? I studied Tony's face to see what was going on in his mind. Did he think the same thing I thought – she had said these words with another man and broken that oath? Did she mean them now?

Tony gazed into Momma's eyes as she spoke. He looked bewitched. In some subtle, mysterious way, she'd managed to gather in his reins, and now she was in complete control, I thought. He looked ready to accept anything and say anything to have her. I hated him for being so in love with her.

The time came for little Troy to produce the wedding ring. In his excitement, he rushed to bring it out of his pocket and dropped it. The tiny clang seemed to echo through the great entry hall and everyone in the audience gasped simultaneously so that it sounded like a giant intake of breath. I saw that Troy was about to cry, but Tony picked up the ring quickly and gave it to him to hand it back. Momma flashed a look of anger and then quickly reverted to her smile.

The rings were presented, the final words were said, and the minister pronounced them man and wife. They kissed and the audience cheered. Momma threw her enormous bouquet at the bridesmaids and it fell right into the hands of Nancy Kinney, the most homely looking of them all. Then she and Tony made their way back through the appreciative crowd of guests and the reception began.

I brought punch and *hors d'oeuvres* to Grandma Jana, who sat in the music room and greeted people. Troy remained close to me most of the time, a little scared by the crowd and the activity. Two photographers wandered through the house taking pictures for the wedding album. A number were taken of Troy and me standing together, both of us looking wide-eyed and uncomfortable, me still clinging to my bouquet of sweetheart roses.

Soon after, the great banquet hall was opened and the guests were drawn in by the music of the orchestra. When most everyone was in the room, the conductor stopped his orchestra and went to the microphone to announce the wedding party. First, all the bridesmaids entered and then Troy followed. After a short drum roll, Momma and Tony entered arm in arm, Momma's face sparkling with excitement. The applause rose to a crescendo and cameras clicked. Momma and Tony took the center of the dance floor and the orchestra began to play a waltz. They danced as though they had been dancing together all their lives.

As they turned and moved gracefully to the music, I couldn't help wondering what my wedding day would be like. Would I have a grand affair like this: a full orchestra, hundreds of guests, tons of food, and a horde of servants? If Momma had her way, I would. Maybe I would even be married here, following the Tatterton tradition, which was now to become my tradition, too. Would my husband be as handsome and as debonair as Tony? Would I be deeply in love or would Momma find me some wealthy aristocrat and convince me to marry him?

And when I put on my wedding gown, would I look anything like Momma did? I saw the awe and the envy in the eyes of the other women as she and Tony danced. Not a strand of her gold hair was out of place; her complexion was perfect. She looked like a goddess, like a statue of Aphrodite come to life.

After a while other couples joined Momma and Tony on the dance floor, and the reception was in full swing. Champagne bubbled all around me. I had two glasses and felt a little dizzy.

I was glad when Troy found me and pumped my hand, urging me to follow him to 'see something'. With the music, the conversations, the tinkle of champagne glasses, and the peals of laughter trailing behind us, we slipped out of the ballroom and down the corridor to a sitting room in the rear. Troy pushed opened the double doors. The floor of the room was covered with wedding gifts, some piled three or four feet high.

'Look at all of it!' he exclaimed. 'Tony said we can help open everything up later.'

I could only nod in awe. There was so much. Troy marched

through the corridors of gifts, touching some, gently tapping on others and then placing his face against the sides of the boxes to listen and get a clue about the contents of each. I laughed and shook my head.

'Are you happy, Troy? Happy now that your brother has a wife and my mother will be living here with him?' He stopped his inspection of the wedding gifts and glanced at me with dark eyes and a somber face. 'Troy? You're not happy?'

He was still silent.

'But why not?'

'Your mommy doesn't like me,' he said, looking as though he would cry.

'What? Why do you say that, Troy?' He shrugged. 'Tell me, please.'

'She looks at me with growls in her eyes,' he said quickly.

'Growls? What's growls?'

He growled like a dog.

'Oh.' I started to laugh, but saw he was very serious. 'Oh, I'm sure she doesn't mean that, Troy. It's just that . . . just that she's never had a little boy before. She's only had me and she's not used to little boys. After a while she will get used to you and you will get used to her.'

He shrugged again, but I saw from the expression on his face that he wasn't very hopeful.

'I'm sorry you're not happy about your brother's marriage, Troy.'

'I'm happy! You're here now, right?'

'Yes, I'm here now.'

'So, I'm happy,' he repeated, clapping his little hands.

'I'm glad about that,' I said. 'In fact, that's the thing that makes me most happy, too.' I knelt down and hugged him.

'Come on,' he said heading for the door. 'Let's get back to the party. We'll miss the cake.'

I glanced back once more at the mountains of gifts and then returned with him to the ballroom.

A special table was rolled to the center. On it was a sky-high wedding cake with the figures of the bride and groom dancing under the word, 'CONGRATULATIONS.' Momma and Tony were brought to the cake for the traditional cutting of the first piece. Momma sliced it carefully and fed it to Tony, who tried desperately to maintain some dignity as Momma stuffed the extra large slice into his mouth, but the creamy icing splattered down his chin and over his tuxedo jacket. Everyone laughed and cheered. I was going to join Grandma Jana to have my piece, but suddenly Momma took hold of my arm.

'It has gone well, hasn't it?' She looked about proudly. 'These people will never forget it. They'll be talking about it forever. How's your grandmother doing?' she asked, gazing at Grandma Jana, who was in deep conversation with another woman her age.

'She seems to be having a good time.'

'I'll rest easier when she goes back to Texas. Who knows what she's saying to these people.' I wondered if Momma feared Grandma Jana would tell me the truth about her past. She turned back to me. 'What's wrong?'

'Nothing, Momma.'

'You look sad. How can anyone look sad at an occasion like this?' She paused and sighed. 'Still worrying about everything, aren't you? Can't help but take after your father, I suppose.' I couldn't help wincing. She could lie with such sincerity. Maybe because she had been doing it for so long, I thought. But how long could I keep what I knew to myself? 'Come with me,' she said suddenly.

'What?'

'Just follow me. Quickly. I want to show you something.' She took my hand and led me out of the ballroom. We went to the stairway and up the stairs quickly.

'Where are we going?'

'To my suite,' she said. When we arrived, she went to her wall safe. 'I had Tony install this for my jewels,' she explained, 'and,' she added turning back to me, a wry smile on her face, 'my documents.'

'Documents?'

She just continued to smile impishly and opened her safe. Then she reached in and produced a very important-looking file. Inside were three long pages of paper clipped together. She handed it to me and I read the title: 'A Prenuptial Agreement'.

'What is this?' I asked.

'It's a contract between Tony and me,' she said proudly. 'I had my attorney prepare it.'

'A contract?'

'Yes. If we should divorce, for any reason,' she said, pointing to some words in the second paragraph of the first page, 'I get half of what he is worth. Half!' she repeated. 'Half of all this,' she said, extending her arms. 'You can read it right there,' she added, pointing to the papers in my hands. I looked down at them, but the words were gibberish to me, not only because I didn't understand the 'whereases' and 'resolves,' but because it was so shocking to learn that Momma and Tony's love affair was written down in legal language like a deed to a house.

'I don't understand, Momma. Why do you need this?'

'Insurance,' she said taking the papers back, obviously not pleased with my confusion. She restored them to her wall safe. After she closed it, she turned back to me. 'There is no man in the world I would trust. Absolutely none. I thought I had taught you that.'

'But aren't you in love with Tony?'

'Of course I'm in love with him. What's that got to do with it?'

'But if you're in love, why do you need such a contract?' I was still dumbfounded.

'Honestly, Leigh. For such an intelligent daughter, you act so stupid sometimes. I told you . . . never trust a man, no matter what. I love Tony and he loves me, but that doesn't mean that some time later on, he might not do something to displease me or manufacture something I supposedly did to displease him, just so he could get his way with me. This is insurance,' she said pointing to the safe. 'He knows he can't send me packing without losing half of what he has and that helps to keep a man under control.

'I wanted to show you this now to make you feel better about the future. You will have everything now, Leigh. You don't have anything to worry about any more.'

'But wasn't Tony upset when you asked for this?'

'He was, but he loves me so much he swallowed whatever bad feelings he had about it,' she said proudly. 'That's why I love him – I'm the most important thing in his life. Understand?'

I didn't know what to say. I had thought love meant trust. Were you really in love if you had to have lawyers and judges looking over your shoulders?

'So, now that you know everything, you can be happy, too,' she said. 'Come on. We've got to get back to the reception. I've instructed the servants to hand out the Tatterton memento now and I want to see the looks on the faces of the guests when they each receive one.

'Be happy, Leigh. Please. Just for one day, put aside any dark thoughts and be happy for me.'

'I'll be happy for you, Momma.' She brushed a quick kiss on my cheeks, then we hurried downstairs. I was stunned by Momma's revelation. Was everything good and true and honest only in storybooks? Nothing seemed to be what it appeared to be. Life was as complicated as . . . as the maze outside. No wonder it's so easy to get lost, I thought.

Grandma Jana left just before the wedding reception actually ended. She was anxious to return to Texas, even though everyone treated her like a queen here. Tony had arranged for Miles to drive her to the airport. I walked out to the waiting limousine with her, since Momma was too busy to say a proper goodbye.

'Goodbye, Grandma,' I said. 'Have a good trip home.'

She stood there staring at me thoughtfully, and then she hugged me to her so tightly, she nearly took my breath away. She looked at me and then her eyes narrowed. For a moment I thought she was going to tell me everything, just blurt out the truth of all of Momma's dreadful lies and why she had been upset to learn of Momma's divorce and new marriage, but her eyes softened and her grip on my shoulders loosened.

'I hope you will be happy here, Leigh, but if for any reason you're not, just remember, you can come to me. I don't live as fancy as all this, but I'm quite comfortable,' she said, sounding far from the ogre Momma often made her out to be. How much of the rest of what Momma had told me about her early life in Texas had really been true, I wondered.

'Thank you, Grandma.'

She kissed me again and got into the limo. I watched it go off and then went back inside. Soon after, guests began to leave.

I heard Momma call my name and saw Tony and her coming down the stairway together. Momma's heels clicked on the marble stairs. How worldly and confident she appeared as she sauntered down arm and arm with Tony. She was wearing her black wool crepe suit trimmed with a mink collar and cuffs. From beneath her jacket peeked a white chiffon blouse that glittered. In contrast to all this darkness, Momma's face was dazzling to behold. She seemed a diamond set against black velvet.

Tony wore a black leather jacket and a bright white scarf. Just like Momma, he appeared fresh and alert. I imagined they were both still buoyed by the day's excitement and the excitement yet to come. They both looked so young and alive and so very happy together.

'Can you believe it's over?' Momma asked. 'You are now looking at Mr and Mrs Tony Tatterton. How do we look together, Leigh?' She squeezed herself up against Tony.

'Wonderful,' I said, in as excited a voice as I could manage, but Momma wasn't satisfied. Her smile wilted.

'Well, we're off. You have everything you need and need to know. I wish I could be here with you Christmas morning when you open your presents, but I know you understand.'

'Try to keep Troy from opening them until Christmas morning,' said Momma's handsome new husband, with his eyes that followed me everywhere and his smile that seemed to mock and know so much.

'You promised him he could open the wedding gifts,' I reminded Tony, my own eyes breaking the stare between us.

'We were going to do that when we got back from our honeymoon,' Momma groaned. 'He'll just have to wait.'

'Oh, I don't see how it could hurt if he unwraps some,' Tony relented. 'Just don't let him make a mess of it.'

'He's sure to, being a little boy,' Momma complained. 'Oh well, I don't want to think of anything that's the slightest bit unpleasant right now. Goodbye, Leigh honey.' She embraced me and even with all my pent-up anger I hugged her back tightly, with a ferocity that I think surprised her. All of a sudden I didn't want her to leave, I needed her in my heart of hearts to be my mother and warm me with hugs and kisses and little touches.

'Have a nice Christmas and New Year in your new home. Don't be afraid to explore,' Tony said. 'It will take you almost as long as our honeymoon to do it.'

'But please . . . stay out of the maze,' Momma warned.

'Okay, Momma. Have a good time,' I choked out.

'May I kiss my step-daughter goodbye?' Tony asked. 'Goodbye, Leigh. See you soon.' His long arms held me and even though through the leather they felt strong and muscular. He kissed me on the cheek, but very close to the corner of my mouth. Momma seemed impressed with how long he held me and how gently and lovingly he kissed me. Then she threaded her arm through his and they were off. Curtis opened the big doors for them and then shut the doors behind them. He nodded at me and walked away.

I heard the voices of some servants and staff echo from the ballroom as they carried things back to the kitchen. Doors were closed and suddenly a great hush fell over the enormous entry way. I looked around. It was as if all the spirits of Tattertons past were sucked back into their portraits and eternal places. The new silence became deafening. I gazed out a front window and saw that the Christmas lights were turned on. The grounds, the hedges and trees were ablaze with reds and greens and blues. It was as though a rainbow had shattered and bits of it had rained down all over Farthinggale.

Mrs Hastings came down and told me Troy was fast asleep. She went off to join the other members of the staff, who were, I gathered, now having a celebration of their own and feasting on leftovers in the kitchen.

I went to the music room where Tony had had the ten-foot Christmas tree placed and decorated. Its lights had been turned on and it looked lovely with its glass angel shining brightly on top. Gifts were scattered and piled around it. There was a fire in the marble fireplace. The room looked all set, ready-made for a family.

But where was this family and who had done all this? It was almost as if the house had a life of its own, each of its rooms coming to life in its own way when its time came. Was everything set on some automatic switch? I wondered. At Christmas, the tree spontaneously lit itself and the fireplace self-started. As if the house were really toying with me, Christmas music suddenly began playing through the speakers built into the walls.

I laughed. I felt so silly all of a sudden. Was there a mechanical Santa Claus set to come down that chimney every Christmas Eve too? Curtis must have been nearby and heard my laughter because he suddenly appeared in the doorway with a look of confusion on his face when he saw I was alone.

'Is there anything I can get you, Miss Leigh?'

Yes, I wanted to say. Get me my Daddy and my Momma. Get me the happiness we once knew. Put us in this warm room together, laughing and smiling, kissing and embracing each other with love and tenderness. Make this a real Christmas for me.

'No, Curtis. Not right now. Thank you.'

'Very good, Miss. Just ring if there is anything you want.'

'Thank you.'

He nodded softly and was gone. I looked at the Christmas tree and the presents and then gazed up at Momma's murals. My heart felt heavy and leaden and my throat ached from holding in my sobs. I left the room quickly and went up to my suite. I was so very tired. I got into my nightgown and then crawled under my covers in my new bed. After I put out the lamp at the side of my bed, I looked through the sheer curtains on one of my windows and saw the moon peeping through a cloud. It drew me to the window.

I gazed out at the vast expanse that was Farthinggale Manor. From here I could look down at the long winding driveway. Tonight, because of the melted snow, the driveway gleamed like a silver metal ribbon. It was easier to be lonely in a place that was as big and as rich as Farthy, I thought. My friends back in Boston would never think so, but I couldn't remember ever feeling as small and alone as I did right this moment.

I looked up and saw the North Star, and I recalled Daddy explaining how sailors depended on it whenever they were lost. Could I depend on it? It twinkled back down at me. Maybe somewhere Daddy was looking up at it too. Maybe he threw me a kiss and that kiss bounced off the North Star and came back to me here at Farthy.

'Good night, Daddy,' I whispered.

'Good night, Princess,' I pretended to hear him say.

And I crawled back into bed, and for the first time in my life, I wasn't so anxious for Christmas morning that I couldn't wait to fall asleep.

I felt myself being jolted awake and opened my eyes to see Troy tugging on my hand.

'Wake up, Leigh. Wake up!'

'What?' I scrubbed my eyes with my fists and gazed around. It would be a while before I was used to waking up in such a big bedroom.

'It's Christmas. Come on. We've got to go down and open our presents. Come on. Hurry.'

'Oh Troy,' I groaned. 'What time is it?' I looked at my clock. It was just seven o'clock.

'Hurry up,' he pleaded.

'All right. Okay, Troy. Give me a few minutes. Girls take longer to get up than boys,' I said, hoping for a small reprieve.

'Why?' He swung his dark brown eyes skeptically at me.

'Because they have to fix their hair and their faces and look presentable. Actually, young men do the same thing.'

He thought for a moment and looked down at himself still dressed in his pajamas, bathrobe and slippers.

'Okay. I'll brush my hair and meet you here in a few minutes!' he exclaimed and scurried off. I laughed and got out of bed. I washed my face free of sleep, and brushed my hair a little, knowing that Momma would never leave her room looking like

I did. But Momma wasn't always right, I thought. More than ever, I was thinking that now. I put on my robe and found Troy waiting impatiently for me in my sitting room. He seized my hand the moment I appeared and led me downstairs. Then he attacked the presents. Mrs Hastings appeared behind me, laughing.

'Merry Christmas,' she said.

'Merry Christmas.'

'I'll see about breakfast, if you'd like,' she offered.

'Thank you, Mrs Hastings. Let's hope we can pry him away from the gifts long enough to eat,' I added. I knelt down beside Troy and helped him unwrap his presents first.

His biggest present was his own television set. There was one in the den, but now he would have one for his own room.

'I've got to get it up to my room,' he said excitedly.

'Wait. There's time for that, Troy. Look at the other gifts first.'

'Okay. And you look at yours, too. I gave you something.'

'Did you?' Momma and I had gone shopping for Christmas presents and spent nearly all our time trying to find something 'right' for Tony, since he had so much. She decided to get him a solid gold tie clip with diamonds on the ends. Then she had 'Love, Jillian' inscribed on the back. I'd had trouble thinking of anything good enough for Daddy. Mittens and silk ties, expensive aftershave lotions, suede gloves, a new pipe holder . . . nothing had the right meaning for a Daddy who wouldn't be opening the gift with me there beside him.

Then I saw something at one of the department stores that was not as expensive as other gifts I could get him, but filled my heart with pleasure and warmth when I thought of him unwrapping it and gazing at it. It was a special photograph to be taken next to a Christmas tree. On the bottom, the photographer embossed 'Merry Christmas'. And you could have your name embossed and the date, too. I bought a handsome light pine frame for it as well.

When I posed for the picture, I smiled as warmly and as lovingly as I could, for I knew it would be the smile that Daddy would see forever and ever, especially when he was lonely and wanted to think of me. I had it wrapped and left it on Daddy's desk at our Boston home so he could find it as soon as he returned from his trip.

I decided to buy Troy an erector set, since he was so good with his hands. It was a toy, but he could do something creative with it too. It even had a little electric motor, so if he made a tiny ferris wheel, it would actually turn. He was very excited about it when he opened the package and saw it. To my surprise, he knew exactly what it was. He got up quickly and gave me a big hug and kiss.

'Thank you, Leigh. Now look at my present to you,' he said. 'I made it myself and wrapped it myself.'

I opened the small package and couldn't believe my eyes. He had made it? It was a little ceramic horse with a girl rider. The girl could be taken off.

'That's Sniffles,' Troy explained. 'My horse. And that's you riding it.'

'You made this?'

'Not the little girl,' he confessed. 'Tony had that made at his factory, but I made Sniffles. I took a picture of her and traced it and shaped it and baked it. Then I painted it myself,' he added proudly.

'It's beautiful, Troy. It's the best Christmas present I've ever received. Thank you.' I kissed him on the cheek. His eyes twinkled and then he went back to unwrapping his presents. What a wonderfully talented little boy he was, I thought. How could Momma not be charmed by him?

'You have other presents,' Troy said pointing. There were at least a dozen different brightly wrapped boxes with my name on them, some from Momma, some from Tony, but a small box caught my eye first, because I saw the emblem of Daddy's ocean liner company on the card's envelope.

Carefully, I lifted the box and ran my fingers lovingly over the top. Troy was impressed with the reverent way I treated it. He put down his next gift and drew closer to me.

'What is it?' he asked in a whisper.

'A Christmas present from my daddy. Somehow, he got one here.'

'Why don't you open it?' Troy's eyes swung from the small box to me and back to the box.

'I will.' Gingerly, taking great care not to tear the paper, I unwrapped the present to find a small dark blue velvet box. I opened it and took out a heavy, gold locket in the shape of a heart with a sparkling gold chain. I pressed the release button and a locket opened to a tiny picture of Daddy and me standing on *The Jillian*. We both looked tanned and happy. I remembered why I looked so happy. We were on the way home and I thought I would find Momma waiting for me at the dock.

'Can I see?' Troy asked. I held the locket out and he plucked it carefully from my palm to gaze at the picture. I saw his eyes widen and then grow small. 'I have a big picture of my daddy,' he said. 'But he's not smiling. I told Tony and he said Daddy's smiling in Heaven and he will always smile as long as I am good.'

'Then I'm sure he will always smile,' I told him. I had him help me put on the locket and then we returned to opening our gifts.

I spent Christmas Day helping Troy set up his toys and put away the clothes he had received as gifts. Late in the afternoon, we watched some shows on his new television set. We had a delicious turkey for Christmas Day dinner, and Rye Whiskey prepared vegetables with sauces I had never before tasted.

Troy kept me so busy that I was relieved when it was time for him to go to sleep. I went to sleep early myself that night. I had promised him that we would ride his pony in the morning, which we did. In fact, there was so much to do at Farthy – swimming in the indoor pool, cross-country skiing, hiking to the ocean and back, horseback riding, and sleigh riding, that the first week passed quickly.

Tony had an enormous library, and my favourite book from its crowded shelves was *Lolita*, the story of an older man's love affair with a twelve-year-old girl, a girl my age! I couldn't believe the things she did and said. There were parts I reread and reread, parts that made me blush and made my heartbeat quicken. I kept the novel buried under the others so the servants wouldn't know I had been reading it, just in case any of them knew what it was about.

I had promised Troy we would spend New Year's Eve in his room watching television. He was determined to stay up until twelve o'clock and watch the people celebrating in Times Square, New York. He held out until almost eleven, but by then, his eyes had shut and his little chest rose and fell in quiet, rhythmic breathing.

A little after eleven-thirty, Daddy called from Florida. He sounded small and faraway. The phone line crackled.

'I loved your Christmas present, Daddy. Yours is waiting for you on your desk at home.'

'I'll be there next week, so I'll call you after I open it,' he said. 'How are you?'

'I'm okay, Daddy, but I miss you,' I said, my voice nearly breaking.

'And I miss you, too. In a few weeks, I'll come by and we'll spend a day together in Boston.'

'I'll be in school by then, Daddy. You'll have to come to Winterhaven. But it's not far from here.' I told him about the different things I had been doing.

'Sounds like quite a place,' he said sadly.

'I'd rather be home with you, Daddy.'

'I know, sweetheart. We will be together soon. I promise. Well now, let me wish you a Happy New Year. I know this past year has not been a happy one, but hopefully, the next one will.'

'Happy New Year, Daddy. I love you.'

'And I love you, Princess. Good night.'

'Good night, Daddy.'

I pressed the receiver against my chest after he had hung up, pressed it so hard it hurt. I didn't cradle it until I heard the television announcer begin to count down: 'ten, nine, eight . . .' Troy moaned in his sleep and then turned over on his side. 'Seven, six, five . . .'

I saw that it had begun to snow again. The snowflakes were large and pretty. They fell so softly, some clinging to the window for a moment before turning into tears and streaming down the pane.

'Four, three, two . . .'

I held my new locket up against my lips and kissed it, telling myself I was kissing Daddy.

'One . . . *Happy New Year, everyone*!'

The camera caught so many different faces – people cheering, people laughing, people screaming, people crying. I wished I was there with them, lost in a crowd of strangers.

Nearly half of the pages of my diary are written upon now. It's a good place to wish myself a 'Happy New Year'. Of course, for me it's more than a new year; it's a new life.

Happy New Year, Leigh VanVoreen.

TEN

The Honeymoon's Over

Troy awoke with a bad cold on New Year's Day, the day Momma and Tony were returning from their honeymoon. By eight o'clock in the morning, he was running a high fever and Mrs Hastings had to send for the doctor. I knew he was very sick because he made no effort to get out of his bed to play. While the doctor examined him, I waited outside in the hallway. Afterward, I heard Mrs Hastings and the doctor conferring in the outer chamber of Troy's suite. The doctor emerged from Troy's suite first, his eyes dark and the lines of his face cut deeply with worry and concern. Mrs Hastings followed, her eye wet with tears. She held her handkerchief against her mouth and shook her head at me.

'What is it? What's wrong with him?' I asked frantically.

'The doctor thinks he's developing pneumonia. Oh dear me, dear me. He's going to call for an ambulance. He wants him in the hospital for X-rays and treatment right away. Mr Tatterton warned me that Troy has so little resistance to germs, but he was doing so well and he was so happy and energetic, I didn't think I let him overdo it,' she cried.

'Now Mrs Hastings, this is not your fault. Whenever he showed the slightest signs of getting cold outside, we always brought him in, and except for last night, which is the most special night of the year, he always went to sleep early. And he's been eating well, too,' I added. 'He didn't get sick after he and I were lost in the maze. You did wonders to prevent that from happening then, remember?'

'Yes, yes. Still, I feel so bad. I'll be right back. I have to see to some of the arrangements. Mr and Mrs Tatterton won't be home until the middle of the afternoon, but the doctor says we can't wait for them.' She shook her head with worry.

'Can I go in to see him?'

'Yes, but don't get too close to him. Oh dear, dear,' she mumbled and hurried to the stairway.

Little Troy looked so much smaller in his large bed with the covers brought up to his chin. I had dolls with heads bigger than his head appeared to be against the large, fluffy white pillow. His small ears, his tiny nose, his closed eyes which looked no bigger than marbles, and his petite mouth slightly open because of his difficulty in breathing, did make him seem like a fragile toy.

His cheeks were scarlet from his fever and his lips looked a little puffy. His hands were cupped into tiny fists, but the rest of his body was buried under the enormous down comforter. I stood by the side of his bed watching him. I didn't want to wake him. Suddenly he started to mumble in his fevered sleep.

'Daddy wake up, wake up,' he said. Then with his eyes still closed, he grimaced. 'Tony . . . Tony.' His face twisted in agony. I went to him and took his tiny, warm hand into mine.

'It's all right, Troy. It's all right, I'm here.'

'Tony . . . I want Tony . . .'

'It's Leigh, Troy. Do you want me to get you a drink of water?'

'Tony,' he muttered and shook his head. Then he squeezed his eyes closed even tighter as if he were trying to deny a picture in his mind. I touched his flushed cheek and became shocked and frightened by how hot his skin really was. It made my heart pound. I looked expectantly at the doorway. Where was the doctor? How could they leave him alone like this, even for a moment?

He swung his head from side to side, moaning softly.

'Troy,' I cried, tears coming into my eyes. 'Oh, my God,' I whispered. I flew out of the room to find Mrs Hastings. She and the doctor were downstairs talking softly with Curtis and Miles.

'Doctor, he's burning up in his bed! And he's moaning like he's in pain!' I exclaimed. The doctor looked at me and then at

Mrs Hastings, wondering who I was. She whispered something quickly in his ear.

'Oh.' He nodded and turned to me. 'Yes, we know, my dear. We have just decided that we will not wait for an ambulance. We are going to take Troy to the hospital in the limousine immediately. Mrs Hastings was just going up to prepare him for the trip.'

'Can I help?'

'No, I think it's best you just stay a good distance away. Don't want to have two patients to rush off,' he said smiling. How could he joke at a time like this? I thought. Mrs Hastings started up the stairs. I was so fidgety and nervous, I could do nothing but wait and watch. A little while later, Miles emerged from Troy's suite with Troy bundled up in blankets, his pinkish face barely visible, and carried him toward the stairs. Mrs Hastings followed close behind, saying, 'Oh dear me, dear me.'

It was hours before Miles and Mrs Hastings returned but the moment I heard them enter, I came running.

'It is definitely pneumonia,' Mrs Hastings declared, her lips trembling. She started to sob. 'It's such a pathetic sight. Oh dear, dear.'

I tried to comfort her.

'You should have something to eat, something hot to drink, Mrs Hastings, and stop blaming yourself. It's no one's fault.'

'Yes,' she said. 'Something hot to drink,' she muttered. 'You're so right. Thank you, dear.' She went off to the kitchen.

'How is he really, Miles?' I asked. Somehow I knew he would tell me the cold truth.

'His fever is very, very high. Troy has a history of sickness and poor resistance. I'm afraid there is serious concern.'

My heart sank. I could feel the blood rushing to my face. My butterflies exploded in a mad frenzy in my stomach, circling and circling, the tips of their paper-thin wings tickling my insides.

'You don't mean he could die, do you, Miles?' I held my breath to hear his reply.

'It's very serious, Miss,' he said and gazed at his watch. 'I have to be off to the airport. Mr and Mrs Tatterton will be arriving soon. I imagine I'll take them directly to the hospital,' he added.

'Poor Tony and Momma. They'll be so shocked,' I said. He nodded and left quickly.

I spent the rest of the afternoon waiting in trepidation. Every time I heard a phone ringing my heart stopped. None of the calls had anything to do with Troy, however. Unable to wait any longer, I had Mrs Hastings call the hospital and ask the nurse on Troy's floor for an update. There had been no improvement. In fact, I gathered from the way Mrs Hastings listened and nodded, her eyes widening, her mouth collapsing, that if anything, he was a little worse.

Finally, I heard a commotion at the front entrance and came out of the music room to see Momma making a grand entrance. The servants were carrying in luggage, and she was shouting orders and complaining to Curtis about the cold weather and the long trip. Tony wasn't with her.

'*Momma!*' I shouted. '*Thank God, you're back!*'

'Amen to that,' Momma said and followed it with a thin, long laugh. She pulled off her gloves. Even though she was complaining about the cold and the trip, she looked fresh and beautiful. She had bright, rosy cheeks and wore a new black sable fur hat and a matching sable fur coat with black velvet gloves and ski pants. Gold drop earrings dangled from her ears. She stepped aside so Miles could bring in the ski equipment.

She hugged me quickly and whispered, 'You wouldn't think a honeymoon could be exhausting, Leigh, but believe me, this one was. I'm absolutely drained, sapped of every ounce of energy. I can't wait to get into my soft bed and close my eyes.'

'But Momma, where's Tony? You know about Troy, don't you?'

'Of course. Tony went directly to the hospital. We left him there,' she said. 'Wait until you see some of the things I've bought in Europe, Leigh,' she said without pausing for a breath. 'After I've had a good rest, I'll show you everything and tell you everything.' She leaned toward me again and whispered, 'And I mean everything.' Then she started for the stairway. 'But for now . . . a hot bath . . . rest . . .'

'But Momma, what about little Troy?' She turned at the foot of the stairway and looked confused.

'What about him?'

'He's so sick and . . .'

'Well, he's in the hospital, Leigh. What more can we do?'

'Did you see him?'

'Certainly not,' she said, shaking her head. 'You don't expose yourself to those things if you don't have to.'

'But . . .'

'You didn't, did you? All we need now,' she said before I could reply, 'is for you to become sick too. I just haven't the strength and energy for that. Not right now, anyway.' She started up the stairway. 'I'll call you as soon as I'm rested,' she added.

How could she be so uncaring and worry only about herself at a time like this? Was she always this selfish? I asked myself. And why was her honeymoon so exhausting? Wasn't it supposed to be the most wonderful time of your life, especially to go somewhere as luxurious as the hotel that she and Tony had gone to where they could do fun things and be together day in and day out, with romantic meals and music. Honeymooners shut the world out and enjoy each other and the miracle of their love, I thought.

How could she leave Tony alone in the hospital, no matter how tired she was? Even if I resented his presence in my life, I had quickly grown to love little Troy. And Troy was almost like Momma's step-son now. Tony was surely very concerned and upset. Wasn't that a time for a wife to be close to her husband, to comfort and to support him? Instead, she had herself brought home and she was going to take a hot bath and go to sleep. She was worried about her beauty rest. Perhaps this marriage was no better than her marriage to Daddy, since the new one was also a marriage built on a lie.

Momma was so different, I thought, and then I thought, maybe she was always this way, but I just hadn't noticed because I saw her only with a child's eyes. But that day I overheard the conversation between her and Grandma Jana aged me faster than I had wanted to age. The rose tint had been peeled back off my world. Now many things that had once been as bright and as colorful as a rainbow were gray.

I went up to my room and sat on my bed looking at the little horse Troy had made me for Christmas. No matter how rich we are, no matter how beautiful or how powerful we think we are, we're all really just as fragile and as delicate as this little ceramic toy Troy made me, I thought. I clutched it tightly to me and said a silent prayer.

Sitting there, I fell asleep, and it was after six o'clock when I awoke. Twilight made my bedroom dismal and full of shadows. I felt a chill as if a wintry wind had slipped into the big house under the front doors and wound its way through the rooms and up the stairway directly to my bedroom. It draped itself over me like some blanket sewn with threads of ice. I shuddered and embraced myself. It felt like a bad omen.

Troy, I thought frantically, and hopped out of bed quickly. The corridor was dim and quiet. My heart began to pound. The house seemed muted, hushed as if it had been deserted by everyone but its ghosts.

Fearing the worst, I glided like a sleepwalker down the corridor to Momma's suite and listened at the doorway. It was just as quiet. I opened the outer door and tiptoed through the sitting room to gaze into her bedroom.

She was still in bed, fast asleep, a thick blanket over her, her golden hair loose and lying over a large fluffy pillow. Boxes and packages covered the floor. Her new mink coat, the mink hat, her ski pants and boots were still where she had draped them over chairs and benches when she had undressed to take her bath. How could she still be sleeping? Didn't she care at all about sweet little Troy?

I found no one in the rooms downstairs. Finally in the kitchen I discovered all the servants gathered around the table talking softly. They turned to me the moment I entered. They were all of one face – dark-eyed, somber, concerned.

'Has there been any news?' I asked, fearful of what their reply would be.

'Oh dear,' Mrs Hastings said. 'Mr Tatterton called a little over an hour ago to say Troy's fever has gone even higher. His breathing is very labored. He's in a critical condition.'

They all stared at me, waiting for my reaction.

'I want to go to the hospital, Miles,' I said. 'Will you take me?'

He looked from Rye to Mrs Hastings to the other servants, not knowing how he should react to my request.

'Your mother might not want you to go,' he finally said.

'My *mother*,' I replied, pounding the word, 'is asleep. I'll be ready in five minutes. Please bring the car up front,' I demanded and left before there could be any further discussion.

I found Tony talking to a nurse in the waiting room of the Boston General Hospital. He had his long, cashmere coat draped over his arm. For once, I felt no anger, hatred or resentment toward him. All of my thoughts were for Troy now. Even so, I thought Tony looked more tanned and handsome than ever.

'Leigh!' he cried as soon as he set eyes on me. He rushed across the waiting room to greet me. 'Is Jillian with you?' He peered over my head and through the entrance way behind me.

'No. She's sleeping,' I replied, unable to hide my disapproval. His face sank, the brightness that had come into his eyes quickly fading.

'Oh.'

'Has there been any change?'

'Some slight change for the better. It's very nice of you to have come to be with me. Thank you.'

'Oh Tony, I'm so worried about him. We had such a good time together while you and Momma were away, but honestly, we didn't do anything that would have made him sick. We were outside a lot, but he was always properly dressed, and whenever he showed any signs of getting cold, we went right back inside. And he had a good appetite and . . .'

'Hold on . . . hold on,' Tony seized my elbows in his hands. 'Troy's been sick like this before. It's just his nature. No one can predict it. I don't blame anyone, least of all you. Stop thinking about it.' He looked at his watch. 'It will be a while yet before the doctor can say anything new about Troy's condition and it's just about dinner time. I know a nice little Italian restaurant not far from here,' he said. 'Hungry?'

'I . . .'

'Sure, you must be. I haven't eaten since early morning. There's no point in us just sitting here. Come on,' he said putting on his coat and then taking my arm into his. I couldn't help my hesitation. I hadn't demanded to be brought here so I could eat dinner in Boston. I wanted to be near Troy.

But, I thought, if Tony felt it was all right to leave for a little while to get something to eat, I suppose it was all right.

'Troy's getting the best possible treatment,' Tony said after we were seated at a small table by the window. 'That little tyke has a way of pulling out of crises when he wants to, and now that you're living with us at Farthy, I know he wants to live and be well more than ever.' He reached across the table to pat my hand reassuringly.

'I hope so,' I said, nearly following it with a sob.

'Let's eat. They have wonderful pasta here. Let me do the ordering for both of us,' he said. How sophisticated he was, pronouncing the Italian words perfectly. The waiter recognized his worldly ways and was immediately impressed. I could see it in the way he listened and nodded. Tony then turned and stared at me for a moment. His penetrating blue gaze rested on me with deep consideration.

'You know you're a baffling girl, Leigh. One second you look positively radiant with happiness, and the next all happiness has fled and you have tears in your eyes. I think you're just as intriguing, or confusing, I should say, as your mother. No man is a match for either of you, I'm afraid,' he added, not sounding bitter so much as he sounded resigned to his fate.

'Did you have a good time on your honeymoon?' I asked, sensing a sour note. 'Momma went right to bed so I didn't have a chance to ask her anything.' His blue eyes narrowed, suspiciously.

'I know I did,' he replied, a wry smile on his face. I waited breathlessly for him to say more. 'Your mother told me she liked skiing and ice skating. She said she loved winter sports but when we arrived in St Moritz, she decided it was too cold to go skiing. Can you imagine?' He laughed. 'Too cold to go skiing. Anyway, I spent the days on the slopes, and she spent them shopping, or by the fireplace in the hotel.

'I finally got her on the slopes one day, but she complained so much and fell down so much, I let her go back to the hotel. As for ice skating at night on their beautifully lit lake . . .' He waved his hand and shook his head. 'That took less than ten minutes to reject.

'She kept complaining about the effect the cold air was having on her skin, and I discovered she hates getting sweaty. So much for a winter sport honeymoon. Or any sports for that matter,' he added with wide eyes.

'But you must have gone to wonderful European restaurants,' I said. I knew Momma was looking forward to that.

'Oh, we did, but your mother eats like a bird. It's a waste to order her a full meal, even a children's portion. I ended up eating her meal and my own every night. Lucky I was getting a lot of exercise, huh?' he said sitting back and patting his tummy.

'No, you look . . . you look good,' I said. I had almost said, 'wonderful'.

'Thank you. Anyway, that's the story of our winter holiday and honeymoon,' he added with disappointment.

The waiter brought us the bread and the salads. It didn't strike me how hungry I was until I began to eat. The cozy restaurant, Tony's casual conversation about Momma and the honeymoon, and the delicious food put me at ease. I relaxed for the first time since I had discovered Troy was so sick.

We talked some more about Europe and I told him about our trips to London. Then I described every little thing I had done while he and Momma were away. I wasn't aware of how much and how long I was talking because he listened so attentively, his eyes fixed on me.

'Oh, I'm sorry I'm talking so much. I don't know what's come over me.'

'That's all right. I'm enjoying it. It's the most you've said to me since . . . since we met.'

A little embarrassed, I swung my eyes away to look at some people coming into the restaurant.

'You look very good,' he told me. 'Like you have been spending time outdoors.'

'Thank you.' I couldn't help blushing. I hadn't learned how to take compliments as nonchalantly as Momma could. She always expected them, however. For me, they were still something unanticipated and something very special, especially when a man as handsome as Tony Tatterton spoke them. He had a way of sounding so sincere. It made me warm and tingly. Then I felt guilty for feeling so good while little Troy lay so sick in the hospital.

'Shouldn't we get back?' I asked. He was still gazing at me intensely, his eyes so piercing and direct.

'What? Oh, yes. Immediately.' He signalled for the waiter.

When we arrived at the hospital, he went straight to Troy's room while I waited in the corridor. Soon, he emerged with the doctor and Tony signaled for me to join them.

'His fever has broken,' he announced happily. 'And he's having much less difficulty breathing. He's going to be all right.'

I was so relieved, I started to cry. He and the doctor looked at each other and laughed, and then Tony embraced me.

'Thank you, Leigh,' he whispered, 'for caring about him so much.' He kissed me on the forehead and I looked up and into his warm blue eyes, my mind reeling in confusion. I had inherited an entirely new family so quickly. It was difficult to sort out my emotions. Whenever I felt good, especially about Tony, I felt I was betraying Daddy, and yet, Tony seemed loving, concerned and caring. He and I had been thrown together by Momma's whim, and maybe he was trying to adjust and sort out his feelings as much as I was. I relaxed in his embrace and lay my head against his shoulder. I can't hate him, I thought. Forgive me, Daddy, but I can't hate him.

'Do you want to look in on him, Leigh?' Tony asked. 'He's not awake, but you can stand in the doorway for a few moments.'

'Yes. Thank you.'

Tony opened the door and I gazed in at little Troy, who

looked even smaller than he had looked this morning. The hospital bed, the oxygen and the intravenous tube made him look so tiny, so fragile. My heart cried out for him. I couldn't hold back the tears that had gathered again in the corners of my eyes. Tony took out his handkerchief and wiped them away.

'He's going to be all right,' he said reassuringly and held me again. I nodded. 'Let's go home,' he said. This time, when we passed through Farthy's great gate, Tony's words rang true: 'Let's go home.'

I was home, for home was not just a building or a house or a place on some street; it was where you had love and warmth awaiting and where people you loved lived. I loved Daddy, but he was on a ship on the ocean and no one lived in our home in Boston now. I loved Momma, despite all her lies and selfish ways, and I knew I loved little Troy and they lived here at Farthy.

I wondered if I would ever come to love Tony Tatterton. The way he held my hand as we walked up the steps to the front door made me think he was more than positive I would.

Momma had finally woken. Tony and I found her sitting at her vanity table brushing her hair. She had just gotten out of bed and was dressed only in a long, evergreen silk robe, one of the things she had bought in Europe.

'Leigh, I called for you at least an hour ago. Where have you been?' she asked. Tony stopped behind me in the doorway and we exchanged a look of disappointment.

'I've been to the hospital with Tony, Momma, to see about Troy.'

'I asked you not to expose yourself to the illness. You can see how it will be bringing up a teenage girl, Tony,' she snapped. 'They're just like wild horses, stubborn and unpredictable.'

'She wasn't exposed, Jillian,' Tony said. 'She was kept a proper distance away, and I thought it was wonderful of her to want to come.'

'You could have called. How could you two leave me here not knowing what was happening . . . where everyone was . . .'

'I did call,' Tony protested, 'but the servants told me you left word not to be disturbed.'

'Well, you of all people should have known how exhausted I was. Anyway, you're here now, so tell me, how is he?' she asked, turning back to the mirror to straighten a strand of hair.

'His fever has broken. He's on the mend.'

'There, you see,' she said pointedly to me. 'There wasn't anything we could do once he was in the hospital. Once he's there, it's up to good doctors and nurses and the miracles of medicine,' she sang as if this had all been a little bedtime story.

'He's still a very sick little boy,' Tony said, 'but the crisis has ended.'

'Well, thank goodness. Are we having dinner now? I've woken up famished.'

Tony and I looked quickly at each other again. Momma caught our glance.

'What?'

'I took Leigh to Leone's while we waited for news about Troy,' Tony confessed.

'You two ate? And without me?' she cried.

'Well, you were home and . . .'

'That's fine,' she said suddenly, her look of disappointment disappearing. 'Just have the servants bring up something light,' she sang, her mood changing so fast it made my head spin. 'I'm not really up to going down and sitting at the table anyway. It will take me at least another day to get back to myself,' she said sounding as if she had been the one in the hospital, instead of someone who had just returned from a wonderful honeymoon in Europe.

'Fine,' Tony said. He stepped forward and leaned over to kiss her, but she leaned away as if he were going to mess up her hair. It was something she often did when Daddy tried to kiss her. Tony looked embarrassed.

'I'm still very tired,' she offered as an excuse. He nodded and left quickly.

The moment he was out the door, Momma beckoned me closer, her eyes wide with emphasis.

'Oh Leigh, you just can't imagine how difficult it has been.'

'What?' I had no idea what she meant.

'Spending these last several days with a man as young and strong as Tony. He never needs to nap and he dresses in a flash,' she said with irritation and envy. 'Somebody up there must like him.' Her delicate eyebrows rose as if in exasperation.

'Then you didn't have a good time on your honeymoon?' I asked to confirm what Tony had told me.

'I did and I didn't. He's so athletic, up at the crack of dawn and expecting me to be dressed and ready for breakfast; and when I complained, he became upset. Can you imagine the lack of consideration? How did he expect me to go down to that dining room without being properly made up and dressed? I sent him down without me, actually glad to get rid of him so I could prepare myself without him watching. He was always finished and ready to go out before I had spent half the time I needed. That annoyed him, but I told him he didn't have to wait for me. I told him to just go right ahead and do his sliding up and down those cold hills.

'You would think that a day of that would leave him exhausted. But no . . . he would return every afternoon actually invigorated and you can just guess what a man of Tony's youth and vitality is like when he is invigorated.'

She saw the look of confusion on my face and smirked.

'He makes love like it's going to be for the last time, practically raping me,' she explained. The blood rushed into my face to hear her make reference to something so intimate. 'And once it's over and you expect to have a chance to catch your breath, he's at it again. I felt like some strumpet.

'Why, even in the middle of the night, he would nudge me awake, shock me out of a restful slumber, and want to be amorous. It didn't matter that I was not fully awake. He was angry because I didn't respond the way he hoped I would.

'Well, I couldn't. I wouldn't. I'm not going to sacrifice my health and beauty to satisfy a young man's animal appetite,' she added determinedly.

I didn't know what to say. Momma made it sound as if lovemaking was an ordeal, but that wasn't the way it was described in books I had read.

'Oh Leigh,' she cried, turning to me and taking my hands into hers, 'you've got to be my best friend, my ally more than ever now. Will you? Will you?'

'Of course I will,' I replied, even though again I had no idea what she meant.

'Good, because Tony likes you and doesn't mind spending time with you. I can see that. It was good that you went to dinner with him in Boston. I'm going to need you to help keep him amused and happy. He requires so much attention and demands so much affection. It's absolutely life draining!' she cried.

'Not that I don't love him. I do. I adore him. I just never expected he would be so . . . so virile . . . so hungry for sex. If I don't find ways to keep him at bay, he'll deplete me, rob me of my vibrancy.

'Yes,' she said before I could react, 'I've seen that happen to other women. Their husbands are so demanding that they become old before their time and then their husbands go looking elsewhere for satisfaction. A woman has to guard her beauty like a precious jewel, keep it encased, protected, permit men to look upon her, gaze at her longingly, but rarely touch because every touch absorbs, takes away, diminishes.

'Tony wants me by his side constantly. He wants me there whenever he has the urge to kiss me, to take my hand, to embrace me, and then, to take me.'

I thought that sounded wonderful – to have a man need and want you that much. And after all, wasn't her big complaint about Daddy that he didn't spend enough time with her, that he didn't want her as much as he wanted his business? Now she found a man who was devoted to her, who worshipped her, and she felt threatened by it. How confusing.

She was quiet for a moment as she contemplated a line under her eyes. Then she sighed and dipped her finger into a skin cream.

'Oh Leigh,' she said as she worked on herself and looked in the mirror, 'I'm afraid you'll have to come home weekends from Winterhaven more often than I had anticipated. Tony wants to go on skiing weekends and take little honeymoons frequently. He expects me to fly off with him for three days here and three days there. Such a vigorous pace will age me.'

She turned to me again and took my hands again.

'You'll help me, won't you? You'll spend time with him, too, and keep him distracted. A young girl has so much more energy. Maybe you'll be able to tire him out so that he won't come at me like some kind of Casanova at night. Oh please, Leigh, say you will.'

I didn't know what to say. What was I agreeing to do? But I saw how much she wanted me to say yes.

'I will, Momma. I'll come home often.'

'Thank you, Leigh. Thank you. I knew you were old enough to understand.' She hugged me quickly. 'It's so wonderful having a daughter old enough to be more like a sister to me.

'Now let me show you all the things I bought in Europe. I bought you some pretty sweaters, too. Did you like your Christmas presents?' she asked without taking a breath.

'I saw that your father sent you something. What was it?' she demanded, her eyes narrowing and filled with suspicion.

'This locket,' I said and held it out. She glanced at it quickly. She didn't ask me to open it.

'Very nice,' she said and turned to all the things she had brought back from Europe.

Troy continued to improve and was a great deal better the following day. I accompanied Tony one more time to visit him before I began my schooling at Winterhaven. Momma was true to all her vows. Beauty had become her religion; she worshipped her own image in the mirror and she proceeded with a new frenzy to win back the vitality she claimed she had lost on her honeymoon. Not only did she refuse to go to the hospital, but she began to rise later and later every morning, and then she spent hours at her vanity table before descending the stairs to have breakfast and meet people.

I saw that Tony grew more and more upset about her, charging up the stairs in the morning to get her to come down and join us for breakfast, and then returning, his face long, his eyes drooping with defeat. Then, the night before I was to begin my session at Winterhaven, I heard them have their first spat. I didn't mean to eavesdrop, but I was on my way to speak to Momma about the wardrobe I was to take to school. It was a little after nine o'clock in the evening, but Momma had already gone up to her suite to rest and read one of her romance novels, something she was doing more and more of lately. I had just entered the sitting room when I heard Tony say, 'We might as well not be married.' I froze in my steps. He wasn't yelling so much as he was pleading.

'I won't have you threaten my health with your lust,' Momma replied.

'But Jillian, making love doesn't diminish your health. If anything, you should feel more complete, more fulfilled as a woman.'

'Rubbish! That's something only a man would dream of saying. Honestly, Tony, you're behaving like a school boy who has just discovered sex. I'm disappointed in your lack of self-control.'

'Lack of self-control!' Tony thundered. 'You were too tired mid-way into our honeymoon, and every day after that you found one excuse or another, and now we've been home three nights, and you still haven't the strength to make love and I'm accused of a lack of self-control?'

'Lower your voice, please. Do you want the servants to hear this?' Momma hissed. 'I told you,' she said in a softer tone, 'I just need a little more time. Please, Tony, please be understanding. Sleep in your own room tonight again. Maybe tomorrow . . .'

'I fear that tomorrow you'll have another excuse,' he said in a tone of defeat. 'I don't know what you're saving it for,' he suddenly snapped. 'Or do you expect to have another, even younger husband some day?'

Before I could turn to leave, he came storming out of Momma's bedroom. He stopped when he saw me standing there, my eyes big. His face softened some, but he said nothing. He simply continued to leave. I waited a few minutes and then went in to discuss my wardrobe with Momma, pretending I hadn't heard anything.

'Remember your promise to me, Leigh,' she said before I left. 'You'll come home as much as you can and spend as much time with Tony as you can. I need help, at least during these early days of my new marriage.'

'But Momma, he won't want to spend his time with me. He married you; he'll want to be with you.'

'He just needs companionship. You'll see. Oh dear,' she said gazing at herself in the mirror. 'All this tension has put bags under my eyes.'

I saw no bags.

'I must get a good night's rest. Sleep well, dear, and have a good first day at your new school.'

'But aren't you coming along, too?' My heart began to race with fear.

'Please, Leigh. You don't need me. Tony's taking care of everything, just as he promised. He'll take you and talk to the headmistress and see that you're comfortable and secure. Then he's going off to his offices. It will work out fine.'

'But . . .'

'I must get some rest,' she snapped off her reading light. 'Good night, Leigh.'

I swung my eyes away quickly, disgusted, angry, angrier than Tony perhaps. I knew why she didn't want to come along. She didn't want the world to know she had a daughter as old as I was. She wanted to continue this charade of youth. She was so determined I would be like a sister to her that in her mind I was her sister, not her daughter. She wouldn't do the things other mothers did; not if she could help it. At this moment I despised her, despised her for everything – for the pain and suffering she brought to Daddy and to me with the divorce, for being so self-centered, and for lying to me all these years. I was so angry, I couldn't fall asleep for the longest time.

When I opened my eyes, I found Tony standing at my bedside staring down at me, smiling. He looked as if he had been standing there for quite a while. I had tossed and turned throughout the night, and my blanket was wrapped around my waist. My nightgown hung low, nearly exposing my breasts to his view.

'Good morning,' he said. 'Didn't mean to startle you, but I could tell you hadn't risen yet, and we have to keep to a schedule this morning. I want to start in about an hour, okay?'

I nodded quickly, pulling the blanket to my chin.

'I'll have Miles come up and get your bags in twenty minutes. See you at breakfast,' he added and left.

I rose quickly, showered and dressed. On my way down to breakfast, I saw that Momma's doors were still shut tight. I didn't bother to go in to say goodbye.

ELEVEN

Winterhaven

It was a clear morning when we set out for Boston and my new school, but the soft blue sky was deceptive because when I stepped out of the mansion, the air was so cold, I felt as if I had stepped into a refrigerator. The bright sunlight reflecting off the hard-packed snow made me squint. Tony laughed at my grimace and gave me his sunglasses.

'Here. Put these on. I have another pair in the limo,' he said.

'But these are a man's sunglasses.'

'No, I got them in Europe. They're unisex, and very expensive, I might add. Your mother bought two pairs, although I don't know when she will use them. She hasn't been out of the house since our return,' he muttered and gestured for me to go in to the car ahead of him. There was a *Wall Street Journal* and a thick folder of papers on the seat. 'I usually read and work on my way into town,' he explained. 'But I'll put all that aside today since I have such pretty company.'

I looked away quickly. I knew he was trying to be nice because he had seen how upset I was about Momma's not coming along, but I wasn't feeling pretty, nor was I in a good mood. I felt trapped, forced to go to places I didn't want to go to and do things I didn't want to do, all because it was what made Momma happy. She seemed always to get what she wanted, and without any of the accompanying hardships or efforts. She was upstairs, comfortably in bed.

'You're going to love Winterhaven,' he said as Miles drove off. 'The main building used to be a church and the bell tower is still there. It chimes for each passing hour, and at twilight, they play melodies.

'All the buildings have names and form a half circle. There's an underground passageway that connects the five buildings. Students use it when snow makes walking difficult. You'll be staying in the main building, Beecham Hall. It houses the dorms and the dining rooms, and the assemblies are held there as well.'

'If it's an all-girls school, how do you know so much about it, Tony?' I asked sharply. I didn't mean to take my anger out on him, but I couldn't help myself. He smiled and gazed out his window for a long moment. I thought he wasn't going to explain, but then he turned back to me, his eyes glassy.

'I used to know a girl who went there,' he replied softly.

'Oh? Was she a girlfriend?' I asked petulantly. He either ignored or didn't hear my irritable, sarcastic tone. His smile widened and he nodded.

'Yes. She was a very pretty, very sweet girl . . . almost angelic, I thought. She was never unhappy, but she had so much compassion and love in her that she cried if she heard a mouse had been caught in a trap.' His eyes grew dreamier and dreamier as he recalled more and more about her. 'She had a soft voice and a small, perfect heart-shaped face. She was childlike, innocent and very gentle. No matter how sad or depressed I was when I saw her, in minutes I felt happy and alive again.'

'What happened to her?' I wondered why he hadn't married such a wonderful person.

'She was killed in a car accident in Europe while on holiday with her parents . . . one of those treacherous mountain roads. I really knew her only a short while, but . . . anyway,' he said quickly, 'she attended Winterhaven, and I would meet her there, so I got to know it well.

'Actually, Jillian reminded me a lot of her. She has that same perfect face, that same soft look, a look artists seek. You have it too, Leigh,' he added turning back to me quickly.

'Me? No, I don't look that much like Momma. My eyes are too close together and my nose is so much bigger.'

'Nonsense,' he insisted. 'You are too modest. Some of it should rub off on your mother,' he said with surprising bitterness. 'She's driving me mad, you know. But,' he said quickly, 'that's my problem. Today, we must see to your happiness and your well-being.' He settled back to enjoy the ride.

Was I being too modest? Was I really becoming pretty or was Tony just saying it to cheer me up? Beside Daddy, no other man really complimented me so lavishly. Was that because I was still young or was it because only daddies and step-fathers would say such things to me? Certainly my hair was becoming as rich and as soft as Momma's, and we had the same color eyes. Was it wrong for me to hope I would be as beautiful, even more beautiful?

'There,' Tony said, pointing when we approached the school, 'see what I mean?'

Winterhaven certainly had an elegant and special look to it. It was nestled snugly in its own small campus of bare winter trees with evergreens relieving the bleakness. The main building was white clapboard, gleaming in the early morning sunshine. I had expected a stone building, or one of brick.

As soon as we arrived, a man from the school came out to collect my luggage and wheel it away on a cart. Tony gestured toward the administrative offices. He saw the look of trepidation on my face. It was a new school with new teachers and new friends to make. I couldn't help being nervous. This was the time a girl needed her mother beside her to comfort her, but mine was probably still in bed, her face covered with overnight creams, I thought disdainfully.

'Don't look so frightened. You'll do fine here. I saw your school grades, and as for making friends, all the girls in this place will trip over themselves trying to get you to be their companions. Except for those who will be terribly jealous and angry that the new girl is so pretty,' he added. His smile gave me strength to climb the steps.

I was surprised by what I found. I had expected something like a posh hotel lobby, but what I saw looked very austere. It was very clean, with highly waxed hardwood floors. The walls were off-white, and the moldings were elaborate and darkly stained. Potted ferns and other household plants were scattered here and there on tables and beside straight-backed, hard-looking chairs to relieve the starkness of the white walls. From the foyer I could see the reception room that was a bit cozier, with its fireplace and carefully arranged chintz-covered sofas and chairs.

Tony led me to the office of the headmistress, Miss Mallory, a stout, affable woman who shone on both of us a wide, warm smile.

'Welcome to Winterhaven, Miss VanVoreen,' she said. 'It's a privilege to have the daughter of the owner of the country's most famous luxury ocean liners attending our school.' She kept smiling at Tony. I estimated her to be in her late twenties, perhaps young for her position, although her high-pitched voice and granny glasses made her seem much older. She had her dark brown hair pinned tightly into a bun and wore no make-up, not even lipstick. She seemed a bit insecure, but from the way Momma had described Tony's influence with the school, I imagined he could have an effect on her future. Tuition at the school was expensive, but it still depended heavily on the contributions rich people like Tony made.

'I know Mr Tatterton is a busy man, so let's move quickly. I imagine he wants to see your living quarters,' she said smiling again at Tony. 'I'll show you your dormitory room myself,' she said, 'and afterward, you and I can get to know each other a lot better when I describe your program to you. I planned it for you personally,' she added, raising her eyebrows to impress Tony. He didn't change expression.

'Right this way,' Miss Mallory said, gesturing. 'I've asked your roommate, Jennifer Longstone, to remain in your room this morning rather than attend class, just so I could introduce you to each other.' She turned to Tony. 'Of course, I don't do such a thing with everyone. And of course,' she said turning back to me, 'if there is any problem between you and Jennifer, anything at all, don't hesitate to tell me and I'll move you to other living quarters.' She smiled again at Tony and led us down the long corridor that connected the administrative offices with the dormitory.

There were a number of bulletin boards along the way, and although most of them were taken up with club announcements and reminders about tests and such, there were also a number of reminders about dorm regulations prohibiting hoarding of food in rooms, forbidding liquor, including beer and wine. Study hour was from seven to eight and after eight, students could go into the recreation room to watch television or play board and card games until curfew, but any form of gambling was prohibited. None of the students were permitted television sets in their rooms and the loud playing of music was forbidden. Of course, smoking was off limits everywhere.

I saw that every prohibition carried the threat of demerits with it. Miss Mallory observed the way I read the bulletin boards as we passed them.

'Yes, you see we have very strict rules at Winterhaven,' she told me. 'We are proud of our girls, proud of their demeanor and their exemplary behavior. Once in a while, we have a problem, but we take care of it quickly. If someone does prove to be incorrigible, the demerit system will terminate her stay here.

'For obvious reasons,' she continued, 'we expect you to be prompt for all your classes and do all your assignments on time, as well as be on time for all meals. A table has been assigned to you, and you are not permitted to change your seating unless the occupants at another table invite you to join them. You can, of course, invite someone to join you as well. Each student is expected to wait at table for one week each semester. We rotate the service, and most students find it not unpleasant.

'But,' she added, stopping at a door, 'I'm sure a girl of your class and breeding won't have any difficulty with any of this.' She flashed a smile at Tony and opened the door.

I was surprised at the plainness of the room because I had expected that girls from such rich and well-known families would have luxurious quarters. Also, the room was much smaller than I had anticipated. The floors were polished hardwood with scatter rugs set down beside the simple, light maple-frame single beds. There were two matching dressers side by side at the center, between the beds. In the corners were two desks with lamps and above them and to the side of each were dark pine shelves. There was a bowl-shaped light fixture at the center of the ceiling. The walls were the same off-white with the darkly stained molding found in the lobby of the building. Behind the headboard of each bed were two panel windows, each with a pale yellow shade and thin eggshell white curtains.

Jennifer Longstone was seated at her desk in the right corner. She stood up immediately and smiled. She was at least three inches shorter than me, with a round face and big dark eyes and what I thought was beautiful black hair. I liked her smile and the way her pug nose twitched. She wore a white blouse and a blue skirt with saddle shoes and bobby sox.

'Jennifer,' Miss Mallory said, 'this is Leigh VanVoreen and her step-father, Anthony Tatterton.'

'Pleased to meet you,' Jennifer said and extended her hand first to Tony and then to me under Miss Mallory's scrutinizing eyes.

'Jennifer is in all of your classes,' Miss Mallory continued. 'I thought you two would like that. Jennifer will show you around after you settle in and then you will report to my office to discuss your schedule. Jennifer, you can then resume your own schedule.'

'Yes, Miss Mallory,' Jennifer replied, but there was a gleam in her eye when she looked at me. I liked her immediately.

'Mr Tatterton,' Miss Mallory said. 'I hope this meets with your satisfaction.'

'Well, it's really Leigh who has to be satisfied,' Tony said gazing at me with his characteristic smile.

'I'm all right,' I said.

'Well, then,' Miss Mallory said. 'We'll leave you two to get acquainted. As soon as you've completed your tour, Leigh, please report to me promptly.'

'Yes, ma'am.'

'I'll see you on the weekend,' Tony said. 'Call if you need anything, however, for I am in town every day.'

'Thank you, Tony, and give my love to Troy.'

'I will.' He kissed me quickly on the forehead and followed Miss Mallory out. Jennifer didn't move or say a word until the door closed. Then she exploded with an energy that overwhelmed and amused me.

'Hi. I'm so glad to have a roommate. Your name's Leigh?

I'm from Hyannisport. Have you ever been there? Oh, of course, you must have been there. Or at least driven through it. Do you want me to help you unpack your things? This is your dresser and closet, but if you need more room, you can use some of my closet. There's room. That was your step-father? He's so handsome. How old is he?' She paused to take a breath and I laughed.

'Oh, I'm talking too much. I'm sorry. You probably have a thousand questions for me. Go ahead, ask away,' she said folding her arms and standing back.

'How long have you been at Winterhaven?'

'All my life. No, I'm joking. Three years. It's a junior and senior high school, you know. I'm sentenced to spend it all here. Where did you go to school before?'

'In Boston at a public school.'

'Public school! You lucky one – classes with boys in them and boys in the hallways and in the cafeteria. Here we see boys only when the high priestess permits a dance.'

'High priestess?'

'Miss Mallory. You know she's only twenty-six, but Ellen Stevens told me she heard that Miss Mallory has taken a vow like a nun, dedicating herself to education. She will never marry. She lives here and never has a date!'

'Ellen Stevens?'

'Yes. Oh, you'll meet everyone at lunch. We have the best table in the junior high wing. There's Ellen and Marie Johnson, whose daddy makes all those automobile tools, and Betsy Edwards, whose father runs the Boston Opera House, and Carla Reeve, whose . . .'

'Is everyone known by what their father does?' I interrupted. It took the wind out of the sails of her excitement.

'Oh, I'm sorry. I just thought you'd like to know. At least, most girls who come here want to know those things.'

'Well I don't,' I said sharply. Her face sagged. 'All right,' I said, 'what does your daddy do?'

'He was a lawyer, one of the best in New England,' she said proudly. And then her smile turned as fragile as paper-thin glass. 'But he died last year.'

'Oh, I'm sorry.'

'I suppose that's why I brag about everyone's fathers.' She dropped her eyes and then raised them quickly as a new thought reinstated her enthusiastic mood. 'But how come you have a step-father and one so young?' I was sure she thought my father had died too and we had much more in common than just our ages and classes.

'My mother divorced my father,' I blurted. I didn't see the point of hiding it. Eventually, everyone would find out anyway. Her eyes widened.

'How sad,' she said. 'Is it hard for you to see your real father?'

'Yes. He works a lot. He runs an ocean liner business. But, he's going to come here to see me this week,' I added, not hiding my happiness and excitement. 'He'll take me to dinner.'

'That's nice,' she said. 'My daddy used to do that,' she added wistfully.

'Not this time, because it's the first time I'll see him in a while, but maybe next time, I'll take you along, if you'd like.'

'Really! I'd love it. And I won't say anything stupid or embarrassing. You'll tell me what to say and what not to. And I won't tell any of the other girls anything you tell me about it. I promise, cross my heart, pinky promise,' she said extending her pinky. I had to laugh.

'All right, I'll tell you some of it, but first, let's get my things put away, before the high priestess comes looking for me.'

Jennifer squealed with delight and hugged me. In just a few minutes she drove away the troubled thoughts that had crowded into the darkest corners of my brain. I knew it was the beginning of a great friendship.

Jennifer gave me the tour, showing me the cafeteria, the assembly hall, the underground tunnels and gymnasium. Then she told me the quickest way to get to each of my classes.

'Our teachers usually make a big thing of students being late to class, so watch out for that, otherwise . . .' She ran her right forefinger across the base of her neck. 'It's a meeting with the high priestess and one of her long lectures about decorum and the need for discipline and order. Ugh.'

'You've had a few, I gather?'

'A few,' she confessed, 'but she's been nice to me ever since . . . ever since,' she added. It was enough. I understood. 'You'd better go to see her now. I've got to make science class. Then we have lunch and you'll meet everyone.'

'Thank you, Jennifer.'

She shrugged.

'Glad you're here. You're my first roommate.'

'Really? But I thought you said you've been here for three years.'

'Just the way the cookie crumbled,' she said and went off to make her class. She was definitely what Grandma Jana would call 'a fresh drink of water'. I hurried back to Miss Mallory's office to get my schedule and first lecture. Now that Tony was no longer present, there was a distinct change in her attitude. She was far more formal and her expression lost its softness. With hard-eyed calculations, she looked me over, weighed me, measured me, guessed at my character, my weaknesses, my strengths.

'When the bell rings at seven each weekday morning, you are to rise and dress as quickly as possible. Breakfast is at seven-thirty, so there is little time to dilly-dally over make-up and hair.

'I must tell you, we don't play any favorites here. You will have to earn the respect of your teachers and your classmates.

'Most importantly, at Winterhaven, we don't flaunt our wealth. I hope you keep this in mind. As I told you earlier, I am very proud of my girls, proud of this school, proud of what it has come to mean.

'I'm sure you will be an asset,' she finally added. 'Well, I see it's just about time for lunch, so you might as well go directly to the cafeteria. Come by if you have any questions or problems. My door is always open.'

'Thank you, Miss Mallory,' I said and left quickly.

The moment I entered the cafeteria Jennifer stood up and beckoned. Our table was the farthest to the right, near the big windows, so we had a view of the front of the school. I hurried over. Jennifer had my seat saved right beside hers.

'Hi,' I said. All the girls studied me just the way I would study a new girl who entered my old school – checking my clothing, my looks, the way I wore my hair. I was sure, however, that Jennifer had filled them in on some things already.

'I'll introduce everyone,' Jennifer declared. 'Leigh, this is Ellen Stevens, Toby Krantz, Wendy Cooper, Carla Reeve, Betsy Edwards, and Marie Johnson.' All the girls nodded and said 'Hi'. I thought Marie Johnson was the prettiest and I understood she was the leader of the group.

'How was your meeting with the high priestess?' Jennifer asked.

'All right,' I said. 'She gave me my schedule.' I held it out and Jennifer confirmed we shared all our classes. Some of the other girls were in some as well.

'Didn't she tell you how distinguished and respectable Winterhaven is and how we are all model citizens?' Marie asked, batting her eyelashes. The other girls tittered. I nodded, laughing myself. 'Well we are when we want to be,' Marie continued looking sly, 'when it suits us.'

'You better get your food fast,' she told me. 'We don't have all that much time for lunch.'

I went off to the lunch line. The food was a lot better than what I was used to at my old school. At least one thing reflected the cost, I thought.

'Jennifer told us your step-father's name,' Ellen Stevens said when I sat back down. 'Does he have anything to do with Tatterton Toys?'

'He is Tatterton Toys,' I said, surprising myself at how proud I sounded.

'I knew it,' Carla Reeve chirped. 'My mother knows him. We have three Tatterton collectibles.'

'Really?'

'Is he as good-looking as Jennifer claims?' Marie asked, her eyes narrowing. She had a much more mature look than any of the others.

'He's very good-looking, otherwise Momma wouldn't have

married him,' I said, not meaning to sound as snobby as I did.

'Momma?' Betsy said. Marie flashed a sharp look at her and she wiped the smirk off her face. Then she turned to me.

'You're lucky,' she said. 'You're sitting with the best group of girls in the junior high wing. We have our own special club. We stick together. I'm having a party in my room tonight after curfew. You can come.'

'But what about the rules?'

'What about them? Don't tell me you believe the things the high priestess told you. She's fast asleep herself by nine o'clock and as far as Mrs Thorndyke, our dorm mother goes, you could explode a bomb at her door and she won't stop snoring.'

Everyone laughed.

'Don't worry,' Jennifer said. 'I'll bring you with me.'

I had just enough time to finish eating before the bell rang and I was off to my first class. School anywhere was more or less the same, I soon found out. Pages to read, questions to copy from the blackboard. I didn't have as much to catch up on as I had feared I would. The teachers were nice about it, asking me to describe the classes I had had at my old school and then taking the time to show me what I should study and review. Because our classes were small, there was a great deal more individual attention than I had in the public school.

That evening, when Jennifer and I went to the cafeteria for dinner, there was a rose on the table at my seat. The girls were all chattering about it when we arrived.

'What's that?' Jennifer asked excitedly.

'It's for Leigh,' Wendy said enviously.

'For me?' I looked at the card, which I was sure they had read already. It said, 'Good luck, Tony'. 'It's from my step-father,' I explained.

'How thoughtful!' Jennifer exclaimed.

'How romantic,' Marie said and gazed at me with a twinkle in her eye. 'Why isn't your mother's name on it as well?' All the girls turned to me to hear my reply.

'I imagine he thought of it at the spur of the moment,' I said. 'And ordered it from his Boston office.'

Marie smiled at the others and all of them, except Jennifer, giggled.

'Why is that funny?' No one said anything, but I saw them look at Marie.

'I would have thought he would sign it "Daddy", Marie said.

'But he's not my daddy. My father is not dead. My parents are divorced,' I announced. I was glad Jennifer had not gossiped, but each of the girls stared at me with lips agape, as if I were a ghost, a ghost of bad taste. All of them came from wealthy, upper class families, families concerned about their lineage. Some had proof their ancestors came over on the *Mayflower*. Divorces weren't tolerated.

When Jennifer and I returned with our trays of food, we found the conversation at the table more subdued. I could see from the looks on the faces of the other girls that they had been discussing me. The warm greeting I had received at lunch chilled. The girls began to argue about what kind of make-up they liked the best. When I started to offer an opinion, no one but Jennifer seemed to be listening.

After dinner we were all supposed to begin our study hour. As the girls rose to leave, Marie leaned over to me.

'I'm cancelling my party tonight,' she said. 'I forgot I have a science test tomorrow.'

I just nodded and watched her join the others.

'She's not cancelling her party,' I told Jennifer. 'They don't want to associate with me because my parents are divorced.'

'Don't worry,' Jennifer whispered as we started out after them, 'they'll get over it.'

'I don't care if they do or they don't,' I said, but in my secret, putaway heart, I was crying. Why did Momma want me to go to school in a place filled with blue-bloods who walked with their noses so high, you couldn't see their eyes? None of them, except Jennifer, would want to invite me to their homes, I thought. Why was I being punished for the things Momma did? Would people always blame me? I shuddered to think of what these girls would do if they knew the truth about my birth.

I wanted to be back home in Boston more than ever, and go to my old school, where my real friends would feel sorry for me, not think me a leper. Now, at a time in my life when I needed friends more than ever, I was thrown in with these spoiled, wealthy girls. I wanted to run away. I even thought about how I would do it. I would go to live with Daddy, even though he was always traveling. Anything would be better than this.

Jennifer was very sweet though and made every effort to cheer me up. We worked diligently on our school assignments, but spent a lot of time talking about fashion and music and boys. Like me, she had never really had a boyfriend, but there was a boy she liked who attended Allendale, an all-boys prep school that occasionally had dances with Winterhaven.

Recreation hour was well underway when we left our room to go watch television, but when we arrived, we didn't find any of the girls from our table, or what Marie had called the 'special club'.

'They're all in her room, having their party. You should go. I don't mean to spoil anything for you, Jennifer,' I said.

'I don't want to go, not if you're not invited,' she replied. 'Besides, they're being horrible. I'm surprised at them, not that they've always been that nice to me.'

'I hate hypocrites,' I declared and something proud sprung into my spine. Jennifer saw the flames of anger in my face.

'What?' she asked, holding her breath.

'Let's go,' I commanded and marched out of the recreation room.

'Where?' Jennifer called, following.

'To Marie's room,' I snapped, not pausing a step.

'But . . . it's so embarrassing. Shouldn't we just ignore them? I mean . . .'

'Jennifer Longstone, I'm tired of ignoring things that make me unhappy. If I am going to attend this school, I am going to be accepted for who and what I am, and none of these snooty girls are going to make me suffer.'

'Lead the way,' Jennifer said. 'It's the last room on the right down the corridor.'

We tramped forward. Aggressively, no longer willing to play humble and helpless, a victim of this or that, I held my head high and proud as we approached Marie's door. We could hear the music, 'Rock Around the Clock'. I pounded on the door. The phonograph was lowered and there was some whispering. Then Marie opened her door.

'Just thought I'd come by and help you study for your science test,' I said. I walked past her. A deadly quiet descended, while the cigarettes burned. The room was full of smoke. Ellen and Wendy were sitting on the floor drinking Cokes, and Carla, Toby and Betsy were on the beds with fashion and fan magazines. For a moment, no one said anything. Then I spun on Marie.

'I'm sorry for how you all feel about my parents getting a divorce, but it's stupid for you to blame it on me and to make Jennifer suffer, too, just because she's my roommate. I had hoped we could all start out as friends. I'm sure no one here is perfect or has a perfect past,' I stated with fire.

'Anyway, I just wanted you all to know you didn't fool anyone. Come on, Jennifer.'

'Wait,' Marie said. She glanced quickly at the other girls. 'You're right. It wasn't a nice thing to do.'

I looked at the other girls. All of them lowered their eyes.

'Anyway, you're here; you might as well stay,' Marie said, flashing a smile.

'Well, I . . .'

'Please,' Marie said. 'Want a cigarette?'

'I never have,' I said staring at them.

'Good a time as any to start,' Marie said. 'Quick, Jen, close the door before old Thorndyke comes by. Ellen, put the record back on,' she commanded.

'Welcome to our special club,' Marie said. 'Anyway with your temper, I'd rather have you on our side. Right, girls?' Everyone laughed. I looked at Jennifer. She was smiling widely, too.

We remained until nearly eleven, talking about school and about music and movies. No one dared ask me any questions about my parents, although Betsy Edwards remembered now that she and her family had once taken a cruise on a VanVoreen ship. I told them about my trip to Jamaica and then we all snuck back to our own rooms.

Jennifer and I lay in bed talking until after twelve. She told me about the day her father died and how empty and alone she had felt. It sounded a lot like I felt the day I learned my parents would divorce. Finally, I couldn't keep my eyes open any longer.

'I've got to go to sleep, Jen.'

'That's all right. I'm tired, too.'

'Good night, Jennifer.'

'Good night, Leigh.' She giggled.

'What?'

'You were so great, the way you pounded on Marie's door and told them all off. I wish I had had the courage to do that before. How did you get so brave?'

'I'm not,' I insisted.

'Oh yes, you are,' Jennifer said. 'You're the bravest girl I know and I'm so happy you're my roommate. Welcome to Winterhaven, Leigh.'

'Thank you, Jen. Good night,' I said again and closed my eyes, exhausted from the turmoil and the effort it took to be happy and safe in a world that could be so mean and cold.

The next day Miss Mallory came to the cafeteria during lunch to find me.

'Mr Tatterton is here, my dear,' she announced, smiling at me in a tight way. 'He's in my office and wishes to speak with you.'

'Is anything wrong?' My heart raced with fear for little Troy.

'Oh, I am sure not,' she said.

When I looked at the others, they were all hiding smiles and containing their laughter.

'Thank you,' I said and followed her out of the cafeteria.

'Please,' Miss Mallory said, 'use my office as long as you wish.' She left Tony and me alone. He was sitting on the leather chair near the desk and looked very distinguished in his double-breasted dark blue suit.

'Is everything all right?' he asked, his gaze steady.

'Yes, fine. How's Troy?'

'He's doing much, much better. I think we'll be able to bring him home in a week or so.'

'That's wonderful, Tony.' I shifted my eyes for a moment because he was still gazing at me so intensely. 'How's Momma?'

'The same,' he said with a sigh. 'Now she's on a new diet . . . lunch consists of a little champagne and cucumber sandwiches. Oh, and she's taking up bridge.'

'Bridge?'

'Yes. Seems the women she admires all play bridge. I'm paying someone to give her instructions and teach her all the fine points,' he said, crossing his legs and meticulously running his fingers down the sharp crease of his trouser leg. He had long, strong fingers and his nails shone.

'So,' he said, 'there's nothing you need? Clothes, school supplies, spending money . . . anything?'

'No,' I said, but I wanted to say *Yes, I need Momma to show some interest in what happens to me too*.

'Okay,' he said, standing. 'Perhaps, I can come by one evening and take you out to dinner before I return to Farthy. Would you like that?'

'Not this week,' I replied quickly. 'Daddy's calling and coming to take me out to dinner.'

'Oh.' His lip curled a bit. Although he tried to keep his blue eyes calm and unreadable, I saw that he wasn't used to being rejected. A man of his wealth and power rarely was.

'Maybe next week,' I added and his eyes brightened again.

'Fine. In any case, I'll be by about five o'clock on Friday to pick you up in the limo. Enjoy your dinner with your father.' He kissed me on the forehead quickly before he opened the office door to leave.

When I returned to the cafeteria, I found 'the special club' all gathered at the window gazing out at Tony, who was standing by his limousine, talking to Miss Mallory. They were all sighing and whispering. As soon as they saw me, they returned to the table.

'He's so handsome,' Ellen said. 'For once, Jennifer didn't exaggerate.'

'When do we all get invited to Farthinggale Manor?' Marie asked, and all of them chimed in excitedly. I told them as soon as I thought the timing was right, I'd have them all over for a weekend pajama party. Suddenly, I was the most popular girl in Winterhaven.

Daddy called on Wednesday and arrived on Thursday to take me to dinner. As soon as I was told he had arrived, I rushed down the corridor and into his waiting arms. He laughed and gave me a big kiss. Then he held me out to look at me.

'You're growing so fast, I hardly recognize you,' he said. 'I'm glad you're in an all-girls school,' he added, looking around and nodding, 'otherwise, so many boys would be following you around I'd have to beat them off with a stick.'

'Oh Daddy.'

'Come along,' he said holding out his arm for me to slip mine through, 'I want to hear all about your new school and new friends and everything that's happened to you since we last spoke.'

He led me out to his waiting cab and we were off to dinner at an elegant restaurant. As I told him everything, he listened attentively, his eyes fixed on me as though he were trying to drink me in, memorize my face. I talked and talked, so excited that he was really here and I was really with him. His expression didn't change until I mentioned the honeymoon. Then his eyes grew smaller and his mouth tighter. He shifted his gaze and became very pensive for a few moments.

An alarm went off in my heart because I sensed that he had something to tell me that would make me unhappy. My teeth came down on my lower lip as I waited for his words. Sadness had rained down on me so often these last few months that I had become an expert about predicting when it would fall again. Finally, he turned back to me, his smile softer, but weaker.

'I know that you are not happy, Leigh, and that your mother has taken you away from many of the things you loved and put you in a strange new world filled with impersonal, cold people who care only about their own comfort and wealth. I deal with the wealthy and influential on a day-to-day basis, so I know how insensitive and selfish they can be. Their money blinds them, keeps them protected and away from reality, permits them to live their illusions.

'I am sorry that all this has happened to you while you are still rather young and impressionable, and just when I am struggling to keep my business alive. Don't think it hasn't torn me apart to be away from you when you need me, too.

'My one solace is that you are bright and firm, that you come from good stock, for the VanVoreens were hardy people who overcame insurmountable odds to build their lives. We are no strangers to hardships and we have not grown soft with success. At least, you have inherited that.'

Oh how I struggled with myself, one part of me demanding I tell him the truth, what I had overheard Grandma Jana say to Momma and what she had admitted, and another part of me screaming not to hurt him any more than he has been hurt. Also, I was terrified of what the truth might do to his love for me. What if he stopped thinking of me as his daughter? Would he stop loving me? If he did I knew I would never survive, that it would be the last and worst blow of all I had received in the past several months. I could only smile and nod and reach across the table to take his hand into mine and reassure him that I would be his daughter, a true VanVoreen.

'Anyway,' he said, coming to the bad news, 'I have to tell you that I won't be able to see you for a while. I am opening an office in Europe to try to capture the growing European market for travelers who want to come not only to America, but to travel to the vacation spots I have been establishing with my travel experts.

'It's a mistake, you see, to think that only Americans have money and opportunity for luxurious vacations.'

'What do you mean you won't see me for a while, Daddy? How long?'

'I won't be back until the summer at the soonest,' he confessed. 'But as soon as I do return, we'll spend as much time together as you want. I promise.'

A lump came to choke my throat. The tears I trapped in the

corners of my eyes burned with their demand to break free and stream down my cheeks. How could I stand it if Daddy, my rock, was gone for so long. With Momma becoming so very self-centered and unreliable, to whom could I go to for advice, for love, for the warmth of hugs and kisses? I forced myself to be the strong little girl he wanted, to be the VanVoreen descendant he believed I was.

'I'll keep writing you letters, of course,' he said quickly, 'and hope you'll keep writing letters to me.'

'I will, Daddy.'

'And as soon as I know when I will return, I will make arrangements for you to meet me.' He patted my hand.

We rode back to Winterhaven sitting very close to each other in the back of the taxi, Daddy's arm around me. I listened to him tell me about his travels, the things he had seen and the people he had met, but I didn't hear his words, just the rhythm of his voice.

Instead, I was thinking about the daddy I knew as a little girl, the daddy who had lifted me on his shoulders to carry me along the River Thames when we toured London, the daddy who took me in his arms and danced with me in the ballroom of his ship, the daddy who held my hand and took me about the luxury liners, introducing me to his crews, showing me how things worked, kissing and hugging me and twirling my hair in his fingers when I sat on his lap.

That daddy was gone, I thought, almost as gone as Jennifer Longstone's daddy. We weren't so different, she and I, and when we lay awake at night telling stories about our childhood days, we were both thinking about times we would never see again, moments we would never have, words we would never hear, kisses and smiles that were as thin as smoke, running off into our memories and lost forever in the maze of storm clouds that had come to block out the blue sky of happiness we had both once known.

Daddy kissed me in front of the school. He kissed me goodbye and hugged me to him and told me again that he would write and think of me all the time, but I knew the moment he got into his cab and started away, that his mind was already racing around with the problems of his business. I didn't hate him for it; I knew he was burying himself in his work to keep himself from being unhappy.

Jennifer was waiting in our room. She wanted to hear all the wonderful details about my dinner with Daddy. I knew she wanted to experience the happiness through me and perhaps recall the happy times she had with her own father. So I didn't tell her one sad thing. I went on and on about the restaurant and the food and the promises Daddy had made. I told her about the funny waiter who spoke in a German accent so thick that I ordered the wrong things, but ate them anyway, and they were delicious. It didn't matter because I was with Daddy, I said. Jennifer laughed.

'Thank you for telling me about your dinner, Leigh,' she said. 'Good night.'

'Good night.'

Jennifer curled up with my happy memories and I turned my back to her and cried as softly as I could, until sleep rescued me from harder tears.

TWELVE

More Surprises

All the girls in the 'special club' knew Tony was picking me up on Friday, so they all accompanied me to the front stoop of Winterhaven and crowded about me like hens. I was so embarrassed by what they might do and say that I was down the steps before Tony was out of the car and opening the door.

'See you Sunday night, Leigh!' a chorus of voices sang out. Then, ringing with giggles, they scampered back up the steps and into Beecham Hall.

'Well,' Tony said, smiling at me as we were driven off, 'looks like I was right – you made a lot of friends fast. Did you enjoy the rest of the week here?'

'Yes, Tony, and I like my roommate Jennifer very much. I'd like to invite her to Farthinggale, and the other girls in my group.'

'Anytime,' he replied. 'As long as your mother approves,' he added ominously.

I asked him about Troy.

'He's getting stronger every day. The doctor says we will be able to take him home either Wednesday or Thursday, so he will be at Farthy when you return next weekend,' he told me. I was anxious to see him, but I was also anxious to spend a weekend at the school. The 'special club' went to movies together and shopped together, and some weekends there were mixers, dances organized between Winterhaven and boys' prep schools like Allendale.

When we arrived at Farthy and I entered the big house, I was immediately impressed with the silence, especially without little Troy scampering up and down stairs and through doors, calling my name or calling for Tony. There was barely a footstep echoing through the great rooms – this in contrast to the world I had just left: a school filled with teenage girls laughing and singing, music coming from the rooms, girls chattering together in the hallways, bells ringing, dishes clanging, friends calling to each other through the corridors – a world of energy, noise, young life. Once again, Farthy seemed like a museum, a house of whispers.

'Your mother's probably in her rooms,' Tony said, looking at his watch. 'She's only just returned from a bridge game, I'm sure.'

I ran up the stairs to see Momma. I was filled with mixed emotions – eager to see her since we had been apart a whole week, anxious to tell her about the girls and the things we had said and done; but also angry, angry and hurt that she hadn't once called to see how I was, and still angry that she hadn't come along with Tony and me that first day. Tony was right – she had just returned from a bridge game and was preparing to take a shower and dress for dinner.

'Oh Leigh,' she said as soon as I entered her bedroom. She looked surprised. 'I forgot you were coming home today, forgot today was Friday. Can you imagine? That's how busy I have been this week.' She stood there in her slip, her hair down. Then she smiled and held out her arms, expecting me to run into her embrace. There was an awkward moment, then she lowered her arms to her sides quickly. 'But wait,' she said, 'let me look at you. You look so much more mature, or is that a look of reproach? Are you angry with me for some reason?'

'Momma, how could you not even call me all week? I called you once and left a message with Curtis. He said you were out with friends, shopping, and in Boston! You could have stopped by the school,' I complained.

'Oh Leigh, how would that look – me bringing all these sophisticated women along to visit my daughter who had been away only a few days. They would think I was babying you. And besides, you don't know what it's like going places with these women. They gossip and chatter so much, we barely have time to do anything. I'm the one who's always saying, "Ladies, please, let's move along or we won't get to do this or do that."

They simply adore me, though. They say I'm the freshest, brightest person they've met in ages and ages.

'No, you must not be angry with me,' she insisted. 'It's not that I haven't been thinking about you. I asked Tony to stop by to see you during the week and he did, didn't he?'

'Yes, but it's not the same thing, Momma,' I protested.

'Oh pooh. You're getting to be as stuffy as your father. It's those puritanical VanVoreen genes you've inherited,' she declared. I was so angry I nearly told her what I knew and demanded she stop lying to me.

'And besides, Tony wanted to do it. You've become very important to him, Leigh, which is something I think is wonderful. You can't begin to understand how much easier this has made my life. Please, don't be angry,' she cajoled and then held her arms out for me again.

I wanted to resist; I wanted to talk and talk until she understood how cruel she had been to me, but she wore that same gentle smile I loved to see when I was a little girl, the smile she wore while she brushed my hair and told me about all the wonderful things that would happen to me, the places I would go, the princes I would meet, the world of magic and love that awaited. She had spun my childhood dreams and fantasies on a magical loom and had made the world outside seem nothing but candy canes and rainbows.

I hugged her and let her hold me. She warmed my cheeks with kisses and stroked my hair and part of me hated that it made me happy, but it did. Then she sat me down on her bed beside her to tell me about all the new friends she had made, each one richer than the next, all from well-known families, pure blue bloods.

'Why do you still look so sad?' she asked, suddenly. 'Was it because of your dinner with your father?' Her eyes grew small with suspicion. 'Tony told me he was coming to take you to dinner.'

'No, Momma. Well, yes, that's part of it,' I confessed, and I told her of Daddy's plans to establish a European office and why that meant I wouldn't see much of him.

'It doesn't surprise me, Leigh,' she snapped. 'And don't think he wouldn't have done something like this even if we hadn't divorced. Oh, when I think of the precious time I've wasted, the youth I've wasted!' Her face burned with frustration and anger for a few moments and then she caught her image in the mirror.

'*Oh, I must not let myself frown!*' she cried with such desperation, I actually jumped. 'Do you know, one of the best beauty experts says frowning speeds up wrinkling.' She sounded frantic. 'I've been reading an article he wrote. People with quiet, happy dispositions age far more slowly than people who are always annoyed and upset. The trick is to keep your anger subdued and to quickly think of something pleasant. He compared it to throwing water on a fire.

'The fire burns, consumes your youth and beauty, if you permit it to, so you have to smother, stifle and extinguish it as fast as you can.' She smiled widely as if to demonstrate.

'Now, I must take a warm shower and give myself a facial before dinner. Then you and I will sit down and you will tell me all about Winterhaven, okay?'

My head was spinning from all the different subjects she had covered in minutes. 'But I want to ask you something, Momma. I've already asked Tony and he said it would be fine with him if it would be fine with you.'

'What is it?' She started to grimace as if preparing herself for a horrible question or terrible demand.

'I've made some nice friends at Winterhaven, especially my roommate, Jennifer Longstone. I'd like to invite them here on weekends.'

'On weekends! Oh, not for a while yet, Leigh, please. I can't have you conducting tours of girls through the estate and being occupied with these new friends. I need you to help me occupy Tony. He wants to teach you how to horseback ride and ski. He told me so himself, and he's looking forward to using the weekends to do it.

'You promised you would help me in this way. You did, Leigh,' she reminded me, her face twisted in a look of urgency. 'I'm sure Tony was only being polite when you asked him. He would much rather have you all to himself, at least for a while.

'And then, we'll let you invite your little friends here one at a time.'

'But Momma, there's so much room. We can have more than one at a time!' I exclaimed.

'We'll see. I'm sure they're all nice and proper girls if they go to Winterhaven,' she added and started for the shower. 'But please, Leigh, no more difficulties. I'm absolutely drained,' she said and followed it with a trail of laughter.

And so my first weekend home from Winterhaven began the way most all of these weekends would. Our Friday night dinners were always quite formal, and unless Tony and Momma were invited someplace to have dinner, they usually had friends to join us. None of the couples ever brought their children along, so except for me and Troy when he was well enough to join us at the table, I was always with the adults who talked about things that I had little interest in.

Sometimes Tony had a movie to show in the little theater. A friend of a friend would get him something that was popular. A few times we had a pianist perform in the music room. On those occasions, Tony and Momma would invite a half dozen or more of their friends to dinner and the private concert. Momma said it was not only chic, but it was her way of supporting the arts and the artists who needed the added income to continue their creative work.

Tony and I did go to a nearby ski hill on Saturdays throughout the winter months. He employed a private ski instructor to teach me the fundamentals and before long, I was following him down the intermediate slope. Tony was a magnificent skier who usually took the most difficult runs. We would have lunch in the ski lodge, sitting by the fire.

Momma never came along with us. While we were away, she would go somewhere to play bridge or have her women friends over to play at Farthy. If she didn't play bridge, she would go shopping or to matinees in Boston.

Troy, still weak from his terrible bout with pneumonia, was kept inside most of the time. At Momma's insistence, Tony hired a full-time nurse to look after him, even though he was no longer sick. In late March when he came down with chicken pox, which was then followed with the measles, Momma never stopped reminding Tony and me how clever she was to insist Troy have personal medical attention around the clock.

Being sick more often than he was well left poor little Troy thin and weak. He would look at me with large, sad, sunken eyes staring out of his small pale face when Sundays came and I was to return to Winterhaven, for he knew he was confined to five more days of little company and enjoyment. Momma treated him like a walking germ, avoiding him whenever possible and, I found out when I returned one weekend, having him fed at a different time so she wouldn't have to be at the same table with him.

In the spring he developed new allergies and had to be taken to see a skin specialist and an allergist almost on a weekly basis. First, they thought it was pollen and ragweed, then they thought it had to do with the fabrics in his suite, so Tony had everything changed: rugs, curtains, linens and quilts, but that didn't solve the problem. He still walked about with a running nose and coughed even on the warmest, clearest days. The hope was he would eventually grow out of the allergies, but until then, he was confined and given heavy dosages of various medicines, some taking his appetite away, some making him tired. He slept a lot, remained thin and small, and looked drained and depressed most of the time.

Naturally, he withdrew into himself, spent most of his time playing with the toys Tony bought him and with creating his own toys. A number of his creations were very good and Tony even made one into a Tatterton toy for children Troy's age.

During the spring months Troy and I started horseback riding. He decided to teach me this himself. We would go for rides along the beach and over the dunes. Troy wanted desperately to come along and to ride Sniffles, his pony, but the allergist absolutely forbid his contact with animals. He couldn't have a puppy or a kitten, not even a hamster. It was so sad to see him standing on a hill, holding his nurse's hand and watching Tony and me start off for a ride along the beach, but there was nothing I could do about it.

That winter and spring Momma was the happiest. I was doing

what she wanted – spending most of my weekends with Tony and freeing her to indulge in her own activities. During the week Tony was very busy, and from what I understood listening to him and to her, they often spent whole days without seeing each other. I wondered what had happened to that driving passion, those magnificent magical moments when the world had looked as though it would end unless they broke apart my loving family so that the two of them could be together all the time.

Daddy's postcards and letters came regularly through the winter months and into the spring. Then, around May, I noticed that the next letter was long in coming. Just when I thought it would never come and had begun to fear that something had happened to Daddy, it arrived. In it he mentioned someone new, mentioned her as if I had always known her.

'And today,' he began in his middle paragraph, 'Mildred Pierce and I had lunch on the Champs-Elysées. It was a magnificent day and the street was filled with cars and people and tourists from everywhere, a veritable parade of fashion. It was the first real day off I had taken in ages. We went to museums and I even let her talk me into going to the top of the Eiffel Tower. Mildred is great company.'

Mildred Pierce? I thought. Who was Mildred Pierce? I thumbed through all the letters Daddy had written just to be sure he had never mentioned her before. Was she a secretary, a relative, some well-known person in his business I should have known? It was very confusing, but there was also something in the way Daddy wrote 'Mildred is great company', that made my heart skip a beat.

How old was this Mildred Pierce? Could she be someone's daughter, someone my own age perhaps, someone who was taking his attention from me? I would have so loved to have had lunch with Daddy on the Champs-Elysées and gone to the top of the Eiffel Tower with him, too. It wasn't fair.

And then I thought it was terribly selfish of me to begrudge Daddy this day which he called his first day off in ages. I couldn't wait until his next letter to see if he would mention her again. He didn't, but he did say he thought his return to the States would be delayed a little and he didn't give a reason, but I sensed something between the lines. Momma would have called my feelings feminine intuition. All I knew was that in my heart of hearts I feared being replaced, feared losing the love of my faraway father. I held my breath every time I opened one of Daddy's letters or read one of his postcards after that.

And then it came in early June. Daddy wrote to tell me he would be returning in mid-July. He said he was anxious to see me and he was anxious for me to meet Mildred Pierce.

I could understand why my father would be happy to meet someone to help fill his time. But he wrote so enthusiastically about this person, it made my heart worry and hurt.

'Mildred and I are very compatible. She's interested in the things that interest me and she is a lovely, gentle person. I'm sure you will like her. Being with her is like being able to push away the gray clouds and bring sunshine back into my life.'

But Daddy, I cried inside, I thought I was the one who brought sunshine into your life. Is this really why you stayed away from me so long, why you lingered in Europe? Has someone stolen that part of your heart I thought had been left for me?

And what if this Mildred Pierce doesn't like me or want to be around me, or was jealous of me? Would you have even less to do with me than you do now? I looked at Daddy's photograph on my dresser for a long time before asking the scariest question. 'If Daddy gets a new family, where do I belong?'

One evening at dinner in mid-June, Tony announced his intention to go to Europe on business. Unlike the times when Daddy would make such an announcement, Momma did not become immediately unhappy, complain and pout. She was very understanding and very interested in what he was going to do.

'There's this company in Europe,' he explained, 'that I recently learned about, a company similar to my own, making different sorts of things for the very wealthy classes in Europe. One of the things I'm afraid of is its expansion to the United States. It might steal away our clientele. I want to learn more about them and see first hand what sort of competition might be in store for me.

'Why don't you come along, Jillian? It could be like a second honeymoon. I don't have to spend all my time on business. There's a lot of sightseeing to do.'

'Europe? Now?' Momma groaned. 'It's too hot and the Continent is overrun with tourists. Besides, I told you I think we should consider redoing some of the rooms in Farthy, and you said I could go ahead and meet with my decorators. I'll have to get started on that.'

Tony wasn't happy, but he left for Europe by himself a few days later. Momma seemed relieved, as if a major responsibility had been lifted from her shoulders. She started on the redecorating immediately, having long meetings with decorators, filling the music room with books and books of wallpaper, carpet, and fabric samples, as well as pictures of furniture. She gathered her experts around her like a queen and her entourage and went from room to room discussing, listening to suggestions, making suggestions. She even had them to dinner, where she continued the discussions of fashions, colors and styles into the evening.

The school year ended and all of us in the 'special club' said our goodbyes, promising to write each other as much as possible. I felt terrible about never having invited anyone, even just Jennifer, to Farthy, but each time they had inquired, I had been forced to come up with another good excuse, leaning heavily on Troy's health problem. I knew they were all very disappointed, especially Jennifer, but there was little I could do. Whenever I had brought it up, Momma would go into a panic, sometimes even a rage. It was too soon . . . wait, wait, *wait!* I grew tired of asking.

But a little less than a week after Tony had left for Europe, Momma surprised me by telling me I could invite Jennifer to spend a few days at Farthy. I called her at home and told her. She squealed with delight. It had been only a week since school ended for the year, but we already missed each other terribly.

She was very impressed with Farthy. I took her horseback riding on the beach and we went swimming every day. She loved Troy, who enjoyed showing her about and demonstrating his toys. Unfortunately, he was not permitted to go swimming yet. There was even some question about his being allergic to the chlorine.

Jennifer was fascinated by Momma. She won Momma over immediately when she told her she couldn't believe someone who looked as young as she did had a daughter as old as I was. Momma asked her dozens of questions about her family and her home in Hyannisport at dinner every night. And then Momma made all sorts of suggestions to her about how to wear her hair, what clothes would be most flattering, what color lipstick to wear. Jennifer listened attentively, her eyes big, nodding as if she were sitting with a movie star. Afterward, she couldn't stop talking about how beautiful and sophisticated Momma was.

We sat up in my room until very late every night talking.

'Your mother is so young-looking and beautiful. Was your daddy heartbroken when they got a divorce?' she asked one night.

I recalled Daddy that morning on *The Jillian* when he came to my room to tell me what Momma had decided.

'Yes, but he blamed himself and kept himself as busy as possible so as not to think about it. Momma always said he was married to his business as much as he was married to her,' I added sadly, for I had come to believe that some of that was true.

'I can't imagine your daddy not wanting to throw himself off the ship when he learned he would lose her,' Jennifer said. Then the smile that accompanied this romantic fantasy wilted and she turned away, her eyes filling rapidly with tears.

'What's wrong, Jen?'

'It's my mother,' she said, weeping. 'She's dating another man, a man who was once my daddy's best friend.' She spun around, her eyes wet, but her face on fire. 'I told her I hated him and he would never be my daddy and I hated her for seeing him.'

'What did she say?' I asked, holding my breath.

'She cried and told me she couldn't help it because she was lonely. It wasn't enough that she had me and my sister. She needed a husband.

'But I don't want another man living in my house and using my daddy's things!' she cried. 'I don't, I don't!' She began to sob. I embraced her and held her and then I told her about Daddy and Mildred Pierce. She stopped crying and listened and soon felt sorry for me.

'Oh Leigh,' she said, 'adults are so very selfish. I'll never be like that when I'm their age. Will you?'

'I don't know, Jen. I hope not, but I don't know.' What was the point in making vows and promises? We could swear on a thousand Bibles that we would never betray each other or the people we loved, but Fate seized us in its grip sometimes and made us forget our dreams. I was tempted to tell Jennifer the truth about me, the truth about Momma and what she had done, but I was too ashamed of it. It was a secret that would burn in my heart only, no matter how painful that fire was.

We were both very sad when it came time for her to go home. She asked Momma if I could come visit her and Momma replied, 'We'll see. There is much we have to do here this summer, dear, and Leigh has to help with Troy.'

Help with Troy? I thought. Since when did Momma worry about how Troy was occupied? What she really meant was help with Tony, but she couldn't say that. Oh, once again my Momma's selfishness made her wants come before mine. It was unnatural, I thought, to put me in charge of entertaining *her* new husband.

One day in late June dawned very hot and I had spent most of the afternoon lounging at the pool and reading. Troy and his nurse had been with me for a few hours since the doctor had put Troy on a schedule of sunshine, now that summer was in full swing. I remained at the pool until the sun started to drop behind the trees and cooler long shadows crept up over the patio to cover the lounge chairs and me. I slipped into my robe, put my towel around my neck, and started for the house. When I entered, I heard Momma's and Tony's voices coming from the living room on the right.

'Leigh!' Tony cried as soon as I peeked in. 'I've missed you! Look how tanned you've gotten in only this short time.'

'Hello, Tony. How was your trip?'

'Quite successful,' he said and smiled at Momma. She sat back on the new Charles II ornately carved and caned armchair she had bought as part of redecorating the room. With her pear-shaped diamond earrings dangling, her hair swept back perfectly, not a strand out of place and her fingers covered with emerald, diamond, ruby and sapphire rings, she looked like a queen. She wore a white lace dress with a sweetheart neckline so that her most precious diamond necklace lay softly on top of her rose-tinted bosom.

'Tony has a wonderful new idea,' she proclaimed. 'And he wants you to be a part of it.'

'Me?' I stepped farther into the room.

'Remember I told you about this European company that was making toys similar in style and purpose to the Tatterton toys?' he said quickly. I nodded. 'Well, they have some of the finest artisans in the world in Europe. What am I saying? They do have the finest. But,' he added, winking first at me and then at Momma, 'I have some of them now.

'In any case during my travels to one of their factories in a small village just outside of Zurich, I discovered they were making something called "Portrait dolls".'

'Portrait dolls?' I slipped onto the settee to listen.

'Yes. Brilliant idea!' he said, clenching his hands into fists and lifting them to punctuate his enthusiasm. 'No group of people are so obssessed and entranced with themselves as the wealthy. They think their money and position buy them immortality, so they all have their portraits painted by the best artists and photographs taken by the best photographers. They will go to any length, spend any amount of money to get it done to their satisfaction.'

'What does this have to do with dolls?' I asked.

'Everything. Imagine a doll that has your face and is your doll! Everyone will want one – mothers, daughters, sisters, aunts; even men will come to want male dolls made in their images eventually.

'And we will be the first to do it here in America so a Tatterton doll will become the thing to have, something special, precious, a personalized collectible. Brilliant!' he exclaimed again, this time pounding his knees with his fists.

I had to admit Tony's fervor took my breath away and the idea did sound very good. 'But how does this involve me?' I asked, remembering what had drawn me deeper into the room and the conversation. Tony gazed at Momma, his smile deepening, and she smiled back and then turned to me.

'Tony wants you to be the model for the very first doll and he wants to do the doll himself,' she said.

'Me?' I gazed from one to the other. Momma's face was locked in her soft, happy smile. Tony's eyes were fixed on me, already with an artist's intensity. 'Why me?'

'For one thing,' Tony began, 'I want to make the first set of dolls for young girls. Not little girls,' he added quickly, 'young girls, teenage girls. That's going to be the biggest market of all for the portrait dolls, I think. Little girls are not old enough to appreciate the extra special art work involved, but most importantly, they don't dote on their own image and worry about how they look as much as teenage girls do.'

'But I still don't understand. Why me, of all people?' I asked. Tony shook his head.

'Isn't it wonderful, Jillian, that she has such modesty?'

Momma looked at me with a twinkle in her eyes as if she understood I was being coy. She had told me often that men like it when beautiful women pretend to be modest. It gives them an opportunity to heap compliments on them without shame or fear of being too flattering, and the woman could draw compliment after compliment by denying and blushing and looking as though she needed the adulation.

But I wasn't doing any of that. I really couldn't understand why Tony wanted me to be a model for a special doll. There were many girls my age, girls who were far more beautiful and who were trained to be models. With his money and investment, he could hire the best in the country, if he wanted to. Why me?

'Tony thinks you are special, Leigh, and so do I,' Momma said.

'You already have a doll's face,' Tony explained. I shook my head. 'Yes you do, Leigh. You can cling to modesty if you like, but why should I go searching for the right look, the right girl, when I have the perfect look and the perfect girl living right under my roof?

'I'm going to have the best photographer in town take pictures of your face, many pictures until we decide on the perfect one, and then, I'll have that picture placed beside the first doll, whose face will be yours too. Then all my rich customers will understand what a portrait doll is and want one for themselves. Your picture will be featured in all my store windows . . . everywhere,' he said.

The idea made my heart beat fast. What would my girlfriends say, the 'special club'? I knew they would all be jealous, but Tony was probably right – each would want a doll made of herself. I sat back and thought about it seriously for the first time – a doll with my face.

'I'm so proud that Tony wants the first doll to be you,' Momma said. I gazed at her for a moment. Why didn't Tony want to use Momma's face? She still looked so young and she had a perfect face, a face everyone agreed was beautiful. What puzzled me too was that Momma wasn't jealous. She looked happy about it.

Then I thought, Momma would never agree to do such a thing anyway. She would hate to have to sit for hours and hours while Tony painted her. Or, was there more to it?

'What do I have to do?' I asked.

Tony laughed.

'Just be yourself, nothing more, your entire self.'

'My entire self?'

'The doll has to be perfect,' Tony said. 'In every aspect. It's not going to be just another doll, molded and reproduced in some assembly line. It's a work of art. That's the point. Think of it as a miniature statue, only made like a child's doll.'

'What does all that mean?' I asked, my voice coming out breathless, almost a whisper. Tony looked at Momma, his smile wilting. Her eyes quickly turned from soft, happy eyes to angry eyes.

'It means you will be a model, Leigh. Why are you acting so stupid all of a sudden? A model, an artist's model. You'll pose.'

'But don't artists' models usually pose . . . in the nude?' I asked, fearfully.

Tony laughed as if I had said the silliest thing.

'Of course, they do,' he replied nonchalantly. 'What of it? It's art, and as I said, this doll is going to be a miniature statue.'

I tried to swallow. Stand in a room somewhere naked while Tony painted a picture of me, a picture anyone could see?

'It's not like Tony's a complete stranger,' Momma said, shaking her head and smiling. 'He's family now. I wouldn't want anyone else to do it but him,' she added.

'And don't think it all won't be done in a very professional manner,' Tony added. 'Just because I am president of my company now doesn't mean I didn't begin as an artist myself. All of the Tattertons do. I was working as a Tatterton artist when my father died and then I had to take over the administrative aspects of the business.

'But this is too important and too delicate to assign to just another artisan at my factory, and as Jillian says, we wouldn't want any stranger copying your image.'

When I didn't reply and there was a long moment of silence, Tony continued.

'Let me explain the process so you can understand what has to be done. First, I'll draw a picture of you. Then I'll paint it in, trying to capture skin tones. After that, I'll work in clay, sculpturing a model to get all the dimensions, and once that is done I will have it cast and duplicated.

'Well,' he said, filling the silence again, 'talk it over with Jillian. I have to make some phone calls and see what's been going on in my absence and then look in on Troy. Don't worry about anything,' he added. 'You'll do fine and become quite famous in the process.' He got up, kissed Momma and then left us alone.

The moment he left, Momma sat back in her chair, looking more matriarchal than ever.

'Really Leigh, I'm surprised and disappointed in you. You

saw how excited, how electrified Tony is with this new idea and how big and important it will be to the Tatterton toy empire, and he wants to make you the center of it all, yet you sat there looking ungrateful, indifferent, whining, "What do I have to do?" like some immature child.'

'But Momma, pose naked?'

'What of it? You heard him – this is art. Look in any museum. Did the man who modeled for Michelangelo's David wear clothes or the women who posed to be Venus?

'When he came in here all excited and proposed the idea to me, I thought you would be thrilled and flattered. I thought you had matured enough not to be giggly and silly about serious art. Believe me,' she said, 'if I were only young enough, your age, and a man like Tony came along and offered me such an opportunity, do you think I would hesitate one moment as you did? Absolutely not.'

'But why can't you be the model, Momma? You're so beautiful and young-looking?'

Like lightning Momma's face changed, growing hard and cold. 'Tony explained that he wants this to be for girls your age,' she snapped. 'Can you imagine my photograph next to a Tatterton portrait doll in the window, a doll made for teenagers? I'm young-looking, Leigh, but I don't look like a teenager, do I? Well . . . do I?' I shook my head, weakly, unsure whether to agree or disagree.

'Maybe you can paint me and do the sculpture,' I said quickly. 'You're an artist.'

'I don't have that kind of time, Leigh. I have social obligations, very important ones. Plus, I do fantasy artwork.

'You won't even have to go anywhere to have it done,' she continued. 'It's all going to be done here at Farthy, and it will give you something else to do this summer. Tony has decided to set up a small studio in the cottage so you and he won't be disturbed.'

'The cottage?'

'Isn't that a good idea?'

I nodded.

'All right then. I'll tell him you want to do it,' she said

standing. 'Isn't it exciting? I can't wait for it to be finished,' she said and left me.

I ran to my rooms to take off my bathing suit, shower and dress for dinner. I felt dazed and confused, my mind filled with contradictions and tugged this way and that by different emotions. I couldn't help but be excited about the idea of my portrait in Tatterton store windows beside a precious doll that was created in my likeness, making me seem like some goddess. My guess was that most of my friends, especially members of the 'special club', would have jumped at this opportunity.

But Tony was Momma's new husband, young and handsome, and to stand for hours before him stark naked!

I stripped off my bathing suit and preened before my full-length mirror gazing at myself, studying my every curve. The veins around my emerging breasts were close to the surface, stretching and growing every day. Would Tony concentrate on such detail? There was a tiny birthmark just under my right breast; would that be on the doll as well? I was sure the doll would be dressed in the store windows, but anyone could strip it and gaze upon its torso. Wasn't it like undressing in the storefront window or on a stage for everyone to see?

How did women become professional artists' models? Did they just sit there or stand there thinking of other things and pretending it wasn't going on?

I put on my robe and went back to the mirror to imagine I was about to pose for Tony. I conjured him before me, paint-brush in hand. He had his palette set up, the canvas prepared. Now he turned his intense blue eyes on me and smiled. He gestured with the brush and I began to untie my robe. My heart pounded, raced, even with this fantasy. I began to pull the material away from my body and then . . .

'Leigh!' I heard Troy shout from my sitting room and I pulled my robe closed. He came running in, more exuberant than I had seen him in weeks. 'Tony told me; Tony told me! He's making a doll of you, a Tatterton doll and someday, I might even have one on my shelf!'

'Oh Troy,' I said, 'you don't want to have a little girl's doll, do you?'

'It's not a little girl's doll,' he said firmly. 'It's a Tatterton toy doll and that's special, isn't it?' He nodded, expecting my agreement.

'I suppose it is,' I said and he smiled.

'But Tony says I can't come see him make the doll with you. He can't be disturbed,' he said sadly. 'But I can be one of the first to see it when it's made.

'It will be the best doll in the world,' he proclaimed. And then after a moment's thought he said, 'I'm going to tell Rye Whiskey.' He rushed out of my bedroom again.

I turned back to the mirror and my own image again. Could I do it? Would I do it? Momma thought I should, but Momma wanted me to do anything to keep Tony occupied and spare her from his constant demands and need for attention.

What would Daddy say? I wondered.

He wouldn't like it; he couldn't like it, not Daddy. How I wished he was home already so I could ask him. But he wasn't home, he was still busy in Europe with his business and with . . . Mildred Pierce.

Mildred Pierce, I thought angrily. He let someone steal away his attention and love, let someone keep him from me longer and maybe even forever.

I untied my robe and let the garment fall to my feet. I would be a Tatterton doll. I might even give Daddy one on his new wedding day.

THIRTEEN

Me . . . A Model?

Tony spent the next week with his marketing people planning out the production and sale of portrait dolls. Every evening at dinner he had something new and exciting to tell us about the project. Momma was more interested in this than she had been in anything else Tony did. I felt myself being swept up in the tide of excitement that rushed over us. Finally, one evening he announced that the cottage had been prepared and he was ready to begin after breakfast the following morning. I felt heat rush to my cheeks and my heart flutter. Momma smiled broadly and Tony proposed a toast to the project.

'And to Leigh,' he said, gazing at me with his cerulean eyes burning brightly. 'The first Tatterton model.'

'To Leigh,' Momma said and followed it with a thin laugh. They drank their wine quickly, like two conspirators who had embarked on a venture from which they had sworn they would never turn back.

'What do I have to wear? How should I brush my hair?' I asked, sounding a bit frantic.

'Just be yourself,' Tony said. 'Don't do anything special. You're special enough,' he added. When I looked at Momma, I saw she was gazing at him with a soft, contented smile on her face. I knew why she was so happy Tony was engrossed in this enterprise. While he was, he wasn't making any demands upon her.

But I couldn't fall asleep that night, thinking about what it was going to be like posing for Tony. I wanted to talk to Momma about it some more, but she went to a bridge game and when she returned, she made it clear that she was exhausted and had to go right to sleep. Tony looked as disappointed as I did about that.

After breakfast the next morning, he and I set out for the cottage. He had decided to walk through the maze. It was a beautiful, warm morning, the fluffy, cotton ball clouds just gliding lazily across the turquoise sky.

'It's a wonderful day to begin something new and significant,' he said. He seemed so energized, so full of enthusiasm that I felt foolish still having butterflies in my stomach. He saw how pensive and nervous I was. 'Relax. This will be easy and once we get into it, you'll actually enjoy it. I know; I've worked with many models before.'

'You have?'

'Of course. I took many art courses at college and had special training here at Farthy.' He leaned toward me and lowered his voice as if he were telling secrets. 'I began when I was eleven.'

'Eleven?' At eleven he was drawing and painting nude people?

'Yes. So you see, you're with a man of great experience.'

He smiled and we entered the maze. Tony moved through it with assurance, never hesitating at any turn, never questioning any choice.

'To other people,' he explained, all these hedges look alike, but growing up with them as I have, I noticed subtle differences. These corridors are as different to me as night and day. After a while, it will become the same for you,' he assured me.

The cottage looked the same from the outside, except all the shades had been drawn in all the windows. Inside, Tony had set up his easel and paints, pencils and pens. He had brought in a long, metal work table. Materials for the sculpture were there, as well as all sorts of carving tools. The furniture had been moved about so as to provide as much free space as possible. There were two large pole lamps, one on each side of the easel, their bulbs directed toward the small couch.

'We'll begin with having you sit there,' he said, pointing to the couch. 'Relax and think of pleasant thoughts. It will take me a few moments to set everything up,' he added. He began to organize his materials. I sat on the couch and watched him as he worked, seeing in his face the same creative purpose and concentration I had often seen in little Troy's face.

I was wearing a plain white, short-sleeve cotton blouse and a light blue skirt. My bangs were cut short, but the rest of my hair was long enough to reach the middle of my shoulder blades and lay softly against my neck and shoulders. I hadn't put on any lipstick.

'Okay,' Tony said turning to me. 'I'm going to begin with your face. Just gaze at me with a slight smile on your face. I don't want the doll to have the wide, clownish smile some toy dolls have. I want this doll to reflect your natural beauty, your soft and lovely expression.'

I didn't know what to say. Was all that true? Was I soft and lovely? Surely, if Tony wanted me for such an important project, he must see these things in me and not be simply flattering me to make me feel good.

He took a long look at me, drinking me in. I fixed my eyes on him as he had instructed and saw the way he measured the features of my face and planned his first lines. I did begin to feel as if I were part of something artistic and soon lost the trembling and quickened heartbeat. Tony looked at me, drew, looked at me, nodded to himself, and drew. I tried to keep perfectly still, but it was hard not to fidget.

'You can move about a little,' he said smiling. 'I don't want to turn you into stone,' he added. 'Loosen up until you feel comfortable.' I did loosen up. 'Feeling better?'

'Yes.'

'I knew you would. We'll work for a while and take breaks. I have the kitchen stocked with great food for lunch,' he said enthusiastically.

'How long will we work every day?'

'We'll work awhile in the morning, have a leisurely lunch, and then work a few hours in the afternoon. Whenever you get tired, just holler and we'll take a break.'

I was surprised at how quickly the first hour went by. Tony looked at his watch and announced it had and then invited me to look at what he had done. I got up and gazed at the canvas. He had outlined my face, drawn in the lines and shaped my lips, eyes and nose. He had just begun to do my hair and neck. Of course, it was too early to make any judgments, but I decided quickly that he did have talent.

'It's nothing yet,' he said, 'but I think I'm getting a good start.'

'Oh yes, it's very good.'

'It's a wonderful experience, doing something artistic,' he said, staring at the canvas, his eyes dark and intent. 'It gives you a sense of accomplishment when you bring something to life out of a blank canvas. This drawing is like the first stages in the making of a baby . . . seeds in my imagination merge with reality and take form, just the way a man's seed attaches itself to a woman's egg and begins the creation of a newborn baby. You and I,' he said turning to me, 'we're giving birth to something beautiful here, together,' he added, his voice in a whisper.

I didn't know what to say. The way he looked at me, his eyes small but bright as coals, his voice so soft, made me tremble inside. He quickly changed expression back to that tight, amused smile and then laughed.

'You look terrified. I'm only speaking in metaphors, making comparisons,' he said and then he tilted his head a bit. 'Tell me, Leigh, did you have a boyfriend while you were at Winterhaven?'

'Boyfriend? How could I? Momma wanted me to come home each and every weekend. You know we spent a lot of time together, skiing, horseback riding . . .'

'Yes, yes, but I thought . . . boys do come to visit there, don't they?' he asked, tilting his head to the side and smiling.

'No. Miss Mallory has prohibited boys from the building unless it's a properly chaperoned dance. There were a few dances, but I never got to go to them,' I said bitterly.

'I see. Well, next year, you'll stay more often and get to meet boys. You're interested in boys now, aren't you? What about at your old school? Did you have a boyfriend there?'

'Not really.'

'Not a steady one, huh? Just someone,' he said and nodded as though I had admitted it. 'How about a cool drink? Coke?'

'Okay.' He went into the kitchen and brought out two glasses of soda. While he drank, he stared at me. I thought he might be still thinking about how to draw this or that, but he was thinking of other things.

'This boy who wasn't really a boyfriend,' he began again, 'I'm sure you kissed him, didn't you?'

'No,' I said quickly. His question made my face redden and he smiled.

'Don't worry. I won't tell your mother.'

'There's nothing to tell her,' I insisted.

'Girls still kiss boys, don't they?' he asked laughing, 'or is that against the new rules. You just rock and roll nowadays.'

'Boys still kiss girls,' I replied, although I wasn't speaking from experience.

'Did you ever French kiss?' He sat on the couch and looked up at me, eager for my answer. I hadn't known what French kissing was until I joined the 'special club' at Winterhaven and heard Marie Johnson describe it.

'No,' I said more firmly.

'You do know what that is, don't you?'

'Yes.'

'But you've never done it. How wonderful. You really are as innocent as you look. You mean when you didn't kiss this boy who wasn't really a boyfriend, you didn't press your tongue against his or he press his against yours?'

'I said no,' I replied. Why was he teasing me so much? He laughed.

'It's not as bad as it sounds, Leigh; although, your mother has come to think so, as well as thinking the rest of it is as bad,' he added, suddenly angry. He stared down at the floor for a long moment and then those blue eyes swung my way, suddenly totally void of expression, as if he wasn't looking at me or didn't see me. It bothered me how empty he could make his eyes, as if he knew how to turn his emotions on and off. Then he blinked rapidly and focused on me again.

'You strike me as a very precocious young girl, Leigh. It's why I thought you would be wonderful as a model. Sometimes, you have a very knowing, very grown-up look in your eyes. I bet you're heads and shoulders above other girls your age, aren't you?'

I shrugged. Sometimes I felt that I was, but sometimes, when all the girls got together and began to tell their experiences, I felt as though I had lived in another world.

'I know you were very upset about your parents getting divorced and for a while you hated me, right? You blamed me for it? You don't have to answer. I understand. In your shoes, I would have felt the same way. I hope the time we spent together skiing and horseback riding has been good for you and maybe helped to have you hate me less,' he said sadly.

'I don't hate you, Tony,' I proclaimed. I really didn't hate him, not now, not any more.

'No? Well, I'm glad. I want us to be friends, to be more than friends.' I didn't say anything. When he gazed up at me now, there was a different look in his eyes from the look he had while he had been drawing me. This gaze went deeper and made me very self-conscious. I allowed my eyes to meet his briefly and then I felt myself blush again and looked away quickly. 'Well,' he said slapping his knees, 'time to go back to work.'

He got up and went to his canvas. I went back to the couch.

'I'm going to draw you from the top down, work slowly, capturing the details,' he explained. 'I'm glad you wore that kind of blouse. I want to see you gradually. It gives me the sense that you're emerging from the canvas, rising up out of the blank page like Venus, rising from the sea.

'I want to do an outline of your torso now. Just stand, with your arms at your sides, please,' he instructed. I did. 'Yes, that's it,' he said excitedly, as if I had done something significant or difficult. 'Yes, yes . . .'

He drew lines rapidly.

'Now, just unbutton your blouse enough to bring it down over your shoulders. Go on,' he said when I didn't move. 'It's all right. Just over your shoulders,' he repeated in a soft voice.

I raised my fingers to my first button and undid it.

'Good. Go on. Fine,' he coaxed. 'Now another.' I did it.

'And another. Go on, one more. There, now lower the blouse over your shoulders softly. Yes, yes.'

His eyes widened and he looked at me longer before turning back to the canvas each time.

'Another button,' he said, gazing at what he had drawn so far. I undid it. Then he glanced my way, looked at his drawing and nodded. 'Just pull your arms out of the blouse and hold it slightly above your . . . your breasts,' he said.

I understood and appreciated what he had said about Venus rising from the sea, but it felt so odd to undress this slowly. It was almost as if I were doing a strip-tease.

I brought my arms out and held the blouse from falling back and down. Tony looked at me for a very long time and then shook his head.

'What's wrong?' I asked.

'I'm not getting your shoulders right . . . something . . .' He approached me and squeezed his chin with the fingers of his right hand as he stared down at me. Then he reached out and peeled the thin straps of my bra off my shoulders. He stepped back again, stared for a moment, went back to the canvas, gazed at it and nodded. 'Just turn around,' he said.

'Around? All the way around?'

'Yes, please.'

I did it and waited.

'Now, let your blouse go.' I released it and it fell to my feet. 'Yes,' he said in a loud whisper. 'The lines in your neck and shoulders . . .'

'What about them?' I asked quickly.

'Nothing bad,' he replied with a slight laugh. 'They threw me for a moment.' I heard him come up behind me and then I felt the tips of his fingers trace the curve of my neck and shoulders. I jumped when I felt him. 'Try to relax,' he whispered in my ear. 'Sometimes, an artist has to make contact with his subject so he truly absorbs the lines and curves in his consciousness. At least, I do.'

'It tickled,' I said. I couldn't see him, but his breath felt so hot on the back of my neck, it made me think his lips were only inches away.

'Do you mind if I do this now?' he asked. He had his fingers on the clasp of my bra. For a moment I couldn't speak. My heart thumped against my chest. 'I want an unobstructed view of your back at this point, okay?' he asked again. I just nodded and then felt the clasp undone, the elastic material snap away, and the undergarment loosen. With the shoulder straps already down, my bra fell clear of budding breasts. I started to pull it back up, but Tony seized my wrists, quickly and roughly at first and then immediately softening his grasp. 'No, just keep your arms at your sides,' he said. He stepped back to the easel.

I stood as still as I could, my heart racing so fast, it took my breath away. It seemed I was standing this way for hours before he spoke again.

'This is coming along fine,' he said. 'Perfect.'

I didn't move. What would he want me to do next? Suddenly, I felt him drape a white sheet over my shoulders. He pinned it around my neck like a cape.

'I know you're nervous,' he said in that voice that was barely above a whisper, 'but I'm not unhappy about that. I want to use it to my advantage, and as I told you, capture you as I would capture Venus rising out of the sea. Take off the rest of your clothing now, but keep this wrapped around you. You'll lower it as we go along, okay? I'll be right back. I want to check on what we have for lunch. It's almost time and I've worked up an appetite.'

Why was he asking me to take off all my clothes if we were going to stop for lunch shortly? I wondered. Perhaps he thought it would be easier for me afterward. Although I was still quite nervous and embarrassed, I felt a warm, pleasing tingle wash over me as I slipped my skirt down and stepped out of it. When I lowered my panties and then pressed the cool sheet against my body, I felt an undulating warmth climb up my ankles, making it seem as if I were stepping into a tepid bath. I saw that the small valley between my breasts had reddened. I wrapped the sheet snugly around my waist and waited for Tony to return.

He called me from the kitchen.

'I have everything ready, Leigh.'

I went into the kitchen. He had made a platter of finger sandwiches and uncorked a bottle of red wine. He poured me a glass and then he poured one for himself. When I didn't move, he pulled out my chair like a waiter in a fancy restaurant.

'Madam.'

'Thank you.' I took my seat and began to eat. Dressed only in this white sheet, I couldn't help feeling foolish sitting at the small table. But Tony acted as if it were quite an ordinary thing. Perhaps it was because of all his artistic experience, I thought. Whenever I moved, the sheet parted, so I held it together with one hand while I ate and drank with the other.

'Do you think girls are more modest than boys?' he asked, obviously noticing my awkwardness.

'No.'

'Did you ever see a boy naked?'

'Of course not,' I snapped. He laughed. I knew he was just teasing me again, but it made my nerve ends twang.

'Now don't tell me there aren't any peeping Janes, just like there are peeping Toms. I know when girls get together, they talk about boys they have seen naked, just like boys might talk about girls. I bet the girls at Winterhaven do when they get together, right?'

I didn't reply, but he was right. At one of our last get-togethers in Marie's room, Ellen Stevens told us about seeing her brother take a shower. Just recalling it now made me blush.

'It's all right,' Tony said, shaking his head and smiling from ear to ear. 'It's only natural to have curiosity about the opposite sex.' He drank his wine.

I took a tiny sip of the wine. I felt flushed. My face grew warmer. He finished his glass and poured himself another quickly.

'There's nothing wrong with modesty,' he continued, 'unless it's taken to a ridiculous extreme.' His face hardened, his eyes turning cold and gray suddenly. 'If you're married and your wife still shuts you out whenever she is dressing . . .'

He looked up at me quickly as if I had said something to disagree, but I was so still and quiet, I was almost like the statue he wanted to create.

'Why would a wife not want her own husband to set eyes on her?' he asked, as if I were the older and the wiser one. 'Is she afraid he will see some imperfection, a wrinkle, a large birthmark? Would you always want the lights out whenever you made love with your husband?' he asked. I didn't know what to say. 'Of course you wouldn't. Why should you?' He looked down and muttered, 'She's driving me crazy.'

I knew he was talking about my mother, but I said nothing. Did Momma think that if Tony saw her naked in a brightly lit room he would know her true age? I wondered. She had such a perfect figure. How could it reveal her age?

I finished my sandwich and sipped a little more wine. Tony seemed in a daze. Suddenly, he snapped out of it and smiled.

'Time to go back to work,' he announced and rose from his seat.

I followed him back to the living room that had been turned into a studio and stood where I had stood before.

'I see the wine has given you a crimson tint. I like that. I'll have to capture that,' he said. 'Does the glow continue down your neck?' he asked and drew closer and ran his right forefinger along my neck line to my collar bone. 'You're truly exquisite,' he whispered. 'A young flower just blooming.' His eyes were piercing, bright. He sighed and shook his head. 'How lucky I am to have you, Leigh. This will succeed only because I have such a beautiful model.'

He returned to the easel and began to draw. After a moment he stopped.

'Just unclip the sheet at your neck and hold it at your waist,' he said, as nonchalantly as he might say, 'turn your head to the left.'

At my waist, I thought. My fingers trembled so when I went to unclip it I couldn't do it. He laughed.

'Here, let me help you,' he said coming forward. He lifted my fingers from the clip gently and undid it. I held the sheet against my body for a moment. Then he peeled it down over my shoulders, over my arms, peeled it from my bosom, all the time keeping his eyes on my eyes. He smiled and stepped back, gazing at me. My heart pounded.

'I love that little birthmark under your breast,' he exclaimed. 'That's the kind of individualistic little thing I can put into the model to make it definitely you. Everyone will look for something that will make the doll more specifically a replica of themselves, don't you see?' He appeared so excited about it that I could only shake my head in astonishment. He rushed back to his easel and continued to sketch.

He worked for more than an hour, stopping often to study me with such intensity and sighing before shaking his head and smiling. Suddenly he stopped and bit down on his lip hard, shaking his head.

'What's wrong?' I asked.

'I'm not getting this right. It's off, unbalanced. I'm not doing justice to your symmetry,' he declared.

'Does it have to be so perfect, Tony?'

'Of course,' he said, a ripple of annoyance passing through his face. 'It's the first and the best.' He looked at his sketch and then looked at me. He turned back to the sketch and nodded. Then he stepped forward.

'I hope you don't mind,' he said, 'but sometimes, we artists see things clearer with our eyes closed.'

'But how can you see with your eyes closed?' I asked.

'We see through our other senses. An artist who paints beautiful birds must listen to them sing and get their songs into the painting as well as their colors and shapes. When an artist paints a beautiful green field, he gets the aroma of grass and flowers into his painting. Understand?' I nodded. It did sound right.

'And through touch,' he said, 'an artist brings depth, texture, fullness to his work. This will be a great asset to me when I transform the drawing into a sculpture. Just relax a moment,' he requested in a breathy whisper. He brought his hands to my waist and closed his eyes. Then his fingers traveled up over my ribs, pausing as they pressed against my bones. 'Yes,' he said. 'Yes.' He moved his hands farther up and the tips of his fingers touched the undersides of my breasts. I started to step back.

'Easy,' he said. 'I'm seeing it all perfectly now.'

I looked into his face. His eyes were still shut tight, but I could see them moving back and forth under the lids.

The tips of his fingers moved very slowly up the sides of my breasts and then came down over the tops. He paused there for a moment, holding his breath. I held mine as well.

The tickling sensation I had first experienced disappeared rapidly and was replaced with a tingling that traveled deep into my body, exploding everywhere. It was as if a dozen fingers were on me, sending the same sensation through my legs and arms and stomach.

The mixture of feelings was bewildering, frightening and thrilling at the same time. I was so confused. Should I pull away, take his hands from my body? Did all artists' models permit the artist to explore their bodies this way? Sometimes when he looked at me so intensely, it felt as if Tony's eyes did touch me, but this was different. His fingers moved under my breasts and over them as if he were shaping me in his mind. My legs grew weak and began to tremble.

Finally, Tony stepped back, holding his hands off me but keeping them in the air just at the height of my bosom. He lingered there for a moment, nodded, and returned slowly to the easel, opening his eyes only when he began to sketch.

He worked with a frenzy now, his lips tight and his jaw firm. I barely moved. My heart was thumping so hard I thought it would burst through my chest. What had he just done? What had I permitted him to do? Did Momma know this would happen? Why hadn't she warned me?

'Yes,' Tony said. 'It's coming now. It's working.' He smiled at me and worked on. Not long after, he stopped abruptly, stepped back to look at his work, and then nodded.

'Okay,' he said. 'We've done enough for today. Why don't you get dressed while I clean up.'

I turned my back to him and began putting on my clothing. When I was finished, he beckoned for me to look at the work.

'Well? What do you think?'

I did see resemblances to my face. He had captured the shape of my head and my chin perfectly, but my torso looked far more mature than I was. My body looked more like my mother's body.

'It's very good, Tony,' I said, 'but you've made me look older.'

'It's how I see you too, you know. This is a work of art, not a photograph. Half of it is in the artist's mind. That's why it was so important for me to touch you, too. I hope you understand, Leigh,' he said, an expression of concern on his face.

'Yes, I understand,' I replied, but I didn't really understand. I didn't understand my own feelings as well. I had felt embarrassed, frightened and thrilled at the same time. It was all so confusing. I made up my mind I would talk to my mother about it, no matter what.

But she was already gone for the evening when Tony and I arrived at the house. She had left a note explaining that she was going to dinner and the theater in Boston with some of her women friends. It came as just as much a surprise to Tony as it did to me.

'Looks like you and I will dine alone again tonight,' he muttered and rushed upstairs to his suite.

Soon after I went up to mine, Troy came to see me. His bouts with the chicken pox and the measles, his allergies and colds had left him so thin and pale. Even the time he spent in the summer sun didn't do much to make his complexion richer. Because he had lost a little weight, too, he looked gaunt and his eyes were drawn and had dark circles around them. Despite his condition he brightened when he came charging into my bedroom to see how the work on the Tatterton portrait doll had gone.

'When will it be ready?' he asked. 'This week?'

'I don't know, Troy. All we did today is sketch in the picture. Tony has to paint and then begin making a sculpture. Did you have your dinner?' I asked. The doctors had put him on a different feeding schedule and he was eating earlier than the rest of us. I knew that pleased my mother, but it made him very unhappy to have to eat alone or only with his nurse.

'Yes. I had to drink that gooey stuff again, too,' he complained.

'It's good for you, Troy, and it will make you stronger so you will be able to live a normal life again. You will get better and be able to ride your pony and swim and . . .'

'No, I won't,' he said with a frighteningly assured and mature expression. His eyes were as sharp and as cold as Tony's could be at times. 'I'll never get better and I won't live as long as everyone's supposed to live,' he added firmly.

'Troy! You must not say such things. That's a terrible thing to say,' I chided.

'I know it's true. I heard the doctor say it to the nurse.'

'What did he say?' I demanded, outraged that a doctor would utter such comments in his presence.

'He said I was as delicate as a flower, and just as a flower would snap in a harsh wind, I would snap if I ever became seriously ill.'

I stared at him a moment. In a strange way his sicknesses had matured and aged him. Right now he appeared to be an old man in a child's body, his eyes had that much wisdom and experience in them. It was as if the months were ticking away like days and the days like hours for him. Perhaps his wisdom gave him a window on the future and he did see his own early death. I shuddered with the thought.

'Troy, he just meant that if you didn't improve, you would be weakly, but you're going to improve. You're just a little boy. You have plenty of time to grow stronger and stronger. Besides, if you died, who would be my little step-brother?'

His eyes lit up with that.

'You will always want me to be your little step-brother?'

'Of course.'

'And you will never leave me here by myself?' he asked with Tony's skepticism.

'Where would I go? This is my home now, just as it is yours.'

His smile washed out the melancholy shadow that had clung to his face. I seized his wrist gently and brought him to me for a quick hug. The tears that gathered in the corners of my eyes started a slow trickle down my cheeks. When he pulled back and saw them, he looked surprised.

'Why are you crying, Leigh?'

'I'm just . . . happy you will be my little brother forever and ever, Troy,' I said. His face became resplendent and he glowed with happiness. I thought he grew stronger, healthier, right before my eyes.

All he really needed, I thought, was someone to love and to cherish him, someone to make him feel wanted. Tony loved him very much, I was sure, but Tony was so involved in all his business activities, he couldn't be the father Troy needed; and my mother . . . she was so involved with herself and so put off by Troy's illnesses, she didn't even see him. I could imagine that when she looked at him, she looked right through him, and Troy being the sensitive little boy he was, surely felt invisible and alone because of all that. It dawned on me that he really had only me now.

In some ways I felt just like him. There were so many times now when my mother looked right through me, had her mind on her own activities and concerns, and my father was preoccupied with a new love. Troy and I were two orphans thrown together in this big house, surrounded by things other children and young people dreamed of having. But things without love and someone to cherish and to cherish you along with them were really only things.

'Will you come into my suite later to read to me, Leigh?' he asked.

'After dinner. I promise.'

'Okay. I've got to go see Tony,' he said. 'Don't forget,' he added and ran out, his little legs wobbling as he charged out of my suite. It made me laugh, but it also made me sad.

I changed and dressed for dinner. Tony was already in the dining room when I came down.

'How are you, a little tired?' he asked.

'Yes, although I don't know why modeling should make me tired. I just stood there,' I said.

'Don't underestimate what you're doing. It's work. You're concentrating too and don't forget, you were nervous today. That can tire you out. Tomorrow, you will be less nervous and as the days go by it will get easier and easier.'

'How much longer will it be, Tony?' I asked. He had said 'as the days go by'.

'A while. I have to spend a lot of time on the actual painting. I want your skin tones perfect and your eyes and hair. And then, there is the actual sculpturing. We can't rush this along,' he said with a smile.

I didn't know what to say. It sounded as if he would spend the entire summer with me standing nude before him in the cottage. Would he have to touch me again and again? Could I ever really get used to that? And what about his other work . . . his business?

'But don't you have other things to do?'

'I have very competent help, and as I told you, this is one of the most important projects Tatterton Toys has ever undertaken.' He patted my hand. 'Don't worry, you'll have time off to do anything you want.'

I nodded. How could I tell him what my real concerns were? Who could I tell? Where was my mother when I needed her? Where was my father?

After dinner, I went up to Troy's room to read to him, but his nurse greeted me outside his suite and told me he was already asleep.

'The medicine he takes tires him out early,' she explained. 'He tried hard to stay up for you, but his eyes shut themselves.'

'I'll just look in on him,' I said, and went to the door of his bedroom.

He would always look tiny and fragile in his king-size bed, but I thought that at least tonight, he had gone to sleep with healthier color on his face. I made up my mind I would try to spend more time with him and help his recovery along. It would take my mind off my own problems.

I read and listened to the radio in my suite and then I tried to go to sleep, but when I put out the lights and closed my eyes, all I could think about was Tony putting his hands on my naked body, his fingers traveling up and over my breasts, his eyes shut tight, but the eyeballs moving nervously beneath the lids, looking like two tiny round animals searching for a way out.

What would it be like tomorrow?

*

When I awoke the next morning, I dressed and went quickly to my mother's suite, but she had her bedroom door shut tight. I knocked gently.

'Momma? I have to talk to you this morning,' I whispered through the door. I waited, but there was no response. 'Momma?' I raised my voice and waited. Still, there was no response. Frustrated, but determined to speak with her about my experience at the cottage, I opened the door, only to confront an untouched bed. Shocked and surprised, I hurried from her rooms and down to the dining room, where I found Tony reading the *Wall Street Journal* and having his coffee.

'Where's my mother?' I asked. 'It doesn't look like she slept in her bed last night.'

'She didn't,' he said nonchalantly and turned the page.

'Well, where was she?' I demanded. He lowered the paper, a look of annoyance on his face. He wasn't annoyed with me; he was annoyed with her.

'She phoned around eleven to tell me she and her girlfriends had decided to spend the night in Boston. I had to send Miles to her hotel to bring her clothes for today.'

'But . . . when is she coming home?'

He shrugged.

'Your guess is as good as mine. Probably better than mine.' His eyes cut sharply toward me. Then he nodded toward Curtis, who had been standing in the corner like a statue, and asked him to bring in our breakfast.

I didn't know what to do. I didn't want to go back to the cottage without first talking about it with my mother, but she wasn't here and Tony was anxious to get started.

'Why don't you just put on one of your loose cotton shifts this morning,' he suggested. 'It will make things easier if you don't wear anything else,' he added. 'It's very warm today.'

Nothing else? No panties, no bra, nothing but my cotton shift? He saw the look on my face.

'Just to be practical,' he added. I nodded. After breakfast I went up to my suite and did as he suggested. Contrary to what he had told me, I didn't feel less nervous this morning, even though it was to be my second session. He was just as animated as the day before when we walked through the maze to the cottage, maybe even more so. He set things up quickly and this time did not ease me into it.

'Today we paint,' he announced. 'Ready?'

I looked at the windows. All had their shades drawn down, but he had opened them a few inches so that there would be a breeze. I looked back at him, his face filled with anticipation. I was tempted to run out of the cottage. My lips began to tremble.

'What's wrong?' he asked, seeing my concern.

'I just feel . . .'

'You poor thing. I'm just rushing onward without considering your feelings. I'm sorry, Leigh,' he said and took me in his arms. 'I know this isn't the easiest thing for you because it's such a new experience, but we did so well together yesterday, I just thought you were over your initial shyness.

'Now just take a deep breath,' he said, 'and think about the wonderful thing we're doing together, okay?'

I closed my eyes and took the deep breath, but my heart was pounding so, I felt faint. He felt my trembling.

'Here,' he said, 'you know what? You don't have to stand right away. I can start with you lying on the couch.'

'On the couch?'

'Yes. I'll help you. Just keep your eyes closed. Go on,' he encouraged. I did so. 'Relax. That's it. Easy,' he said and I felt his fingers take hold of my loose cotton shift just below the waist. He lifted it slowly, gently. 'Raise your arms, please,' he whispered. I did so and the shift came up over my head, rising softly, as softly as it would had a delicate and tender breeze been lifting it. I kept my eyes closed even after Tony brought it past my raised hands. He put it aside and then took my shoulders and softly guided me to the couch.

'Lie there. Make yourself comfortable,' he said.

I lowered my head to the pillow he had placed against the arm of the couch and opened my eyes. He was standing before me, looking down, smiling.

'Good. See, how easy it will be.'

He returned to the easel and began. Time seemed to pass

more slowly than it had yesterday. We didn't take a break until lunch. When he announced we would eat lunch, he handed me the sheet I wore yesterday. I clipped and draped it around me. Again, we had sandwiches and wine. Tony talked about some of the exciting marketing ideas he was developing for the portrait dolls. The more he talked, the more relaxed I became. He surprised me though when we returned to the work.

'You don't have to stand. I need a rear view now,' he told me.

'What should I do?'

'Just lie down on your stomach,' he said. I hesitated. 'Go on. I'll take the sheet off you when I'm ready.'

I did as he asked. He set up another canvas and then he came to the couch. First, he stroked my hair.

'Are you okay?' he asked.

'Yes.'

'Good. Then let's begin again,' he said and reached under my chin to unclip the sheet. He lifted it from me and stood looking down. 'Perfect,' he muttered, almost inaudibly. He returned to his easel and worked. Hours seemed to go by before he groaned as he had yesterday.

'Not right,' he said. 'Just not right.' I looked at him. He was staring at me, his fingers pinching his chin. Then he approached me. 'Just relax.' He brought the palm of his hand to the small of my back. He ran it up to my neck and then back down, only not stopping where he started, but going over my buttocks. Then he stood up, sighed, and returned to his canvas.

He worked with a new frenzy. Touching me truly inspired him. This time when he stopped for the day, he looked exhausted. He seemed barely able to speak.

'We're finished for today,' he declared. I put on my cotton shift and joined him at the easel. Once again, I thought he had captured my likeness well, but the body he had drawn and painted was more my mother's than my own. He saw my look of surprise.

'It's how I see you,' he explained. 'It's how you are on the tips of my fingers.' The look in his eyes made my heart flutter.

He kissed me on the forehead and said, 'You're wonderful. You could turn anyone into an artist.'

I didn't know what to say. His words embarrassed and flattered me at the same time, but having him hold his eyes on me so intently made me quiver. Finally, he gathered his things together and we left the cottage. I followed him through the maze, through the long shadows and corridors. My body was in such turmoil, caught in the midst of a storm of feelings. When we finally came out of the maze, I felt as if I had left a dream world and re-entered reality.

I hurried into the house and up to my suite, not even stopping to see if my mother had returned from Boston. I had to close the doors quickly and catch my breath. My body still tingled with the memory of Tony's fingers running over me, turning me into the woman he wanted me to be.

FOURTEEN

Oh, Daddy

I heard my mother coming up the stairs to her suite. She was laughing and talking quite excitedly to one of our maids. I hurried to my door just as she went by.

'Momma,' I called. She turned quickly.

'Oh Leigh. I was just talking to Tony about you downstairs. He said everything was going wonderfully. I'm so happy. Give me a minute to shower and change and then come to my suite so I can tell you all about this wonderful play I saw in Boston and this fabulous hotel my friends and I stayed in. It was luxury beyond luxury,' she said and swept on toward her suite.

'Momma,' I cried, stopping her. 'I want to talk to you now.'

'Now?' She shook her head at me. 'Really, Leigh, you must give me a little time to myself so I can make myself presentable again. You know how I despise traveling.'

'But Momma . . .'

'I'll let you know when I'm ready. It won't be long,' she promised and went on before I could offer any further protest.

But it was nearly two hours before she finally did send for me. She had showered and dressed and done her hair and make-up first because two of Tony's business friends were coming to dinner with their wives.

'Now what's so urgent?' she asked as I came into her bed-room. She was at her vanity table making some finishing touches on her hair and looked at me in her mirror.

'It's about my modeling for the portrait doll,' I said. She seemed not to be listening. I waited as she played with some loose strands. Finally, she turned to me.

'What?'

'I can't go on with this, Momma,' I said and started to cry. She jumped up and went to her door to close it quickly.

'What is it? You can't do this now, make a scene. You want one of the servants to hear you? And our guests will be arriving any moment for dinner. What's wrong?' she exclaimed, her voice frantic.

'Oh Momma, it was hard enough to stand naked in front of Tony while he drew me, but when he touched me . . .'

'Touched you? What are you talking about, Leigh? Stop sniveling like a child and talk sensibly.'

I wiped my eyes quickly and sat on the bed facing her. Then I quickly explained what Tony had been doing and why he said he was doing it. She listened attentively, her face barely changing expression. All that she really did was narrow her eyes some and pull her mouth in slightly at the corners.

'Is that all?' she asked when I was finished. She returned to her vanity table.

'All? Isn't it enough?' I cried.

'But he hasn't done anything to you, has he? You said yourself he tried to make you comfortable each time. He sounds very considerate to me,' she said and started to turn back to the mirror.

'But Momma, does he have to touch me to paint me and create the model?'

'It's understandable,' she said. 'I once read about this blind man who sculptured beautiful things using only his sense of touch.'

'But Tony isn't blind!' I protested.

'Nevertheless, he's only trying to enhance his senses,' she said and put on her lipstick. 'What you're doing is wonderful for both of you. He seems so involved, so pleased. To tell you the truth, Leigh,' she said turning back to me, 'before he got involved with this project, I thought he was going to drive me mad. He was at my door night and day, demanding my attention. I never realized how possessive he was and how much he needed to be occupied. A man like Tony could exhaust one woman to death!' she declared. Then she smiled. 'Just think about the doll and what it will mean. Everyone will be talking about them and about you.'

'Momma, I have been thinking about the doll and the pictures Tony has painted.'

'So?'

'They're . . . they're not right.'

'I can't believe that, Leigh. I know Tony's a fine artist; I've seen some of the things he's done.'

'I'm not saying he's not a fine artist, Momma. He has drawn my face well and the picture really looks like me, but . . .'

'But? But what? You're not making any sense and we have to get ourselves ready for dinner,' she said, her face twisting with anger.

'The rest of me doesn't look like me. It looks like you!' I cried. She stared at me a moment. Relief rushed like a wave over me. Finally she understood why I was so upset. But suddenly, she smiled.

'That's wonderful,' she declared. 'Absolutely marvelous.'

'What?'

'How clever. He's combining both of us into this wonderful new work of art. I guess it was to be expected – the man is completely obsessed with me. He has me on his mind night and day,' she said playing with her hair. Then she turned back to me. 'You must not blame him for it, Leigh. He simply can't help it.

'Now you can understand why I run away sometimes, why I need relief, why he must be distracted by one thing or another. It's so difficult for a woman when a man literally worships the ground she walks upon.' She sighed. 'Sometimes, I long for him to be more like your father.'

She looked at her diamond watch. 'You're not going to dinner dressed like that, are you? Put something more formal on tonight. These people are very wealthy and important. I'd like you to make a good impression.' She looked at herself in the mirror again.

'Then you think everything is all right?' I asked her.

'Everything? Oh, yes, of course. Don't be a baby about this, Leigh. It's not going to be that much longer before Tony is finished and hopefully on to other things that will consume his energies just as much.' She paused, looked at me a moment, and then got up and went to her jewelry box to choose her rings.

I rose slowly from the bed and started out. When I looked back, I saw her shaking her head at her first choice. She had already put our conversation to sleep.

Perhaps my mother did say something to Tony about our discussion, because when we returned to the cottage the next day, he refrained from touching me. In fact he became more and more intense about his work, at times giving me the feeling he wasn't actually looking at me; he was looking at some image in his mind and simply staring in my direction. We spoke little until we broke for lunch and even then, he was distracted, getting up often to check something on the canvas and then returning to the table.

He spent almost half a day on my feet and hands, studying and measuring, often muttering to himself as he contemplated his drawings. One afternoon, I grew bored and actually fell asleep for a few minutes. If he had noticed, he said nothing. By the end of the first week, he had drawn and painted me from all angles.

Every night at dinner the work was the main topic of conversation, even when we had guests; although I noticed Tony and my mother left out the fact that I was posing in the nude.

I didn't complain again to my mother about posing, but I couldn't help wishing it would all soon come to an end. Then at the beginning of the second week, Tony announced he would start the actual sculpturing and create the model for the doll. Since the paintings were completed I wondered why he needed me.

'Now we get to three-dimensional work,' he explained. 'I need you more than ever.'

He put the paintings up on a row of easels for reference and began what he promised would be the final stages of the process.

I didn't understand what he meant until he began his work.

Then it all started again. Those times he had touched my body to enhance his ability to draw and to paint were nothing compared to what he was doing now. It seemed he stopped every five or ten minutes after he began to work with the clay so he could come to me to feel me or as he said, 'experience me artistically'.

He would hold my head in his hands and stand there, his eyes closed, his head back, and then he would rush back to his table to form the clay. He traced the lines in my face, lingered over my ears and gently pressed the tips of his fingers against my closed eyes. When I looked into his face while he was doing some of this, I saw an intensity and concentration that both amazed and frightened me because his face was flushed and his eyes were maddeningly wide.

The doll's figure began to rise out of the mound of clay on the table just the way he had described Venus rising out of the sea. I watched it taking shape and anticipated his every touch. After he finished my shoulders, he returned to trace my raised collar bone, his fingers moving softly across my body. He confirmed every inch of the way down my torso before bringing himself to outline it in the mold.

When he reached my breasts, I stiffened. He stood before me, his eyes closed again.

'Easy,' he whispered. 'It's working. My fingers are carrying you from here to the sculpture and drawing you out of it, just as I hoped they would.'

He cupped and traced my bosom, keeping his fingers on me for what seemed longer than ever. I couldn't keep myself from trembling again, but if he felt it, he didn't acknowledge it. Finally, he lifted his hands from me and returned to his sculpturing. On and on it went, following the same procedure. Every time he returned to my body, I felt as if I were sinking into a pool of soft, warm clay myself, rather than rising out of it.

Toward the end of our session, he was on his knees, tracing the small of my stomach, running the palms of his hands over my thighs again and again, stroking me as if I were made of clay and he was reshaping me. I wanted to protest, to question, to end it, but I was afraid that whatever I did would only prolong the process, so I kept my eyes closed and endured.

Finally, he told me to put on my clothes.

'I just want to make some finishing touches and we will call it a day,' he said.

After I dressed, I looked at the sculpture. Just like in the drawings, there was a strong resemblance to my face, but the doll's figure was more like my mother's.

'I won't need you for a few days now,' he said, looking away from me. 'I'm going to do the fine work from my drawings and paintings and then I'll have you back for one final session to confirm everything. All right?' His eyes cut quickly to my face, then away again just as quickly.

I nodded. The day had left me strained, tense and exhausted. I felt confused, torn between a yearning for something I couldn't describe and a desire to get away from the cottage and never return there.

Tony had been right that I would grow adept at moving through the maze. Now I ran down its green corridors and around the turns, bursting out of the maze on the other side, feeling as if I had just escaped from a madman. I rushed to the house. As I hurried to the stairway, Momma came out of the music room, one of her lady friends beside her.

'Leigh, how did it go today?'

I looked at her and shook my head, unable to speak, afraid that if I began, I would burst into tears and embarrass her. She saw the expression on my face and followed her question with her thin, silvery laugh. It chased me up the stairway to my room where I threw off my clothing quickly and ran a warm bath. I didn't feel relaxed and clean again until I had been soaking in it for at least fifteen minutes. I was almost asleep in the water when I heard my mother come in. She came to the doorway of my bathroom.

'What is wrong with you, acting like that in front of Mrs Wainscoat,' she raved, pacing frantically before me, throwing her hands up in the air. 'You don't know what kind of a gossip that woman is.'

For once I ignored her hysterics. 'Oh Momma, it was worse than ever today. Tony . . . had his hands all over me, everywhere!' I cried. She shook her head and I could see she wasn't listening. What would it take to get her to listen – to hear my cries for help? 'Whatever he had to do to the clay, he did to me – pressing, touching . . . for minutes at a time.'

Momma only fumed. 'He's just told me he's nearly finished and he won't be needing you but one more time,' she said. 'Is that true?'

'Yes, but . . .'

'Then *stop* crying like a baby. You did it and I'm sure it will be wonderful.

'Anyway,' she went on, 'I didn't come up here because of that. You had a phone call today and you have a date tomorrow. Your father has returned. He wants to have lunch with you in Boston.'

'Daddy's back?' Oh, thank Heaven, I thought. Thank Heaven. Now there will be someone to listen to me and help me. Daddy was home.

I was so excited the next morning that I took extra special care in dressing and then preened before the mirror for a guilty moment. I looked in the glass, surprised at my similarity to my mother. Was that the cause of Tony's behavior – was it my fault all along? I felt shame at the thought for a while then I decided that whatever was the true cause I couldn't be to blame. Tony was adult – and he was my step-father!

I brushed my hair down, stroking it until it shone, and tied it back with a pink ribbon the way Daddy liked it. I put on just a suggestion of lipstick and chose a light blue skirt and blouse, both in a beautiful, airy fabric. I put on the pearl earrings Daddy had brought back for me from the Caribbean.

When I gazed at myself in the mirror, I hoped I would look more grown up to him. It was important, for I wanted to tell him everything that had happened and especially tell him about my posing for the portrait doll. I had secret hopes that he would ask me to come with him now, get me a tutor perhaps, and take me on one of his trips. If I could only show him that I was old enough to be more on my own. He would understand my need to get away from Momma and Tony. The only thing I regretted was I would be away from little Troy, but I had to do it. I just had to.

When we drove away from Farthy and passed under the great archway, my heart pitter-pattered in anticipation. What would Daddy look like? Would he still have his full beard? I couldn't wait to inhale his aftershave and smell the aroma of his pipe, to have him embrace me and hold me against his tweed jacket while he rained kisses on my hair and forehead. I wanted and needed to see him so much, I never once thought about the truth about him. Nothing seemed further from my thoughts than the knowledge he was not really my father.

When we reached the hotel, I asked the receptionist to let Daddy know I was there. I was going to run into Daddy's arms and hold him as tightly as I could the moment he came downstairs.

I stood waiting, watching the indicator that told what floor each elevator was presently on. I saw one moving down . . . five, four, three, two . . . the doors opened and Daddy stepped out, but I didn't run to him as I had planned.

He was holding a woman's hand. She was a thin woman with gray and black hair cut just below her ears, and she was very tall, as tall as my father. She wore a dark blue cardigan suit and thick-heeled shoes. Daddy smiled at me, but he didn't release the woman's hand. She smiled too and they both began walking toward me. I waited, my heart pounding. This had to be the woman he had written about in the letters, the woman he said made him happy, Mildred Pierce.

'Leigh,' Daddy said finally, holding his arms out to me. I embraced him, but I didn't hold on to him. Instead, I stepped back quickly and looked at Mildred Pierce more closely. Unlike Momma, she had pale skin, a hard, bony face and deep dark eyes. Her thin lips looked as if they would snap like rubber bands when she smiled and stretched them. Daddy kept his hands on my shoulders.

'You look older and more beautiful than ever,' Daddy said.

'Thank you, Daddy,' I replied. They were the words I'd

wanted, waited to hear, but right now they almost didn't matter. I was still staring at the woman beside him.

'Leigh, this is Mildred,' Daddy said.

'Hello, Leigh. I've heard so much about you. I couldn't wait to meet you,' she said and extended her hand. She had long, thin fingers, and her hands were not anywhere as soft and feminine as my mother's hands.

'Hello,' I said. I shook her hand quickly.

'Are you hungry?' my father asked. 'I have reservations for us here at the hotel. I thought that would be most convenient. Actually,' he said taking Mildred's hand again, 'Mildred thought that. She's a wonderful planner, what we call a details person.'

'Oh Cleave. I just do what seems most efficient.'

'Just like her to belittle her work. Mildred's an accountant, Leigh, so she knows about efficiency.'

'Let's not talk about me,' Mildred said, taking my hand and leading us toward the hotel restaurant. 'Let's talk about you. I want to know all about you. I have two children of my own, you know.'

'You do?'

'Yes. They're both in their twenties and both married with children of their own, so I don't have anyone to baby anymore.'

'I'm not a baby either,' I snapped.

'Of course you're not, dear,' Mildred said. She winked at my father. 'Anyone can see you're a young lady.'

We entered the restaurant and the *maitre d'* took us to our reserved table. Daddy pulled out Mildred's chair and the *maitre d'* pulled out mine. Now that we were seated, I looked at him more closely. There were no major differences in his appearance, although he looked much happier than he did the last time I had seen him. His beard was trim, his cheeks rosy. I thought his hair was cut shorter, but he wore the same suit and tie, what Momma had despairingly come to refer to as his 'uniform'.

'So tell me, how was this school you attended?' Daddy asked.

'It was all right,' I said.

'Just all right?'

'It's a good school,' I confessed. 'But I like being in a public school more and none of my teachers are as good as Mr Abrams,' I added quickly.

'Mr Abrams was the tutor I employed whenever we took Leigh on a voyage during school session,' Daddy explained to Mildred. She nodded with approval.

'I can't wait to go on another voyage,' I said. Daddy nodded, a smile around his eyes, but he didn't make the offer I had hoped he would make instantly.

'And how is your mother doing?' he asked.

'She's happy, I suppose. Busy with her bridge and theater and friends.'

'And Mr Tatterton? His business must be doing well.'

This was my chance to talk about the portrait doll, I thought, but I didn't want to do it in front of this woman I hardly knew. I decided I would wait until Daddy and I were alone.

'I guess so. I missed you, Daddy,' I said quickly. I didn't want to talk about anything else but him and me. Again, he nodded without saying any of the things I had hoped to hear. I wanted him to tell me how much he had missed me and how much he wanted me to be with him. I wanted him to explain how we would be together more and I wanted him to propose a trip, a plan for us to spend time together, but instead, he looked at the menu.

'Let's order. I'm starving,' he said.

I didn't care about eating. I didn't care if we never ordered.

'We had the London Broil yesterday,' Mildred said. 'If you like that, they do a very good job with it here.'

'You were here yesterday?' I asked quickly, my insides twisting with surprise and disappointment.

'Oh . . .' She looked at Daddy.

'Yes, Leigh. We've been back a little over a week, but I didn't want to call you until I could spend time with you. We've had so much to do.'

I didn't know what to say. How could he have been here so long and not call me? What about all those words he wrote in his letters, at least the earlier ones, telling me how much he missed me. What happened to the promises and pledges of love? I didn't even try to hide my look of hurt. They looked at each other again.

'I was a bit overwhelmed with work,' Daddy continued. 'I have a new and wonderful cruise planned. Actually,' he said turning to Mildred and taking her hand, 'it was Mildred's idea, a wonderful idea.' He turned back to me. 'We're going to have cruises to Alaska. To Alaska! I know you think people won't want to go there because everyone thinks it's freezing there, but the summers in Alaska are probably the most beautiful summers in the world. Mildred has been there then!' he exclaimed. 'She can tell you.'

'I don't care about Alaska,' I said sharply. The tears were stinging behind my eyes, but I kept them trapped.

'Now, Leigh, that's not very polite.'

'It's all right, Cleave. I understand how Leigh feels. You should tell her all of it,' she said, her face tight and serious.

'All of it?' I looked at my father. He sat up straight.

'It wasn't all business that occupied us since our return from Europe,' he said. 'Two days ago Mildred and I got married.'

I wanted to get up and run out of the restaurant and the hotel. I wanted to run and run until I collapsed. My stomach felt as if it had dropped to my feet. My heart seemed to shrink in my chest and my chest became an empty chamber echoing with the tiny beats. Daddy was holding Mildred's hand to his lips and looking at her so lovingly. Then he turned back to me.

'We thought it would be best for everyone if we just went out and did it ourselves, no public ceremony, no receptions, no extravagant affair. Mildred is so practical when it comes to things like that, and in that way, she is a lot like me,' my father said. With every word he seemed to drift farther and farther away from me, like a leaf being carried away in the wind, rising and falling on an invisible sea and drawn toward the horizon until it was barely visible, a dot against the gray sky.

'We haven't even told my children yet,' Mildred explained. I imagined that was supposed to make me feel more important.

I had learned about their marriage before her children had learned about it; but I didn't care.

'We're off to Maine tomorrow,' my father said.

'Maine? Tomorrow?' The words bounced around in my head. They seemed unreal.

'That's where Mildred's children live. We're just going to surprise them with the news.'

'Like you surprised me,' I said bitterly. Daddy blinked.

'I wrote you letters,' he said softly. 'You must have had some idea.'

I did, I thought, but I wouldn't admit it to myself. I refused to see it, hoping for another world, a world that just included Daddy and me, a world in which I was the most important thing in his life, a world like the happy one I once knew. But that thin dream had burst. It fell out of the air like a single tear.

'I know it's hard for you, dear,' Mildred said. She reached across the table to put her hand on mine. 'You've been through quite an upheaval, but I assure you, I will do anything I can to help make your life easier and more pleasant. In time I hope you will think of me as a second mother, someone to whom you can come for advice and comfort.'

I looked into the eyes of this stranger, a woman so unlike my real mother. She seemed so hard and so stern. Even her smile was an efficient little movement in her face. Confide in her: the woman who had stolen my father from me, the woman who was going to take him to another family? Which children would he care more about now? With whom would he spend more time?

'And that's one thing Mildred is good at,' Daddy said, turning to her again, 'giving advice. She's given me some wonderful advice these last few months. To tell you the truth, I don't know what I would have done without her.'

But why didn't you feel that way about me, Daddy? I wondered. Why didn't you ever say you wouldn't know what to do without me? Why did you let me go so easily?

'Mildred has planned everything out carefully and wisely,' Daddy continued. 'So you need not worry about me any longer.'

Worry about you? Why aren't you worrying about me? I cried silently.

'After we go to see her children, we're going to honeymoon in Alaska as a way to plan the cruise and enjoy ourselves. Isn't that efficient? Then we'll be doing some traveling again. Off to Europe on business and back to Boston just before the winter. But we won't be staying in Boston all winter. Some of it we'll spend in the Caribbean. In the spring we'll vacation in Maine with Mildred's family and then next summer . . .'

'But what about me?' I finally cried.

'Oh, we'll see you whenever we can,' Daddy said. 'Mildred will plan that out, too.'

Mildred will plan that out? Why had my father permitted this woman to take his life over completely?

'That's right, dear,' she said. 'I'm working on when we can take you along with us on a trip and when you can come stay with us. We would take you to Maine with us tomorrow, but . . .'

'I don't want to go with you to Maine,' I snapped.

'Now Leigh . . .' Daddy raised his eyebrows.

'I don't care.'

'But you should care,' Daddy said. 'If you want to be considered a young lady, you have to show some courtesy,' he chastised. Mildred stared at me, her eyes cold. I looked down at my menu. My chest felt so heavy. It was as though it were filling up with the tears that had built up behind my eyes.

'Now then,' my father said, 'what would you like to eat? Leigh?'

'You should think about the London Broil,' Mildred said.

'I hate London Broil,' I blurted, 'and I hate being here, and I hate you.'

I couldn't help it. It all just rushed out over my tongue, and once the words had escaped, there was no turning back. I got up from the table and ran from the dining room, ran through the hotel lobby and out the front door. Miles was asleep in the front seat of the limousine. I woke him when I banged on the window. He sat up quickly, shocked by the tears streaming down my face.

'What is it? What's wrong?'

'Take me back to Farthy,' I said getting in. 'I want to go back.'

'But . . .'

'Please, take me home.'

He started the engine. I looked out the side window and saw Daddy on the front steps looking for me. He didn't see the limousine until Miles backed out of the parking lot. Then he charged down the steps.

'Leigh!' he called. Miles began to slow down.

'Just drive, Miles,' I commanded in my mother's sharp tone of voice. He obeyed and the car surged forward away from the hotel. I looked back once and saw my father standing in the center of the parking lot, his hands on his hips. Coming up behind him was his precious new wife. I turned away and cried so hard my ribs ached. By the time we arrived at Farthy, I was feeling drained and exhausted.

I ran up the steps and into the house, not pausing a second before rushing up the stairs to my suite. Once there, I threw myself on my bed. I didn't think I had a single tear left but I cried a waterfall of tears until I cried myself to sleep. I felt myself being shaken and awoke to find Troy at my side. He was dressed in his little sailor's outfit. I sat up and wiped my eyes. I caught a glimpse of myself in the mirror and saw that my cheeks were tear-streaked.

'Didn't you have a good time with your daddy?' Troy asked.

'Oh Troy,' I moaned and embraced him to me.

'What's wrong, Leigh?' He looked up at me with his eyes big, inquisitive and concerned. 'Why were you crying?'

'My daddy's not the same, Troy. He has a new wife.'

Troy fluttered his eyelashes. I could almost hear his thoughts.

'You have another mommy?'

'No. She's not my mommy; *never, never, never!*'

He stared at me. He had no mother and no father. It was not hard to understand why he was confused by my anger. I was sure he wished he had the chance to have a new mother and father and here I was throwing a new mother back as if she were a fish too small.

'My daddy doesn't love me as much as he did before,' I

explained. 'His new wife has her own family and he has new children too.'

Troy's eyes brightened with some understanding. He nodded.

'You want to come play with my electric train?' he asked, hoping to cheer me up. I smiled and kissed him. Funnily enough, I was suddenly very hungry. My emotional turmoil had drained me, but now my stomach churned. I had been too nervous at breakfast to eat much, and of course, I ran out of the restaurant before a thing was served.

'I'll just go down to the kitchen and ask Rye to make me something for lunch,' I told him. 'Then I'll come play with you.'

'I'll come with you,' he offered. He waited while I washed my face, scrubbing away the lines drawn by tears and pain. I ran the brush through my hair, took his hand, and started out just as my telephone rang. It was my father.

'Leigh, please don't hang up,' he said quickly, anticipating my first thought. 'Will you listen to me?' he asked when I didn't reply.

'Yes, I'll listen, Daddy.'

'I'm sorry, sorry that I didn't come to see you as soon as I had returned and sorry that I broke the news of my new marriage the way I did at lunch. It was insensitive of me and I apologize. Mildred is very upset about everything. She wanted so much to get you to like her. Really, she did. You believe that, don't you?' he asked.

'Yes, Daddy,' I said dryly.

'Mildred says all that's happened to you this last year is a considerable emotional burden on top of the normal emotional burden teenagers carry these days. She's very wise when it comes to these things, you see. She has a daughter of her own, as well as a son. I hope you will meet them someday soon.'

When I didn't reply, he continued.

'I'd ask you to come with us to Maine, but . . .'

'I can't go to Maine, Daddy. I'm modeling for a new Tatterton toy, a portrait doll,' I said, 'and I'm very busy with it.'

'Oh?'

'I would have told you all about it if we had been alone,' I snapped.

'You could have spoken about it at lunch. Mildred is my wife now and she wants to be a mother to you.'

'I have a mother.'

'Well, at least a good friend, then. So, you're modeling. Sounds exciting. Are you enjoying it?'

I hesitated. Should I blurt it all out over the phone, make him feel terrible for not meeting me privately? Would he come to Farthy immediately, come charging into the house and demand an audience with Tony and my mother, and then bawl them out and take me away with him?

But I would go off with him and his new wife and her children, his new family. Would I like that?

'Yes, Daddy,' I said. 'I'm enjoying it. It's going to make me very famous,' I said petulantly. He was silent a long moment.

'Well, I'm happy for you, Leigh. Would you like to try again, meet us for dinner tonight, perhaps?'

'No, Daddy. I can't tonight. I have to go to sleep early because I have an early morning session and I have to be fresh and wide awake all over,' I said. I thought he might ask why I said 'all over', but he didn't.

'Perhaps when we return from Maine then,' he said.

'Perhaps.'

'Leigh, please believe me when I tell you I love you.'

'I believe you, Daddy,' I replied quickly.

'You'll always be my little Princess, no matter what,' he added in the voice that brought back a hundred memories. How I wanted him near me now, to hug me and kiss me just the way he often did when he returned home from a cruise or business trip. But all he was, was a tiny, faraway voice on a phone.

'Bye, Leigh. We'll call you when we come back.'

'Bye, Daddy.' I lowered the receiver slowly. My body began to shake with dry sobs. Troy came running to me and embraced me.

'Don't cry, Leigh. Please, don't cry.'

'I won't, Troy.' I held my breath a moment and then smiled. 'I'm all right. Come,' I said, 'let's go see what Rye Whiskey can fix for me.'

I took his hand and we went out.

Later that afternoon, my mother came to Troy's suite looking for me, curious about my day with my father. She was surprised to hear that he had remarried and wanted to know all about his new wife. I didn't tell her I had run out on them.

'She's tall and thin and her nose is long and bony,' I said. She smiled at that. 'She has a poor complexion, pock marks on her forehead, and her hair looks like she rarely washes it. It's dull and full of gray streaks.'

'I'll never let my hair turn gray,' Momma said quickly. 'It's so unnecessary for a woman to go through that.'

'She has no figure,' I continued, enjoying the way I ran down my father's new wife, 'but Daddy likes her because she is an accountant and she is very efficient.'

'Just the kind of woman he would like. You must have had a dreadful time, poor thing.'

'And she has her own family with grown-up children!' I exclaimed.

'Really? Extraordinary! What happened to her first husband?' she asked. I didn't know what to say.

'They didn't tell me that.'

She nodded in understanding.

'Are you going to see them again soon?' she asked.

'No. They're off to see her family and then they're going on a combined business trip and honeymoon.'

My mother burst out laughing. Even Troy, who had been sitting quietly by his trains and listening to me, looked up with a confused, but wide smile on his face.

'Isn't that just like him? He'll make his own honeymoon into a tax deduction.' She started out of Troy's suite and turned. 'Oh, did you tell him about your modeling for the portrait doll?'

She had tried to ask the question nonchalantly, but from the way her body had tensed, I suddenly realized she had more than a passing curiosity in my answer.

'Yes.' I refused to elaborate. If she so badly wanted to know what I had told Daddy, then let her ask! I wasn't going to make things any easier – she hadn't for me.

She studied me for a moment. Was it my imagination or had her eyes suddenly filled with apprehension? I studied her eyes more closely. Yes, there was definitely apprehension . . . and fear! I watched her swallow over the lump in her throat and she could barely get her next words out, 'What did he say?'

I gave her a pointed stare. 'He thought it was wonderful. What else would he say?'

Relief washed over her beautiful features. She knew I hadn't told Daddy the truth. 'You're a very wise and intelligent young lady for your age, Leigh. I'm proud of you. Oh, Tony and I are going out for dinner. We've been invited to the Ambersons'. You know who Mr Amberson is, don't you?' She didn't wait for me to answer. 'He's a multimillionaire who owns tons of paper mills. He's got oodles of money and can have anything his heart desires. Anything!'

Was that all she cared about? Money? Possessions? Had her love for luxury and wealth overpowered her love for me? I wondered more and more with each passing day.

'By the way,' she continued as she breezed out of Troy's suite, 'Tony told me to tell you he'll need you for just a little while tomorrow morning and then he's finished with his work here. Isn't that exciting?'

Before I could answer she was gone, heading to her suite to bathe and dress for dinner.

I slammed the door of the suite in anger. Troy looked at me with scared eyes. How I wanted to scream at Momma! Once again she had told me what to do without thought or consideration of my feelings.

With each passing day the web Momma had ensnared me in was becoming tighter and tighter. Where would it all end? I fearfully wondered.

Tony wasn't at breakfast the following morning. Momma explained that he had risen early and had already gone to the cottage to work. I was to follow as soon as I was finished with my own breakfast. I ate slowly, while she described their dinner at the Amberson's. After a while I stopped listening and her voice droned on over my thoughts. I was feeling much more nervous about this final session with Tony than I had felt about all the others. Maybe it was just a result of all the dramatic and terribly emotional things that had been happening to me.

Finally, I left the table, went up to my suite and made some final touches on my hair, and then started out for the cottage. It was a bright morning, warmer than most. The ocean breezes were very slight and the clouds seemed pasted to the aqua sky. Even the birds which were usually quite active and noisy were placid. They stared down at me with jeweled eyes in anticipation. I heard the whir of lawn mowers on the far corners of the grounds and caught the cry of a tern, but other than that, the world seemed like a gigantic painting on a gigantic canvas.

All this made the stillness and isolation of the maze even more intense. The shadows were darker, deeper and longer. Cool spots were cooler and the scent of the freshly cut hedges was pungent. Instead of feeling as if I were moving through tunnels though, I felt as if I were dropping deeper and deeper into a world of mystery. I looked back once and saw the roof of Farthy just before it disappeared behind a tall hedge. For no reason I could figure out I panicked and ran the rest of the way, bursting out by the cottage. I stopped and caught my breath. Then, feeling foolish, I wiped my face with my handkerchief, brushed back my hair, corrected my posture and went to the cottage.

Tony was hovering over the clay model, his hands over it as if he were about to seize it and press it to him. He looked up sharply when I entered and straightened quickly.

'I couldn't wait for you this morning,' he said. 'I was that eager to finish up. Just sit there,' he said pointing to the couch. 'All I want to do this morning is make some final touches on the doll's face. So,' he said as I took my seat and faced him, 'you went to see your father yesterday.' He began working with a tiny tool.

'Yes.'

'But all didn't go well?' he asked. I shifted my eyes to him quickly. He saw I was wondering how he knew that. 'Miles told me,' he added softly.

'I didn't say anything to your mother though.' He winked. 'I gather from what you told her that neither did you.'

'I didn't want to upset her.'

'Yes. So what happened to upset *you*? Just turn a little to the right. A little more. Fine.'

'My father remarried,' I said.

'And you didn't know about it until then?'

'That's right.'

He shook his head.

'Men can be such fools.' He smiled. 'Didn't you get along with the new woman?'

'I was too upset about things. I suppose I was unfair,' I added. I had been thinking that I should have given my father and his wife another chance by going to dinner with them. Now he was off to Maine and I couldn't do anything about it.

'I can't imagine you being unfair to anyone, Leigh. There's no one sweeter or more considerate. I see the way you are with Troy,' he said smiling. I didn't say anything. 'I know I'm a poor substitute,' he continued, 'but I wish you would think of me as you would a father. I know you think me too young, but I have a great deal of experience. My wealth and responsibilities have aged me far beyond my years.' He smiled again, shifted his position, studied me, worked and then stopped and studied me some more.

'Anyway,' he said after a while, 'if you ever have any problems you can't discuss with your mother, I wish you would come to me.'

'Thank you, Tony,' I said.

'I'd enjoy helping you.' He worked with other tools, scraping, making fine touches, studying me, working, on and on like that for well over an hour. Finally, he stood up and announced he was finished.

'That's it,' he said. 'Your job's over. Now I've got to get this cast. I think I'll turn the actual painting over to one of my best artists.'

I was finished? No more nude modeling? What an easy final day, but I realized I hadn't seen the finished sculpture.

'Can I see it now?'

'Of course,' he said, stepping back. He gestured toward the clay figure. I got up slowly and walked around to face it. The moment I looked at it, my face turned beet red and I gasped.

My head was reeling. I felt hot all over then cold. My face was perfect but he had sculptured every detail and every part of my body with such exaggeration, it looked pornographic. Everyone could see this . . . boys . . . everyone.

'What's wrong?' he asked, his eyes narrowing to tiny blue slits.

'Tony you can't show everyone this. It's embarrassing. Dolls don't have . . . have . . .'

'Genitals? No, dolls don't, but a portrait doll is a work of art, I told you.'

'*No!*' I cried. 'I can't let you put my face to this. I can't,' I said.

'But it will be only your doll. No one else will have this one. They'll want their own.'

'But they'll be looking at this one to see what theirs will be like.'

'It will be dressed when they look at it.'

'But then why did you do this?'

He looked at me and then at the doll as if the answer were on the doll's lips. Then he reached out and caressed the clay figure. As he did so his eyes became dreamy and faraway as I had seen happen before.

'Because . . . as I said . . . it's a work of art.'

'No, I won't let you put my picture beside it. *I won't!*' I insisted. He stared at me a moment. Then his eyes turned cold, even colder than before. They lost their faraway look and focused hard on me.

'All right,' he said angrily. 'I'll change it. You're finished now. You can go,' he snapped.

I walked to the door. When I looked back, I saw he was standing there staring down at the doll, his face as hard and as still as a sculptured one. I left the cottage and hurried on through the maze. Before I was halfway through, I began to run the rest of the way, fleeing the image of myself naked and exposed for everyone to see.

FIFTEEN

Angel

Although I had looked forward so much to my summer vacation, I was happy when it drew to a close and I would return to Winterhaven. I missed Jennifer. I had told her about the portrait doll, but I hadn't told her about my nude posing. And I never got to visit her. After I finished my work for the doll, Momma found one reason or another why I shouldn't leave. I asked her again, weeks before I was to return to school, but she said I would see my friends soon enough. A few days later she decided she wanted to take me to New York City to shop for new clothing for school and new clothing for herself as well. It was a whirlwind trip because almost as soon as we arrived, she decided it was too hot to stay. After only one night in New York and shopping in just two department stores, we returned to Farthy.

Throughout most of August Tony did a great deal of traveling, establishing new markets across the country for his toys and especially for portrait dolls. I had yet to see the finished product. He had done as he said and turned the fine art work over to one of his better artisans, a man he had imported from Europe, a man who had worked on these dolls there. Tony told my mother and me that he didn't want us to see it until it was completely done, down to the last eyelash.

The changing weather caused Troy to develop a new allergy. It got so bad that for one week at the end of August, he had to be in the hospital. The doctors did dozens of tests on him, trying to find the best antidotes for his problems. I had Miles take me to visit him every day, but Momma never went once. She always seemed to have something else to do, some place to go, people to see.

Finally, the day came when I was packed off for my return

to Winterhaven. Our private school began a week earlier than the public schools. It had been one of the warmest summers on record, but toward the very end of August, the weather made an about-face. Autumn came charging in on the heels of the wind and the rain, turning the leaves into the rainbow colors of fall almost overnight. Temperatures sunk and the hazy blue sky became a deeper and sharper blue.

I didn't mind. I always loved fall, loved the colors and the brisk breezes. The air was fresh and filled me with energy and hope. I had received two phone calls from Daddy, one on his return from Maine, just before his honeymoon, and one right after that. Each time, he left me with the promise of seeing me, but something happened with his schedule or his business that made it impossible. We left it that I might spend my Christmas holiday with him and Mildred.

Jennifer's mother had remarried, too, and she was just as unhappy about it and just as eager to get back to Winterhaven and the 'special club'. She was waiting outside our dorm when Miles drove me up. She ran to the car and we hugged and kissed and talked so quickly and so much, we both grew hoarse. She helped me unpack my things and then we went around to see the other girls. Everyone but Marie had arrived. She was coming a day later, directly from Paris.

That first night back, Jennifer and I sat up in bed talking into the wee hours. I finally told her about my modeling experience. When I described the way I had first undressed and how Tony slipped the sheet from my body gradually, she grew quiet, her voice then dropping to a bare whisper.

'But he's so young-looking,' she said. 'I don't know if I could have done that. How did you do it?'

'I don't know. My mother talked me into it,' I told her. 'You know she's an artist and artists don't think much of that sort of thing,' I explained. I didn't tell her about Tony's method of touching me and then painting and sculpting. I just couldn't confess to that. Even so, what I described was enough.

'You must promise not to tell anyone in the "special club", Jennifer. I don't want the others to know the details. Let them think the doll's body was created from Tony's imagination. They will laugh anyway when they see it.'

'Why?' she asked quickly.

'Because it looks older than I do, more mature. Especially here,' I said indicating my bosom.

'Why did he do that?' Jennifer asked, her eyes wide.

'I don't know. I don't understand men, not my father, not any man.'

Jennifer grew quiet. I thought she was thinking about her own father, but she surprised me.

'I met a boy the last week of the summer,' she said, 'and we had two dates.'

'Jennifer Longstone, you never told me a thing about it in your letters and phone calls,' I cried sitting up quickly. 'What boy? What's he like? How old is he?'

'It happened so fast I didn't have time to tell you, and anyway, I didn't want to make a big thing out of it until I was sure he really liked me. His name is William Matthews. He's sixteen and he attends Allendale so he will be at the dance this coming weekend. Are you going to be able to stay?'

'Yes. My mother has agreed to let me stay every other weekend.'

'Oh, that's wonderful because William's roommate will be coming too, and when I told William about you, he said you and his roommate would be perfect together.'

'Jennifer, you didn't. What did you tell him?'

'Just the truth . . . that you're beautiful and smart and fun to be with.'

'Oh, Jennifer.'

'It's all right. I didn't make any promises. I wouldn't do that without talking to you first. William's roommate's name is Joshua John Bennington. William says he's very shy, but very good-looking and one of the brightest boys at Allendale. Also, he's very rich.'

'You sound like a matchmaker. Since when did you get so sophisticated about boys, Jennifer Longstone?'

'Since the last week of the summer,' she whispered and then

went on to tell me about her two dates with William, the second one occurring at her house where they were alone together.

'He kissed me, Leigh,' she confessed. 'It was the first time I let a boy touch me. Did you ever let a boy touch you, Leigh?' she asked.

I thought again about Tony running his hands over my body, but I was still ashamed to tell her about it.

'No,' I said quickly. 'I don't think I could unless I loved him and he loved me,' I said. Jennifer nodded, looking a little guilty.

'I like him a lot,' she admitted. It made me think there was more to her story.

'What happened?'

'I liked it, Leigh. But I made him stop when he went too far,' she added quickly. 'I did,' she emphasized. 'That's the secret, knowing when to stop. That's what Wendy Cooper told me and Wendy ought to know. She's been going steady with Randolph Hampton for almost a year now and Randolph's nearly seventeen!' We were both quiet a moment and then Jennifer said, 'But it's hard to stop, Leigh. Things happen inside you and you have to argue with your own body. You'll see when it happens to you,' she promised.

I thought about the way I had trembled under Tony's touch, experiencing feelings I had never had. But I had been mostly embarrassed. I wondered if I always would be, even when I did these things with the man I loved.

Jennifer had really surprised me. Of all the girls in the 'special club', I would have thought her the least likely to do these things with a boy. There's no way to be sure about anyone, I thought, not a best friend, and certainly not a father. Summers were short, yet so much seemed to happen over summers. Everything in and around my life was happening so quickly now. I felt like I was on a runaway roller coaster.

'Oh Leigh, it's so good to be back with you and have someone I can talk to again. I hate my mother now and I can't talk to her about anything that's important to me anymore. Do you hate your father?'

'I don't know,' I said. I really didn't know. 'Sometimes I do and sometimes, I feel sorry for him. It's all so confusing, I hate thinking about it anymore.'

I said good night and turned over to go to sleep, but Jennifer's confessions had rekindled my memories of Tony touching me, studying my body with his fingers, and stroking me as if I were the clay for him to mold. How could my mother think that my permitting him to touch me like that was all right? Didn't she think I would feel things as Jennifer did when her boyfriend touched her, or did she think I was still too young?

I looked over at Jennifer, who was already asleep and probably dreaming about William Matthews. Her first experiences were exciting, the kind of experiences all of us girls had talked about and dreamt about having. I wanted a boyfriend too, someone to love and cherish me the way men and women loved and cherished each other in romantic movies and novels. I didn't want to be thinking about Tony Tatterton gazing down at my naked body while I stood obediently before him. What kind of romantic moment was that?

It took all my powers of concentration to drive the images from my mind so I could turn into the arms of Sleep, but finally, I was able to do it.

The next morning the dorms of Winterhaven exploded with life and energy. Everyone was excited about beginning classes in a new school year. The showers ran continually, hair dryers were blowing everywhere, girls were shouting to each other, borrowing clothing, jewelry and ribbons from each other. It felt good to be back. I didn't think I would be as happy as I was, but here at Winterhaven, with all the girls chattering away, with bells ringing and girls scurrying about not to be late, I would try to forget the sad and ugly moments of the past few months.

The 'special club' gathered together as always for the walk to the classrooms. Marie Johnson was due any moment and we were anticipating her arrival. And everyone was talking about the upcoming dance with the boys of Allendale. It was the traditional way to start the new school social year. I was so happy that I would be able to attend it. Of course, the main topic of conversation was what to wear. Everyone had an opinion about that.

We started down the corridor. Other girls waved and called to us from their rooms as we passed by. During the day all the dorm rooms had to be left unlocked so they could be inspected to see if the beds were made and clothes were hung up.

Just as we reached the lobby, Marie came bursting in, her chauffeur right behind her struggling with her luggage. She had earrings as big as ice cubes on her lobes and she had her eyebrows trimmed with eye shadow over her lids. She wore a white cotton tennis sweater with a matching cotton blouse and long flowing dark blue skirt.

'*Jeunes filles!*' she cried. '*Comment allez-vous?*'

'Marie!'

Everyone rushed to greet her. She looked so much older.

'I can't believe I'm back in this place,' she said, looking around with an expression of disgust. 'And look at you all. The rat pack.' Then she laughed. 'I missed you, each and every one of you.'

She took turns hugging each of us.

'I tried to arrange arriving last night, but it just couldn't be done,' she said quickly and sighed. 'I'm going to have to rest a while, but don't worry about me. Miss Mallory has been contacted and I'm excused from all my morning classes. Tonight, you're all invited to my room. I have little presents for all of you and I will tell you every detail about my summer in Paris . . . especially, the men.'

'Men!' Toby cried.

'Well, young men. *Au revoir*,' she said and gestured to her chauffeur to follow.

I walked toward my class with my friends, not letting them know that there was a storm brewing inside me. I knew there were dreams and pains I could never share with the 'special club'.

Suddenly nothing became as exciting as the upcoming dance with the boys of Allendale. Jennifer spoke with William on the telephone one night and called me to her side so I could say hello to William's roommate, Joshua. I didn't want to do it, but she beckoned and beckoned and pleaded until I gave in. Then she handed me the receiver. I scowled at her.

'Say hello,' she coached.

'Hello,' I said and this deep, soft voice replied.

'Hello.' There was a long pause before he went on. 'This is a bit embarrassing. William wanted me to speak with you before the dance and . . .'

'And Jennifer wanted me to speak with you,' I said, seeing how hard it was for him, too.

'Yes, I . . . I do look forward to meeting you. From what William has told me, Jennifer speaks so highly of you.'

'Jennifer exaggerates.'

'Oh, I don't think so. Anyway, I just wanted to say hello and tell you I look forward to seeing you at the dance,' he added. I thought he sounded very grown up.

'Me too,' I replied and hated the sound of my voice because I sounded so young. I thrust the phone back at Jennifer, practically stabbing her with it in the chest. She took it and finished her conversation with William. As soon as she cradled the receiver, I was at her.

'How could you do that? It was so embarrassing trying to have a conversation with someone I've never met. I'm sure he doesn't want to have anything to do with me now. I sound like an idiot on the telephone.'

'No you don't.'

'I like to see the person I'm meeting for the first time,' I complained, but Jennifer stood there with her Cheshire cat grin. All the rest of that night I replayed Joshua's words. I hoped he looked as good as he sounded.

Now wearing the proper dress and looking my best became so very important. I could think of nothing else. I finally settled on my pink chiffon with a waist bow on the back. I had hesitated because of the spaghetti straps. I still thought my shoulders looked too bony, but I decided I would wear a lace shawl as well and keep it on if I felt too self-conscious.

Winterhaven was hosting the dance. Downstairs, the decorating committee had removed most of the tables from the large dining room. The rugs had been rolled and put aside. Colorful streamers and festive paper decorations had been hung from the ceiling, and spinning where a more sedate chandelier had once hung was a large, mirrored ball. I would have never believed that a room which was sunny and bright by day, since it faced east and south, could be converted into a passable ballroom.

With Marie leading the way, jabbering on and on about the balls she attended in Paris, the 'special club' marched down. The night before Marie had given us all a lecture about the boys of Allendale, emphasizing that most were very rich and sophisticated. Her advice was to be coy, let the boy do most of the talking, pretend to be impressed, and bat our eyelashes. She even demonstrated the way a woman called a *femme fatale* would do it. She said they were beautiful, but dangerous women who usually destroyed the hearts of the men who fell in love with them. Marie knew boys from Allendale well and claimed some deserved to have their hearts broken. I hoped Joshua John Bennington wasn't one of those. Neither Jennifer nor I had told the others about him and William Matthews. We wanted to surprise them with our little secret.

By the time we arrived, the music had already begun; the band was playing 'Rock Around the Clock'. Some of the balloons had broken free and were floating over the center of the dance floor. All of the other boys from Allendale were standing in a herd across the room, some sipping punch, others standing and gazing at us with cool eyes and placid smiles, each deciding who he was going to ask to dance.

The eyes of the other girls in our club popped when a tall, blond-haired boy with fair skin and blue eyes came across the room quickly to greet Jennifer.

'Leigh,' Jennifer said taking William's hand and turning him to me. 'This is William Matthews. William, Leigh VanVoreen.'

'I'm pleased to meet you,' he said, extending his hand. I thought he had a pleasant face with soft, gentle features, and I was very happy for Jennifer. Behind us, the members of the 'special club' were whispering madly.

'I'm pleased to meet you.'

'My roommate is standing over by the punch bowl shivering in terror,' William said.

'Oh William, don't tease him,' Jennifer said. 'Or Leigh,' she added with wide eyes.

'Ladies,' William Matthews said, holding his arms out to escort us both to the punch bowl. I took his left arm, gazed back once at the amazed 'special club', and walked across the floor. A tall, black-haired boy with a very tanned face and bright hazel-green eyes looked up. I thought he was very handsome with a quiet, underlying manliness that made my heart flutter. There was a tenderness in his gaze, but the way he glanced at me with his eyes moving rapidly over me, scooping me in, titillated me. I felt a tingling sensation through my spine.

'Leigh,' William said with a little more force and volume than necessary, 'this is my roommate, Joshua John Bennington, the famous telephone conversationalist.' He followed that with a laugh and Jennifer poked him in the shoulder.

Joshua swung his eyes toward the ceiling and shook his head.

'I'm sorry my roommate is such a clown,' he said and extended his hand. 'Pleased to meet you.'

'Me too,' I said and almost bit my lip to prevent myself from uttering that infantile phrase again. 'I mean . . .'

'Jen and I are going to dance while you two get acquainted,' William said. 'Be careful, Leigh, there is a mile-long trail of discarded women behind him. Joshua, you're on your own,' he warned and winked. Then he took Jennifer onto the dance floor. I watched them for a moment.

'He's a good dancer,' I said.

'William's good at most everything he does. He's one of those perfectly accomplished guys who makes the rest of us feel inferior,' Joshua said.

'Oh,' I said quickly, 'you have no reason to feel inferior.' Even I was surprised at how enthusiastically I had said it. He widened his eyes and his smile.

'Don't believe that story about discarded women. I didn't even attend one of the dances last year,' he confessed.

'You didn't? Neither did I.'

'Really?' He smiled, his eyes more relaxed. 'Some punch?' he offered.

'Yes, please.'

After he poured my glass, we went to a bench to sit and talk. I learned that his father was an estates attorney, that he had two brothers and a sister, and he lived just outside of Boston. His family had a home in West Palm Beach, Florida, as well as a beach house on Cape Cod. Once he started to talk about himself, he never stopped. Every once in a while, I looked toward the 'special club'. Some had found partners and were dancing. Toby and Betsy hadn't and were staring at me with daggers of envy.

He asked me where I lived and I told him about Farthy. He had heard of Tatterton Toys, but his family didn't own any. When I mentioned Tony, I said 'step-father,' but Joshua didn't ask me about my real father or why my mother had remarried. I thought that was very courteous.

We danced, ate the refreshments, and danced some more. Jennifer and William were with us most of the time. Finally, when she couldn't hold back any longer, she asked me to go to the girls' room with her. The door wasn't closed behind us before she blurted out with her questions.

'Do you like him? Are you having a good time? What's he like?'

'Yes, I like him. He's very nice and *soooo* polite,' I said. 'But I love it. He makes me feel . . . like a lady.'

'I'm so glad,' Jennifer said and we hugged and laughed. Before we could leave the bathroom, however, Marie, followed by the others, came storming in. She stood before us, her hands on her hips.

'All right, you two, what's going on here? How come no one in the "special club" knew you two had boyfriends from Allendale?' she demanded.

'He's not my boyfriend,' I said quickly. 'I just met him tonight.'

Marie turned to Jennifer.

'I met William at the end of the summer, but he hasn't asked me to go steady or anything,' she replied. Marie bit down on the corners of her mouth.

'You should have told the rest of us you had dates anyway,' she said. 'Members of the "special club" don't hide things like this from each other. We trust each other with our hearts. That's what makes us special,' she added, her eyes shooting daggers.

'But . . .'

'We all feel like idiots, not knowing. It's a kind of betrayal of trust,' she added, folding her arms across her bosom.

'That's silly, Marie. We told you . . .'

'It's not silly.' She turned to the others. 'Does anyone else here think it's silly?' They were all of one face, Marie's face – angry, jealous, spiteful. 'You should have told us,' she repeated. 'But it's just like you not to share. You didn't invite anyone else but Jennifer to your precious estate home, did you? You think you're better than the rest of us.'

'I do not. I told you . . .'

'Have a good time,' she snapped and turned. The rest of them moved along with her as if they were part of her tail, a clump of envy glaring back.

'Oh Leigh, I'm sorry,' Jennifer cried. 'I got you into trouble with the others.'

'I'm not in any trouble, Jen. They're just jealous, that's all. Forget about them. We'll do just as Marie said. We'll have a good time. Besides, it's as much my fault as yours. I didn't say anything to them either.'

Jennifer nodded, but I saw she was very upset.

'Come on,' I insisted. 'Forget about it.' I took her hand and led her out of the bathroom.

But the rest of the night was a nightmare for us. The others didn't stop glaring at us spitefully. None of them would talk to us and before the dance ended, they were whispering things about us to other girls and laughing aloud.

Joshua sensed something was wrong, so I told him.

'Just like me,' he said, 'to be the cause of someone's problems.' I was surprised at how quickly he accepted blame.

'Oh no, it's not your fault and it's a very stupid reason for them to argue and be angry. They're not really our friends if they would do this.' I glared back at them across the dance floor. 'Besides,' I said, 'I would much rather you be my friend than any of the so called "special club".'

'Really?' Joshua's eyes lit up.

'Yes. I hope you will call me and come see me whenever there is an opportunity.' I couldn't believe how brazen I was about him, but I was angry and I did like him.

'Oh, I will. I will.' He beamed.

We danced again and again and when the slow dance came, he held me firmly against his body and his lips grazed my temple. I looked up at him and for a moment, he held his eyes on mine. We must have looked very romantic, because when I gazed at some of the other girls from Winterhaven who weren't members of our 'special club', I saw them looking at Joshua and me with dreamy expressions in their eyes and sighs on their lips.

Miss Mallory announced the end of the dance and advised the clean up committee to be up early in the morning to do their job. Future parties, she warned, depended on how well they performed.

The boys began to leave. Jennifer and I walked out with William and Joshua, both of us holding hands with our dates. As soon as we walked out of the building, William pulled Jennifer into the shadows to give her a good-night kiss. Joshua and I watched. Then we turned to each other. I couldn't help my feelings. I wanted him to kiss me, too. Without realizing it, I was squeezing his hand. He looked puzzled for a moment and then he led me toward another shadowy area where he kissed me softly on the lips.

'Good night, Leigh. I had a wonderful time,' he said.

'So did I. Good night.'

He joined William and they were off with the others. Jennifer and I waved until they were gone. Then we looked at each other and laughed. She and I hugged, held hands, and re-entered the dorm.

When we arrived at our room, we found a note on our door

that read, 'KEEP YOUR SECRETS AND YOURSELVES AWAY FROM THE REST OF US.'

I ripped it off the door and tore it up.

Jennifer went to her bed to sit down and mourn, but the moment she did, she jumped with a scream.

'What?'

'Look,' she pointed.

Our beds were soaked. It smelled like they had scooped water out of the toilets and thrown it over them.

'Ugh,' Jennifer said. She started to get sick and ran for the bathroom.

When I had told her I didn't understand men, I had made a gross understatement. I didn't understand anybody, men or women. Cruelty, selfishness, jealousy, evil in many forms festered like a blister under everyone's heart, probably, even my own. Right now I wished I could punish each and every one of the 'special club' by sticking needles and pins in them.

I started to strip off the bedding. We would have to turn over the mattresses.

Jennifer came out of the bathroom, tears streaming down her cheeks. I smiled.

'How can you be happy after this?' she asked.

'I'm not thinking about this. I'm thinking about Joshua John Bennington's hazel-green eyes,' I replied. She stared at me in amazement for a moment and then she smiled too. And then we both laughed.

We laughed so loud and hysterically that some of the other girls came out of their rooms to see what was happening.

'It's nothing,' I screamed in the hallway, *'we just had such a good time tonight.'*

Doors slammed down the corridor.

Jennifer and I looked at each other and laughed again. We laughed so hard and so long, we were too tired to make our beds properly and fell asleep on the unmade mattresses, our feet still moving to the music, our eyes still full of the ballroom lights.

*

The school year was different for us without our being part of the 'special club'. Some of them, like Wendy and Carla, couldn't help but be friendly again, even though we were never invited to any of their parties and meetings. It didn't matter as much as we feared it would because we were so involved with William and Joshua.

Every weekend I remained at Winterhaven, the four of us managed to get together to do something, even if it was just to study in the library. We went to movies and to restaurants and took walks on the docks. The weekends I had to go home, Joshua called me twice a day.

I told Momma about him, but she didn't seem very interested. She was very upset about herself because she couldn't lose four pounds no matter whose new diet she followed. She had even hired a dietician to help Rye prepare foods, something he didn't appreciate; but when that didn't bring about the results Momma wanted as quickly as she wanted them, she fired her.

Tony was very busy because his business was growing in so many ways. When I asked about the portrait doll, he said it was nearly ready, but he had decided to hold off showing it until the Christmas season, deciding it would be a wonderful new item for their stores. My mother told me that he was secretly keeping the doll from me until my birthday.

Troy's allergies improved and Tony hired a full-time tutor for him because he was so precocious. He was sure to be skipped along when he finally did enter grade school since he was already reading and writing.

One weekend early in October, I caught Momma in one of her better moods. She had been to a dinner party at which an editor from *Vogue* attended and told her she was beautiful enough to be a cover girl. He was even going to send a photographer around to take some sample shots to show. While she was in such high spirits, I asked her if I could have a birthday party and invite Jennifer, William and Joshua, as well as a few other girls we had become friendly with since being ostracized by the 'special club'. She agreed and even took charge of the arrangements. My birthday would be on a Monday, but we decided to have the party on the Sunday before.

That Saturday night Tony took my mother and me to dinner for our private celebration. Troy was permitted to go along. We had a wonderful time. Tony had arranged beforehand for the restaurant to make a special birthday cake for me, and the chef himself brought it out. The waiters and waitresses gathered around our table and sang 'Happy Birthday'. Momma and Tony kissed me and then little Troy gave me a present, one he was proud of because he had picked it out himself. It was a gold locket. He had put his picture in it, too. On the back he had the jeweler inscribe, 'For my sister, Leigh'.

'Oh, how sweet,' I said hugging him. 'I love this, Troy. I'll try to wear it always,' I told him and he looked so proud but dignified in his sports jacket and tie.

Later that night, not more than an hour after we had returned from the restaurant, I heard a knock on my outer door. It was Tony. He stood there holding a package wrapped in pink and blue paper.

'I wanted to do this privately,' he explained, his blue eyes capturing my own and holding them for a long moment. 'It's too special for us to share it with anyone at first.'

'Thank you, Tony.' I took the package from him and sat on the settee to unwrap it while he stood by, his hands behind his back, watching me. My fingers were clumsy because I was so excited. I didn't let on that I knew what was in the box, for Momma had already given it away.

I lifted the lid and looked down at my portrait doll. I thought it was truly a work of art, the doll's face so like my own it was as if I were looking into a mirror that miniaturized whoever gazed upon it. The expression on the doll's face was lovely, an exquisite smile, its eyes so bright and lifelike, I had the eerie feeling it could speak to me.

'Its hair feels so real,' I said in a whisper.

'It is real hair,' Tony replied, his lips curling into a smile. 'Your hair.'

'What?'

'Do you remember when Jillian took you to her hairdresser two months ago? I was in cahoots with him. He saved every strand of your hair that he cut and gave it to me and I had this done.'

'Really?' I was impressed.

The doll was dressed in a dress much like the one I had worn to the first school dance. Everything on it was authentic, even the tiny gold bracelet and the tiny gold locket, an exact replica of the one Troy had given me.

'If you look behind that locket with a magnifying glass, you'll see it says, "Love, Tony".'

I turned it over and saw the tiny words. How precious, I thought.

Everything about the doll was beautiful. Of course, her body was still much more developed than mine, but I remembered what Momma had said about Tony's combining the two of us.

I admired the detail work in the fingers and hands and had to turn my own palms over to compare. He had carved the same lines in the doll's palms. I wanted to undress it, and look for other things, but I didn't want to do that in front of him.

'It's beautiful, Tony, and a work of art, just as you said it would be.'

'I'm glad you like it. I have copies being made for the window displays, of course, but this is the original and it's yours forever. Happy birthday, Leigh,' he said, leaning down to kiss me. I turned my cheek, but he kissed me quickly on the lips.

'Well now,' he said standing. 'I have some things to do in the office. I'll see you later.'

'Thank you, Tony.' I held the doll in my arms as he left. Then I went quickly into my bedroom, closing the door behind me. I looked at the doll's body and breathed a sigh of relief. Although the bosom was vivid and there was even that little birthmark that was under my breast, he had done what I had asked about the genitals.

I smoothed down the dress and went off to show it to Momma.

'Oh, it's so beautiful, Leigh!' she exclaimed, turning it around and around in her hands. 'But I just knew it would be. Tony was so determined. It will be the hit of the Christmas season – portrait dolls by Tatterton. I so like the ring of that, don't you?

'Some day, I might just have him make one of me,' she said and sighed. 'Although I could never sit still as long as you did. I just don't have that kind of patience. He'll just have to do it from memory or photographs. Once I lose this excess weight, that is. Don't you think that's a good idea, Leigh?'

'Yes, Momma,' I said and left her dreaming about photo sessions.

I set the doll beside me on my bed and stared into its eyes. They twinkled as if she were truly alive and knew some deep secrets, perhaps the secret of my future.

'How I wish you could talk as well as look beautiful. Then you could be my guardian angel.'

What a good name for the doll, I thought, Angel.

'That's what I'll call you from now on,' I told her. I thought her smile widened, but of course, it was only my wild imagination fed by my hopes and dreams.

What a wonderful birthday this was turning out to be. If only Daddy were home and not married again with another family . . .

It was as if he heard me across the country. The phone rang and it was he, calling from San Francisco.

'I wanted to be sure to get you, Princess,' he said. 'I have an early departure tomorrow. My present will arrive in the morning. I hope you like it. Mildred picked it out,' he added. I closed my eyes, trying to ignore those last words.

'Where are you going this time, Daddy?' I asked, unable to hide the critical and unhappy tone in my voice.

'We're developing a cruise to the Hawaiian Islands. There's a real market for such a thing on the West coast. Mildred did a great deal of research on it. She's becoming of inestimable worth. Oh, Mildred says Happy Birthday.'

'Tell her thank you. When will you return?' I asked, thinking about our tentative plans to spend the Christmas holidays together.

'Not for months, I'm afraid. There's the establishment of offices, work with travel agents and hotel chains, the hiring of employees. But as soon as I return, I'll plan another holiday for all of us. Are you having a birthday party?'

'Yes, Daddy.' I was about to say, 'I wish you could come,' but I held back. Why wish for something that could never come true?

'Well, next year, I will be there for your birthday. That's a promise I'll be able to keep because Mildred has decided we should plan our calendar a year in advance. Everything all right?' he asked when I didn't respond.

'Yes, Daddy.'

'Well, happy birthday, Princess. I'll think of you all day tomorrow and I'll send you post cards. Good night.'

'Good night, Daddy,' I said. I heard him hang up, the click traveling thousands of miles and falling on my ear like a tear drop made of lead.

I felt the warm trickle of my own tears and brought my finger to my cheeks. The tip glistened. I brought it to Angel's face and touched her cheek.

Surely, she wanted to share my tears, too.

SIXTEEN

At the Cottage

Momma went overboard with my birthday party. She was determined to do all she could to impress all my friends from Winterhaven, not that they needed anything special to excite them. Once they were driven through the great arches and approached Farthy, they were already sufficiently impressed. Jennifer and I decided I should invite Wendy and Carla, since they had remained friendly even after Marie and the others excluded us. Of course, that hardened the distance and heightened the wall between us and the others, but neither Jennifer nor I cared anymore.

It was a beautiful October Sunday, a little warmer than usual. The grass was still quite green and plush, as were the hedges. With the fall colors in the background, the sky crystal blue and spotted here and there with candy cotton clouds, the day promised to be wonderful. I had no idea how elaborate my party was going to be. Late that morning a five-piece band arrived and set up in the ballroom. The staff brought out long serving tables and tables for the guests. With caviar as one of the appetizers, solid silver bowls of punch, decorations designed by a Boston decorator, professional musicians, memento presents for all my guests, waiters and waitresses everywhere, and a movie to be shown in the small theater, my party was truly overwhelming and quite unlike any birthday party I had ever had when we were all together and living in Boston. Even Tony was taken by surprise.

Troy was so excited he tried hard to get out of taking his morning nap. Under the threat of not being able to attend the party, he finally agreed to rest. Momma dressed up as if it were a party for adults. She put on her expensive diamonds and one of her most expensive designer black dresses, and spent most of the morning preparing her hair and make-up. She took a position in the great entry hall to greet my guests as they arrived. After they met her, either Troy or I escorted them into the great ballroom.

When Joshua arrived, I took his hand to make a big thing of introducing him to my mother. My heart hardened when she didn't even notice I was treating him as someone special, and I realized she had never listened to me when I had spoken about him before.

'This is Joshua Bennington,' I repeated when she had greeted him quickly and turned to give one of the maids an order.

'Do I know your family, Joshua?'

'I don't think so, Mrs Tatterton,' Joshua replied politely. I groaned with disappointment and took Joshua through the big house, showing him the music room with the murals, the grand piano, the gigantic fireplaces, and then snuck him away for a quick look at my suite.

'It's beautiful,' Joshua said. 'I've never been in a house quite like this. It's a . . . a castle.'

'Much too big to be a home,' I said. He nodded and then his eyes fell on Angel. I had her propped up against a pillow on my bed.

'What's that?'

'That's Angel. Angel, meet Joshua Bennington. You remember him. I've been talking about him enough,' I said. Joshua's eyes widened and then he laughed. He stepped closer to the doll.

'It looks just like you.'

'It is me,' I explained. 'It's the newest Tatterton toy, a portrait doll. I modeled for the very first one.'

'It's beautiful. Just like you, Leigh,' he said and blushed after his own words. How wonderful to have someone besides Tony or my father tell me that, I thought.

'Thank you, Joshua. Afterward, if you like, you and I will sneak away from the others and I'll show you the English maze and the cottage where I modeled.'

'Yes, I'd like that,' he said.

I took his hand and led him back downstairs where my party was just getting underway.

The band was very good because it played up-to-date songs. There was so much food and everyone thought the memento Momma had designed was very clever. She had a globe put in a glass cube and on the cube she had inscribed, 'Leigh, we think the world of her.' I was embarrassed by all this extravagance, but Momma went about, relishing the role of hostess, questioning everyone about his or her family, introducing Tony and bragging about Tatterton Toys. She wanted to be sure they all took home good stories about Farthy and Jillian Tatterton. In some ways she reminded me of how she used to be when we had first started going on Daddy's cruises and she would mingle with the passengers.

Finally, she announced the showing of the movie in 'Our private movie theater'. My friends couldn't believe their ears. She had somehow gotten one of the newest movies before it even reached the movie theaters.

'Oh Leigh,' Jennifer said, rushing over with William, 'I'll never forget this birthday party.'

'Neither will I!' William exclaimed.

Momma had Tony direct everyone to the theater. I squeezed Joshua's hand and indicated that he and I should remain behind to take seats in the rear.

'Once the movie's underway,' I whispered, 'we'll sneak out so I can show you the maze and the cottage. Unless you want to stay.'

'Oh no. I want to go with you.'

'Good.'

The private little theater was designed just like a regular movie theater with soft cushion seats and a big screen. There were two big doors in the back. Momma even had the maids go up and down the aisle with bags of popcorn. Joshua and I sat in the last row on the aisle. Jennifer and William sat with us. I had already told her of my intention to sneak out with Joshua for a while.

The lights came down and the picture was begun. We waited a good fifteen minutes into the movie before I poked Joshua and the two of us snuck out. I didn't see Tony anywhere, but I could hear Momma down the long corridor, laughing in the music room. She was speaking to someone on the telephone. I led Joshua to a side entrance and we burst out into the daylight and hurried across the grounds toward the maze.

'What is that?'

'An English maze. It's very easy to get lost in there, but don't worry, I know my way through it. Now it's fun for me.'

He held back, his eyes full of wonder as we entered.

'Are you sure you know how to get out once we go deep in?' Joshua asked skeptically. I laughed.

'I'm sure. Don't worry. Besides, would it be so terrible for you to get lost with me?' I teased.

'Oh no, I . . .'

I laughed and went forward. He held tightly to my hand as I took us through the corridors and around corners, moving to the right here and to the left there swiftly and assuredly until we came out on the other side and faced the cottage.

'Doesn't it look like a little storybook cottage?' I asked, stopping to breathe it all in: the beautiful warm way, the pretty little fence and lush green lawn and the cottage itself, straight off the pages of a book filled with nursery stories. 'It's so special.'

'Yes, it is,' Joshua said softly, his eyes full of excitement.

'Come on.' I took his hand again and led him down to the front gate. As we drew closer, I was surprised to see that the windows still had their shades drawn.

'We'll go inside for a moment and then we'll go back before anyone misses us. After I had first seen it,' I explained, 'I used to dream of living in it with the man I love. At least, for weekends. We would come here to escape from the world and have only ourselves.' I glanced at Joshua to see if he felt anything like I did. He had his eyes fixed on the cottage, but then he looked at me and smiled warmly.

We went up the short walkway to the front door. When I stepped in, I was surprised to find that Tony hadn't removed any of his art materials and supplies. The room was still set up like an artist's studio. But it had been so long since we had completed the work here, I thought. Why didn't he take everything out?

'Oh,' I said in disappointment. 'I thought it would have been turned back to the way it was.'

Joshua came in slowly behind me. I went directly to an easel. There was a canvas on it, a painting of me lying naked on the couch. I didn't look at it long because I was embarrassed about it, but I realized there was something different about this painting. I didn't recognize it as one of the paintings Tony had done while I modeled here, and my mother, who had invaded Tony's images of my body, also pervaded the face in the painting. It was truly a mixture of the two of us.

'Wait,' I said as Joshua started to approach. 'I don't want you to see this.'

'What? Why? What is it?'

'It's something . . . personal,' I replied and quickly covered the painting with the white sheet. 'I'm sorry.'

'It's all right,' he said quickly, even though his eyes were wide with confusion.

I looked about quickly to be sure there was no other evidence of what had gone on here. I saw some canvases in a carton on the right, but they were stacked so that no one could see what any of them were. Breathing relief, I sat on the couch.

'So this was an art studio,' Joshua said looking around. 'And Tony Tatterton created the portrait doll himself?'

'Yes. He painted and sculpted it here.'

'What a talented man.' Joshua sat beside me. 'I can see how this could be a very cozy little place,' he said nodding. 'A hideaway.'

'I used to love to come here. I still do. I just wish Tony had taken all this out and restored it to what it was. I don't understand why he hasn't.'

'Maybe he wants to do more work here,' Joshua suggested. The idea had never occurred to me. Perhaps he would talk my mother into coming here to pose or perhaps he would do another girl my age.

'Maybe. But I wanted you to see it the way it was . . . my make-believe home.'

'It can still be that,' Joshua said softly. 'You can make believe anything is anything.'

'Can we pretend to be two people desperately in love who live here on weekends?' I asked him.

'We don't have to pretend,' he replied, the desire behind his hazel-green eyes rising to the surface. We had kissed only half a dozen times, and always quickly to say good night or goodbye. But our lips never lingered long on each other's and we never held each other very closely so we could kiss each other more than once. Joshua leaned a little closer and so did I. Then our lips touched and he brought his hands to my shoulders, drawing me to him. I held him at his waist.

'Happy birthday, Leigh,' he whispered.

He kissed me again, longer this time. A moan escaped my lips and my body tingled right down to the tips of my fingers and toes. I thought about Jennifer's descriptions of her moments of love with William, how he kissed her and touched her. It was different when someone likes you very much and you like him and you let him touch you, I thought, thinking about Tony touching me in this very room. It had to be different and do different and more wonderful things to you.

Joshua backed away, unsure about kissing me so long and hard. I could read the indecision and the hesitation in his eyes. He was so sweet and so shy, but beneath that shyness a passion slept. I could sense it in the way his lips trembled against mine and in the way his fingers slipped across my shoulder until they touched my neck.

'I like you, Leigh. I like you more than any girl I ever met.'

'I like you too, Joshua.'

He started toward me and I closed my eyes. As he kissed me, his fingers drifted down the side of my arm. I tingled in anticipation. He was so close to touching my breast. When he started to draw back again, I realized he wouldn't. He was too unsure of himself, but I had to know the feeling, had to know if it would be different.

I twisted my shoulders and nudged his hand with my upper arm, directing him. For a moment he looked confused and then he brought his fingers to my bosom and pressed them around my breast, his palm just caressing the tops. It did feel different because I wanted it. The tingling grew stronger, traveling with electric speed down to the small of my stomach where Tony's fingers had lingered so long and had traced the lines of my thighs until he touched me and touched me. Right on this very spot! I thought. I couldn't stop thinking about that, no matter how much I wanted to think about Joshua. It invaded my mind, ruining my moments of love. I groaned in disappointment.

Joshua thought I was disappointed in him and pulled his hand away quickly.

'No,' I said taking his wrist. 'I'm not mad at you.'

'Leigh,' he whispered. I saw such desire in his eyes, a deep, intense look that made me want to hold him and kiss him. I brought his hand back to my bosom, but just as I did, the door of the cottage flew open. We both jumped.

It was Tony!

'WHAT ARE YOU DOING HERE?' he screamed. *'And on that couch!'* he added as if it were some special piece of furniture. *'Why did you bring him here? Why aren't you with your guests watching the movie!'*

Joshua stood up quickly.

'We . . .'

'I just took a walk with Joshua through the maze,' I said quickly, 'and decided to show him the cottage.'

Tony looked from him to me.

'And what were you showing him on that couch?' he demanded, his eyes tiny slits of anger. He looked wild.

'Nothing,' I said, my heart pounding. He stared at me a moment and then relaxed his posture.

'It's not right for you to have left your own party,' he said more calmly but still breathing hard. 'No one knows you have, not even your mother, but I advise you to go back immediately,' he added, looking pointedly at Joshua.

'Yes sir,' Joshua said. He looked terrified. He turned to me and I started around the couch. Tony stepped back as we headed through the doorway.

'Leigh,' he said seizing my arm to hold me back. I looked up at him. 'I won't tell your mother about this, but I want to talk to you about it later.'

'Yes, Tony,' I said and hurried to join Joshua. Without speaking, we walked quickly to the maze.

'I'm sorry if I got you in trouble,' Joshua said.

'Don't worry. It's nothing. He's just being . . . trying to be a father to me,' I explained. 'He feels he has to.'

Joshua just nodded, but he was very shaken. We hurried through the maze and back into Farthy through the side entrance. Then we slipped back into the movie theater. Jennifer and William were kissing in the dark. They broke to look at us when we sat down.

'Have a good time, Romeo?' William asked Joshua. He said nothing. He slid down in his seat until the movie ended and the lights came on.

After the movie my guests began to leave. Their cars arrived, some chauffeur driven. I stood at the doorway thanking them for attending and for their gifts. Joshua and William and Jennifer were the last to leave.

'I hope everything will be all right with your step-father,' Joshua whispered.

'Don't worry. I'll try to call you later,' I promised.

Jennifer and I hugged and then they were all gone. Even with all the servants moving about, cleaning up Farthy, folding up chairs and tables, there was a deep emptiness in the great house. Troy's nurse had convinced him to take a nap; my mother was up in her room resting from what she called 'the ordeal', and as far as I could tell, Tony had not yet returned from the cottage. I wondered what he did there now and thought about that painting I had discovered and concealed on the easel. Why was he still doing these pictures? Was he planning a different doll?

'Excuse me, Miss,' Curtis said, approaching, 'but delivery men brought this a little over an hour or so ago.' He handed me a package. It was my birthday gift from Daddy and Mildred.

'Thank you, Curtis,' I said. I decided to take it up to my room before opening it.

Once there, I sat down on the settee in the sitting room and unwrapped the box. I took out a ceramic, hand-painted ballet dancer. It was a music box. After I wound it up and placed it on the table, the dancer moved to some of the 'Nutcracker Suite'.

Daddy's birthday card read 'Mildred and I found something beautiful for a beautiful young lady. Happy birthday.'

I sat back and watched the dancing doll, while I recalled other birthday presents and other birthdays, especially the last one when Daddy had given me this diary. I had been so happy then, so unaware of the storm of unhappiness and sadness that would burst upon us and rain torrents and torrents of tears.

Suddenly, my reverie was interrupted by Tony's presence in the doorway to my sitting room. I had the impression he had been standing there a while, staring in at me.

'What's that?' he asked.

'A present from my father,' I replied staring at him. He looked different. Strands of his usually neatly brushed hair were wild. His face was flushed, his jacket open and baggy, his tie loose. It was as if he had run back from the cottage.

'It's very nice. Imported?' he asked coming farther in.

'I guess so.' He took it into his hands and turned it upside down.

'Yes, it's made in Holland. I saw many like it during my travels.' He put it down again. 'Your mother really throws a great party, huh?' he said smiling. I saw he was trying to be friendly, make small talk, but I was still angry about the way he had burst in upon Joshua and me.

'Yes,' I said. I put the music box back into the package and stood up. 'Well, good night. I'm going to put this in my bedroom,' I explained and went in, expecting he would leave; but he followed me.

'Leigh, I'm sorry I frightened you at the cottage, but I saw you two going into the maze and followed, naturally curious as to why you would leave all your guests.'

'I just wanted to show Joshua some of the grounds,' I replied, keeping my back to him.

'That's understandable, but you should have waited until you could have taken other guests, too.'

'I didn't want to take any other guests to the cottage,' I said turning.

'Leigh, I'm not your real father, I know,' Tony pursued stepping closer, 'but you're a young girl, just blossoming. You've been somewhat protected up until now, and young men with far more experience can take advantage of a girl like you. Believe me, I know about these things.'

'Joshua's not like that,' I snapped.

'Maybe, but there's no sense in not being careful and I wouldn't feel right knowing that . . . well, I wouldn't feel right not giving you some advice. Now, as I told you at the cottage, your mother need not hear a thing about this. It's just between you and me.'

He stepped closer until he could reach out and take my shoulders in his hands.

'I'd like there to be something special between us, to always have something special between us,' he said, his eyes feasting on me. His fingers tightened until they actually began to hurt.

'Tony.' I grimaced but he didn't loosen his grip.

'Actually,' he whispered, 'your mother wants me to help her with you, expects me to take on this responsibility. She feels overwhelmed being the parent of a young daughter. I don't mind. You're too beautiful and too precious not to care for and protect. Please, let me protect you, let me care for you.'

'I appreciate what you want to do for me, Tony. Thank you,' I said. I just wanted to end the conversation. His gaze was fervent, and his fingers tightened even more.

'I mean, I know what goes through a man, especially a young man, when he kisses you and puts his hands on your shoulders like this,' he said. His fingers relaxed and moved down my arms. He smiled. 'You don't understand what sort of power you possess over a man.'

'Power?' What was he talking about now? Why was he so

intense? It had been an incident; it was over. Why dwell on it so long and so passionately?

'Yes, power. You have it already, the same sort of power your mother has. Your beauty and her beauty are mesmerizing. Any man who looks at either of you feels himself weaken, feels all his resolve dissipate like smoke. But he wants to be a slave to your beauty. It fulfills him to be twisted and turned, squeezed and caressed. He lives for that,' he said, his voice so low, I practically had to read his lips. 'Can you understand? Do you understand?'

'No,' I said, shaking my head. I tried to step back, but he held my upper arms too tightly.

'When a man is as close to you as that boy was in the cottage, and you let him touch you,' he said, the fingers of his left hand lifting from my arm and settling over my breast, 'it turns his heart into a small furnace, sending heat pulsating throughout his body. Soon, he can't control himself. It's not his fault. He becomes a puppet and you become the puppeteer,' he said, his fingers still caressing my breast.

He held me so firmly with his right hand, I couldn't move. The small veins in his forehead lifted against the skin. He was touching me just as Joshua had touched me.

How long had he been watching Joshua and me before he had decided to interrupt? He had seen us go into the maze, so he had followed us, I thought. Why hadn't he yelled to us when he first saw us, if he thought it was so wrong for us to have left the other guests?

'You must understand your powers, Leigh, so you don't misuse them.' He brought his fingers to my collar bone. 'I saw how that boy kissed you and you kissed him. You can't expect it to end with that. It's as if you were lighting a match in a pile of hay, thinking you would have just a tiny little flame for a while and then put it out.

'But once it's begun, it spreads too quickly, it breaks free, runs on its own and consumes you as well as the hay. I want to show you, warn you, teach you,' he said. 'You must never be afraid of me. You must trust me and permit me to help you. Will you, Leigh? Will you?' he demanded.

I didn't know what to say. Show me? Warn me? Teach me? What did all that mean?

'I already told you, Tony. I appreciate your concern for me.'

'Yes,' he said. 'My concern. Yes.' He drew me into his strong arms and kissed the top of my head. 'My beautiful portrait doll, my special work of art.'

He held me long and tightly. Finally, his arms relaxed and I backed away. He ran his fingers through his hair and smiled.

'We're friends again, then?' he asked.

'Yes, Tony. We're friends.'

'Good. Nothing would sadden me more than losing your friendship and affection now, especially after we have been so successful together,' he said and gazed at Angel. 'Look at her, at the way she looks at us. I've captured a piece of your beauty in her face, painted a note of your exquisite melody and whenever I look at her, I can hear that tune. It's my greatest artistic achievement. I understand now how an artist can fall in love with his own creations.' He turned back to me and I remembered the painting in the cottage.

'Tony, why are you painting me again? Are you planning another doll?' I asked.

'Painting you again?'

'Yes, that painting on the easel, the one I covered up with the sheet.'

'That's not a new painting, Leigh.'

But I was positive it was. I had seen all the paintings and none of them had Momma's features so clearly included.

'Why is the cottage still set up like an artist's studio?'

'I just haven't gotten around to restoring it. Actually, I sort of like going back there from time to time and reliving the moments we spent together creating this wonderful work of art. The cottage has become a very special place for me now.' His face hardened, his lips tightening, his eyes growing smaller. 'That's why I was so disappointed you took a stranger there today.'

'Joshua's not a stranger, Tony,' I said quickly.

'Still, I had hoped you would think the cottage special. Before you ever bring anyone there again, please ask me first, all right?' I nodded. I was tired and wanted to end this strange conversation. He looked at the doll again. 'I'm sure your doll feels the same way,' he said and smiled.

'Anyway, I really came in to wish you happy birthday one more time.'

'Thank you, Tony.'

He stepped closer again.

'Happy birthday, Leigh,' he whispered and kissed me quickly on the lips. 'Sleep well,' he added, turned and left.

As soon as he was gone, I closed my door. He had left me in such turmoil and confusion. I didn't know what to think. I washed and prepared myself for bed, happy to crawl in under my soft blanket, beside my Angel. The events of the day paraded by. It had been a wonderful party. All my friends had such a good time, and Joshua had kissed and held me so romantically before Tony had interrupted. I had a real boyfriend, a special boyfriend.

Remembering I had promised to call him, I sat up and dialed his number.

'This is Joshua,' he said. He never said hello.

'It's Leigh.'

'Is everything all right?'

'Yes. My step-father left a while ago. He was concerned, but he's not going to make any big deal over it, and he's not telling my mother anything. Don't worry, and anyway, I don't care. We didn't do anything wrong. I wanted you to kiss me,' I confessed.

'And I wanted to kiss you. It was a wonderful party, Leigh. The best party I have ever attended.'

'It was wonderful because you were here and we could spend time together. Will you come see me at school next weekend?'

'Of course. William and I are already planning something to do.'

'I can't wait. Good night, Joshua.'

'Good night, Leigh.'

'Angel says good night too,' I added laughing. I brought my portrait doll to the receiver as if she could really hear him and speak.

'Good night, Angel.'

Joshua laughed, too.

After I cradled the receiver, I held Angel close to me. I put out the lights and closed my eyes, expecting to remember Joshua's kiss and the way it had made me feel, but instead, I saw Tony standing before me, his eyes fixed pointedly on my face, his lips glistening, his smile tight. In my mind it was his hand, not Joshua's, on my breast.

'I want to show you, warn you, teach you,' he had said. Why did those words make me tremble? He was only trying to be a good step-parent, wasn't he? Yet did he have to touch me *there* to demonstrate?

I wished I could tell my mother and ask her what she thought, but how could I do that without telling her everything: Joshua and I sneaking away from the party and going to the cottage and kissing and my permitting him to touch me?

No, no, I thought, she would only say that Tony had done the right thing.

I wouldn't talk about all this; it was better to simply forget it. No one but my doll Angel would know how Tony Tatterton had held me and touched me and kissed me in my bedroom tonight, but I felt sure this was only the beginning. There would be many more secrets kept between my portrait doll and myself.

I finally fell asleep with her in my arms.

If Tony ever did say anything to my mother about the cottage incident, she either forgot it or didn't think much of it, for she never mentioned it. Joshua and I stopped talking about it, too, although we didn't forget the way we had kissed and had held each other. My body would tremble whenever I dreamt of him holding and kissing me like that again. We did kiss when we went to the movies, but it wasn't the same because we weren't alone. There weren't many opportunities to be alone. Boys were forbidden to be in our rooms at Winterhaven and girls were forbidden to be in boys' rooms at Allendale.

My mother permitted me to remain at Winterhaven many more weekends than I had expected. Joshua, I, William and

Jennifer became the talk of the school. We were always going places, doing things.

Marie and the 'special club' softened toward us, too. Before Christmas we were all speaking to each other openly, inviting them to our room and once again, being invited to all of theirs. One day Marie formally asked us to rejoin them. We said we would, but the truth was we didn't have the time to spend with them as we first had. All our weekend time was spent with Joshua and William.

The portrait dolls became a huge Christmas item for Tatterton Toys. Tony ran advertisements in magazines and newspapers throughout the country. The Boston newspapers produced articles on the dolls and I saw myself featured on the pages. Just as Tony had predicted, most of the girls at Winterhaven wanted portrait dolls, too, and soon dozens of them had put in their orders. Tony was ecstatic about it, and every weekend that I returned to Farthy, he had much to show me and tell me about the project.

During the winter months, he did some more traveling, establishing new markets for the dolls in Canada, France, England, Spain and Italy. He was happy about the success he was having competing with the European companies who had been doing similar things. Momma joined him for only one trip, the trip that included a week at St Moritz and the Palace Hotel.

Unfortunately, that was the week of the school's play. I had a big part, but neither she nor Tony could attend. I had secretly hoped Daddy might come because he had written to tell me he would be on the East coast around March for meetings in New York City and Boston, but he never answered my letter inviting him.

I half hoped he would come anyway, that I would peep out through the curtains and see him and Mildred come in and take front row seats, but he never showed up. A week after the play, another letter arrived full of apologies, and I learned that he had been unable to keep to his schedule and hadn't yet gone to New York. He was still on the West coast. He said he had seen an advertisement for the Tatterton portrait doll and he thought it was beautiful.

By the time spring came, the portrait dolls had become a multi-million dollar part of the Tatterton Toy empire. Tony never stopped thanking me for being the first model. He told me he was setting aside a share of the profits in a trust fund in my name. Momma thought this was all wonderful and reminded me how silly I had been for hesitating to pose.

'Tony has made you a star after all,' she told me. 'Isn't that sensational?'

I supposed it was. I was the envy of all the girls at school, I had a wonderful doll myself, and now I was even making my own fortune because of it. Tony turned out to be a considerate and sincere person after all, I thought, and the negative things I had felt about him, the things that he had done and said that had frightened me, all drifted away. The world that had turned gray and dreary after my parents divorced became bright and happy again. Sunlight had broken through the clouds. I had friends, a boyfriend, a fascinating home and everything any girl my age could ever want – clothing, jewelry, records, anything.

It wasn't the same for Momma. Despite her enormous wealth, despite her being married now to a handsome, bright and wealthy businessman, she was always complaining about one thing or another. She was still upset about her weight and what she thought were imperfections in her figure. Finally, in late May, she announced she was going to Switzerland to a 'wonder spa' she had learned about from her wealthy friends. She would be there for at least a month, or 'however long it took'. The best thing for me was she said I could stay at Winterhaven straight through until the school year ended.

She left the last week in May. Two weeks later my second year at Winterhaven ended. Joshua, William, Jennifer and I made all sorts of plans for the summer. I hoped I would be able to do half of what we dreamt of doing. I thought I would begin by inviting them all to Farthy the very first weekend back, but when I told Tony, he said it would be better if I waited for my mother's return before I went anywhere or had friends come visit.

It was our first argument and we had it at our first dinner together. Even little Troy became very upset.

'I'm not a little girl, Tony. I don't have to have my mother's permission for every single thing I do,' I complained.

'No, but it's not going to be that much longer before she returns and it would be better if she decided something like this,' he said softly.

'Why? It's not a major decision in my life. I just want to invite some friends for a weekend. It's not that we don't have the room or can't afford the expense,' I insisted.

'Of course we have the room and can afford guests. But you're still a minor and decisions about where you go and who you see must be made by your legal guardians,' he replied. 'Besides, after what happened once when you were alone with a young boy . . . I would have to spend all my time acting as chaperone and . . .'

'That's not fair,' I cried.

'Still, it's an enormous responsibility. I would feel much better if we wait until Jillian returns. It's not that much longer and besides . . .'

'I'll be bored to death until Momma comes home!' I cried. That was when little Troy's eyes filled with tears too.

'No you won't,' Tony said suddenly smiling. 'I'm taking a short vacation and with the weather so wonderful, there will be much to do. We'll go horseback riding. I've filled and started heating the outdoor pool . . .'

'It's not the same thing!' I declared. I threw my napkin down on my plate of food. 'I feel trapped.'

'Now Leigh, please don't have a tantrum. Everything has been going so well while your mother's been away, I would hate . . .'

'I don't care. It's not fair,' I repeated and got up from the table.

'Leigh!' Tony cried, but I ran out of the room and upstairs to my suite, throwing myself over my bed. I held Angel and sobbed until I could sob no more. Then I sat up and wiped my eyes and gazed at my beautiful doll. She looked so sympathetic and sad, too.

'Oh Angel,' I said, 'why can't I be like other young people my age and live in a normal home with a normal family, so I could do things girls my age want to do? I don't care about all this wealth. What good is it if it doesn't make me happy?'

I sighed. Of course, my doll couldn't answer, but it made me feel better talking to her.

I stood up with Angel in my arms and went to the window that overlooked the front grounds. 'It's going to be like being in prison, Angel. My friends can't come here and I can't go to see them until Momma returns. What will I tell Joshua when he calls? What will I tell Jen? It's embarrassing.

'How can Tony think I would be happy just being with him? I like to go horseback riding and swimming, yes; but I would like to do some of that with my friends and not my mother's husband.'

As if he heard me speaking about him, he suddenly appeared below, walking briskly down a garden walkway, heading for the English maze. In moments he disappeared within. I was sure he was going to the cottage. But why? Why did he keep it as an art studio still? Why had he lied to me about the new painting when I had asked him? He said he wasn't designing a new kind of portrait doll. Then what was he doing?

Out of curiosity as well as boredom and frustration, I put Angel back on my bed and hurried downstairs, slipping out a side entrance of Farthy to follow him. I didn't want Troy to see me and want to know where I was going or what I was doing. He'd cry to come along.

Daylight lasted much later now, but the bright orange sun dropping reluctantly below the horizon made the world seem so dreamlike and ethereal. The birds had already settled in, only a few still chirping. There were no terns crying. The blue sky was turning inky in the east and I thought I could see the first twinkling of a distant star as it emerged slowly out of the great vastness of space.

I hurried over the grass and slipped softly like a spy into the long, wide shadows cast by the tall hedges. I looked back only once at the great house. I had left the light on in my suite and saw my wallpaper and curtains. Then I turned, listened, and stepped into the maze.

Never did it seem as quiet in these corridors or as dark. I

realized I had never gone into it this late in the day and never at night. How would I find my way back? Would it be too dark in the middle, even now? I hesitated. How did Tony get through it and how would he come back?

Still driven by overwhelming curiosity, I continued down the first corridor, turning quickly around the first and second corners and then moving as quietly as I could through the center of the maze. The only sound was the soft crunch of my feet over some fallen twigs and my own heavy breathing. Finally, I stepped out on the other side and confronted the cottage. The shades were still drawn, but I could tell that the lights within burned brightly.

Could it be that Tony had another young model, someone he wanted kept secret? Was he afraid I would be jealous? Or that Momma would be angry and jealous? Hovering in the shadows now cast by the trees, I scurried down to the small fence and listened. There was some soft music playing, but I heard no voices.

Carefully, I passed through the front gate and went to the first window. It was difficult to see within because the shade had been drawn so tightly. I could make out only the legs of the easel. I moved down to the second window. This would offer me a much better view of what was going on within because the shade was short of touching the bottom by at least four inches. The window looked in on the room from a rear perspective. I would be looking toward the front door from behind the easel.

I knelt down slowly and peered over the bottom of the window frame through the opening. Tony wasn't in the room, but the painting I had discovered when I had brought Joshua to the cottage was there.

I gasped when I saw what Tony had added to it.

He had drawn and painted in himself lying naked beside the female figure that combined so many characteristics of my mother with me. Why did he do that? What did it mean?

Before I could rise and leave, he emerged from the kitchen.

I gasped again. He was stark naked!

He stopped abruptly and looked my way. I felt icicles dripping down my neck and for a moment, I couldn't move. Did he see me?

Without any hesitation, I jumped up and ran as fast as I could to the front gate, opened it and scurried as quickly as my feet would permit until I was charging down the corridor of hedges in the maze.

SEVENTEEN

Trapped in a Nightmare

Because of my excitement and the dim light, I made a few wrong turns and found myself running in circles through the center of the maze. Frantic, wet with perspiration, I stopped to catch my breath. My heart was pounding so hard, I thought it would shatter from the effort and pressure. I took deep breaths and tried desperately to get a hold on myself so I could think calmly and restore my sense of direction. Leaning too far back, I got my hair caught in some branches and screamed because I didn't know what was happening. I thought someone had grabbed me. Once I understood, I pulled myself loose quickly and continued.

Carefully I chose one turn and then another, forcing myself to move slowly and accurately through the hedges until I saw the familiar entrance on the Farthy side and shot out. I stopped again to catch my breath and listen. Had Tony seen me? Was he in pursuit? I heard no footsteps, nothing.

Still, I hurriedly returned to the house and ran upstairs to my suite. As soon as I entered, I shut my door and leaned back against it. Behind my closed eyelids, I once again saw that new painting. Tony's left hand completely covered my right breast and he was smiling down at me, his cerulean blue eyes painted so brightly they looked absolutely luminous in the picture.

Then I again envisioned him emerging naked from the kitchen. I assumed he had taken off his clothing because he had been using himself as a model. There was probably a mirror set against a wall, I thought. What other reason would he have for undressing while he worked?

He hadn't shouted out or quickly dressed to pursue me. Perhaps he hadn't seen me peeping through the window after all. I decided not to say anything about it. When my mother returned, I would tell her. She should know about something like this. It was so bizarre.

I relaxed now that I was safe in my own room. My body was still sticky with sweat, my silk blouse clinging to my arms and chest as if it had been glued to me. I felt ratty, dirty, not only from the flight through the hedges, but from what I had seen. I shook my head and shuddered. Then I embraced myself like someone caught in a snow storm and hurried across my suite to my bathroom to run a warm bath. I shook in some bubble bath powder and watched the water turn aqua, the sweet scent circling around me like smoke.

I went to my dresser and chose a nightgown. After I hung it up on the bathroom door, I sat down at the vanity table and brushed out my hair. Some tiny twigs and leaves fell on the table. Looking in the mirror, I saw my face was still quite flushed, my cheeks bright red as if they had been slapped. I sat back for a moment in a daze. Then I remembered my bath and got up quickly. I stripped off my clothing as fast as I could and lowered myself into the soothing, tepid, perfumed liquid. It embraced me and I closed my eyes and lay back, moaning with pleasure.

I might have fallen asleep in the water for a few minutes. I don't know; I lost track of time. Suddenly, I opened my eyes and realized the bath had cooled down considerably. I rose out of it immediately and dried myself. Then I put on my nightgown and slipped under my soft blanket, searching for the security and warmth of my own bed. I just wanted to go to sleep and forget the whole day.

When I gazed out the window to my left, I saw a slice of the silvery moon gleaming through some gauze-like clouds. Above it a single bright star blinked like the light of a ship anchored for the evening somewhere far out on the inky ocean. The moonlight flowed into my room, turning my furniture into ghost-like silhouettes, but Angel's eyes twinkled reassuringly. I reached out and took hold of the doll's little hand. Then I closed my eyes and let myself sink into sleep, anxious for the peace and the darkness.

Suddenly, my eyes snapped open. I sensed I was not alone. I didn't move; I listened keenly and waited. There was the distinct sound of someone else's heavy breathing. Gradually, in tiny increments of movement, I turned in my bed until I was completely on my back, looking up. In the same silvery moonlight that had soothed and sent me into sleep, stood Tony Tatterton, his naked chest glistening. I was trembling so hard, I thought I would stutter when I spoke, but my words came out straight and true.

'Tony, what do you want?' I demanded.

'Oh Leigh, my Leigh,' he whispered. 'It's time to bring the painting to life. It's time for me to do what I promised: to show you, to teach you . . .'

'What do you mean? What do you want? I'm sleeping now. Please, leave,' I begged, but he didn't. He sat on the side of my bed. I was afraid to lower my eyes, to follow the lines of his body, for I could sense without looking that he was naked again.

'You're as beautiful as your mother,' he said, reaching out to stroke my hair. 'More beautiful. Men will seek you everywhere you go, but you are like a precious work of art. You shouldn't be touched and misused by anyone. You're too special; yet you have to know what it means and what can happen. You have to be prepared and be aware. I can do that for you. I'm the only one who should do that for you, for in a way, I have created you.'

He brought his hand to my face. I tried to pull back, but I was already against the pillow.

'I have lifted you from the canvas and like Pygmalion, filled you with life and beauty. Everyone who feasts his eyes on the portrait doll, feasts his eyes on your beauty, beauty I carved with these very fingers,' he said, running the tips of his fingers along my jawline and down to my neck.

'Tony, I want you to leave right now. Please, get out of here this moment,' I demanded in a shaky voice. I couldn't help it. My heart was thumping and I was swallowing my own breath, gasping for enough air to form words and demands.

He acted as if he didn't hear me. Instead of leaving, he peeled away my blanket, folded it neatly down my body. I reached up to tug it back, but he caught my hand and brought it to his lips.

'Leigh,' he moaned. 'My portrait doll.'

'Tony, get out. What are you doing?'

I raised my head and shoulders and saw that he was indeed completely naked. He slipped in beside me, his hands on my thighs, forcing my nightgown up my body. I wanted to speak and tell him I was almost his daughter, and he shouldn't be here doing these things, but I couldn't catch my breath. He had brought my nightgown over my waist.

I pushed out to keep him away, pressing on his forehead, but he was so strong and determined.

'Tony, what do you think you're doing? Get off me. Please, stop!'

He drove his head down until his lips touched my neck, making a trail all around my throat, savoring the taste and feel of my flesh. I shivered, wanting him to stop, but my small hands and weak arms had no effect on his broad shoulders and chest. He had brought my nightgown up so it was just under my arms. When he pressed his chest against my naked bosom, I could feel his steady heartbeats, thumping, making it seem as if I were a part of him. He had his lips to my ear.

'You must experience, understand, be aware,' he whispered. 'You will know and be prepared. It's my duty, my responsibility, part of the artistic process involved in creating you,' he said, convincing himself that what he was doing was right and necessary.

'No, stop!'

I tried beating him back by pounding his shoulders and neck with my tiny fists, but it was like flies on a horse's back – just a minor annoyance. I felt his legs slip in between mine. My panic rose. He had slid his hands down and embraced me, holding my arms firmly against my body. His lips moved along my collar bone and dropped between my breasts. I felt the wetness of the tip of his tongue.

'Show you . . . teach you . . .'

'Tony!'

My body trembled and shuddered, but I could move my hands only a tiny bit because his strong arms were holding me like vices. He pressed forward, driving himself firmly between my legs and then using his thighs to push mine apart.

'You must understand . . . I'm responsible . . . responsible . . . please, don't fight me. Let me show you . . . teach you . . .'

'STOP!' I cried one final time, but it was a futile cry. He forced upon me what should only have been given in love. His thrust was hard and accurate, opening me to him. A hot, searing pain came and went. I felt myself go dizzy and faint. Perhaps I did faint for a few moments. My body was totally at his command, moving as he moved. For a moment I felt detached from it, my head falling back against the pillow, the rest of me beneath him. He was doing what he wanted. In his own mind he was sculpting me in another way.

My cries were as tiny as a doll's cries. I bit down on my lower lip and tried to endure. The heat rose from my legs and stomach in continuous, rhythmic waves, traveling higher and higher until it overwhelmed me. I thought I was sinking into the bed beneath him.

Finally, he loosened his hold around my arms and torso and brought his fingers to my lips and cheeks, following them with his own lips.

'Do you see? Do you feel it and understand the power? Now, I have turned you into a woman,' he claimed. 'I have completed my greatest work of art, made you into a living portrait doll.'

I moaned, swallowing my cries. My cheeks were wet with tears. I kept my eyes shut tight. I felt his lips press down on them softly and then felt him kiss my lips. After a long moment of silence, he lifted himself away. I dared not speak or move for fear he would return. I heard him sigh deeply before I felt his finger trace a line between my breasts and down my stomach. He kept it there for a moment.

Then he murmured, 'My portrait doll. Sleep well.'

I heard his departing footsteps and opened my eyes just as he passed through my doorway and out. The moment the door closed, my tears burst forth and my shoulders shook. I embraced my naked body and sobbed. Finally, I sat up. I stared through the darkness in disbelief, questioning what had happened. Maybe it was only a nightmare. I wanted to deny it, but my body, still trembling from his kisses and his violation would not permit me to ignore or pretend.

What would I do? Whom would I run to? Momma was still away. My father was off with his new wife building a business. There were only servants here and little Troy. I got out of bed and went to the bathroom, bracing myself against the wall as I went along. I put on the light and gazed at myself in the full length mirror. My face was streaked with tears and beet-red. My neck and shoulders were blotchy from his forced kisses and caresses. The sight of myself this way hammered home what had happened. I grew dizzy again and had to sit down.

I thought about calling Jennifer or Joshua, but I was too ashamed. What would I say? What could either of them do anyway? I had no one but myself. I had to come to my own aid. Finally, after a series of deep breaths, I was able to stand up again. I put out the light and returned to bed. What else could I do? I couldn't go ranting and raving through the halls of Farthy.

I reached for Angel. She looked shocked, saddened. I held her in my arms and pressed her to me, searching for the comfort I needed so desperately. Ironically, the doll Tony created was here to soothe me after the terrible thing he had done. But there was more of myself in this doll than there was of him, I thought. And now she despised him as much as I did.

'Oh Angel, we have only each other. Tony was right about one thing . . . we are both portrait dolls.'

I closed my eyes and let sleep take me back into its arms and turn me away from this hard and shocking world.

The warm sunlight caressed my face and tugged my eyes open. I blinked rapidly, focusing in on where I was and what had happened in this room the night before. When I sat up, I somehow expected everything to be in disarray, expected the world to be as topsy-turvy as I was; but nothing was changed around me. Everything in the room was as neat and orderly as it had been. The sunlight was beaming cheerfully through my windows. Even Angel looked bright and restored.

Had it all been a nightmare? I looked down at myself as if there would be some evidence. My arms were sore where Tony had clamped them against my body in his vice-like grip and my thighs ached, but other than that, there were no tell-tale scars or marks of his passion. Yet I felt that all the scars were within me. It had been no nightmare.

I rose slowly and sat for a while on my bed, wondering what I would do. I would run off to join Daddy if I knew where he was, I thought; but he could be halfway across the world by now for all I knew. I decided to shower and dress. I didn't want to go downstairs and confront Tony, but I couldn't remain in my suite all day. I supposed I could claim to be ill and have my meals brought up, but it would only bring him in here too, I thought, and there would still be a confrontation.

Besides, I wasn't up and around for more than ten minutes before I heard Troy at my door. He was here to remind me of promises I had made to him the day before, promises concerning things we would do together. I turned my face from him when he spoke, afraid he would see the horror and the terror in my eyes and be frightened by it. But he was too excited about our proposed activities to notice anything.

'You said you would go to the beach with me today, Leigh. Can we go right after breakfast? Can we? Please? We can look for seashells.'

'All right,' I said. 'Just let me shower and dress. Go down and start your breakfast.'

'Tony's already downstairs,' he said.

'Good.' I thought perhaps Tony would eat and be gone by the time I arrived, so I took my time showering and dressing. It looked like it was going to be a very warm day, so I decided to put on a pair of shorts and a short-sleeve blouse for my walk to the beach with Troy.

Unfortunately, when I arrived at the dining room, Tony was still sitting there reading his newspaper and sipping coffee. My heart skipped a beat when he lowered the paper to look at me.

I gazed at him with as much fury in my eyes as I could muster, but he didn't seem to see it. He smiled brightly.

'Good morning, Leigh. It's going to be a beautiful day. Troy tells me you and he are going for a walk on the beach. I might just come along.'

I looked at Troy. He was drilling a half a grapefruit with his fork. His nurse reminded him not to play with his food. Without saying a word, I took my seat. The maid poured me my orange juice immediately. I glanced at Tony and saw how he was still smiling and watching me. His hair was neatly brushed and he wore a white and blue short-sleeve shirt and a pair of light blue slacks. He looked so chipper and well rested.

How could he be this way? I thought. Did he think I would just forget what he had done? Did he think by his pretending nothing was wrong and nothing was different, he could get away with it? Surely, he must expect I was going to tell my mother everything. She would want to divorce him and we would leave this place.

But he didn't act the least bit concerned. He folded his paper neatly and sipped his coffee.

'Troy's putting away a good breakfast this morning because he knows he needs energy if he's going to do all the things he plans to do with you today, Leigh,' Tony said and winked. 'Right, Troy?'

'Uh huh,' he said and chewed vigorously on a chunk of grapefruit.

'I thought perhaps you would like to do some horseback riding today, Leigh. I've already asked Curly to have Stormy and Thunder ready for us after lunch. How's that sound?'

I glanced at Troy's nurse and Troy. Both were occupied with other things and not listening to Tony. Then I glared at him.

'How can you even suggest such a thing?' I demanded through clenched teeth. He shrugged.

'I thought you might like it today. It should be a wonderful day for a ride. I thought you loved horseback riding.'

'I do love horseback riding. That's not the point,' I snapped.

'Then what is?'

'You expect me to go horseback riding with you after . . . after what happened last night?'

The nurse looked up sharply. Tony's smile faded, but he replaced it quickly with a look of confusion.

'What do you mean? What happened?'

I looked at the nurse. The maid had paused as well and turned a keen ear in our direction.

'I don't want to talk about it now,' I said and drank my juice.

Tony sat back in his chair.

'Oh well,' he said. 'Perhaps you'll feel better after lunch. If you do, everything will be ready. It can be only a short ride anyway, for me. I had some things turn up at the office this morning, unexpected things, and I have to go into Boston tonight.'

'You can go right now for all I care,' I said quickly. Tony didn't respond. He shook his head, grimaced, and went back to his paper.

What an act, I thought. Did he really expect to get away with it? I decided not to pursue it at the moment, for Troy's sake as much as my own. He was already rambling on about our walk on the beach and the things he was planning to do with the sea shells we would locate together. I had to smile and be happy for him.

Tony finished his coffee and rose.

'I'll see you two out at the beach perhaps,' he said. Then he excused himself and left the table. I finished my breakfast and then started out for the beach with Troy before Tony could join us.

Troy's endless happy chatter kept me from thinking dark thoughts, for every time my mind went back to the horrible events of the night before, Troy would ask me a question. He was full of inquisitiveness this morning and his verbal energy kept me from drifting away.

'What makes the clouds move, Leigh? See,' he said pointing. 'That big one was over there and now it's over here. Do they have wings?'

'No,' I said smiling. 'It's the wind that pushes them along.'

'Why doesn't the wind blow right through them?'

'I suppose it does sometimes. That's why there are small ones, pieces from bigger ones,' I replied, and ran my fingers through his soft hair. He swung his little pail as he walked, pounding the soft beach with determined steps.

'If I were up there, would the wind push me, too?'

'If you were light enough to float, it would,' I said.

'And would it break me into pieces like a cloud?'

'Only if you were made of air. What makes you think of such things?' I asked, wondering what sort of dreams he had. He shrugged.

'Tony says there arc places that have winds so strong they lift people off the ground and twirl them about like clouds.'

'Oh Troy,' I said stopping and kneeling to embrace him. 'Not here. You're safe here.'

'The wind won't blow you away either?' he asked skeptically.

'No. I promise,' I said, even though in my heart I felt a terrible sort of wind had tossed me about and burst whatever bubble of happiness I had found here.

He smiled and broke free, running toward the water.

'Look! Look at the blue shells!' he cried and began to fill his little pail.

I took a deep breath of the fresh sea air. It seemed to clear my lungs and wash out the anxiety and the heaviness I felt in my body. I looked back to be sure Tony wasn't following us. I didn't see him and assumed he must have realized I wouldn't tolerate him near me. Convinced Troy and I would be left alone, I joined him to sift through the shells and fill his pail with the more beautiful ones.

Tony wasn't at the house when Troy and I returned. When Troy asked after him, Curtis reported that Tony had to go to Boston much earlier than he had anticipated. Curtis said he had left a message for me, however – my horse would be ready if I wanted to ride in the afternoon.

I didn't. I spent the day reading and playing games with Troy in his suite. Just before dinner, I took him for a walk through the gardens. We brought along pieces of old bread and fed the birds at the fountains.

Tony did not return for dinner, which made me happy. And

then Curtis came in with news of a telegram my mother had sent announcing she would be returning from her European spa late in the day tomorrow.

Oh, thank Heavens, I thought. I would tell her everything, every little detail, so she would understand what a horror I had gone through and what a horrible man she had married. I was positive that we would be leaving this place in a matter of days. Tony would pay for what he had done to me. When my mother was angry at a man, she could be a most formidable opponent. I made up my mind that no apologies, no promises, no expensive gifts, nothing would get me to forgive him. I half expected he would come begging me for that forgiveness once he discovered how soon my mother was to return.

As darkness fell, I became more and more anxious. Wherever I was in the great house, I kept an ear toward the front entrance, anticipating Tony's arrival. As the hours ticked away, the tension built within me, ticking like a grandfather clock and building toward that moment when he would come home and surely look for me. No matter what I tried to do to distract and occupy myself, it didn't work: not listening to the radio, not watching television, not reading, not talking to Troy, nothing kept my mind from turning back to the events of the night before.

Finally, more out of fear than out of fatigue, I retired to my suite; but the moment I closed the door behind me, I felt trapped and vulnerable. After all, it was here where it had happened, where he had come and where he might come again. Only my mother's bedroom suite had a lock on the door. It was something she had insisted be built in, for she prized her privacy; and also, I realized now more than ever, her opportunity to be away from her demanding young husband.

An idea came to me. I put on my robe, slipped my feet into my slippers, scooped up Angel, and left my suite. I went directly to my mother's suite, closing and locking the outer door behind me. Not only did I feel safer because of that, but just being in my mother's room, smelling her jasmine scents and seeing her make-up, her clothing and her shoes, gave me a sense of security. I put on one of her nightgowns and dabbed some of her jasmine perfume on my neck. Then I crawled into her bed just the way I used to when I was very little in Boston. Her sheets and pillowcases and her blanket smelled as fresh and clean as she always demanded they be.

'Oh Momma,' I moaned. 'I wish you were really here.' I set Angel down on the pillow beside me and turned off the lamp on the night table.

The moon was larger tonight, its silvery light brighter and unhampered by passing clouds. A small patch of stars had gathered at the moon's feet and I imagined a kingdom in the sky ruled by a beautiful princess, the moon, who had dozens of handsome suitors always at her beck and call, the stars. Up there, there was always soft, sweet music and there was no cruelty and meanness, no children with parents who despised each other, no men twisted and deceitful and no jealous women and girls looking to harm each other.

'It's the world we should have, Angel,' I whispered. 'The world we belong in.'

I closed my eyes and tried dreaming of it, dreaming of a world with candy-coated streets, with happy children, bright and handsome as little Troy, laughing and playing safely; a world of warm, cheerful homes filled with loving families, with Daddies who rushed back after work to be with their children and their wives. It was a world without the harsh winds Troy feared so, a world without gray skies where all the girls my age had portrait doll faces and devoted boyfriends.

If I could only drift away, rise slowly toward the moon and be part of that world . . .

I fell asleep, but awoke hours later to the sound and the sight of the lights in the sitting room being turned on. I sat up quickly in my mother's bed. Tony was standing in the doorway, his face and body in shadow. Suddenly, he laughed. I couldn't speak; my heart began to pound.

'Locking me out again,' he said and laughed again. Could it be that he thought I was my mother, that he misread the telegram and thought she had returned tonight? He held a key up in the light.

'I never told you I had a copy made for the time when I

finally grew tired of your . . . your ridiculous antics: shutting me, your husband, out of your bedroom, keeping me away from you, denying me my conjugal rights. Well, I'm tired of it now, tired of being made the fool. When we first met, I was handsome and desirable enough. Now that we're married and you made me sign that ridiculous marriage contract, you think you can drive me away. Well, I won't have it. Not any more. I've come for what is rightfully mine and what you should rightfully want as well.'

He stepped farther in.

'Tony,' I said in a loud whisper. 'I'm not Momma. I'm Leigh.'

He paused and there was a long moment of silence. Because he had moved from the light into the darkness, I couldn't see his eyes or the expression on his face, but I felt his confusion.

'I'm sleeping in my mother's bedroom tonight. She's not home yet. Now go. You've done enough to make me hate you forever!'

Suddenly he laughed again, this time with a cold, sharp tone.

'So, you want to be your mother,' he said. 'You want to be just like her. You crawl into her bed, wearing her nightgown and her perfume. You dream of being Jillian, being my wife after all. This is your fantasy.'

'*No!* That's not why I came in here. I came in here to keep you away from me! Get out!'

'Just like your mother, you refuse to admit to what you really want, what you really need. I understand. It's a family trait,' he added and laughed.

'Get out,' I pleaded desperately.

'You locked me out just the way she does,' he snapped. 'It's not right. I won't have it.' He came closer. When he was only a few feet away, I smelled the whiskey on his breath. That frightened me even more. I cringed, pulling the blanket up against my body.

'Please, go away, Tony. I'm afraid of you and I can't stand what you did to me. Just thinking about it makes me sick. Please, just leave.'

'Oh, you must not feel that way. You must fight these fears. Is that why you lock your door and find excuse after excuse to stay away from me?' he asked, confusing me with my mother again.

'No, Tony. I'm not Jillian. I'm Leigh. Can't you understand? Don't you listen?'

'Still full of anger, but anger is a passion. Don't you see? You're full of desire, full of yearning and lust. You must not ignore that voice within yourself,' he said and sat down quickly on the bed. I backed away, thinking I would hop off the bed on the other side and run from him; but he was too quick, anticipating my avenue of escape. He reached out and seized my wrist, turning it until I could keep my hands clasped to the blanket no longer. I cried out in pain and he released me, but he leaned over my legs and waist.

'It's a beautiful night, a romantic night, a night lovers dream of having.'

'We're not lovers, Tony,' I moaned through my tears.

'Sure we are. Forever and forever, I am linked to you through my work.'

'*Get away from me!*' I cried when he put his hand on my thigh. 'My mother will know of this, of all of it. She will know what you did to me last night and she will hate you forever and ever and leave you,' I said, spitting my words. Anger was better than fear.

But he laughed again.

'You're going to tell your mother? Tell her what? What she already knows, or should I say, hopes. Who do you think drove me to you, pushed me forward, encouraged me? Who suggested I use you as my model, my nude model? I'm not stupid. I know why she's done this; but I've accepted it, desired it myself. You are beautiful, and will be more beautiful than she is. Don't you think she knows that too and don't you think it eats away at her?'

'No,' I screamed. 'These are all lies.'

'Are they?' He laughed. 'She thought you and I made love in the cottage and tolerated that.'

'Liar!' I swung out at him, but he caught my tiny fist in the air and held it.

'We don't keep secrets from each other. I tried to get her

jealous, to get her to want me more, so I told her, told her how you got excited and demanded I make love to you once I had you pose and once I touched you. Do you know what she said? She said at least you learned from a master, from a consummate lover. Oh, I knew she was just flattering me, but she really wasn't upset.'

'She wouldn't say that,' I said, shaking my head. 'She wouldn't.' I pulled my wrist free. 'You don't even know her. You say you don't keep secrets from each other, but she has kept a big one from you,' I said as spitefully as I could. 'You don't even know her true age. You think she's years and years younger than she really is. She would never confide in you completely.'

'Oh, I know her true age, my sweet,' he said calmly, so calmly it made my heart sink. 'I looked into her past fully. Unfortunately my love for her blinded me and I waited until after the wedding to do so. She'll never know how betrayed I felt – that she would have kept such a thing from me – me who worshipped the very ground she walked on. No, I let her live in her dream world. What harm does it do?'

'No, you're lying again. Get away, get out!' I pushed at him, but he took hold of both my wrists this time and pulled me to him, kissing me roughly on the lips. I struggled to break free, but he was too strong. My mouth was left with the taste of his whiskey and it made me sick.

He stood up on his knees to lean over me and press my hands back to the pillow.

'You're more beautiful now because you're fresh and far more innocent. You're right: there's no deceit in you. You are truly the portrait doll,' he added, and brought his lips to my neck again.

Once again, I twisted and turned beneath his body, and once again he fit himself between my legs, taking me the same way. It was like a recurring nightmare. I cried; I pleaded, I begged, but his ears were closed to everything but the voices he heard within himself, voices of desire and lust that would not be denied.

All throughout his forced lovemaking, he confused me with

my mother, alternately calling me 'Jillian' and then moaning, 'Leigh'. I closed my eyes and turned my head away from him to deny what was happening, what he was doing to me. My body lifted and fell beneath his. There was no way I could stop it.

Opening my eyes before he was finished, I saw Angel on the pillow beside me. I struggled to get my right hand free of his and worked it loose enough to take hold of my precious portrait doll and turn her face away, for in her eyes, I saw my own terror and sorrow.

After that, I just squeezed my eyelids shut and waited for it to end.

After he had spent himself, he lay over me for some time before rising like a sleepwalker and leaving me. I didn't move. My wrists ached and my face felt as if he had brought sandpaper to it. I wept until I thought my heart would break. Finally, when I had cried ten waterfalls of tears, I closed my eyes and pulled the blanket back over me and Angel. Then I turned, buried most of my face in the soft pillow, and waited for sleep.

In the morning I rose with the first rays of sunlight and scurried out of my mother's suite and back to my own, where I crawled into bed. Troy came looking for me, but I told him I wasn't feeling well. He went running out to tell Tony and the servants. Moments later, Mrs Carter, one of our older maids appeared to see what was wrong. All I told her was I wasn't feeling well. She said she would bring up some breakfast.

'Do you want me to have Mr Tatterton see you?'

'No,' I cried quickly. 'I don't want to see anyone until my mother arrives.'

'No doctor?'

'No one, please,' I pleaded.

'Very well. I'll bring you something hot to drink and something hot to eat. Perhaps that will make you feel better,' she said.

Make me feel better? No food, no doctor, not a roomful of friends could make me feel better, I wanted to tell her; but instead I turned away and pulled my blanket up to my chin. Troy looked in on me again, disappointed that I wouldn't be coming out of my suite to play with him or take a walk. I ate a little of the hot oatmeal Mrs Carter brought up and sipped some sweet tea.

Tony didn't come to my suite. I was prepared to throw him out, to shout and be hysterical and draw the attention of all the servants if necessary. Perhaps he anticipated that and stayed away.

Mrs Carter returned with some lunch. Again, I ate like a mouse, nibbling at a sandwich, drinking a little juice. Late in the afternoon, she returned and asked again if I would like her to send for a doctor.

'No, a doctor can't help me,' I replied. 'Just send my mother to me the moment she arrives.'

'Very well,' Mrs Carter said, shaking her head. She took away the tray of dishes and food. I dozed off a few times until the late afternoon. Finally, I heard a commotion in the corridor outside my suite and knew Momma had arrived from Europe. I waited with great anticipation, positive the servants had already told her about my not leaving my suite all day and not eating very much.

The outer door burst open and Momma came in quickly, sweeping through my bedroom and up to my bed like a gust of fresh air. I pulled the blanket down and gazed up at her. Her hair was swept up in a stylish chignon and she wore a dark blue silk suit, the jacket buttoned snugly about her waist. She looked svelte, her complexion clear and smooth, her eyes bright and happy. Crystal earrings in the shape of tiny icicles dangled from her lobes. They captured light around them and glittered.

'Leigh VanVoreen,' she declared, her hands on her hips, 'how dare you be sick the day I return. Now what's wrong with you? It's summer. People don't get colds in summer.'

'Oh Momma,' I cried. 'Momma.' I sat up. 'A terrible thing has happened. And twice!'

'What is this nonsense, Leigh? I thought you were sick. As soon as I came through that front door, that Mrs Carter came running to greet me, wringing her hands and crying about how sick you are and how you wouldn't let her send for a doctor and how you refused to see anyone. Do you have any idea what it's like traveling to and from Europe? How tired I am?

'It's been an ordeal, you know,' she said twisting and turning herself so she could catch her image in my vanity mirror, 'losing the weight and getting the imperfections out of my body. But it's over, and I've been successful. Everyone thinks so. What do you think?' She turned to me with an expectant look on her face, ready to be lavished with compliments. But there would be no compliments today . . . only bitter truths. I wasn't going to allow Momma to escape the truth any longer!

'Momma, I've gone through a far more terrible ordeal right here at Farthy. Tony came into my room twice and . . . forced himself on me,' I cried. 'He . . . he . . .' Why was she letting me go on? Did I have to tell her every last, ugly detail? I looked at her with tears in my eyes, expecting her to rush to my side, wrapping her arms around me and consoling me with warm hugs and kisses . . . promising to make everything better . . . safe . . . as it had once been.

She came to my side with an amazing burst of speed. At last I had gotten her attention! At last she would listen to me! But then I noticed her eyes – always her eyes! Already they were narrowing to dangerous slits, glittering with coldness. Oh, how I was frightened! My tears immediately stopped and my stomach grew cold, my butterflies fluttering with full force. She didn't believe me! Momma's eyes always revealed her true emotions.

'*What?*' she incredulously demanded. 'What kind of ridiculous story is this? Forced himself on you? Really, Leigh. I've heard that teenagers fantasize, but isn't this a bit much?'

I shook my head furiously. 'No, Momma. This isn't a fantasy. It happened. It really did.' Now that I had her full attention I couldn't lose it. I had to make her listen! 'Let me tell you all of it, please. Please, listen.'

'I'm listening,' she said, her face contorting with annoyance.

'The night before last, I followed him through the maze to the cottage.'

'Followed him? Why?'

'I was curious as to why he was still working there, why he had kept it as an art studio.'

'You shouldn't be following him about like that, Leigh,' she said, convicting me of an indiscretion without hearing the rest of it. I ignored her and continued.

'When I got to the cottage, I peered in a window and I saw that he had painted another picture of me . . . of the two of us, only he had painted himself in it . . . naked!'

'Really?' she said.

'A moment later, he appeared, naked.'

'Was he alone?' she asked quickly.

'Yes, but . . . anyway, I got frightened and ran home. After I went to bed, he came in here . . . naked, and he attacked me, forcing me to make love to him.'

She stared at me, a skeptical look still on her face.

'He did! And then, last night . . . I went to your bedroom to lock myself safely within and he came to me again. He had a key. At first he thought I was you, but it didn't matter. He forced himself on me again. Oh Momma, it was horrible. I couldn't fight him.' Her expression didn't change. 'Momma, don't you hear what I'm saying?'

She lowered her shoulders and shook her head.

'I was going to speak to you about all this after I had settled in,' she said. 'I had hoped it could wait until I regained some of my strength.'

'Speak to me about all this? But how did you know?'

'Tony picked me up at the airport, Leigh. He told me how you have been behaving. He didn't tell me about your following him to the cottage, but he told me you asked him to come into your suite and when he arrived, he found you stark naked on your bed.'

'What? He's lying!'

'He said you took hold of his wrist and pulled him onto you, begging him to make love to you, but he broke free, bawled you out and left.'

'Momma, listen to me . . .'

'He also told me about your going to my suite to pretend you were me so he would not refuse you a second time. He said you had even put on one of my nightgowns and sprayed yourself with my perfume.' She looked at me with triumph, sniffing the air. 'That is my nightgown, isn't it? And you are wearing my perfume.'

'Oh, Momma, I did all this just to be close to you. I was so afraid.'

When she looked at me again I could see her disbelief. She didn't even attempt to hide it! In that moment a surge of hatred flowed through my blood. Never before had I felt this way toward Momma. Never! But why shouldn't I? She didn't believe me! She was choosing to disregard her own daughter's words over those of a man she hadn't even been married to for a year! All she cared about was Tony . . . disgustingly wealthy Tony . . . her young and horrible husband.

I looked at Momma with cynical eyes. Oh yes, I could see it all. Momma wasn't about to jeopardize her position as mistress of Farthinggale Manor. So what if she had gotten Tony to sign a settlement agreement, entitling her to half his fortune? Without his name she was nothing . . . *nothing!* If she chose to believe me and divorced Tony, she would lose the respectability and privilege she had as Mrs Tony Tatterton. Invitations would no longer arrive. Boston society would close its doors in her face and she'd be reduced to being a poor girl from Texas, allowed only to look in from the outside. As much as I wanted Momma to be happy, because deep down part of me still loved her . . . because I knew she needed to have a man in her life to give her a purpose . . . I couldn't allow Tony to get away with what he had done to me. I couldn't. I tried one last time.

'Momma, I'm telling you the truth.'

'Really, Leigh. Your story is so outrageous. What do you expect me to believe?'

'I expect you to believe me, not him! He's a madman.'

'He said you tried everything to get him to make love to you and when nothing worked, you . . . you betrayed me. You told him about my age,' she concluded. She looked more hurt than angry.

'Momma, I . . . no, I said that because . . .'

'How could you? There was no one I trusted more than my own daughter.'

'Momma, he already knew. He didn't care!'

She shook her head.

'Really, Leigh, you must get hold of yourself. I was a teenage girl; I know what you're going through. Your body is developing quickly. Overnight, you have become a woman with a woman's needs and here is handsome Tony Tatterton, the man you modeled in the nude for. It's understandable, and I'm partly to blame for not seeing how mature you've become, but you have to learn to control your fantasies and drives.

'You see how well I can do it. Remember what I told you about a man wearing you out and remember what I told you about being a good girl.

'I'm sure that after a day or so, everyone will get along with everyone just as before. Tony doesn't harbor any ill feelings toward you. He is very understanding when it comes to these things. That's why our marriage is going along so well.'

She smiled.

'Oh, I can't wait to soak in a hot bubble bath,' she said.

'Momma, you must believe me . . . please . . .'

'Now, Leigh,' she snapped. 'I insist you stop talking about this. One thing leads to another. Next thing you know, the servants will be talking about it, spreading horrible rumors.'

'They're not rumors. I'm not fantasizing or lying!'

'Leigh,' she said, her eyes small, 'do you expect me to believe that my husband would turn to my daughter, a girl just becoming a woman, when he has me? Really,' she declared. 'Now get hold of yourself. I want you to bathe and dress and come down to dinner.'

'But Momma . . .'

'I absolutely insist. Besides,' she added smiling, 'I have so many nice things I bought in Europe to show you and I want to tell you all about the spa and the people I met.' Her smile evaporated.

'I was very upset when Tony told me you revealed my true age to him, Leigh, but I can forgive you because it doesn't seem to matter to him as much as I feared it would. He really is a wonderful man. But I won't be able to forgive you if you keep up this . . . this performance. So please, get yourself together and be down for dinner.' She relaxed again and sighed deeply.

'Oh, there's nothing like coming home after a long trip,' she sang and left me.

Home? Had she just referred to Farthinggale Manor as home? Hell was the better word! I stared at the spot Momma had just vacated. What had just happened? Was I dreaming? Was I trapped in another nightmare? Momma *refused* to believe me. Instead of helping me she stayed behind the glass walls of her vain and shallow world, obsessed only with herself. *Herself!* Gone was the momma I had always loved and adored, replaced by the stranger from my nightmare. I turned to my portrait doll.

'Oh Angel,' I cried. 'If only you could talk. You're the only witness.'

But somehow, I thought, even if Angel could talk, Momma would find a way not to believe.

She either didn't want to or didn't care. For me, it was one and the same.

EIGHTEEN

Confrontations

I got up and dressed to go down to dinner. Even though I had eaten very little all day, I had no appetite, but I stupidly hoped that somehow I might still get Momma to see the truth. All she had to do was take a good look at my face, I thought. I had little enthusiasm when it came to brushing out my hair. It reflected my inner feelings, looking dull, drab and listless. I saw the fatigue and the emotional exhaustion in my eyes. With drooping shoulders, I left my suite and descended the stairway.

To my surprise Momma was already at the table with Tony. I heard their laughter as I approached the dining room. As soon as I entered, they stopped and turned my way. Tony glanced at my mother and then smiled at me.

'Leigh, feeling better?' he asked, turning his face into a mask of fatherly concern.

I said nothing. I went to my seat and spread my napkin on my lap, feeling the weight of their eyes on me.

'I was just telling Tony,' my mother began, her voice light and cheery, 'about the Walston twins. You remember them, I'm sure. I've mentioned them before. They're from Boston and their daddy has this estate home in Hyannisport as well. One of their legs equals my entire body. The Walrus twins is what all of us at the spa called them. To see them in the steam room when they sat together!' she said, throwing her head back and laughing. 'I mean, every woman there felt twenty pounds thinner the moment she looked at them.

'Anyway, the funniest part of all this is when it came time for them to leave, it was discovered that they had both gained five pounds apiece instead of losing. Seems they were smuggling in cakes and fudge from the nearby village. Can you imagine spending all that money and gaining five pounds?'

Tony shook his head and laughed along with her. I couldn't believe how happy they seemed. Nothing I had said to Momma had taken hold. The rest of the evening continued this way. Momma told story after story about the rich women at the spa. Tony was a perfect audience, laughing at anything she said that was meant to be funny, growing serious when she grew serious.

After she finished criticizing her fellow dieters, Tony went on and on about the success of the portrait dolls. Every once in a while, my mother would turn to me and widen her eyes to express her amazement and try to force an expression of appreciation out of me. But I refused to give in to her wishes. This once my wants and needs just *had* to come first. I knew what had happened to me was important, shattering. It broke my heart that she could shut out my pain so easily.

'I'd like you to see some of the things I bought in Switzerland, Leigh,' my mother declared after coffee was served. 'They're in the blue room. I brought an expensive gift home for you, too.'

She rose to tell Curtis something as she left the dining room, and Tony and I got up as well. On the way out behind her, Tony took hold of my right arm at the elbow to keep me back so she couldn't hear what he had to say.

'I just want you to know, Leigh, that I don't harbor any resentment toward you for what you told Jillian. She and I understand how it is with a girl who is literally exploding into womanhood.' He smiled, his blue eyes soft and forgiving. His casual tone of voice was maddening. For a moment a lump came to choke my throat. I swallowed hard and bit down even harder on my tongue.

'Coming Leigh?' Momma called.

'Yes,' I said and then I spun on him with fury. I allowed my eyes to meet his, sending fire and hate. A flame of anger shot through my chest. With ice in my words, I spoke. 'You might have fooled her for the moment, but in time she will believe me, for someone like you can't hide what he really is forever.'

He shook his head with a look of pity on his face that only infuriated me more.

'I had hoped now that Jillian has returned, you would have a different attitude, but I can see everything they tell me about bringing up teenage girls nowadays is true. Nevertheless, I want you to know that I will always be understanding and sympathetic and never ridicule you.'

'You're despicable,' I said behind clenched teeth. He continued to smile. Then he tried to take my arm to walk out with me, but I pulled away. 'Don't touch me. Don't you ever try to touch me again.'

He nodded and gestured toward the entry way. I hurriedly joined my mother. Tony didn't follow us into the blue room where Momma had piled her purchases. I sat on the settee and watched as she unpacked sweaters, blouses, skirts and leather belts. She had bought works of art, small sculptures, jewelry boxes and ivory hand mirrors. She gave me an elegant gold watch with diamonds. Every item had a story that went along with it, how she discovered it, what the store was like, what the other women thought when she bought it. She bragged about how the others followed her about, doing whatever she did, buying whatever she bought.

'I found myself suddenly thrown into the role of guide,' she boasted. 'Can you imagine? All these terribly wealthy and well-traveled women depending on me to tell them what was chic, what was real art, and what was a good buy. Really, I should have taken a commission.' She paused and looked at me as if for the first time.

'You do look a little tired, Leigh. You should get some sun tomorrow. You shouldn't lock yourself up in your suite like that. It's not healthy. The air could be stifling and stale and that kind of air can do unbelievable damage to your skin. I had long discussions with experts at this wonderful spa,' she said quickly before I could interrupt. 'Did you ever notice that Swiss women have such perfect complexions? Some of it is a result of their diets,' she continued, as if I were a student in a class, 'and some of it is because of their exercises, their fresh air, their steam baths and mud packs.

'I've already asked Tony to have a steam room built in my bathroom,' she concluded.

'Momma, I look this way because I went through a terrible experience. If you will just listen to me, really listen . . .'

'You're not going to start all that again, are you, Leigh?' she said, pursing her lips in a pout. 'I really can't stand it. I don't know how I'm still going on the little sleep and rest I've had since I left Switzerland. I've forced myself to be full of energy just for you and for Tony, but I'm tired now and I'm going up.'

'Momma.'

'Good night, Leigh. I hope you enjoy your watch.' She left me sitting there, surrounded by all the opened boxes and packages. I stuffed my new watch back into its box. Who cared about it? What did precious and expensive things mean now? Did she think gold, silver and diamonds made everything right, no matter what?

I felt so frustrated, resembling a poor dumb person unable to get her thoughts and feelings out, her screams trapped in her own ears, all the doorways leading from her mind shut tight. I might as well be invisible, I thought. Momma won't look at me, won't listen to me, won't see the truth. She was blinded by the glitter and the glamour of her own life.

Afterward, it was always the same whenever I tried to bring up the terrible thing that had happened to me. She wouldn't listen, or she would skip right on to another topic. Finally, I gave up. Most of the time, I went off alone to walk the beach or go horseback riding. The ocean air, the sound of the sea and the wonderfully hypnotic and meditative sight of the waves coming in and going out soothed and calmed me. I read, wrote in this diary, listened to my records and spent time with Troy.

Jennifer called a number of times, but I didn't call her, nor did I call Joshua. He had called late in June to tell me he was going on a vacation with his family anyway and would be away for nearly a month. He had hoped to see me before he left, but I just couldn't see him. If he looked in my face he would see all that had happened, and hate me for it, I just knew it. I found solace and comfort in my solitude. Nature proved to be the mother and the father I no longer had, soothing my bruises, stroking me with her warm breezes and filling me with a sense of security I couldn't get back in the big house with its dark corners and giant rooms.

Whenever I went for walks with Troy, I would follow behind him and listen to his childish babble, not really hearing his words so much as his innocent, happy voice. Those little rhythms were melodious and delightful. I loved to sit with him and look out at the ocean and answer his questions while I stroked his soft hair. In a way I wanted to be back in his world, a child's world, the world of dolls and toys and candy canes, a world without hard truths and ugly realities. All the bogeymen could be chased away with a warm embrace, a soft, reassuring kiss, a promise for tomorrow.

Momma submerged herself in her social life again, attending her afternoon bridge parties, going to shows and shopping in Boston, hosting dinners for wealthy acquaintances and attending their dinners. She tried on a number of occasions to get me to join her and Tony when they went to a dinner at some rich estate. She claimed she wanted me to meet the sons and daughters of the upper classes, but I declined every time.

Tony kept his distance, barely talking to me, even avoiding looking at me, especially when he was with my mother. If I were alone and I saw him in the house, I would go the other way. Thankfully, the house was so large, it was possible to get lost in it whenever I wanted to. And I could wander the grounds, stay at the outdoor pool, go for a horseback ride and stay away all afternoon, or take one of my beach walks and avoid any contact with him.

Then, at the start of the third week in July, he announced he was going to Europe for a quick business trip. Momma gave him a list of boutiques to go to and things to get her. He remarked that he would look for something special for me, too, but I didn't reply.

A few days later, Daddy called from Houston, Texas. He was on his way back to the East coast and wanted to make arrangements to see me. I had been writing him continually, trying to get him to call or write me back, but he hadn't responded until now.

'I was on the move a great deal, Princess,' he explained. 'All your letters are probably one day behind me. Is everything all right?'

'No, Daddy. I've got to see you,' I said desperately. He was silent on the other end for a moment.

'What is it?' he asked.

'I can't talk about it over the phone, but I need to talk to you. I really do,' I emphasized.

'Your mother can't help you?'

'She . . . no, she can't help me,' I replied. My voice was dry, unemotional, deadly honest.

'All right. I'll call you as soon as I get to Boston and we'll all meet for dinner. I'm due there the day after tomorrow.'

'Daddy, try to meet me by yourself,' I pleaded.

'Leigh, I'm married now and Mildred is a part of everything I do. She likes it that way. She gets very upset if I exclude her from anything, and she wants so much to get to know you. Won't you forget that we married so quickly and give her a chance?' he begged.

'It's not that this time, Daddy. I . . . have some very personal things to discuss.'

'Mildred is part of my personal life, Leigh,' he insisted. Once again, Daddy was clay in the hands of a woman, I thought.

'All right, Daddy. Call me as soon as you arrive,' I said. I had no choice and no one else to turn to.

'Right. See you soon, Princess,' he said and hung up.

Knowing that Daddy was coming the day after tomorrow buoyed me. Surely, after I told him what had happened to me, he would demand that I remain with him. He wouldn't even permit me to return to Farthy that night and he would tell my mother that he was willing to go to any lengths now to win me away from her legally. I didn't know how much better my life would be, but at least I would be away from Farthy and Tony.

I was cheerful and energetic for the first time since Tony had forced himself on me. I did laps in the pool, went for a fast horseback ride, and took Troy for a long beach walk, collecting seashells. I had the best appetite I had had in weeks, asking for seconds and eating dessert. Momma noticed a change, but I didn't tell her about Daddy's impending arrival.

I woke up early on the morning of Daddy's arrival in Boston. I thought I would have Miles drive me into the city the moment Daddy phoned. I had already dressed, eaten breakfast, and taken a short walk with Troy by the time my mother came down. In the afternoon, she was having some friends over for bridge and I knew that meant she would spend hours preparing herself.

Just before lunch, Curtis called me to the phone. I was standing outside with Troy, watching the gardeners work.

'Is it my father?' I asked eagerly.

'He simply said he was calling for Mr VanVoreen,' Curtis replied in his usual nondescript manner of speaking. I hurried into the house and to the nearest phone, which was in the living room off right.

'Hello,' I said. 'This is Leigh.'

'Miss VanVoreen. My name is Chester Goodman. I work for your father and he has asked me to call you.'

'Yes?' I said, impatient with the formalities. I didn't care what his name was. All I wanted were the details.

'He sends his regrets. He won't be able to see you today.'

'What?' I felt the color drain from my face. My chest felt so cold and empty, I was sure my heart had stopped beating. 'Why? I must see him. I must!' I insisted. 'Please, tell him, put him on the phone. I demand to speak with him.'

'I'm sorry, Miss VanVoreen, but he is no longer here. One of the VanVoreen ocean liners has broken down in the Pacific. There is a rescue operation on the way and he had to fly out to the coast on an emergency.'

'Oh no!'

'He said to tell you he will phone you the first chance he gets. Miss VanVoreen?'

I didn't reply. I cradled the receiver and sat back in the chair by the telephone, dazed. Didn't Daddy hear the desperation in my voice? Why couldn't he see to it that he met with me first somehow or why didn't he simply take me along with him? We could have talked on the airplane. Why was his business more important than his daughter?

A frightening thought suddenly occurred to me. Maybe he knew; maybe he had always known that I wasn't really his daughter and maybe that was why he didn't put me at the top of his list of most important things.

I buried my face in my hands.

'Leigh?'

It was Troy, standing in the doorway.

'Are you coming back out now?'

I looked up at him.

'No,' I said. 'I'm not feeling well. I've got to go up and lay down a while.'

'Will you come out later?'

'I don't know, Troy. I'm sorry,' I said and walked to the stairway. I didn't look back. I couldn't stand the sight of any more sadness.

It seemed to take me forever to go up the stairway. I was walking in such a stupor, I didn't realize I had reached my suite. Suddenly, I found myself standing in the bedroom. I went to my bed and lay back on the pillow. My head had begun to ache and my stomach felt funny. It felt as if there were a dozen butterflies in it, all trying to find a way out. Their wings tickled as they flapped about frantically.

I felt just as trapped. How could I ever feel any worse than this, I thought?

But I did, and as soon as the next morning. I hadn't gotten my eyes open a few seconds before it came over me: this wave of nausea. Wave after wave came, building and building until I had to get up quickly and run to the bathroom to vomit. I felt so sick I thought I was going to die. Finally, it subsided and I made my way back to bed to rest until I felt strong enough to get up again.

What was it? Something I had eaten? Why would it come and go like that anyway? I wondered.

And then something struck me. I had forgotten all about it because I had been so occupied with other things this past month and a half.

My period was overdue.

And now morning sickness! Oh no, I thought. I'm pregnant!

*

I waited three more days before telling my mother, hoping and praying what I feared wasn't true, but the nausea greeted me each morning and even recurred sometimes during the afternoon. There was no mistaking the calendar either. No matter how hard or long I looked at the dates, I confronted the same fact: my period was long overdue and I had never been irregular before.

Finally, I realized I could avoid it no longer. Oddly enough, when I envisioned telling Momma, my first thought was that this would now confirm what she had refused to believe: Tony had raped me. I couldn't have gotten pregnant myself. Of course, I would have rather she went on doubting me than having this proof, but since it had happened, there was no point in not using it to drive home the truth, once and for all.

She was getting ready for a charity cocktail party she was hosting here at Farthy in the afternoon. I found her seated at her vanity table, studying a new way to wear her hair. She didn't acknowledge me when I entered, nor did she hear me when I called to her.

'Momma, please!' I exclaimed. Her eyelids fluttered and she spun around.

'What is it, Leigh? Can't you see I'm getting ready for my guests? I don't have time for any nonsense,' she barked.

'This isn't nonsense, Momma,' I said, my voice heavy, cold. She saw how serious I was and put down her brush.

'Very well, what is it now?' She batted her eyelashes and looked at the ceiling, barely tolerating me. 'Whenever I'm in the middle of something important, you have some sort of emotional crisis. I don't know what's wrong with teenage girls today. Maybe you're eating too much sugar,' she concluded.

'*Momma, will you listen to me?*' I felt like running over to her and taking hold of the strands of her precious hair, forcing her to see me, to hear me.

'Stop shouting. You have my attention. Only please be considerate enough to make it fast.'

I swallowed back the lumps in my throat and took a deep breath.

'When I first told you what Tony had done, you didn't believe me. You wouldn't believe me!' I said. I couldn't help the way my voice rose and my eyes widened. The more I talked, the angrier I became myself. Momma's expression of annoyance and impatience fanned the hot coals of my anger, turning them into small flames. 'I kept trying to explain, to get you to understand that it wasn't any teenage fantasy, but you wouldn't listen.'

'And I still don't want to listen to this. I told you, I'm . . .'

'Momma!' I screamed. *'I'm pregnant.'*

When the words came out of my mouth, they surprised me, but there they were. We were both silent, startled by the truth. There would be a baby. Tony's evil act would have consequences and now God would make us all pay for one madman's lust.

Momma simply stared at me a moment and then a tight, small smile appeared on her face. How I wanted to wipe it off! She sat back in her chair, folding her hands on her lap.

'What did you say?'

The tears were streaking down my cheeks and this time I was helpless, could not swallow them back.

'My period is long overdue and for the past few days, I've been having morning sickness. He made me pregnant.' She didn't speak; she looked at me as if I had just spoken in some foreign language and she was waiting for me to translate. 'Don't you understand what I'm saying, Momma? Everything I had told you was true, and now I'm going to have a baby, Tony's baby!' I cried, driving the reality home as firmly as I could.

'Are you sure? Absolutely positive about the dates?'

'Yes. You know I always keep good track of that,' I replied firmly. There was no point in pretending what was happening was not. I would not do as my mother did: I would not live in a world of illusions just to keep myself happy.

She shook her head, her eyes turning small and hateful.

'It's your own fault, you little fool.'

'What?' I couldn't believe my ears.

She sat back nodding, confirming her own thoughts.

'You flaunted yourself about, tempting him, tormenting him

with your young, blossoming body. And now, you have the result, the horrible, embarrassing, terrible result.'

'I didn't flaunt myself about, Momma. You know . . .'

'Yes, I know. Don't you think Tony came to me continually, complaining about how you batted your eyelashes at him. And then, while I was away, you invited him into your suite. What did you expect him to do with you lying there naked, tempting, inviting, demanding he make love to you or you would . . . would make up stories about him?'

'What? Did he tell you such a lie? How can you believe that story?' I demanded.

'And now look what you have done,' she said, not listening to me. She resembled an actress who had been rehearsing and rehearsing these lines and refused to do anything but recite them. 'What if this gets out? Just think what it will do to me, what my friends will think. Why, we'll never be invited to a single dinner. We'll be ostracized from society . . . and all because my daughter is a promiscuous, sex-driven, selfish, inconsiderate . . . jealous. Yes, that's what you are,' she said, obviously very satisfied with her explanation, 'and that's what you've been. You're jealous of me, of my looks and the fact that I married such a young and handsome man, instead of remining chained to your father, an old man who didn't deserve me.'

'That's not true!'

'Of course it's true. He told me how you behaved in the cottage, how you tried to seduce him during the modeling sessions.'

'Lies, these are all lies!' I cried. Why was she doing this? What had happened to our mother-daughter relationship? 'I didn't want to be the model. Don't you remember? You made me do it. And afterward, when I came to you . . .'

'Yes, you came to me to try to get me to dislike Tony. You tried to make me jealous. That's what you were doing,' she concluded, her eyes lighting up. 'You thought that by making up these stories about his touching you . . .'

'He did, Momma! Those weren't stories!!'

'He did, but not the way you wanted me to think he did.

And when all that didn't work, you enticed him into your bedroom and when he resisted, you spit the truth about my age at him, trying to drive a wedge between him and me!' I saw she would never forgive me that. She would never believe that Tony had already known.

'Finally, because he is only a man, he succumbed, and now, look at what you've done, what you've accomplished. Well, I hope you're proud of yourself, little Princess!' she hissed. Never did she look as ugly to me.

'Momma, none of this is true. You can't seriously believe it.'

'And after I tried so hard to bring you up right, to understand how women and men should be with each other, how a woman has to hold on to her virtue to win the respect and admiration of men. *I told you,*' she screamed, '*good girls don't go all the way!*'

Her scream vibrated through me, shattering whatever feelings of love and respect for her remained. It broke, splintered and disintegrated like a plate of bone thin china, the parts falling through my memory – fragments of loving conversations between us, slices of images, pictures of happier times, the broken sounds of tinkle bells and music from precious music boxes, unfinished laughter, half smiles, little kisses on my cheeks and forehead, our hands parting.

I couldn't stand it any longer. I wasn't the jealous one; she was. I wasn't the one who had been promiscuous; she was. I wasn't the one who lied and betrayed. I wasn't selfish and blind to anything that didn't please me; she was. And now, to keep her little world the way she wanted it, she was painting me as evil. I was to be the guilty person, even though I was the one who had been violated.

'*You liar!*' I screamed back at her. 'You hypocrite, sitting there and condemning me for being promiscuous and going all the way. I know the truth about you. I overheard Grandma Jana talking to you just before you married Tony and I know Daddy isn't my real father, that you slept with another man and got pregnant and married Daddy without telling him the truth so he would think I was his child. I knew, but I kept it a secret buried in my heart of hearts, even though it burned and hurt.'

'Why that's . . .' She sat back, a dazed look on her face.

'That's true,' I said. 'All true. But your mother helped you find a husband, a man who would love and respect you.'

'This is ridiculous,' she said, emerging from her daze and looking about as if we had witnesses to convince. 'What sort of story do you want to spread now? Is this another way to try to get Tony away from me?'

'Stop it! Stop lying!'

'How dare you shout at me like this? I'm your mother.'

'No, you're not,' I said, shaking my head and backing away from her. 'No, you're not. I have no mother and I have no father.' I allowed myself to be just as ugly with my words as she had been with hers. 'You thought you could have it all, didn't you? Only the finest!' I spat out. 'A handsome young husband, a luxurious estate, a designer wardrobe and a *specially selected mistress for your own husband!'* I lowered my voice to a purr the way Momma had done on countless occasions. 'Tell me, Momma, when did you first get the idea? On your honeymoon? When you returned to Farthy?' My questions became frenzied and I didn't allow Momma to answer as she had done with me so many times. 'When did you realize that your beauty wouldn't last forever and would start *fading*!' I laughed in her face. 'That's right, fading! With each passing day you grow older and older, Momma. But you've always known that, deep in your heart of hearts. *I can't stand you anymore!* You don't care about anything but yourself and your precious face. Well let me tell you something Jillian Tatterton, the game is over! You're going to be a grandmother! Does that make you feel young? No matter how young you look, you'll never escape the fact that you're a grandmother and the only person you have to blame is *yourself*!' I turned and ran from her suite, ran from her lies and hypocritical eyes, ran from a woman I no longer recognized or loved. I slammed the door of my room behind me, but I didn't cry. I wouldn't cry again in this evil place. I hated this place, hated what happened here, hated what it had turned me into. All I knew was I had to get away, get away from its sins, lies and its false smiles.

I threw open my closet door and grabbed a suitcase. Without planning what I would take, I grabbed something here, something there, throwing the garments into the suitcase roughly. I didn't care about my beautiful clothes or my precious jewelry; I didn't care about pictures or mementoes. I just wanted to get away as quickly as I could.

I closed my suitcase and started out, but I paused at the door and turned as if someone had called out to me. Angel stared at me across the room. She looked as sad and as lost as I did. How could I leave her behind? I scooped her into my arms and charged out of my suite with my suitcase swinging in my hand. My mother hadn't come after me and she wasn't in the corridor. I hurried to the stairway.

It was only when I reached the bottom of the staircase that I stopped to question what I was doing, where I was going. I couldn't just walk out of Farthy. I was miles and miles from anywhere.

Grandma Jana, I thought. I would go to her. She would understand. She knew who and what Momma really was. I would tell her all that happened. She would be sympathetic. I had to go south and make my way to her home, but that took money. I looked in my pocketbook for my wallet and found I had barely twenty dollars, not enough to finance a trip to Texas. I recalled where Tony kept some money in his office and went in to get it. Why not? I thought. If anyone should pay, it should be Tony.

There was nearly two hundred dollars in a desk drawer. Hardly a fortune, but enough to get me on the road. I stuffed the money into my purse, straightened up and gazed into a mirror. I brushed back my hair, wiped my cheeks with a handkerchief, and took a deep breath. I didn't want to look as desperate as I felt. I intended to go out and casually ask Miles to drive me into Boston. If he thought something was wrong, he might go back into the house to ask my mother first.

I left the office, closing the door quietly behind me. The house was quiet. I gazed up the stairway at the second floor, and saw no one. My mother probably had gone right back to getting ready for her party. After all, nothing came before her looks and she had her wealthy friends coming, people she had to impress. Curtis emerged from the music room and paused to look my way, an expression of curiosity on his face because he saw me standing with a suitcase. I smiled, trying to make everything look casual, and he nodded and went on to the kitchen.

Then I stepped out the front door. The bright sunlight made me squint, so I shaded my eyes with my hand. It was very warm and there were big, high clouds scattered across the deep blue sky. A slight, soft breeze caressed my face. The world welcomed me, encouraged me to come out of the dark, enchanted kingdom called Farthinggale. When I arrived here I thought it was like a storybook. Now I knew the *truth*: that it was a nightmare come to life!

Lucky for me, Miles was in front polishing the car. I didn't have to go looking for him and attract the attention of the groundsmen. He looked up sharply when I started toward him.

'I'm not early,' I said and smiled. I looked at my watch and then held it toward him for him to see the time.

'Huh?' He put his polishing rag down and looked at me with a puzzled expression. 'I'm supposed to take you somewhere this afternoon?'

'To the train station, Miles. Don't tell me, my mother forgot to tell you this morning.'

'No, she didn't. I . . .'

'Just like her when she has one of her charity affairs. She gets so excited and flustered, she forgets everything else,' I said. I knew he would believe that. 'I'm going to visit my grandmother. Everything's been arranged. I'm afraid we will have to leave immediately so that I will not miss my train.'

'But . . .' He looked up at the house.

'Miles?' I lifted my suitcase to indicate he should take it.

'Oh.' He took it hurriedly and put it into the trunk of the limousine. 'I can't understand why Curtis didn't remind me. He always reminds me about trips.'

'Perhaps Momma didn't think to tell him either,' I said. 'Shall we go?'

'What? Oh, yes.' He opened the door for me and I slipped in quickly. Then he got into the limousine and started the engine. I watched the front doorway, half expecting my mother to suddenly appear and start screaming, demanding to know what was happening. But she didn't emerge, and Miles started down the long, winding driveway. I gazed out the side window and suddenly saw little Troy and his nurse coming back from a walk to the beach. In my excitement and anger, I had forgotten all about him and what my leaving would mean to him.

'Oh no,' I muttered. 'Troy. Miles,' I cried. 'Please, stop for a moment. I forgot to say goodbye to Troy.'

As soon as the car came to a halt, I stepped out and called and waved to Troy. He paused and came running toward me, his little pail swinging in his hand.

'Leigh. I got the biggest shell you ever saw,' he cried. 'Look.' He stopped before me, out of breath and put his pail down. He had a pink and white conch set on top of a variety of small shells.

'That is big.'

'And you can hear the ocean's roar.' He picked it up and handed it to me. 'Listen.'

I put it to my ear and nodded, smiling.

'Sounds like it's going to come out and get me all wet,' I said, pulling it away as if I were really afraid. He laughed.

'It's not really in there.' He took the shell back and placed it in his pail. Then he looked at the limousine. 'Where are you going, Leigh?'

'I've got to go away for a while, Troy.' I took his little hand into mine and squatted so I could look into his eyes. 'You be good and try to rest and eat right while I am away, okay?'

'But when are you coming back?'

'Not for a while, Troy.'

'A long while?' I nodded. 'Then I want to go with you.'

'You can't, Troy. You've got to stay here where you can be looked after.'

'But where are you going?' he asked again, his eyes already filling with tears.

'To see my grandmother.'

'How come you never went before?' he asked, his clever little mind quickly working up skepticism.

'I was always too busy,' I lied. He tilted his head slightly. He could see I was lying, I thought, but I couldn't help it.

'Aren't you really coming back, Leigh?' he asked softly.

'Of course,' I said. I smiled and squeezed back the fat tears that wanted to burst out.

'No you're not,' he said pulling away from me. 'You're leaving me and Farthy. You're not coming back; you're not.'

'I will, Troy. I promise. Somehow, someway, I'll come back to you.'

'Promise?'

'Cross my heart. Come, kiss me goodbye. Please,' I begged. 'Otherwise, I will have a horrible trip.' I grimaced, resembling someone already in great torment.

He relented and put his small arms around my neck. I kissed his cheek and held him tightly. Then he pecked mine like a tiny bird and pulled back. I stood up, smiled down at him, and headed back to the car.

'Leigh!' he called. 'Wait.'

I paused at the door. He reached into his pail and took out the conch.

'Take this with you,' he offered.

'Oh no, Troy. You keep it here.'

'No,' he said shaking his head vigorously. 'Take it with you and you won't forget me.'

'I can't forget you, Troy. You don't have to worry about that,' I said, but he stood there, stubbornly holding out the conch. I took it. 'Okay, thank you.'

'Put it to your ear and you'll hear the ocean and me,' he promised and turned to run back to his nurse. I watched him for a moment and then got into the car.

'Please, let's go, Miles,' I said. 'As fast as we can.'

He smirked, still a little suspicious, and then started away. We rolled on through the main gate and under the great arch, but I didn't look back. Instead, I put Troy's conch to my ear and listened to the ocean and heard his little cry.

He was calling after me. 'Leigh . . . Leigh . . .'

And then I pulled it away and closed my eyes and Farthy fell back behind me, flickering out like a dying candle.

NINETEEN

A Visit to a Circus

I had never traveled anywhere all by myself, but I didn't show Miles any of my fear and indecision. Right after we arrived at the train station, he took my suitcase from the limousine trunk and waited for my instructions.

'I can take it from here, Miles,' I said.

'Oh no, Miss Leigh. I'll bring it to the porter. Where are you going?'

'It's all right, Miles. I want to be on my own. I like the idea of traveling alone,' I explained and smiled warmly so he wouldn't see my nervousness. He hesitated a moment and then put my suitcase down.

'Well, you have a good trip, Miss Leigh,' he said.

'Thank you, Miles.' I took my suitcase quickly and walked into the station, stopping to wave goodbye to him once more. Would I ever see him again? He stood there staring after me, but he didn't follow me to be sure I was safely on my train.

I turned and looked around. People were rushing about everywhere and announcements were being made concerning different trains and destinations. The hustle and bustle was exciting, but also frightening as well. I saw a tall, red-headed policeman standing by a news stand talking with the man by the cash register. He looked young and had a friendly face, so I went directly to him.

'Excuse me,' I said, 'but could you tell me where I would go to buy a ticket to Texas?'

'To Texas?' he asked smiling. 'Texas is a big state.' The news stand attendant laughed. 'You know where you're going in Texas, right?'

'Yes sir, I do.'

'Well,' he said, 'just make a right at this first corridor and at the end of the corridor, you'll find the ticket booths.'

'Thank you,' I said.

'Say, that's a pretty doll you're carrying, as pretty as you,' he said. I forgot how tightly I was holding on to Angel. I smiled and started away. 'Not running away from home, are you?' he called to me.

'Oh no, sir.'

He and the news stand attendant laughed again. When I arrived at the ticket booth, I asked for a ticket to Fullerton, Texas. That was really all I knew about Grandma Jana's home. I thought once I arrived there, I could call her to come get me.

The ticket seller smirked.

'Fullerton, Texas?' He looked at his charts. 'Don't have any train stop there, Miss. What's it near?'

'Oh, I'm not sure. I think . . .'

'Houston? Dallas? El Paso?'

I began to panic. If I didn't choose one, he would surely think I was a girl running away from home. He might even signal to the policeman and nothing would be more horrible, more embarrassing and degrading than being brought to Farthy in a police car right in the middle of Momma's charity affair.

'Dallas,' I said quickly. All I wanted to do was get to Texas. Once I was there, I would call Grandma Jana. I was sure she would see to it that I was brought to her home, no matter how far away I was.

'Okay, Dallas. Well,' he said, 'the best I can do for you is send you to our hub city, Atlanta. You'll have quite a lay-over there, however; unless you come back and leave early in the morning tomorrow.'

'No, I don't care about the lay-over,' I stammered.

'I see. Round trip, I imagine?'

'No,' I said quickly. 'One way.'

'You want general seating, a car, a sleeper?'

'A car,' I replied.

He nodded and began working on my ticket. 'That will be one hundred and sixty-two dollars.'

One hundred and sixty-two! That didn't leave me much money for anything else. Perhaps I should have chosen general seating, I thought, but I didn't hesitate. I didn't want the ticket seller to know that I didn't have much traveling money. I counted it out quickly and he gave me the ticket.

'You leave from platform C, in about fifteen minutes. That's down to the right and over. You can't miss it.'

'Thank you.' I took my ticket and started away. Now that I actually had the ticket in my hand and I was heading for the train platform, the reality of what I was doing set in. My heart was thumping so hard, I thought I would go into a faint and make a scene. I imagined a crowd of people clustered around me, the young policeman holding everyone back. It frightened me even more to imagine it, so I hurried to the platform and then took the first available seat on a bench. Because there was still some time before the train left, there weren't many people here. I saw a woman with two little girls two benches down from me. She was reading to them from a children's story book to keep them occupied. I couldn't help remembering the way Momma would read to me.

How different the world was when I was very little and we were all living in our Boston home, I thought. Watching this mother and her children made me wonder about the baby I was carrying. Was it a boy or a girl? When I gave birth, should I keep the child or give it up for adoption? What would Grandma Jana's advice be? Could I give up the baby once I had held it in my arms? But wasn't I too young to be a mother, and if I did become a mother, what kind of a mother would I be?

I knew I would never be a mother like mine. I'd rather give the child away than be that, I thought. I set Angel down beside me and closed my eyes. The rumble of trains approaching and leaving other platforms made the floor quake. Soon, more and more people began to arrive. When a man in a suit and tie sat down beside me, I hugged Angel to me. The man smiled but then immediately opened a newspaper and began reading.

My heart began to thump again. It was getting closer and closer to my departure. I looked back. Was I making the right decision? It would be easy to change my mind. I could simply call and have Miles return. Soon, he would be arriving at Farthy himself and he would either mention taking me to the train station or be asked where he had gone. Momma would find out and send him right back to get me, but he wouldn't arrive in time.

There was no returning, I thought, and when the train came rumbling in, I got up immediately to enter as soon as the doors opened. I found my car quickly and took a seat by the window. Then I put my suitcase overhead, set Angel beside me snugly and waited anxiously. There was room for at least three other people, but only an elderly gentleman came into my car. He nodded, smiled, took his seat and immediately began reading his newspaper.

Finally, the train began to pull away. My heart thumped in rhythm with the thump of the train's wheels as they turned on the tracks. The station disappeared behind us and we shot out into the twilight, heading south, heading away from the only world I had ever known.

'Ticket miss?' the conductor said. I had it clutched in my hand and handed it to him quickly. He punched it and smiled. I sat back and looked out the window as the train snaked on, carrying me into tunnels of darkness and over hills toward new horizons. We seemed to be riding into the approaching night, the darkness crawling towards us. I caught glimpses of stars peeping down between clouds. They never seemed farther away than they did now.

The train rocked on. From time to time, I saw the lights of other cities or houses out in the distance, their windows a warm yellow. Within those houses, families sat together having dinner. Those children felt safe and secure with parents who loved them. They weren't as rich as I was, and their homes could fit in one corner of Farthinggale Manor and be lost, but they would be going to sleep in their own beds tonight and their parents would kiss them good night. Mothers would tuck in little children. Daddies would kiss them on their cheeks or foreheads and promise them an even brighter or happier tomorrow.

I had no one to promise me a happier or brighter tomorrow,

no one but Angel. She and I sat like two lost children being pulled into the unknown. We were tired and hungry and already, quite lonely. Even though the gentleman across from me eyed me curiously when I placed Angel firmly in my lap, I kept her there, hugging her tightly to me as the train rolled on. I was determined. There was no turning back, not now, not ever. Soon, the monotonous rhythm of its wheels put me asleep.

I awoke with a start in the middle of the night. It was dark in the car, but there were lights on the outside of the train and lights in the corridor, so after my initial confusion, I remembered exactly where I was and what I had done. The gentleman across from me was asleep with his newspaper opened on his lap. His body rocked from side to side with the train. I curled up again and closed my eyes. In moments, I was asleep once more.

I awoke with the first light of morning and looked out over the farms and flat fields. The elderly gentleman was already awake.

'How far are you going, miss?' he asked.

'Atlanta.'

'I get off at the next stop. You've got a good five hours more. You can get some breakfast in the dining car. Very pretty doll,' he said nodding toward Angel. 'I don't think I've ever seen one that pretty,' he added with a smile of admiration.

'Thank you.'

'Going home?'

'Yes,' I said. I thought it was better to say that. In a way I might be going home, I reasoned.

He stretched.

'Me too,' he said. 'Been on the road nearly a month. I'm a salesman, wholesale shoes.'

'That must be hard for you, being away from your family so long.'

'That it is. Nothing like going home. Of course, all my children are grown, so there's just me and the good woman. It's nice though. We have five grandchildren,' he added, smiling proudly.

I smiled back at him and then I thought, soon Momma would

have a grandchild, only she would never be able to appreciate her grandchild the way this man appreciates his grandchildren, for hers was fathered by her new husband. The twisted and dark world of Farthy would follow my baby forever, I concluded. It was almost a reason not to have it.

But maybe I could find another world, a world very different from Farthy, and bring my child into that world. If only I could, if only I could, if only I could. I chanted it like a prayer in rhythm with the train's wheels. Then my stomach churned with hunger.

'I guess I will get some breakfast,' I said standing.

'I'll watch your doll for you,' the gentleman offered.

'Oh no sir. She goes everywhere I do,' I said. 'And besides, she's just as hungry.'

He laughed and I went out to find the dining car.

We stopped at his stop while I was having something to eat, so he was gone by the time I returned. I spent the next three and a half hours alone, staring out the window. When I heard the announcement for Atlanta, my heart began to pound again. The first leg of my long and sad journey was over. I was far away from Farthy and by now, Momma was surely frantic and angry. I wondered how she would handle it. Would she call the police or would she be afraid of a scandal? Would she try to contact Tony in Europe?

One thing was sure, I thought. She didn't let what happened interfere with her charity affair at Farthy. No one who attended would be able to tell anything was wrong by looking at her face and she would instruct the servants, Miles and Curtis especially, not to mention one word about it to anyone.

I could just hear her.

'She will be back once she's over her tantrum.'

'No I won't, Momma,' I pledged. 'No I won't.'

I stood on the platform for a few moments reading all the signs that instructed passengers where to go for different destinations. The Atlanta terminal was bigger than the one in Boston and there seemed to be twice, maybe three times the number of people rushing about. I found an information booth in the large lobby and showed my ticket to the girl behind the desk.

'You have to go down the corridor on the left there and make the first right. You'll see the signs, but this train isn't scheduled to depart until eight P.M. Don't you have anyplace to go until then? It's hours and hours.'

'No,' I said. 'It'll be all right.'

'Suit yourself,' she said and turned to someone else. I bought a magazine and then followed her directions and arrived at my platform. It was much wider and longer than the one in Boston. There was a small lounge area off to the right, so I went directly to it and sat on a bench toward the rear. Then I counted my money. I didn't have much left, and hoped I had enough for lunch and dinner.

'I bet I could turn one of your one dollar bills into a five dollar bill,' someone said and I looked up and into the most radiant black eyes I had ever seen. The young man standing in front of me had thick, rich ebony hair and bronze skin. He was tall and handsome with broad strong shoulders that made the seams of his thin short-sleeve shirt strain.

'Pardon me?'

'Just trust me with one of those one dollar bills a moment and I'll show you,' he said sitting down beside me. I don't know why I did it, but I handed this stranger one of my precious dollars. I knew that unsuspecting travelers, especially young girls like myself, were targets for con artists everywhere. But he had said he would turn my one into a five and not vice versa and I liked looking at him.

From what I could see, he had nothing in his hands and of course, he had no sleeves in which to hide anything. He folded my dollar very carefully in his palm right before my eyes. He made it as small as he could. Then he turned his hand over so I could see only the top of his closed fist. He held it in front of me and smiled.

'Okay, you touch my hand,' he said. His eyes twinkled.

'Touch your hand?' He nodded. I put my finger on his middle knuckle and then took it off quickly. He laughed.

'It's not goin' ta burn ya. Okay, that was good enough

anyway,' he said and turned his hand over, palm up again. Then, before my eyes, he unfolded the bill and there it was – a five dollar bill!

'How did you do that?' I asked, my eyes wide.

He shrugged.

'Magic, how else? Anyway, here it is, five dollars,' he said handing it to me. 'The way you were counting your money, right down to the penny, you look like you needed an extra four dollars,' he said.

'Is that right?' Heat came into my face. 'Well, I'm not accustomed to taking money from strangers, even magic money,' I replied thrusting the five dollar bill back at him.

'Okay. I won't be a stranger then,' he said, leaning back and holding his palms up. 'My name's Thomas Luke Casteel, but most everyone just calls me Luke. And you are?' He extended his hand.

I stared at him, not knowing whether I should laugh or get up and walk away. He was too handsome to be a con man, I thought; rather, I hoped.

'Leigh VanVoreen.' I shook his hand.

'There, now we're not strangers and you can keep the magic money.'

'I really don't need it. I have enough to get where I have to go. I must insist you change this back to my one dollar bill.'

He laughed.

'I don't know the magic to change it back. Sorry.'

'You're being very foolish, giving away money like that.'

He shrugged.

'Easy come, easy go. Besides, it was worth far more than four dollars to have seen your face when I performed my trick,' he said, fixing his eyes on me. I felt myself blush.

'Are you a magician?'

'Not really. I've been working in a circus nearby and I picked up a lot of stuff like that from the carnies.'

'Carnies?'

'Carnival people. They're wonderful people to know. They stick together through thick and thin and help each other all the time, and some of them have traveled all over the world and know a great many things. Just sitting around and listening to them talk, I learn a lot. You'd be surprised how much I already know, and knowledge and experience is what makes you older,' he added proudly.

'You don't look that old.'

'Seventeen. You don't look very old either.'

'I'm almost fourteen.'

'Well, we're not much older than Romeo and Juliet, you know,' he said. 'The duchess told me about them. She was a professional actress in Europe. Now, she does the knife-throwing act with her husband.'

'You mean, she stands there while he throws knives around her?'

'Yep.'

'I could never do that. And what if her husband got mad at her?' I asked.

Luke laughed again.

'That's a big joke around the tents. It's not as dangerous as it seems. There's a technique to it, just as there is for most anything in the circus, but that's what I love about the circus – the illusions, the make-believe world, the excitement.'

'It sounds like fun. What do you do, magic tricks?'

'No. I just took on a part-time job, just for a short while, just to be around it. I want to be a circus barker one day. You know, the man who calls to the people.' He jumped up and cried out, 'Come one, come all, to the greatest show on earth. We have one-eyed giants, a snake lady, the smallest man in the world, the bearded lady, Boris the lion tamer, the greatest acrobatic team in the air!' he recited as if he were standing on a platform. People nearby turned our way, but he didn't seem to care that he was attracting attention.

'How'd I do?'

'Very good.'

'Thanks. I practise all the time, but it's hard because where I come from, people don't know much about circuses. They don't know much about anything,' he said sadly.

'Where are you from?'

'A place in West Virginia known as the Willies. It's in the

mountains above the town of Winnerrow,' he said, and I saw that despite what he had said about the people back there, he had a warm feeling in his heart for his home.

'Why do they call it the Willies?' I asked. It seemed like a strange name for a home.

'Oh, living on the mountainside is enough to give anyone the willies – especially when the wolves howl like the wind and the bobcats screech. Up there, wild things roam at will. Gotta keep your eye on your puppy dogs,' he added, and laughed.

'You don't make it sound very nice. No wonder you left to work in the circus.'

'No, I'm just kiddin'. It's not that bad. Actually, I miss the peace and quiet of the woods. Most of the time, you hear only the birds singin' or a nearby crystal clear brook babblin'. And I miss the smells – the rich green leaves in summer, the pine needles, the wild flowers. It's great to look eye to eye with squirrels and the like, and when the sun comes up in the morning and lifts its head above the mountain or peeps through the trees, you feel . . . I don't know . . . alive, I guess.'

'Now you make it sound wonderful,' I said. 'Which is it?'

'It's both. So, where are you going?'

'I'm going to Texas,' I said. 'Fullerton, Texas, to stay with my grandmother.'

'Oh? Where you from?'

'Boston and Cape Cod.'

'How can you be from two places?' he asked. I laughed, but he looked hurt. I saw he was a very sensitive young man and didn't want to be thought stupid or foolish.

'My family has a few homes,' I said. 'I grew up in Boston, but I've been living in a home outside of Boston,' I explained.

He nodded.

'Sounds like you were right.'

'What do you mean?'

'You didn't need me to change your one to a five,' he said sullenly. I stared at him a moment and then I shook my head.

'Yes, I did,' I confessed. His eyes widened with interest.

'Huh?'

'I didn't take much money with me when I left and I had no

idea how much things cost,' I added. He nodded, thoughtfully.

'Sounds like you left in a rush. Did ya?' he asked, but I looked away. 'Say, what's that you're holdin' on to so tightly?' He leaned over so he could get a better view of Angel. 'A doll!' he said with amazement. My eyes flared.

'It's not just a doll; it's a special doll, a collector's doll. It's a work of art and it's called a portrait doll,' I said sharply.

'Oh, I see. Excuse me. Well, can I get a better look at it? I promise to be careful.'

I fixed my eyes on him. He looked sincere so I handed Angel to him. He held her gingerly and studied her face and features. Then he whistled through his teeth.

'You're right. This is truly a work of art. I never seen such detail in a doll.' He lowered her and gazed at me. Then he looked at her again. 'Wait a minute. This doll looks a lot like you.'

'It's supposed to,' I said, taking her back carefully. 'I told you – it's a portrait doll. I . . . I modeled for it.'

'Oh. Say, that's something, and those clothes, they look special too.'

'They are.'

'Well, that explains why you're holdin' on to it for dear life.'

'I'm not holding on to it for dear life,' I snapped. He laughed again. When he smiled, his eyes brightened warmly. There was nothing snide or conniving in his smile; it was nothing like Tony's sneer. Luke's smile gave me a warm, safe feeling.

'I'm just kiddin' ya. So where do you have to go?'

'Texas. Dallas, Texas.'

'That's far. When's your train leavin'?'

'Not until eight P.M., I'm afraid.'

'Eight P.M.! That's hours and hours. You can't just sit here all that time. It's dusty and dirty and noisy here. Don't you know nobody in Atlanta?' I shook my head and he thought a moment. 'Well, let me ask you somethin'. Would you like to see the circus? I can get you in free and it would pass the time away and then I can bring you back to the station.'

'I don't know. I . . .'

'Have you ever been to a circus?'

I thought. I had been to one in Europe when I was very little, but I barely recalled it.

'No,' I said.

'Well that fixes it then,' Luke said, slapping his hands together. 'Come on.' He reached down for my bag. I remained seated. 'Come on, I won't hurt you and you'll have fun.'

I thought about his offer. I did have a terribly long time to wait and he was so handsome and friendly. Why not? I decided and stood up.

'Great. I just took a friend to the station and was on my way back,' he explained as he led me out. 'The circus ain't far from here. It's only goin' to be here another two days and then it's off for Jacksonville.'

'Sounds like a lot of traveling,' I remarked. He walked so straight and assured through the train station. I admired him for being so confident at his age. Unlike the boys I knew, even Joshua, Luke had a maturity about him. I expected he had grown quickly because he was on his own.

When he stepped out of the station, he turned me toward the parking lot and indicated a battered old, light brown pickup truck.

'That's my Rolls Royce,' he said. 'Ain't much, but it gets me where I gotta go. I bet you're accustomed to finer vehicles,' he added, winking. I didn't reply. He opened the door for me and I got in. There were three empty beer bottles on the floor. He scooped them up quickly and dropped them in the back of the truck. The seat was ripped and there were wires dangling from the dashboard. He got in quickly and started the engine. It spurted and stalled. 'Come on, Lulu Belle, you should be impressin' our passenger, not bein' stubborn. Just like most women,' he said, 'she's moody.'

'Men are just as moody,' I retorted. He laughed. The truck started and we were on our way to his circus.

'Is your family involved in the circus business now?' I asked him.

'My family?' He laughed again. 'Hell no. My daddy's been somethin' of a farmer and a moonshiner most of his life. Ma's a hard workin' woman. She raised six of us and it took its toll on her, I'm afraid,' he said, his face turning soft and sad. 'You know what they say: it ain't how far you've traveled, it's how rough was the road.'

'Six is a lot to raise. How many boys and how many girls?'

'All boys, which made it harder, I suppose. She never had a daughter to help her with the housework.'

'Where are your brothers?'

'They're spread out all over the place. Two went bad already. Before I left the Willies, we heard Jeff and Landon were in county jails for shopliftin'.'

'I'm sorry,' I said. I had never known anyone whose brothers or close family members were criminals. I couldn't help being afraid and wondering if I hadn't made a mistake getting into the truck with him.

'Yeah, Ma's takin' it hard,' he said, shaking his head.

'What's a moon . . . moon . . .'

'Moonshiner? Boy, you sound like you live behind some tall, thick walls. Moonshiners make moonshine whiskey, bootleg whiskey. They got their own homemade stills and they make this cheap whiskey and sell it all over the place. Most of the time, nobody bothers them, but once in a while, federal agents pop up. Ma don't like Pa doin' it, so he don't do it as much. Lately, he's been doin' odd jobs, handyman jobs. He's a good carpenter. Speakin' of dolls and such, you should see the wooden figures he carves when he's a mind to. Why he can sit on our porch for hours and hours and work on a dumb piece of wood, turnin' it into a rabbit or squirrel that looks so real, you'd expect it to jump out of your hand.'

I laughed. He had such a colorful way of speaking, yet he sounded real, down to earth, honest. I couldn't help liking him and in a way, envying him for the simple life he had led and the simple world he had grown up in.

He made a few turns and soon I saw the orange circus tents ahead of us. There were crowds of people coming and going. Luke waved to a man directing the traffic and turned so he could drive through an opening in the barriers created with ropes and posts. We bounced over the field, past the elephants that looked at us with little interest, and then stopped behind a smaller tent.

'I work here,' Luke explained. 'I care for the animals, feed 'em, wash 'em down. It ain't much, but it keeps me around the circus. Come on. We can put your suitcase and your doll in the tent. I have a mattress in one corner. That's my space. Nobody bothers it.' He saw the hesitation in my face and added, 'One thing about circus people; they never steal from each other. That's what I like about them – their code of ethics. Much better than the world outside.'

I got out and followed him into the tent. There were pails and cleaning equipment, bags of feed, ropes and other tools stored in it. In the rear was a bed of hay with an old mattress dropped over it to form a make-shift bed.

'I sleep here,' he explained. 'That's my stuff.' He pointed to a duffle bag. 'Why don't you put your doll into your suitcase and just leave it right there next to my bag.'

I nodded and opened my suitcase. He stood over me, looking down as I carefully wrapped Angel and placed her in the suitcase. I closed it and he put it beside his bag.

'There. Now let's go have some fun. I don't have to do any work for a while,' he said. I followed him out and to the carnival area where there were rides and games and food stands. It was a wonderful day to go to a circus and carnival. There were just enough clouds in the sky to keep the sun from beating down, yet it was warm with a slight breeze. Everyone knew Luke and from the way most waved to him and greeted him, I thought they liked him very much.

As soon as we entered the carnival area, he talked me into going on the ferris wheel. Although it wasn't a very big one, we still had a wonderful view of Atlanta when we reached the top. The seat swung back and forth, taking my breath away. I squealed with delight and Luke laughed and embraced me to give me a sense of security. I did feel safe under his strong arm.

'Want a beer?' he asked after we got off. 'I can get it free,' he said, winking and nodding toward the young man at the beer concession.

'No thanks,' I replied. He bought me a soda pop.

After that he tried his luck at darts. He became very upset when he didn't win anything, but I told him not to put down any more of his money on the game.

'Try another, if you want,' I advised. 'My father used to tell me that when something's not going right, just put it aside for a while and do something else.'

He nodded, thoughtfully.

'You're right, Leigh. I get stubborn and stupid sometimes and lose everything in anger. It's nice having someone sensible beside me,' he said, his eyes soft. When he looked at me like that, with such intensity and with such sincerity, all sounds around me died away. It was as if we had drifted into our private world for a moment, risen above the crowd, just the way we had on the ferris wheel.

'Come on,' he said, taking my hand excitedly and pulling me along. We stopped at the baseball game. The object was to knock three milk bottles off a basket. You had two chances for a quarter. Luke took the balls into his hand and wound up to throw. Then he stopped.

'Touch it for good luck,' he said handing me the ball.

'I don't usually bring good luck,' I said.

'You will to me,' he insisted. He made me feel good about myself. I held the ball for a moment and then he wound up again and threw it. He hit the bottles squarely in the middle and the three burst away from each other and off the basket.

'A *winner*!' the man behind the counter announced, and then he reached back and took a pudgy, little black teddy bear from the shelf and handed it to Luke.

'For you,' he said handing it to me. 'It's not as beautiful as your doll, but it's a lucky one.'

'It's very beautiful and very cuddly,' I said pressing it to my cheek. 'I love it. Thank you, Luke.'

He smiled and led me off. He bought a foot-long hot dog and had it covered with all the fixings. We started eating the hot dog. We had fun eating at it from both sides. Our noses bumped when we reached the middle and we laughed and laughed.

'I've got to feed the elephants,' he said. 'And then we can

go in and see the clown show and acrobats, all the circus acts, okay?'

'Sure.' I followed him back to the work area. He found a wooden case for me to sit on and watch as he worked. He took off his shirt and seized the pitchfork. The sun glistened off his smooth, muscular back. He had wide shoulders that tightened and displayed their strength as he scooped up large bites of hay and dropped it in front of the appreciative elephants. He worked right beside them, beside their enormous legs, any one of which could crush a man to death, and he stood inches from their thick, muscular trunks, but he didn't seem afraid and the elephants took great care not to nudge him. After he fed them their hay, he filled large pails with water and placed them in front of each elephant, who immediately dipped his trunk into them. It was funny to see and I couldn't help laughing.

'Ain't they some beautiful creatures?' Luke asked me when he was finished. 'They're so big and strong, but so gentle. If people had their strength, they'd be going around bashin' each other all the time,' he added bitterly. 'Well. Let me wash off a bit and then we'll go to the show. You all right?'

'Yes, fine,' I said, still hugging my soft teddy bear.

'You can leave that with your suitcase,' he said. 'If you want.'

'Okay.' I went into the tent and put the stuffed animal with my suitcase. When I came out again, I saw Luke over by a water hose, running the water over his head and upper body. He wiped himself vigorously and then returned.

'Just let me brush my hair,' he said. 'Can't go around lookin' bad when I'm with such a beautiful woman,' he added. Although he smiled when he said it, I sensed he meant it and that made my heart flutter. He went into the tent and then emerged with his hair brushed neatly. He had such rich, soft ebony hair. I felt like running my hand over it.

'Ready, M'lady?' he asked offering me his arm.

'Yes, I am.' I put my arm through his and we walked to the show tent. We could hear the barker calling the crowd to the next show and Luke's eyes lit up. As we joined the line moving through the front entrance, I felt the excitement building. There was the sense that we were about to see the greatest show on earth. Children were laughing excitedly, but even their parents looked flushed and happy with expectation.

The ticket taker just nodded at Luke and we entered free. He hurried me around to what he said would be the best seats in the house. Once we were seated, he bought us bags of peanuts, a soda for me and a beer for himself.

'How can you drink so much beer, Luke?' I asked him. 'Doesn't it make you woozy?'

'Woozy?' He laughed. 'Naw. This stuff ain't nothin' compared to the moonshine I grew up on,' he replied, but I saw how it was beginning to make his face red. He saw the concern in mine.

'But you're probably right about this too,' he said, raising the cup of beer. 'I won't drink any more today.'

That made me feel better and I turned to the show. The music started and the clowns came rushing in, slapping and falling over each other, squirting each other with water guns and dropping water-filled balloons on each other's heads.

While the clown show went on, a young girl, no more than my age surely, dressed in a gold costume that glittered with multicolored sequins, performed acrobatics on a palomino horse, somersaulting, standing on her hands and on her head, and flipping this way and that, taking the audience's breath away. The announcer pointed out one act after another: jugglers, magicians, tumblers.

A drum roll introduced the trapeze artists and two handsome men and a beautiful woman ran to the center of the tent to take their bows and begin their climb up the ropes. My heart pounded in anticipation. There was something to see everywhere I looked. When I turned to Luke, I saw that he had been staring at me, a small, warm smile on his face, his eyes bright with appreciation.

'It's exciting, isn't it?' he said. 'See why I love it?'

'Oh yes. I never realized . . . it's a wonderful show.'

'This is only the beginning,' he said. 'We'll see it all.'

Even in my excitement, I realized he had entwined his fingers around mine to hold my hand softly, but I didn't mind it; I welcomed it. The music and the laughter, the spectacular performances and constant banter about the various acts, the applause and air of excitement turned hours into minutes and minutes into seconds. I lost track of time and place. While I was in the circus, I didn't even think about my situation, about my running away from home. It was as if the world had stopped turning.

We had more to eat, hamburgers and bags of French fries. Luke started to order another beer, but when he saw my face, he stopped and bought himself a soda pop, too. Then we had ice cream cones with candy sparkles. Luke paid for everything eagerly, even though I offered to use some of my money.

'Your money is all magic money,' he said. 'It's not fair. As soon as you give it to the vendors, it will disappear in their hands.'

'Luke, I can't let you pay for everything. You work so hard for your money.'

'I don't mind. I don't have much to spend it on, and never do I get a chance to spend it on someone as beautiful and nice as you, Leigh,' he said. We were holding hands again. For a moment I couldn't speak. Even though we were in the tent and surrounded by hundreds and hundreds of people, I again felt as though there was no one around us. Before I knew what was happening, he leaned forward and kissed me quickly on the lips.

'Sorry,' he said. 'I got so excited, I . . . I . . . couldn't help myself,' he stuttered.

'It's all right.' I turned back to the show, but my heart was pounding so hard, I thought it could be heard above the laughter and clamor around us. Luke said nothing, but every once in a while, we looked at each other and smiled.

It wasn't until after the final act of this show ended that I thought about the time. I looked at my watch and screamed.

'Luke, look at the time! I'm going to miss my train!'

'Don't worry,' he said, but his face was twisted with concern. We tried making our way out quickly, but the crowd was large and people were bunched up at all the exits. Frustrated, we waited our turn. As soon as we emerged, we hurried across the grounds to the work tent. Luke shot in and out with my suitcase and teddy bear in hand. Then we got into his pickup truck.

It didn't start. He tried it again and again. He pounded the dashboard angrily and got out to lift the hood and fiddle with the engine. It took a while, but finally, he got it started and we were off to the station. Neither of us spoke very much; we were both thinking too hard about the time and the ride. Because the show had broken at the circus, there was a lot of traffic and quite a tailback on the highway. Luke was constantly losing his temper and then apologizing. I tried calming him down. He did his best to weave in and out of lanes, but it took us nearly twice as long to return to the station as it had to come from it.

When we pulled into the parking lot, I had less than five minutes. Luke couldn't find a place to park; all the spaces seemed taken. Finally, he just stopped the truck.

'I don't care if they give me a ticket,' he said. 'Come on.'

He scooped up my suitcase and helped me out of the truck. Then we ran to the station. The lobby seemed to have triple the number of people in it than it had when I had first arrived. It was the rush hour. We ran down the corridor to my platform and gate, but when we arrived, my train was pulling out.

'Oh no,' I cried.

We stood there watching the train speed away. I was stuck in Atlanta. Luke turned to me.

'I'm sorry,' he said. 'I should have watched the time.'

'It's my own fault.' I took my suitcase from him and looked toward the lounge with its hard benches.

'Wait,' he said, taking my arm. I turned back. 'I can't let you sit here all night. I don't have much to offer, just a mattress on a bed of hay, but . . .'

'What?' I didn't absorb what he was saying immediately. I was still stunned.

'Of course, I'll sleep on another bed of hay. You can't stay here,' he pleaded.

What more can happen to me? I thought. I felt I resembled a leaf at the mercy of the wind, tossed and turned this way and that, a lone leaf already carried so far away from where it had blossomed and grown.

Luke took my suitcase back and then grasped my hand in his. I said nothing. I let him lead me away and back into the night.

TWENTY

Someone to Watch Over Me

Still in a daze, I followed Luke to his truck. He opened the door and helped me in and then we started back to the circus. I just sat there, clutching my suitcase to me with my left arm and hugging Angel against me with my right.

'Don't worry, Leigh,' Luke said with assurance. 'I'll be sure to get you to the train on time tomorrow. There's a gas station up ahead on the right and it has a payphone on the side. Do you want me to pull up there so you can call your grandmother and tell her you're gonna be a day late?'

I didn't respond. I barely heard him speak. I felt like someone stuck on a merry-go-round, spinning from one side to another but getting nowhere.

'Leigh? Don'tcha think you should call her so she won't worry when you're not on the train?'

'Oh Luke,' I said, unable to hold back the river of tears that sought to flow freely over my cheeks. 'My grandmother doesn't know I'm coming. I'm running away!'

'What?' He slowed down. 'Running away?' He turned the truck onto a side road away from the traffic and stopped. 'So that's why you didn't have much travelin' money. Well, why are you runnin' away from home, Leigh? Sounds to me like you were livin' high on the hog back in New England.'

I cried harder. He slid over on the seat and embraced me tenderly.

'Hey, take it easy. It's all right. If a sweet and lovely person like you wanted to run away, it has to be for a good reason.'

I couldn't control my sobbing. It seemed to have a mind of its own, making me shake and quiver in his arms. It made me cold and my teeth chattered. Luke tightened his embrace and ran the palm of his hand up and down my arm to warm me.

'Easy,' he said and kissed me softly on the forehead and then brought his lips down my cheeks to kiss back the tears. I caught my breath and swallowed. 'I've run away a hundred times myself. Heck, in a sense I'm runnin' away now, but I always manage to find my way back somehow. You will too. You'll see,' he added with encouragement.

'I don't want to find my way back,' I snapped. He nodded.

'Boy, it must've been bad.'

'It was bad,' I said. I took a deep breath, sat back and told him all of it – my parents' divorce, what I learned about my mother when I overheard her conversation with Grandma Jana, what Tony Tatterton was like, what Farthy was like, and what it was like modeling for the portrait doll. Then, I cried again and told him how Tony had raped me and how my mother wouldn't believe it when I told her.

'And when I found out that I was pregnant, I ran to my mother, thinking now she would have to believe me, but instead of helping me, she blamed it all on me. On me!' I moaned through my tears.

Luke had turned off the engine and sat back against the door of the truck listening as quietly as a church mouse. An overcast night sky made it very dark in the truck. We were away from the headlights of other cars and street lights. He sat there in a dark silhouette, but I could sense how somber and thoughtful he was when I paused.

'I thought these kind of things happened only to the hillbilly people, people in the Willies. I guess bein' all that rich ain't always what it's cracked up to be,' he said. Then his voice turned stern. 'I wish I had that Tony Tatterton right here. I'd twist his head until his neck twanged like a broken guitar string.'

I laughed. I couldn't help it. He had such a colorful imagination.

'See? I knew I could make you feel better. Anyway, I'm sorry now I fed you all that junk food at the circus. You ain't in no condition for that. I'm taking you right to this diner I know on the way back to the circus. It's all homemade cookin', just like my ma's. In fact, the place is called Ma's Diner.'

'Oh, I'm not hungry now, Luke. I'm just very tired.'

'Sure. It's understandable. I know what,' he said, snapping his fingers. 'I'll get you a room in a motel so you can be comfortable. A bed of hay in a circus tent ain't no place for a girl who's havin' a baby,' he declared firmly and reached for the ignition key.

'Oh Luke, I can't let you spend your money like that. I saw how hard you work for every penny.'

'You ain't got no say about it,' he replied and started the truck again. I realized there was no arguing with him. When Thomas Luke Casteel had made up his mind about something, he was stubborn and determined. 'You need a proper night's rest and comfortable bathroom facilities. Some of these places got television, too,' he added, and headed the truck back to the main highway.

He asked me to tell him more about Farthy, so I described the size of the rooms, the maze, the Olympic pool and tennis courts, the stables and the private beach. He whistled through his teeth and shook his head.

'I knew there were rich folk, but not that rich. Sounds like this Tony Tatterton owns his own country.'

'Just about.'

'And he makes all this money making toys for rich people?' he asked incredulously.

'Yes,' I said. 'But they're very expensive toys.'

'Like your doll, I guess. Why did you take it along if he made it?' he asked.

'I couldn't leave Angel behind! I held her when I cried and I held her when I laughed. She knows my secret thoughts and secret dreams and all the terrible things that happened to me. Tony Tatterton made her, but she's more me than him,' I explained.

'Angel?'

'That's what I call her. My guardian angel,' I said softly, expecting him to laugh at a young girl's tender and fragile world of make-believe. I imagined most boys his age would, but he didn't laugh. He smiled.

'That's nice,' he said. 'It's beautiful. Just like you. Know what?' he added, turning to me. 'That's what I'm gonna call you from now on . . . Angel. It fits you more than Leigh does.'

My heart, that had sunken and become cold, warmed again in my chest. I felt myself blush. Then I sniffed back a tear.

'Now, why are you crying?'

'I'm crying because I was lucky to meet someone like you, someone nice. Most girls my age are afraid to travel alone because there are so many bad people out there waiting to take advantage of them, not help them. I'm sure that might have happened to me, too, if I hadn't met you.'

'Yeah, but if you hadn't met me, you'da made your train,' he reminded me. 'When I get caught up with circus acts . . .'

'But I wanted to see the circus with you and I had a wonderful time there, Luke.' I did – because it had made me forget all my troubles for a while.

'Did you? I'm glad about that. I had a wonderful time too. It was like seein' it all for the first time when I saw it again with you. You got a fresh, clean way of lookin' at things, Angel. It kinda makes me feel . . . I don't know . . . more important, bigger, bein' with you,' he said, nodding after he said it.

I looked away. I didn't want him to catch a glimpse of my face, for I was embarrassed to show him just how much I liked him and how much better his simple, but sweet words made me feel. He wasn't someone with a great deal of formal education; he wasn't rich, and he didn't dress fancy like the boys at Allendale, but he had a hold on the world that I admired. I felt safe with him because he was able to deal with hardship and crisis. Luke Casteel was only seventeen, but he was a man.

He drove the truck up to a motel. The blue neon sign flashed 'Vacancy'.

'You don't have to do this, Luke,' I said, putting my hand on his.

'I know. I'm not doin' it because I have to. I'm doin' it because I want to. Now you just sit here with Angel and be patient. I'll be right out with the key to your room,' he said and went into the motel office. I sat back and closed my eyes. He was right: I was so tired, I did need a comfortable night's rest. The excitement of traveling, the day at the circus and the shock of missing my train all left me exhausted. I actually drifted off while he was in the office getting a room. I awoke with a start when he jerked open the truck door and hopped in.

'4 C,' he announced, dangling the room key. 'Nice room with two double beds and a television set.'

'I don't think I could keep my eyes open to watch television. You should have gotten a cheaper room.'

'They're all the same price here,' he explained and pulled up in front of the room. He took out my suitcase and opened the door. Clutching Angel to me, I followed him in.

It was a small room with drab gray walls and dusty-looking light green curtains. It had two double beds with a scratched-up wooden table between them and two night stands, one on each side. Each stand had a small lamp on it, the yellow shades stained and dusty. There were closets at Farthy that were twice the size of the room, but I didn't care. The soft mattress looked very inviting. Luke set my suitcase down and went into the bathroom, turning on the lights and inspecting everything.

'Looks like it all works. Sure you don't want somethin' to eat? What about a nice hot cup of tea? There's a restaurant a half mile down the road. It'd just take me a few minutes to go get you a warm drink. And maybe a muffin, huh? You gotta have nourishment,' he said with a look of concern.

'All right,' I said. 'I'll wash up and get into bed.'

'Great. Be back in a jiffy.' He slapped his hands together and rushed out.

I had to smile again at his enthusiasm. He wanted to do things for me and he was sincere. I had put myself in a terrible spot, but I had met a true guardian angel. Maybe it all had to do with magic after all. Maybe by running away from the evil world of Farthy, I had escaped from the evil spell that had fallen over me.

I showered and changed into one of my soft, silk nightgowns and unpinned my hair. It felt ratty and dirty from all the traveling, but I was too tired to wash it and brush it out. I promised myself I would do it in the morning. Then, with Angel beside me, I crawled under the covers of one of the double beds. It smelled starchy and the sheets were stiff, but I was far too exhausted to care. Luke knocked softly on the door and then came in with my hot tea, a corn muffin and jam, and a bottle of beer for himself. He put everything on the small night stand by the bed and pulled the one chair up to the bed to sit on and drink his beer while he watched me drink and eat. He looked as concerned as he would were he really the expectant father. His dark eyes twinkled tenderly, lovingly.

'Aren't you hungry, too, Luke? Surely a beer is not enough.'

'Naw, I'm still too excited, I suppose. Sometimes beer calms me down.' He smiled and gestured at Angel. 'That doll does look like you. You both have such beautiful hair,' he said stroking Angel's hair tenderly.

'Angel's hair is really my hair.'

'No foolin'?' I shook my head and his eyes widened. Then he leaned toward me. 'I never seen anything as precious and as lovely as the two of you lying there together,' he said softly.

'Thank you, Luke. You're very nice.' He stared at me a moment and then stood up.

'You going to be all right here?' he asked.

'Why? Where are you going?'

'Back to my tent.'

'Well, why can't you stay here? There's another bed and you paid for the room, Luke. You shouldn't have to go back to a bed of hay.' I know I sounded a bit desperate, but I had never stayed in a motel room before, much less stayed in one by myself.

'Sure you don't mind?'

'Of course I don't mind.'

'Well, then okay. I guess I can get up early enough to water and feed the animals.'

'You can watch television, if you're not tired yet,' I said lowering my head. Now that he was going to stay with me, I could relax. 'It won't . . . bother me . . .'

Sleep came over me that fast, but I woke with a start in the middle of the night and forgot where I was. I couldn't help crying out in fear. Seconds later, I felt Luke beside me in the dark.

'Angel, Angel,' he said, stroking my hair. 'It's all right. You're safe. It's Luke. I'm right here with you. Don't you worry about a thing. I don't want you to ever worry about a thing,' he added in a whisper. I realized where I was, but I was still so sleepy that I only vaguely felt his lips on my cheek and heard his words. The words seemed more like words in a dream anyway, words whispered by my guardian angel.

'I want to take care of you from now on, protect you, love you. Never again will anyone, even someone rich and powerful, hurt you. I'll take you to a world where no one evil can reach you, a world in which you will be surrounded only by soft, happy and natural things, where the music comes from song birds and the diamonds are the stars and the gold is in the sunlight and autumn leaves. Will you come with me, my Angel? Will you?'

'Yes,' I muttered. 'Oh yes, yes,' I said and then I was asleep again.

I awoke in the morning and found Luke beside me in my bed. I had fallen asleep in his arms and I had never felt as safe or as happy. His eyes fluttered open and he gazed upon me for a moment before smiling. Then he kissed me softly on the lips.

'Good morning,' he said. 'How do you feel?'

'Much better. But why . . .'

'Why did I get into your bed? You had a bad dream, I think, and woke up screaming. I calmed you down and fell asleep beside you. Did you forget all of it?' he asked with some disappointment. 'All I said and you said?'

'I think so, although there are words in my mind that seem like dream words.'

'They weren't dream words; they were mine and I meant them,' he said with that tight look of determination again. 'I told you I wanted to look after you, to protect you, always and forever, and I meant it.'

'What are you saying, Luke?' I sat up, holding the blanket against me, for I was in my thin, silk nightgown. He sat up, too.

'I know you're carrying your step-father's baby, but no one

else has to know that. Let everyone think it's mine. I want it to be mine because I want you to be mine.'

'What do you mean?' I understood, but I had to hear him say it.

'I mean I want to marry you, to have you forever and forever as my angel. Oh, I know a life in the circus wouldn't be a good life for two young people just getting started, especially if they were expectin' a baby. But I thought it all out,' he continued excitedly. 'I want to take you back to the Willies with me, start all over. I got plans and ideas. I want to earn enough money and get my own farm started, and I can do it too, Angel.

'Oh, I ain't sayin' it won't be hard in the beginnin',' he went on before I could interrupt, 'real hard. We'll hafta stay with my folks for a spell, but I'll work day and night earnin' enough money to get us that down payment so we can start our own home.

'You'll love it there, Angel. I promise you will. It's not what you're accustomed to, by no means, of course,' he said, speaking very quickly, 'but it's a pure, free life, a life in nature, a life away from corruption and people who care more about themselves than their loved ones.'

'Luke, you want to be the father of my baby? You want this?' I asked, still disbelieving.

'As long as it means I'll have you, too, Angel. Don't go to your grandmother's,' he pleaded. 'It doesn't sound like you'd be happy there anyway. You hardly know her and she's old, set in her ways. Besides,' he said, striking at a fear I harbored in my own heart, 'what if she doesn't believe you? What if she thinks you're just like her daughter? She might send you back.

'I'll never send you back, Angel,' he concluded firmly.

'But you can't return to the Willies to work. You love the circus, Luke,' I cried. I had seen it in his eyes.

'Not half as much as I love you, Angel. Nothing as special or as sweet and precious has ever come into my life before. I feel so complete when I'm with you, so hopeful. I don't doubt I can do everything I dream of doin' as long as I have you. You make me feel important, just as important as anyone else. I'd work myself to the bone for you. Won't you say yes? Please.'

I was speechless for a moment. Nearly fourteen years ago, my mother had become pregnant and then tricked the man I thought was my daddy into marrying her, never telling him the truth. Would he have wanted her the way Luke now wanted me, if he had known the truth? How different would my life have been in the beginning? How different was it going to be for my baby having a father who knew and accepted the truth? I really believed Luke's love for me was so strong and so full, there was enough of it to spill over and embrace my baby too.

I felt hope sweep back all fear and trepidation. This handsome, loving young man wanted me no matter what, wanted me even though he had heard my story and knew my condition. He loved me so much he was willing to consider my baby his baby and give up things he wanted just to please me.

I never knew such unselfishness. Why couldn't my daddy have had half Luke's love for me and have been willing to sacrifice some of his business interests in order to help and protect me? Why couldn't my mother have cared more for me more than she cared for herself? My parents claimed they loved me, but they didn't love me the way Luke did. His was a more honest and sincere love because he was willing to sacrifice for me.

And then I thought love means not only sacrificing, but wanting to sacrifice, getting pleasure out of giving to your loved one more than you give to yourself. How lucky I was to have found someone who loved me this way.

I looked at Angel. She seemed to be smiling. Perhaps she was my guardian angel after all; perhaps she had brought Luke to me or me to him. And now Luke wanted to be that same guardian angel.

Luke saw the way I was gazing at Angel.

'What's she tellin' you?' he asked softly, hopeful.

'She's telling me to say yes, Luke,' I whispered, as much to myself as to him.

His dark eyes brightened. What a handsome smile he had. He was the kind of a young man who would only grow more and more good-looking with every passing year and he would be my husband.

'She's telling me to say yes,' I repeated, looking into those beautiful eyes.

Luke embraced me and we kissed.

A journey that had begun in anger, fear and hopelessness had suddenly become a journey of love and hope. My tears were different. They were tears of happiness and they were warmer. I held on tightly to Thomas Luke Casteel. My heart beat happily. There was magic in the air.

The circus management was not upset about Luke's abrupt departure because he explained that he was going to marry me and start a new life back in his home town. He told them he had obligations and responsibilities now and the news spread quickly through the carnie population. By the time we had gone back to his tent to gather his things, a crowd of well-wishers had appeared. It was an unusual crowd, to say the least. I found myself being introduced to and congratulated by the bearded lady, the Siamese twins, midgets, the fattest man in the world, the tallest man in the world and the strongest man in the world, as well as jugglers, fire eaters, acrobats, and the knife thrower and his wife. Then the magician, the Amazing Mandello, appeared with his glamorous assistant and asked me to give him my hand. I looked at Luke, who nodded, so I did so and suddenly, I felt a ring in my palm.

I opened it and saw a pretty imitation rhinestone.

'A gift from the Amazing Mandello,' he announced. 'Your wedding ring.' The audience that had gathered around us oohed and ahhed as if he had handed me something truly valuable. They all lived in a world of illusion, but I didn't mind. I felt as if I had entered their world, a world in a rose-tinted bubble.

'Oh thank you. It's beautiful.' Back in Farthy I had real diamond rings and bracelets and necklaces, but here at Luke's circus, amidst all these friendly, happy people, I thought this ring was the most precious and wonderful I had ever received.

All of these people liked Luke so much and wished him the best.

'We'll be stopping at the justice of the peace right down the street on our way out,' Luke announced. There was a murmur of excitement. Someone said, 'Let's go,' and the whole crowd of circus people followed us to the home of the justice of the peace. It was surely a wedding he and his wife would never forget.

The judge couldn't conduct the wedding in his office. Our guests even crowded his spacious living room and spilled out onto the porch. The Siamese twins, two men in their twenties who were attached at the waist, played piano. They squeezed themselves onto the piano stool and began a rendition of 'Here Comes the Bride'. I looked around me, into the eyes of the bearded lady, the smiling faces of the jugglers and midgets and acrobats and thought about Momma's wedding.

It seemed a hundred years ago, but I remembered how nervous and uncomfortable I was following those elaborately dressed bridesmaids down the great stairway. I recalled the sea of faces below . . . all those wealthy people, the men in expensive tuxedos, the women in designer gowns and bedecked with precious jewels, one trying to outdo the other.

My mother had promised me a wedding just like hers with a costly reception, but here I was in the home of this ordinary justice of the peace, marrying a young man I had just met, and surrounded by circus people. Never in her wildest imagination could Momma have envisioned this, I thought.

And yet, I wasn't upset about it. I didn't mind not having the famous and upper class people around me; I didn't care that I was wearing one of my simple summer dresses, instead of a custom-made wedding gown and that as soon as this was over, we would be off without any reception, no music and dancing and fancy foods.

But I knew that no amount of money, not a hundred more rich people, not a mountain of food could have made Momma's marriage any happier or her life any better. The guests she had at her wedding didn't look at her and Tony as warmly as Luke's circus friends looked at us. Momma's well-wishers weren't anywhere as sincere. I felt a real pouring-out of hearts. When these people kissed and hugged me, they meant it. They were a special, happy lot, many of whom had overcome their peculiarities and made those peculiarities work for them. They were show people who lived to give other people pleasure, lived to dazzle and amuse. In a way they did live in a world of magic, the magic of smiles and laughter, the magic of the lights and the music. No wonder Luke had been so comfortable among them, I thought.

'Well now,' the judge said when he took his position before us and looked around him, 'I guess we can begin.'

The judge was a tall, thin man with a red mustache and hazel eyes. I knew I would never forget his face, for he was about to utter the words and make the pronouncements that would tie me forever and ever to Thomas Luke Casteel. Luke's future would be my future, his pain, my pain; his happiness, my happiness. In a real sense, our lives resembled two trains that had approached each other from different angles and joined to continue their journey. It was significant that we met at a train station, I thought.

The judge's wife, a short, plump woman with a jovial face, stood beside him, her eyes wide with amazement, too.

The judge began, and when he reached that point where he asked if I take Thomas Luke Casteel to be my loving husband, to have and to hold until death did us part, I closed my eyes and thought about Daddy holding me in his arms when I was no more than eight or nine and promising to build me a mansion when I got married, 'a castle on a hill for you and your prince'. I heard my mother rattling on and on about the day I get married, what I must wear, how I must act, who I must invite. My whole life seemed to flash by in seconds, the words, the pictures, the smiles and the tears all falling away until I could hear only the pounding of my own, excited heart.

'Yes,' I said turning to Luke and looking into his deep, dark eyes and seeing the promise of love, 'I do.'

'And you, Thomas Luke Casteel, do you promise to have and to hold Leigh Diane VanVoreen, to love and to cherish her through sickness and through health until death do you part?'

'I do,' he said with a manly firmness that nearly took my breath away. He looked ready to fight to the death to make me happy.

'Then by the power vested in me, I pronounce you man and wife. You may kiss the bride.'

We kissed like two lovers who had run across a long field to leap into each other's arms and hold each other forever and forever. The circus people cheered and surrounded us. I had to kneel down so the midgets could give me a good-luck kiss. The acrobats had located rice and passed out handfuls to many of the others so they could rain it down upon us as we left the judge's house.

We got into Luke's truck and waved to them. Everyone was on the front lawn waving and smiling and throwing kisses, everyone but one woman in a purple dress, a matching bandana around her forehead. There were long, silver-leaf earrings dangling from her lobes and she had a dark face with eyes even darker than Luke's. She looked serious, somber and stood back from the crowd.

'Who is that woman, Luke?' I asked and pointed.

'Oh, that's Gittle, the Hungarian fortune teller.'

'She looks so serious, so worried,' I said with trepidation.

'She always does,' Luke explained. 'That's her act. People take her serious that way. Don't worry. It doesn't mean anything, Angel.'

'I hope not, Luke,' I muttered as we drove off. 'I hope not.' I looked back and waved as we bounced out of the judge's driveway and turned onto the main highway. In moments it was all behind us and Angel and I were off to another life, another world, which was hopefully a much happier one than the one we had known at Farthy, the life we had left behind forever.

I looked back once more. There were storm clouds on the horizon behind us, but we were riding away from them, rushing down the highway as if in flight from the threat of rain and wind and cold. Off in the distance before us, the sky was bright blue, warm and inviting. Surely that meant all that was sad and ugly was in back of us. Even my memory of the somber face of the fortune teller couldn't survive the glow of warmth in the promise spread out by the welcoming sun.

I squeezed Angel to me.

'Happy?' Luke asked.

'Oh yes, Luke. I am.'

'So am I. I am as happy as a pig in . . .'

'In what?'

'Never mind. Got to watch what I say from now on. I want to be a better person and all because I have you.'

'Oh Luke, don't make me seem like some royalty. I'm just another person trying to be happy in a world that could rain down pretty hard at times.'

'No you ain't. You're my angel and angels come from Heaven. Say,' he added smiling. 'If we have a girl, that might not be a bad name for her: Heaven. What do you think?'

I loved him for saying, 'If *we* have a girl . . .'

'Oh yes, Luke. Heaven would fit her real fine.'

'Why, we'll give her your name, too. Then, we can call her Heaven Leigh Casteel,' he said.

He laughed and we rode on toward the sunlight and the promise.

TWENTY-ONE

The Willies

The trip to Winnerrow and the Willies was a long, hard one in Luke's old truck. Shortly after we had started out, his engine overheated and he had to walk a mile to get some water from a gas station. He kept apologizing for making me wait in the truck on a hot day. I told him it was all right and that nothing could make me unhappy now. Even so, he insisted we stop at a small restaurant just outside of Atlanta so I could get something cool to drink and he could get a cold beer. He downed it quickly and ordered another.

'Don't you worry about drinking too much beer, Luke?' I asked him.

He paused as though it had never occurred to him before.

'I don't know. Where I come from, it just seems natural to drink moonshine and beer. We hardly ever think about it.'

'Maybe that's because you're drinking so much you can't think about it, Luke,' I suggested gently.

'You're probably right.' He smiled widely. 'You're lookin' after me already,' he said. 'I like that, Angel. I just know I'm goin' to be a better person all on account of you.'

'It has to be on account of yourself, too, Luke.'

'I know,' he said. 'I promise you this, Angel. I'll do all I can to make you happy, and if anything I do makes you unhappy, why you just don't hesitate to bawl me out. Besides, when you bawl me out, I feel good,' he added and kissed me on the cheek. It made me tingly and warm to hear a young man like Luke tell me he wanted me looking after him. I felt as though he and I were growing up years with the passing of minutes.

While we were at the restaurant, I saw some postcards on the counter and decided to buy one to send to my mother. I thought it just might be the last thing I say to my mother for a very long time, so I thought carefully and then wrote.

Dear Momma,

I am sorry that I had to run away, but you wouldn't listen to me. During my travels I met a wonderful young man named Luke. He is handsome and gentle and very loving and he has decided to marry me and be the father of my child.

Luke and I are on our way to his home, where we intend to build our own lives.

No matter what you said to me or what you did, I still wish you happiness and hope that you will find it in your heart to wish me the same.

Love,
Leigh

I put a stamp on it and dropped it in the mailbox outside the restaurant. Then, we were off again.

Luke drove all day and all night. I kept asking him if he were tired, but he said he had more energy now than ever before in his life and he was so anxious to get to Winnerrow, he didn't want to stop for anything but gas, food, and the bathroom. Miles and miles slipped by and I fell asleep a few times. By the time the first light of morning peeped over the horizon, we were in the hill country, steadily climbing, the truck straining as we wound around and around. Shoddy, unpainted little buildings heralded yet another country town off the beaten track, until those too were left behind us. I noticed that the gasoline stations became more widely spaced, and the newly constructed motels were replaced by little cabins tucked away in shadowy dense woods.

We went down the mountains again and reached a valley. Here were the broad green fields on the outskirts of Winnerrow; neat farms with fields of summer crops that soon would be harvested.

'After these farms,' Luke said, 'you'll see the homes of the poorest in the valley, those not much better off than true hillbillies. Up there,' he pointed toward the hills ahead of us, 'are the coal miners' shacks and moonshiners' cabins.'

I gazed up toward the hills excitedly. The tiny homes dotted the mountainside and looked so peaceful and set back, almost as if they had grown there and were part of the natural surroundings.

'There are rich and well-to-do people here, too,' Luke explained, nodding toward the deepest part of the valley. 'See where all the richest mountain silt is driven downward by the heavy spring rains. It ends up in the gardens of Winnerrow families, providin' fertile soil for those who need it least. They have all these spectacular flower gardens and grow the best tulips, daffodils, irises, roses, and anythin' else their rich little hearts desire,' he added bitterly.

'You don't like the town people very much, do you, Luke?' I asked. He was silent for a moment and then he spoke through his teeth.

'We'll drive down Main Street and you'll see that's where all the winners live. Maybe that's why they call this place Winnerrow.'

'Winners?'

'The owners of the coal mines built their big houses here on the backs of the losers: miners who still die from black lung and the like. You also have the owners of the cotton gins that make fabric for bed and table linens and owners of cotton mills with their invisible airborne lint that so many workers breathe into their lungs. And no one ever sued an owner for damages,' he added angrily.

'Did you or any of your family ever work in the mines or mills, Luke?' I asked.

'My brothers did for a while when they were younger, but they couldn't hold down any sort of work long and took off on their own. My pappy wouldn't do that work. He'd rather scrounge out a livin' in the earth, take odd jobs here and there, or sell moonshine. And I can't say as I blame him.

'One thing I should tell you right off, Angel: the townspeople don't like us Willies folk much. They make us sit in the back in church and keep their children away from our children.'

'Oh, that's terrible, Luke. Why take things out on little children?' I cried, thinking how hurt they must feel. Now I, too, understood why Luke was so bitter about the townspeople. 'No one should feel better than anyone else.'

'Yeah, well, you tell that to the mayor of Winnerrow,' he said smiling. 'I bet you could. I can't wait to get dressed up and take you to church, Angel. Can't wait,' he said, shaking his head.

We arrived at a fork in the road and Luke made a right turn that took us away from the macadam road and onto a hard packed dirt and gravel road. It went on and on through the woods and finally became only a dirt road with ridges and bumps that made the truck toss and turn so hard, I had to grab hold of the door handle. As we drove on, my nostrils were tickled with the scents of honeysuckle and wild strawberries, and raspberries on the vine. It was cool and fresh and crisp here in the mountains of Virginia, and it made me feel more alive. It was as if the mountain air washed away all the polluted air I had been breathing in the stale, cold and dreary rooms of Farthy; for that was the way I remembered it right now.

'Almost there, Angel. Hold on. Wait until Ma gets a gander at you.'

I held my breath. Where did his family live? How could they be so far back in the woods? How could they have a house with pipes leading to a sewer system or to a water system? And where were the electric wires and telephone wires? All I saw were trees and bushes.

Suddenly, I thought I heard the sound of a banjo being played. Luke smiled widely.

'Pa's on the porch, strummin' away,' he said.

We turned around a clump of thick trees and stopped. There it was – Luke's home. I couldn't prevent my gasp of surprise. Two small hound dogs sprawled in a pool of sunlight sprang up and began barking excitedly.

'That's Kasey and Brutus,' Luke said. 'My dogs. And that's home sweet home.'

Home sweet home! I thought. The cabin was built out of old wood full of knotholes. It looked like it had never known paint.

The roof consisted of rusted tin that had wept a million tears to stain the old silvery wood. The cabin had drainpipes and rain barrels which I realized were meant to catch water.

Across the front of the cabin was a sagging, dilapidated front porch on which were twin rockers. A man I easily recognized as Luke's father sat with a banjo on his lap. He had the same coal-black hair and dark complexion, and although he looked like he had traveled a rough road, he still possessed handsome facial qualities – a straight Roman nose, strong cheekbones and strong jawline. He looked rugged, but when he saw it was Luke, he smiled in a soft and gentle way.

The woman sitting beside him and crocheting looked much sterner. Her long hair was tied in a ponytail that reached half way to her waist. When she stood up, she appeared to be about my mother's age, but after she came off the porch and closer to the truck, her face added years to my first estimate. I saw she was missing some teeth and she had weather-worn wrinkles around her eyes and temples. The lines in her forehead were cut deeper, harsher than the lines in my mother's face.

But Luke's mother had once been a very pretty woman probably. She had Luke's dark eyes, and although her hair was stained with gray strands, it looked like washing it in rain water kept its body as healthy and rich as it ever was. She had a proud, firm look, Indian proud, with high cheekbones and she was nearly as tall as Luke. I saw that her hands, which could have been as soft and as dainty as my mother's, were rough and manly-looking because of the short fingernails and calluses.

'Ma!' Luke exclaimed and hopped out of the truck. She embraced him eagerly, a mother's pride and pleasure lighting her eyes and softening her suspicious look. Luke's father set his banjo down on the rocking chair and bounced down the porch steps quickly to greet and hug his son.

'Howdy, Luke,' his father said. 'Didn't expect ya back so soon this time. What changed ya mind?' he asked, still holding on to Luke's shoulders.

'Angel did,' Luke said.

'Angel?'

Luke's mother and father turned my way.

'Angel, come out here and meet Ma and Pa. Ma,' Luke continued as I got out of the truck, 'I want ya to meet my wife, Angel.'

'Yer wife!' his mother exclaimed. She looked me over from head to foot as I approached, her expression of disbelief turning to an expression of disappointment. 'Ain't she a bit young and fragile lookin' fer a Willies wife?' she asked herself aloud. I stood in front of her and Luke's father, waiting for a proper introduction.

'Angel, I want ya to meet my ma, Annie, and my pa, Toby Casteel. Ma, this is my Angel. Her real name's Leigh, but she's more an angel than a Leigh.'

'Is that so?' his mother said, still eyeing me with disbelief.

'Welcome to our home,' his father said and hugged me.

'When ya go an' do this, Luke?' his mother asked, still staring at me.

'Just yesterday in Atlanta. We met and fell in love and were married by a justice of the peace, all right and proper, and we had the biggest and best crowd of wedding guests you ever did see – all my circus friends. Right, Angel?'

'Yes,' I said. I felt so self-conscious under Luke's mother's intense gaze. Any mother would be suspicious and would look critically upon the woman her son brought home, I thought, but Luke's mother looked shocked and disappointed.

'How old are ya?' she asked me.

'I'm nearly fourteen,' I said. I felt tears come to my eyes. Even here, in the poorest part of the world, people found fault with me.

'Well yer age ain't no problem,' Luke's mother said, 'but it takes a lot a grit ta live in the Willies, child. Let me see ya hands,' she demanded and reached out, seizing my fingers and turning my hands over. She ran her callused fingers over my soft palm and shook her head. 'Ya never seen a real day's work ya whole life, didja, girl?'

I pulled my hands back sharply.

'I can work as hard as anyone,' I replied. 'I'm sure your hands were as soft as mine once.'

There was a moment of heavy silence and then she smiled.

'Well now, ya got pride like a Casteel. Knew there had ta be some reason my son chose ya.' She turned back to Luke, who stood beaming with pleasure. 'Welcome home, son. What are ya plans now?'

'Angel and me are goin' to live on with you and Pa for a while, Ma. I'm goin' to get a job with Mr Morrison in Winnerrow and learn carpentry. He was always after me to work for him. Then I'm goin' to build us a fine house, maybe in the valley where I'll work the land, raise cows, pigs, and horses, and make us a clean and decent life. I'll build a house big enough for all of us and you and Pa can come down off this mountain and live like people should live,' he added.

His mother hoisted back her shoulders, whatever smile there was in her face evaporating.

'We ain't no lower or worse than those people in the valley, Luke. Ya never talked down about the Willies life before. It was where ya was born and raised and ya ain't no worse off fer it.'

'Didn't say I was, Ma. I just wanna do big things now,' he said, taking my hand. 'I got responsibilities.'

His mother continued to eye me with suspicion.

'Well now,' Pa Casteel said, 'this calls fer a celebration, right, Ma? Let's cook up those rabbits.'

'The rabbits is fer Sunday,' she replied.

'I'll go huntin' fer more.'

'Took ya long enough ta go huntin' fer these,' she snapped, but he remained undaunted.

'I'm back now, Ma,' Luke said. 'There'll be plenty a meat on the table again.'

'Um,' she said skeptically. 'All right, better bring in yer things, Angel,' she told me.

'All she got is one suitcase,' Luke said.

'One suitcase?' Annie Casteel's eyes widened with new interest. 'She looks like she should have a truckload of things. Well now, ya come on inside and watch me put up a rabbit stew and tell me all about yourself.'

'I'll break out the apple cider, Luke,' Pa said behind us.

'Now don't ya go and get yerself and Luke all soggy and

plastered with that rotgut licker, Toby Casteel,' she warned. Luke's father laughed. Luke and he followed Annie and myself up the rickety steps and into the cabin. My expectations had been lowered considerably the moment I had set eyes on the cabin, but I was still not prepared for what I found inside.

The cabin consisted of two small rooms, with a tattered, faded curtain to form a kind of flimsy door for what I imagined was to be a bedroom. There was a cast-iron stove in the center of the big room. Next to it sat what looked to be an ancient kitchen cabinet stacked with metal bins for flour, sugar, coffee, and tea.

'As ya kin see,' Annie began, 'we ain't got a castle, but we got a roof over our heads. We got fresh milk from our cow and fresh eggs when our chickens have a mind ta lay 'em. The hogs and pigs roam at will and snuggle down under the porch at night. You'll hear 'em snortin', along with the dogs and cats and whatever else decides ta make its bed under there,' she said, nodding toward the floor.

I believed she wasn't exaggerating. The cabin floor had at least a half inch space between each crookedly laid floorboard. As I gazed around, I realized there was no bathroom. Where did they go to the bathroom? How did they take a shower or a bath? I wondered. Luke's mother read my thoughts. She smiled at my look of curiosity.

'If ya wonderin' about the toilet, it's outside.'

'Outside?'

'Don't tell me ya never heard of an outhouse, child?'

'Outhouse?' I looked back at Luke.

'Don't you worry, Angel. First thing I'm going to do is build you your own outhouse. I'll be startin' on it as soon as I get back from town tomorrow.'

'What's an outhouse?' I asked softly.

Luke's mother laughed.

'Ya sure got yerself a city girl, didn't ya, Luke? An outhouse is a bathroom, Angel. Yer go out ta the little buildin' when nature calls and ya sit on a board with two holes.'

I might have turned a little pale. I don't know. But Luke's

mother stopped smiling and looked reproachfully at him. He dropped my suitcase and embraced me.

'I'm going to build you a real nice one, Angel. You'll see. And it won't be for all that long anyway. Why in no time, I'm going to have enough money to start our home in the valley.'

'You know anything about makin' a rabbit stew?' Annie Casteel asked. I looked up and saw her lift two dead rabbits by the ears out of a small ice box. I gasped and swallowed hard. 'Well, after I skin 'em, I'll show ya my ma's recipe.'

'Ma makes the best rabbit you ever tasted,' Luke said.

'I never ate rabbit, Luke,' I said, swallowing back my gasps.

'Then you're in for a treat,' he replied. I nodded hopefully, took a deep breath and looked around me. Luke's mother and father were about the poorest people I had ever seen, yet when I looked at Toby Casteel, I saw a bright, happy smile on his face, and when I looked at Luke's mother, I saw pride and strength. I was confused, tired, and frightened. Life had thrown down another challenge just when I thought I was beginning a magical life of happiness. But I saw there was no time nor place for tears here. There was only work, the battle to survive. Maybe there was some good to be had. Maybe I would grow stronger, leaner, tougher so I could face down the evil in the world we had just left.

'Someone's got ta peel those "taters",' Annie Casteel said and pointed at a bushel of potatoes on the floor.

'I'll do it,' I volunteered, even though I had never done it before. She looked at me skeptically, which only made me more determined. 'Where's the potato peeler?' I demanded. Luke's mother smiled.

'We ain't got no fancy tools, Angel. Just use that pocket knife there and don't cut too deep. Luke, ya go an' put Angel's things behind the curtain.'

'Behind the curtain? But where are you and Pa goin' to sleep?' Luke asked with a look of concern.

'We'll do fine on the floor pallets. We've slept on 'em before, right Pa?'

'That ain't no lie,' Pa said.

'But . . .'

'No don't go arguin' about it, Luke. If I know ya, ya'll be startin' fer a baby right away. Suspect ya might have already,' she said, gazing at me as if she had the power to see my pregnancy in my face. 'All Casteels are made in beds,' she added. 'I'm hopin' and prayin' that's always gonna be true.'

'All right, Ma.' Luke pulled back the curtain to reveal a big brass bed with a saggy old stained mattress over coiled springs. What a difference between that and even the bed in the cheap motel we had slept in last night, I thought; but it was to be our first marriage bed. It would have to do.

There couldn't have been two more different worlds than the world of Farthinggale Manor and the world of the Willies. I had set out to run away from Farthy and I had come so far it seemed that my mother and Tony and all that I had left behind was on a distant planet in another solar system. I was shocked and afraid, but I was determined not to go back.

Despite her rough manner of speaking and critical eyes, I found Annie Casteel easy to talk to. She really listened when I spoke, absorbing the story of my life with interest and amazement on her face. Of course, I didn't tell about Tony's raping me. Luke wanted me to keep the secret of my pregnancy even from his parents. Annie wanted to know why I had run away and I explained that my mother's new husband had been making advances and my mother blamed it all on me.

'Without a Daddy who cared and a mother who believed me, I felt lost and alone and decided to leave. I was on my way to my grandmother's when I met Luke and fell in love,' I explained. She nodded and passed me the carrots to scrape and wash clean. But when I told her about the portrait dolls and Angel, she insisted I stop working and take Angel out of the suitcase so she could see something that fine and expensive. Her eyes lit up with pleasure.

'When I was a little girl, my pa had to whittle me a doll out of a thick branch. I never had anythin' dainty and sweet, and I never seen nothin' like this, even in the store windas down in Winnerrow. And then, after I got married, I had no cause ta buy one fer I had six boys and no girls. After a while, I gave up tryin' ta have a girl.

'I hope when Luke and ya have a baby, it's a girl,' she said and I saw that this tough, hard woman of the Willies could be as soft and gentle as any woman I had met. I felt sorry for her, sorry that her life was so hard and there were so few opportunities for her to be a woman, to dress up and be pretty, to keep her skin soft and let her fingernails grow.

'I hope so, too, Annie,' I said. She stared at me a moment and then replied.

'Ya call me Ma,' she said and I smiled. 'Now let's get this stew cookin'. If I know them two, they'll be brayin' like mules fer somethin' ta eat sooner than ya think.'

'Yes, Ma.'

I used an outhouse for the first time in my life and sat down at the small plank dinner table and ate something I had never dreamed of eating. But it was delicious. After dinner, Pa played his banjo and Luke and he sang old mountain songs and drank moonshine. I saw they were both starting to get tipsy. Pa got Luke up to do a jig and then he did one himself. After a while Ma bawled them out for acting stupid. Luke looked at me quickly and I shook my head. It was enough to sober him up quickly.

Just before we went to bed, Luke and I sat out on the porch and listened to the sounds of the forest – the owls hooting, the coyotes howling and the peepers croaking in the swamps. I did feel a sense of peace and security sitting with Luke, holding his hand and looking up at the stars, even though I was miles from civilization as I had known it and living in a shack.

When we crawled under the quilt together, I hugged and kissed Luke lovingly. He was stirred, but he didn't take me the way a husband should take his wife.

'No, Angel,' he whispered. 'We'll wait until after you have the baby and I've given you a proper home and we can sleep and make love away from anyone else's ears.'

I knew what he meant. The old springs squeaked even when we just turned toward and away from each other. On the other side of the curtain, Pa snored, and under the floorboards, just as Ma promised, the hogs snorted and the dogs whimpered. Something scratched at the wooden piers. I heard a cat hiss and then, all was as still as it could get with the wind whistling through the trees and the cracks in the floor and walls of the small cabin. Pa's moonshine put Luke to sleep very quickly. It took me a while longer, but I finally closed my eyes and slept my first night in the Willies.

In the morning Luke got up bright and early and drove down to Winnerrow to get that carpentry job. Pa was working with some farmer named Burl, building a new barn with him and earning some money. After breakfast, Ma sat down to continue her crocheting. I decided to take a wash cloth, pail and detergent and do what I could to clean up the cabin. Ma seemed amused by my efforts, but when she came back in and saw how I had cleaned the windows and shined up whatever appliances she had, she nodded with approval.

Afterward, she took me out to her small garden and I helped her weed while she talked about her past, what life was like for her growing up in the Willies. She told me about her other sons, Luke's brothers, and I saw how upset she was about two of them being in prison.

'We're poor and we never put on airs,' she said, 'but we always been honest folk – 'cept, of course, for the moonshine, but that ain't the government's business anyway. All them revenuers is tryin' ta do is protect the big businessmen who make licker and sell it for outrageous prices. Folks up here could never afford it and would have none if it wasn't fer the moonshiners.

'Not that I approve a drinkin', mind ya. It's what got ma other boys inta trouble. I jist hate ta see some poor Willies man hunted down fer makin' his own whiskey. Understand, Angel?'

'Yes, Ma.'

'Um,' she said, watching me work. 'Yer jist might make a Willies wife yit. At least yer don't mind gettin' yer hands dirty.'

It was funny how that made me feel proud. I thought about the expression on my mother's face if she could see me now. She would die if she touched something dusty in Farthy, but here I was with my fingers in the soft, cool earth. And I didn't feel all that worse for it, I thought. But I did want to look pretty for Luke when he returned from his first day of work in Winnerrow.

'But it's all right to clean my hands up later and maybe rub in some of that lotion I brought with me, isn't it, Ma?'

How she laughed.

'Of course, child. Damn, don'tcha think I'd like ta look like one of them fancy rich Winnerrow women?'

'Well, maybe I can help you do that, Ma,' I said. 'Let me brush out your hair later and you can use some of my hand cream.'

She looked at me oddly.

'Um,' she said. 'Maybe.'

She seemed afraid of the idea, but she let me do it, let me brush out her hair and trim it some. Then we took out her best dress and one of my nicer ones and got ourselves as dressed up as we could to greet Luke and his father when they returned from work. Pa came home first.

'What's this?' he said when he saw us on the front porch as dolled up as we could get. 'It ain't Sunday, is it?'

'Now Toby Casteel, it don't have ta be Sunday for me ta look decent, does it?' Ma snapped. He looked pinched and confused, turning to me to understand what he had said that got her to bite at him so quickly. 'It wouldn't hurt ya ta clean up and put on some decent clothes fer dinner once in a while yerself. Yer still a handsome man.'

'I am? Well now, I guess that's true,' he said, winking at me.

'Oh it is, Pa,' I said and his face lit up. He went behind the cabin and bathed in rainwater and then got into some of his best clothes, his 'Sunday clothes'. The three of us sat on the porch and waited for Luke's arrival.

Not long after we heard his truck grinding its way over the rough mountain road. Every once in a while, he pressed down on his horn.

'Uh oh,' Ma said. She flashed a look of warning my way. My heart began to pound. What was it? What did it mean?

Luke came tearing into the front yard, his horn beeping. Then he hopped out of the truck without closing the door. He had a six-pack of beer clutched to his stomach, three of the bottles already emptied.

'It's celebratin' time,' he cried, and laughed.

'What in tarnation . . .' Pa said.

'Confound him,' Ma spit.

Luke stumbled around, smiling stupidly. Then his eyes focused clearly on the three of us, all dressed up.

'What the . . .' He pointed at us as if there were someone standing beside him. 'Look at them . . . what the . . . oh, yer all celebratin' too.'

'Luke Casteel,' I said standing up, my hands on my hips. 'How dare you come home like this? First, you could have driven the truck off a cliff or something, and now you look so foolish, I could cry.'

'Huh?'

'Tell him,' Ma coached.

'Here we are getting started, making things work, and you come home drunk.' I spun around, tears streaming down my face, and rushed into the cabin.

'Huh?' Luke repeated.

I flopped on our mattress and cried. Moments later, a much more sober Luke Casteel followed me in. He knelt beside me and stroked my hair.

'Oh Angel,' he said. 'I was just celebratin' for us. I got the job and found out I could buy lumber at a discount when I'm ready to start our new home.'

'I don't care, Luke. If you have something to celebrate, you should wait for us to celebrate it together. I told you I was concerned about your drinking and you promised to cut down. Now this happens.'

'I know, I know. Oh, I'm so sorry,' he said. 'I'm going to take the remaining bottles of beer and heave 'em off the cliff,' he vowed. 'And if you don't forgive me, I'll heave myself off after 'em.'

'Luke Casteel,' I cried, turning to him. 'Don't you ever talk like that. Ever!' My eyes flared. I could see how surprised he was.

'Boy, are you beautiful when you get real angry,' he said. 'I ain't never seen you this angry, but I don't want you to be angry. I promise,' he said raising his hand. 'I won't do any more drinkin' and drivin'. Will you give me another chance?'

'Oh Luke Casteel, you know I will,' I said and we hugged and kissed.

'I got some lumber in the truck,' he said. 'And I'm goin' to start on your outhouse right now.'

I followed him out and watched him start to unload. Ma flashed me a look of approval for sobering him up so quickly. Then she turned to Luke.

'What's that lumber fer?' she asked him.

'Angel's outhouse,' he said, and that made Ma and Pa Casteel laugh.

'Go ahead, have a good one on me,' Luke said, 'but when you see it, you'll stop.'

Luke did put all his love for me in his work and he built as pretty an outhouse as could be. Afterward, he painted it white and insisted that we call it a bathroom instead of an outhouse. Ma teased him whenever she could.

'I'll be goin' ta ma outhouse. I mean, bathroom,' she would say and Luke would swing his eyes away and shake his head.

Summer passed into fall. Luke made other improvements on the cabin, trying out some of the carpentry skills he was learning. He built Ma some cabinets and shelves and reinforced the porch and the porch steps. He closed up some of the leaks in the walls and floor, but his job in town began to take up more and more of his time. Pretty soon, he was coming home after dark and he was dead tired, almost too tired to eat dinner. Sometimes he would have whiskey on his breath. Whenever I mentioned it, he claimed he had to have a snort or two in order to get through the day.

'He's trying to get the work of two men out of me, Angel,' he told me one night after dinner. We would take a walk down a path through the woods that led to a clearing on a ridge overlooking the valley. It gave us a breathtaking view. We could see the lights of houses for miles and miles. 'All the Winnerrow businessmen eventually take advantage of the Willies people,' Luke explained. 'I'm holding down my temper because I want to get started on our own home as soon as I can, but it's gettin' harder and harder.'

'I don't like you drinking up your troubles and frustrations, Luke. Can't you find a different job?'

'There ain't that many jobs for us mountain folk. That's why I left the Willies so many times.'

'I've been thinking, Luke. Maybe I should try to get in touch with my daddy. He owns a steamship company and I'm sure he would have a good job for you.'

'What kind of a job? Working in the engine room of an ocean liner and bein' away from you most of the time?'

'I'm sure he could give you an office job, Luke.'

'Me? An office job? I'd feel like a wild squirrel put in a cage. No sir, not me. I need the outdoors or the excitement of the circus, which is even a freer life.'

'Do you want to go back to the circus after the baby is born, Luke?' I asked. 'I'll go with you, if you want.'

'Naw. Circus life is hard and you're travelin' all the time. I'll stick this out until we have our stake,' he said.

'I could write my daddy and ask him to send him some of my money. There's money in a trust fund for me back at Farthy, too.'

'We don't want any of that money,' Luke snapped. It was the first time he ever got angry at me. Even in the dark with only the starlight, I saw how his eyes blazed with vexation. 'I can take care of my own.'

'I didn't mean to say you couldn't, Luke.'

He nodded and immediately felt bad about raising his voice to me.

'I'm sorry I snapped at you, Angel. I'm just tired.'

'Ma's right, Luke. You should take a day off. You work around here even when you get time off from your job. Let this be the Sunday we all get dressed up and go to church. Please, Luke.'

'Well, okay,' he said, relenting.

Ma was happy about us going to church, but when we arrived there the following Sunday, I saw what Luke had meant about the townspeople looking down on the Willies people. As soon as we entered the church, you could cut the air with a knife. The fancy townspeople all turned and glared at us, their glares meant to keep us back in our place. Ma and Pa Casteel moved quickly to seats beside other Willies people I recognized, but I didn't budge.

Luke looked at me curiously. He was so handsome in his suit and tie with his hair slicked back, and even in my sixth month of pregnancy, I thought I looked just as pretty as these women and girls from Winnerrow. My dress was as expensive, if not more expensive than most of theirs, and no one had hair as soft. The rainwater shampoos had made mine even richer than it had been when I first arrived in the Willies.

I saw two empty places down front and tugged Luke toward it. He held back a moment and then looked at my face.

'I thought you wanted me to tell off the mayor of Winnerrow, first chance I got,' I said. He smiled widely.

'Darn if I didn't,' he said and followed me to the seats. The people in the pew sat back as if a wind had come gushing in and over them. They were all wide-eyed, curiosity mixing with outrage, but I stared them down until their eyes lowered and they relaxed. The minister took his place at the pulpit and preached a fine sermon about brotherly love, which I thought fit the day.

Afterward Ma came up to me and said, 'I was right when I first laid eyes on ya, Angel. Ya got the grit of a Casteel woman. I'm proud a ya.'

'Thanks, Ma,' I said.

After church on Sunday, the Willies people would gather for a ho-down. They would fiddle and dance and eat the food each family contributed. I helped serve and then sat back and watched as Luke and Pa sang and played the banjo. The men danced and the women clapped.

A thousand years ago, I had a birthday party at Farthy. My mother had hired an expensive band and caterers. My school friends were all dressed up and all came from the best and richest of families. We had the movie in our private theater. At the time I thought it was the greatest party I had ever seen.

But here in Winnerrow with these simple mountain people

singing about their dreams, or singing funny songs about their mountain heritage, I felt even happier. No one could put on airs here. I felt at home, at ease, comfortable.

Of course, I saw how many of the mountain girls looked longingly at Luke, for dressed up he was as handsome as a movie star. One girl, Sarah Williams, flashed her green eyes at me when she did get him to dance. She practically pulled him onto the dance floor, and kept looking my way and smiling. Sarah had fire-red hair and was almost as tall as Luke. She clung to him very tightly and I couldn't help being jealous because she was a pretty girl with a slim figure and no belly sticking out like mine. As soon as the dance ended, he returned to me, literally breaking out of Sarah's grasp.

'Sarah's a pretty girl, Luke,' I said looking away.

'Maybe so, Angel, but I have eyes only for you,' he said, and turned me around so I could look into his dark eyes, eyes full of love and hope and pride. 'I shouldn't a let her pull me out to the dance floor,' he added, reproaching himself. 'It's the moonshine creepin' up on me, just like you warned me it would.'

'I don't mean to sound like some old nag, Luke.'

'You ain't. No way.' He shook his head when one of the other girls called to him.

'Oh Luke, I feel like I'm stealing you away sometimes by making you the father of my child.'

'Hush now,' he whispered, putting his finger on his lips. 'That's our child and you ain't stealing me away from nothin' I don't want to get away from myself.

'You look tried, Angel,' he added. 'Let's go on home. I had enough to eat and drink.'

'But you're having so much fun, Luke.'

'I'd rather be home alone with my Angel,' he said.

My heart was full again. When we returned to the cabin that night, we were all laughing and talking excitedly until we went to sleep. Luke and I crawled under our quilt and hugged each other. I never felt more secure or happier. Once in a while the baby would kick and Luke, who was pressed up beside me, would feel it too.

'Don't know if it's a boy or a girl,' he said, 'but whatever it is, it's got your pride and courage, Angel,' Luke said. 'I'll never forget the way you stared down them rich folk today.'

'And I'll never forget how handsome you were and how many girls made eyes at you, Luke Casteel.'

'Oh, come on now.' With his cheek to mine, I could feel him blush.

'Looks like we'll have plenty to tell our child when he or she is old enough to listen and understand, huh, Luke?'

'Oh, that's for sure,' he said. He kissed me and held me and we closed our eyes and drifted off to sleep.

It snowed late in November in the Willies. With the night came the smothering cold to settle down on the mountains like an ice blanket. The wind would blow through the cabin unmercifully at times, and I would wrap myself up in our quilt and sit beside Old Smokey, the coal stove. When Luke came home at night, he would hug and rub me, cursing the cold. Ma and I crocheted new quilts and Luke bought me long johns to wear. I was a sight with my stomach out and we had a good laugh about it.

On Christmas Eve we had the best meal we could afford. Pa had gotten a turkey from Simon Burl. It cost him a full day's work, but he was proud of it. Ma and I had knit gloves and sweaters for Pa and Luke and Luke brought home presents for everyone: new combs for Ma, a real corncob pipe for Pa and something so special for me, he wanted me to unwrap it with him behind the tattered curtain that served as a wall for our bedroom.

I sat on the bed and carefully undid the ribbon. Then I lifted the box cover off and peeled away the tissue paper to find the most beautiful doll's clothes I had ever seen, clothes for Angel. He had bought her a wedding outfit: a wedding veil with the filmy mist flowing from a tiny jeweled cap, a long dress made of white lace, lavishly embroidered with tiny pearls and sparkling beads, white shoes made of lace and white satin, and even sheer stockings that were to be fastened with a tiny garter belt.

'Oh Luke, it's all so beautiful. I can't wait to dress her,' I cried.

'You never had a proper wedding in a proper wedding dress, but I thought at least Angel should have one,' he said.

'How sweet of you Luke.' I dressed Angel in her new finery and noticed the locket around her neck, the one that said 'Love, Tony'. I wouldn't let that hateful thing stay on Angel's neck. I ripped it off and threw it as far into the woods as I could. Then we brought her out to show Ma and Pa.

Afterward, while Ma and I were cleaning up the dishes, she leaned over and whispered to me.

'I never thought my Luke would turn out this way, Angel. I was always afraid he'd be jest like his brothers, 'cause he likes his nip of the snake, but you keep him from going too far. If he hurts ya, he hurts terrible inside hisself. As long as he has ya, he'll never git inta real trouble. I think it was his lucky day, the day he found ya.'

'Thank you, Ma,' I said, my eyes filling with tears. She smiled and hugged me, really hugged me for the first time.

Somehow, even though we were as poor as could be and we lived in a cabin the size of a bathroom at Farthy, I was happy. I was even thinking it had been the best Christmas of my life. Angel's eyes sparkled in the light of the oil lamp. She was happy, too.

The next month was a hard one for us. It snowed almost every day and it was bitter cold. Old Smokey pumped out as much smoke as heat, but we had to keep her stoked continually. Every night Luke would apologize to me for the weather and spend hours rubbing my toes and my fingers, but somehow, we got through it and went into an early February thaw. There was one cloudless day after another, the sun beaming down and melting the ice off tree branches. At night, the melted snow and ice gleamed like diamonds, turning the forest around us into a jeweled wonderland.

The way I figured my pregnancy, I was only weeks away from giving birth. Ma was as good as a trained midwife, having delivered dozens of Willies babies as well as five of her own. Luke wanted to take me into town to see the town doctor, but

I felt safe with Ma and didn't see why Luke should spend nearly two months' salary on a doctor that would only do the same thing when the time came.

The baby was active and I found myself out of breath often. My lower back ached. I wanted to do my fair share of the work, but Ma insisted I rest more. She encouraged me to walk as much as I could, however.

When the weather let up some and winter eased its grip on the forest, Luke and I would take our nightly walk to the ridge overlooking the valley. From our mountain view, the unobstructed winter night sky was spectacular.

If there is something for me to remember more than anything, I suppose it would be this early February night. I was all bundled up. Even though it wasn't as cold as it had been, Luke insisted I wear the sweaters and the coat, the sock hat Ma knitted for me and gloves I made myself after she taught me how. But when we arrived at the ridge, I slipped off my woolen gloves so I could hold his hand in mine and feel the warmth in his fingers.

We stood there quietly for a moment, both of us dazzled by the thousands and thousands of stars spread out before us across the deep black night. Houses below us threaded through the valley, their windows lit and looking like stars themselves. They twinkled with the warmth of families around fireplaces. I could almost hear the laughter and the music and the quiet talk.

'Someday,' Luke said, 'someday soon, one of those houses down there in the valley is gonna be ours. I swear it, Angel.'

'I know it will, Luke. I believe in you.'

'We'll be sittin' in our livin' room and I'll have my feet up and I'll be smokin' my pipe and you'll be knittin' or crochetin' and our baby will be playin' on the floor between us, all of us warm and safe.

'That's all I want, Angel. Is that too much of a dream?'

'I don't think so, Luke.'

'Ma and Pa think it's as far out of reach as those houses below,' he said sadly.

'That's only because it has been for them, but it won't be for us, Luke.'

He nodded and embraced me, holding me to him. We stood there with the stars above and before us, two small people alone in the winter night, whispering their love for each other. My baby kicked.

'Feel it, Luke?' I asked, putting his hand on my stomach. He smiled.

'I think it's a girl, Luke.'

'Maybe. I love you, Angel.' He turned to me. 'I love you more than any man has ever loved a woman.'

My baby kicked again and my stomach felt hard. I had more pain tonight than I had ever had. The last few days, I had woken with pain in the night and even in the morning, but I didn't complain because I didn't want Luke to worry and stay home from work. The pain might only mean it was getting close, I thought, although Ma didn't seem happy about it.

'I think she wants to come out and join us, Luke. It's getting close to the time.'

'Well, there'd be no better time than now,' he said. 'With the heavens blazing so, with all these stars, it's a good night for a baby to come, especially if it's a girl and we name her Heaven.'

A sharp pain nearly brought me to my knees, but I grimaced and bore it so Luke wouldn't see and be worried. He was so happy and hopeful, I didn't want anything to change his mood. But I couldn't help being a little frightened, even though I imagined it was expected of any woman having her first child, especially a woman as young as I was.

'Oh Luke, take me back to the cabin and hold me, hold me like you never held me before,' I said. He kissed me and we began to return to the cabin.

'Wait,' I said, stopping him.

I turned back once to get a last glimpse of the stars.

'What is it, Angel?' Luke asked.

'When I close my eyes tonight, I want all those stars to appear behind my lids. I want to feel as if I'm falling asleep in Heaven.'

He laughed and then we made a turn in the forest and they were gone.

Epilogue

I turn the page, but there is nothing more written, not on the next page or the next. Finally, I find a paper folded between the last page in the diary and the cover. I open it carefully, for it is so old, it feels like it would crumble in my fingers if I were too rough with it. It's a letter from a detective agency.

Dear Mr Tatterton,

As you know, I did locate your step-daughter in the hills of Virginia. In my last report, I described the conditions under which she was living and I did report that she was pregnant.

I am afraid I have bad news. Yesterday, my assistant, whom I left on the case, called in to report that he had learned of your daughter's death. Apparently, she died in childbirth. He told me that she did not have professional medical attention and gave birth in her mountain cabin. I am sorry.

He did report that the child lived and it was a girl.

I await further instructions.

Sincerely yours,
L. Stanford Banning, P.I.

For a moment I can't catch my breath. The air is so stale and so stifling in this old, dusty suite.

'Annie!'

It's Luke calling.

'I'm in here, Luke.'

In a moment he is in the doorway.

'Everyone who is coming has arrived, Annie; and they're all

asking after you. It's time,' Luke says. I nod. 'What have you been doing?'

'Just sitting here, reading.'

'Reading what?' He comes farther in.

'A story, a strange, sad, but beautiful story, my grandmother's story.' I hold back my tears, but Luke sees them in my eyes.

'Annie, let's go. This place is haunted by sadness and sorrow. You don't belong here.'

'Yes.' I smile. How handsome Luke is, as handsome as his grandfather must have been. He reaches out for me and I take his hand and stand up. We start out and I stop.

'What's wrong?'

'Nothing,' I say. 'I just want to put this back. Somehow, I feel it belongs here among all the other memories.' I put the diary back in the cloth bag and return it to the drawer. Then I look around once more and hurry to join Luke.

We descend the great stairway. I pause. I thought I heard a little boy's laugh. I even think I hear him calling: 'Leigh! Leigh!'

I smile.

'What is it?' Luke asks.

'I was just imagining my father as a little boy calling after my grandmother to play with him.'

Luke shakes his head.

We continue down the stairs and through the great entry hall. Is that music behind me? Angel's birthday party? A piano concert for wealthy guests? My father practising his Chopin? Or is it just the wind finding its way into the great house? Maybe it's all of it.

I go out with Luke and close the great door behind me, leaving the question and the answer with all the others in the great house of Farthinggale Manor.